THE SEEKER'S CHEST

MARIE ANDREAS

OTHER BOOKS BY

MARIE ANDREAS

The Lost Ancients
Book One: The Glass Gargoyle
Book Two: The Obsidian Chimera
Book Three: The Emerald Dragon
Book Four: The Sapphire Manticore
Book Five: The Golden Basilisk
Book Six: The Diamond Sphinx

The Lost Ancients: Dragon's Blood
Book One: The Seeker's Chest

The Asarlaí Wars Trilogy
Book One: Warrior Wench
Book Two: Victorious Dead
Book Three: Defiant Ruin

The Code of the Keeper
Book One: Traitor's Folly

The Adventures of Smith and Jones
A Curious Invasion
The Mayhem of Mermaids

Broken Veil
Book One: The Girl with the Iron Wing
Book Two: An Uncommon Truth of Dying
Book Three: Through a Veil Darkly

Books of the Cuari
Book One: Essence of Chaos
Book Two: Division of Chaos
Book Three: Destruction of Chaos

DEDICATION

For Laura, Liesel, and Katie Schilling.
For believing in and helping with the faeries.
Thank you.

Acknowledgements

It seems like a book is written by a single person, perhaps two, but, in fact, it takes an army to bring a world to life. I have been so very blessed to have so many wonderful and supportive people who have helped me along this path.

I'd like to thank everyone who has ever supported me, read chapters, edited, let me cry on their shoulder, and/or bought me supporting and soothing beverages. I could never have done this without ALL of you. I can't list you all here, but you mean the world to me.

My editor extraordinaire- Jessa Slade of Red Circle Ink—thank you for reining in my wild stories. My beta readers: Patti Huber, Lisa Andreas, Lynne Mayfield, and Laura and Liesel Schilling. Typo hunters Lia Fairfield and Rossinna "Soapy" Ippolito. Any errors or mistakes are completely mine. And possibly the fault of Crusty Bucket rampaging through the book.

Thank you to The Killion Group for their formatting mojo and the spine and back magic on the print cover.

And to my very talented artist- Aleta Rafton, thank you for again bringing Taryn to life.

CHAPTER ONE

—◆—

"LET LOOSE THE KITTAHS OF war!" Garbage Blossom yelled as she tore out of the cottage and into the clearing. Again.

When she first yelled it two days ago, after coming to break up a wonderful, romantic, and well-deserved retreat for myself and the love of my life, Alric, I thought she was serious. She and her faery companions had hunted us down and demanded we follow them to the distant south where—according to them—the evils of the world were brewing.

Keep in mind, Alric, myself, the faeries, and several of my friends had just saved the world. We were tired. I'd found out an awful lot about myself and was not ready to start coping with any of it yet. And she wanted us to go fight far away? *No.*

Of course, since the faeries found our hidden cabin, they had all yelled their war chant repeatedly with different emphases. They were trying out a new battle cry. Whether there really was danger in the distant south, or more importantly a danger that we actually had to go do something about, were extremely different things.

"Seriously, do we have any chocolate around here? If I must, I'll go find a town and buy some." Alric shut the door of our cabin after getting all the faeries outside. Again. The moment we opened the door, they'd come swooping in until we chased them out.

Even frustrated and annoyed, Alric was too damn good-looking for my own good. He was a high-lord elf, a member of a species that, up until a short while ago, the world thought had vanished. Nope, they'd just gone into hiding for a thousand years. Alric was tall with lean muscles that spoke to extensive hand-to-hand and sword training. Unnaturally soft, white-blond hair drifted past his shoulders, and his bright green eyes missed nothing. I was glad he wasn't trying to dye his hair anymore. When I'd first met him, bringing him in as a wanted man with a bounty I desperately needed to collect, he'd been trying to hide who and what he was with a hideous dye job.

And he personally didn't like chocolate, so I knew this wasn't him wanting a snack.

However, the faeries loved chocolate, especially my original three: Garbage Blossom, Leaf Grub, and Crusty Bucket. My friend Harlan brought some of the new substance to share a few months ago, and the girls ate more than they weighed. Afterward, they crashed into the heaviest slumber I'd ever seen. Alric was hoping to drug the flying maniacs into silence.

"Kittahs! Kittahs! Bring out the warrior cats!" The chanting was getting louder and was starting to rattle the windows of our cottage.

"We don't have any, sorry." Alric might not be fond of chocolate, but I was. The small bit Harlan had snuck into my pack when Alric and I left the others a week ago was gone almost immediately. "At least they don't actually have their cats with them right now." During our last couple of battles, we'd found out that the faeries had taken street cats and trained them to be their steeds in battle. With armor and everything. I'd thought it was a bit odd at the time, since the faeries can fly extremely well. Then came a battle in a place where their ability to fly didn't exist. Granted, the entire thing had smacked of prophecy, but I was still impressed that they'd prepared their cats for such a battle. Now I wished they'd go back and stay with them for a bit. When the faeries first invaded our peace and solitude, they'd had a fleet of their war cats with them. The cats got bored after the first hour and vanished. Most likely back to roaming the streets of Beccia.

That might be something. "Maybe we can send them off to get their cats again? Tell them we want to see how ready they are in full armor?" I started picking up belongings as I spoke; this idea had merit. "Tell them they need to first show each cat and armor to Covey and Harlan."

Alric had been watching the chanting from the window but dropped the curtain to turn to me. "How is that going to help? They will come back, you know. It will be worse."

"Ha!" I waggled a shirt at him as I stuffed it into my pack. One advantage of a spur-of-the-moment escape trip—not a lot to pack back up. "We'll be gone by then. There's an entire world that we can go explore. No more relics, no nasty people trying to kill us, just us. Out there." I waved toward the door and the hypothetical world beyond the clearing of chanting faeries.

He stepped forward and looked down at me. "They will find us eventually." He rubbed my arms and gave me a lingering kiss. "But it would be nice to get on the road again, without being chased, and it should slow them down enough to give us a few days of peace." He turned and started gathering his things as well.

I smiled and finished packing. The past two years had been full of danger, mayhem, violence, and faery shenanigans—it would be nice to have something of a normal life again. I still had a house in Beccia, but I'd enjoyed being alone with Alric the past week. A few more weeks spent alone with him could be more than nice. We'd started off in one of the elven traveling houses more than a week ago. But it wasn't in great shape and collapsed in on itself when the faeries all landed on it upon arriving. So Alric found us this cottage to stay in. It was closer to Beccia than I would have liked, but cute and hidden. Of course, the faeries had just followed us over. "Hey, what about that elven traveling house you had? It's close to town, but no one would expect us to be going out into the woods to grab it. It would make traveling a lot nicer. It seemed more stable than that first one."

The traveling house he had was gorgeous, a relic from before the elves went into hiding. When I'd seen it, the little house had been locked into an open position and looked like a small house with all the amenities we'd need. It just happened to be decorated in early elven glamour and could collapse down to the size of a small cart.

"It's newer than the other one. We could go after it, but if we see anyone we know on the way, we're taking off in the other direction and living off the land." He finished packing up his stuff and dropped the packs into the closet where the faeries wouldn't see them. "I have nothing against any of our friends, but I think some more time with just you and me would be better." The look in his stunning green eyes made me want to bolt the door and drag him back to bed.

I shook my head to push the thought aside. The goal here was to escape the flying loons outside. "Shall I bring them in?"

Alric pulled up a chair and placed it in front of the closet, sat, then nodded.

I flung open the door. "Girls! We need you!" The chanting had reached screeching levels and none of them responded. "Girls!" Nope, nothing. I closed my eyes and focused on my original three. Then I imagined a huge pile of ale bottles.

We'd found out a while ago that I could mentally reach out to the faeries. Words didn't really work, but images did. Especially booze. The silence in the clearing was almost painful in its suddenness. But it only lasted long enough for all the faeries to swarm me as I took a few steps back into the cottage.

"Where is?" Garbage Blossom, the orange, de facto leader of the mob, hovered in front of me with her hands on her hips and her weird, one-eyed glare. She thought by almost closing one eye and making the other as wide as possible, she looked fierce. I hadn't the heart to break the truth to her.

"I was trying to get your attention. There's no ale here. But…" I held up my hand as the muttering started. "There is back in Beccia. And we have an important task for you. All of you."

They still looked annoyed, but Garbage particularly enjoyed being needed and doing important things. Almost all the rest of the faeries hovered closer at her nod. Crusty Bucket was flying upside down and facing the woods outside the door, but even she nodded.

I loved my little blue faery, but she was her own special case. She'd follow where the rest of them went, so her not paying attention wasn't crucial.

"Alric and I need you to get your war cats. Full armor. They all have to be inspected by Covey and Harlan first before you can bring them back here." I paused. Covey might chase them off. "Covey and Harlan might act like they have no idea why you're doing this, but that's part of this plan. Don't give up until all of the cats have been inspected by both."

Garbage was slowly nodding. "For great battle?"

Crusty spun toward us but she was still upside down. "Sing at them? If no listen?" Sneaky little faery.

"Yes, great battle will be coming." I turned to Crusty. "In this case, yes. Sing until they fully inspect the war cats. Can you do this?" Faery singing was considered torture by most civilized people, but it might help keep the faeries focused on Harlan and Covey and delay their return so we could get away far enough to avoid them for a while.

All the faeries watched Garbage as she hovered in front of me with her arms still folded. With a sigh, she pulled out a tiny black bag out of the pocket in the front of her overalls, pulled out her war stick from it, and held it high. "We do!"

The rest of her flying armada grabbed their own bags, withdrew their own war sticks, and yelled. War sticks looked to be little more than four-inch-long sticks with a branching prong. But I'd seen the serious damage the faeries could do with them.

Garbage flew out of the cottage, then yelled a battle cry and streaked off. The rest followed except for Crusty. She turned right side up, flew over to me, and patted my cheek. "We do right. Battle kittahs!" With a deranged spin in the air, she flew out and followed the others.

Alric got up from his seat and turned to take the packs out of the closet. "Good job, that was—"

"Wait." I cut him off and kept one hand up as I listened for any suspicious faery noises. "I don't trust them." We waited a few minutes and finally I nodded. It wasn't that I thought the faeries didn't believe me, but they could get distracted sometimes, and I didn't want them coming back and catching us leaving. I could usually use my two constructs, Bunky and Irving, to ensure a bit of focus and compliance, but they were guarding my house right now.

"I think we're clear. But we need to move quickly." I grabbed my pack and Alric grabbed his. The horses weren't tethered, but something about elves and horses made them not need to be. Both animals were nearby and enjoying a patch of sun.

"Let's ride to the north first. At least a few of those faeries are developing tracking skills." He secured his pack and then turned to help me, but mine was already fastened behind my saddle.

"They learn from the best. I told you to watch what you do around them. They soak up information as well as ale."

The faeries were originally just thought to be nuisances. Then we found out they'd been around far longer than almost any other species. And that they had lost powers that were creeping back. The more they learned, the more frightening they were.

Alric shook his head and swung up on his horse. "I'm still not sure which revelation was more unexpected: what they can do, or who you are." He winced as the words came out. He'd been avoiding the subject at my request.

"I thought we weren't going to talk about it yet?" I got on my horse, but he hadn't moved yet.

His face softened and his sharp green eyes mellowed. "I know, but it is who you are. I accept and love all of you. I think you need to talk about it, though."

I hated it when he was being too nice. And while I agreed with him logically, finding out that the lost Ancients had actually been dragons who could shift into human form and that they weren't dead, just misplaced in time, and oh yeah, I was one and I was the one who misplaced them was a hell of a thing to find out. Emotionally, I was completely fine with living in denial a bit longer. A few years longer might be even better.

"This isn't really the time." I looked around just in case any faeries had drifted back this way. "We can talk when we're in that house of yours and far away from here. I promise." I left just how far was far from here undefined.

He looked ready to argue, then shrugged, and turned his horse down the trail. "Fine. But you do need to talk about it."

I smiled, nodded, and followed him out. I really wanted to sort it out in my head before talking to anyone about it, even him. Aside from really needing a rest, and genuinely wanting to spend time alone with Alric, part of the reason I wanted to be away from my friends was to sort things out. None of them had looked at me in any judgmental way, but I felt it in my soul. What kind of person sends all her people somewhere into the future? It was done from a place of fear, panic, and extreme loss. Twenty-five hundred years ago, my people, now only known as the Ancients, were losing a long battle against the syclarions. My parents had been murdered. I was a young magic user with far more power than training. In a final attempt to save my people, I created a staff of powerful items. It was designed to push the syclarions out of existence. I succeeded in destroying many of them and reducing the powers and advancement of the rest.

My people were flung somewhere into the future, I went twenty-five hundred years into the forward, locked in my human state with no magic and no memory.

These were things that were going to require many nights at my favorite Beccian pub, the Shimmering Dewdrop. Since that was in direct conflict with my current goals, I would just keep ignoring the entire situation a bit longer.

The ride back to Beccia wouldn't be a long one, made shorter since the traveling house was on this side of the town. Although our final battle had taken place far from the drunken little town, we'd moved closer when we took off on our own.

I was lost in my thoughts, watching Alric and his horse veer away from the path into town and toward the deeper forest where he'd left his traveling house.

"Halt and give us all your money!" shouted by a group of random thugs, was not expected.

CHAPTER TWO

———

THEY'D POPPED UP ON THE heavily forested trail branching into ours right in between Alric and me. That I hadn't noticed three men on horseback said something about the distraction of my thoughts. But I was surprised that Alric hadn't noticed them, either.

He turned at the leader's words. His sword, which was nowhere to be seen a second ago was in one hand, and the other hand was ready to throw a spell. When he got a good look at the man in front, he swore, and the sword and the spell ball vanished.

"Damn it, Grillion, what in the hell are you doing?" His sword had gone back to wherever it was the spirit swords went when they weren't needed. I had one as well, and I had no idea where mine stayed when I didn't need it. I was just grateful it wasn't popping in and out of my life at inopportune times at this point.

The man broke into a wide grin and motioned to his partners. "Getting bonus points by sneaking up on one of the sneakiest elves I ever knew. Even if he never told me he was an elf. Or blond." The tall, skinny human smiled at me. "Grillion's my name, and charm's my game."

I looked over his head to Alric. He rolled his eyes and nodded, so I gave a slight smile. "I'm Taryn."

"How did you know it was me?" Alric ran a self-conscious hand through his light hair. Obviously, this person knew him when he was dying it black.

"We've been following you since you left that cottage—I only heard your voice at first and thought to sneak up on you. I'd heard rumors about the elves coming out of hiding and some great hero named Alric. Figured you being an elf would go far in explaining your stealth skills when we worked together."

He turned back to me, still holding my hand, and kissed it. "Ah, lovely Taryn, why are you hanging out with this thief and scoundrel?"

Alric rolled his eyes. "First off, she's with me. Secondly, you really came back up here to find me based on tales? What if Cirocco was still looking for you?"

"It was worth a shot." Grillion let go of my hand with a shrug. He also dropped his smile. "I heard he hadn't been around much and hoped I could reach you and get back out before he came around. I have a sweet setup in Notlianda down south. Small kingdom, actually doing legitimate and legal work." The proud look on his face told me that wasn't common for him.

"You actually have to work? You left with a fair amount of those gold wall plates." Alric gave his friend a questioning look.

One of Grillion's friends, a short dark man, burst out laughing. "He didn't have those for long. I'm Hass, since Grillion is too busy to introduce us. That's Fealk. He doesn't talk much." He nodded to the tall human, or most likely a human-giant breed. The man had a shock of red hair, huge doe-like eyes, and arms the width of my waist. He smiled, gave a slight nod, and then held still. I'd seen bar stools that exuded more character.

Both Alric and I said our hellos. "What gold wall panels?" I turned to Alric. "Was this in Beccia?" I knew that Alric had been in town for a few weeks before I met him; whatever he had been doing during that time was *why* I met him. Cirocco had put a bounty on him. There'd been nothing about a friend and the bounty was just for Alric. I could see the mage crime lord getting pissed if someone stole gold from him.

"They were found in a cave on the outlying part of the main ruins, the part over the valley that collapsed a year ago. Yeah, Grillion should be a wealthy man somewhere." Alric shook his head and laughed. "A woman or gambling?"

Grillion's scowl went deeper and he folded his arms. "Three women and some gambling. But what do you mean it collapsed? There were still a lot of pieces left."

I was pretty sure I knew what section Alric was talking about. "That entire area, if it's the one I think it is, was extremely unstable. I'm a digger. Or was. Anyway, some folks were trying to get Alric and made it more unstable than it had been. A huge section is now on the valley floor. Most likely anything you were looking for is dust now."

"Damn it." Grillion waved his hand in the air. "That wasn't why we came up here, but it would have been a sweet bonus. Suffice it to say, I'm back to working for a living and have been hired to get you, and the lovely Taryn, to follow us back south."

"Someone in the southern continent knows of me?" I disliked that idea, more so because there were now two groups trying to get us to go south. I might just relocate to the frozen north if this kept up.

"Yes, they do. Spoke highly of you, not so much of Alric, but as I figured the person they were speaking of was the one I knew—I understood. Yes, here you go, milady." He held out a fancy, albeit slightly crumpled, letter.

I looked to Alric. We might be able to outrun them. He knew the forest better than anyone. He nodded toward the letter and I took it with a sigh. The wax seal was some outrageous flower with loops running through what could be initials but it was too ornate to tell.

The writing inside was almost as bad. I went down to

the signature and started swearing.

"What does it say?" Alric leaned forward.

"I haven't read it yet, but it's from Qianru." I shared my annoyance with Alric and then read the letter. Qianru had been one of my patrons from when I was an official digger in the ruins around Beccia. She'd also been a spy of sorts for her people from the south. She'd left to go back and report in and see if the Dark had made further moves several months ago. She hadn't been here for the final relic battle, nor did she have a clue what I was.

Her letter had a tone of ordering me about, even as she was asking for my assistance. There were signs of a growing power within the Dark, a group of elves who had tried a thousand years ago to take over all their people. Many of her fellow spies, sent to find out what was happening, never returned. So, she wanted us to come and help. I held up the letter. "Didn't we send faeries down with her and Locksead who were supposed to contact us if there was trouble? It sounds like the Dark are alive and well down there."

"Her faeries took off actually," Grillion said. "At least she said she had faeries, but I never saw them. Not that I really want to, after our friends in that cave." He looked to Alric and gave a shudder.

I raised an eyebrow, but Alric shook it off. I'd get the story out of him later.

"How well do you know her? Or did she just hire anyone who would be willing to come north?" Alric's friend might be claiming he wasn't here to find more of the gold tiles, but I had a feeling that was his real reason for traveling here. He didn't strike me as a letter runner. Not to mention three men for one little envelope seemed a bit of overkill.

I looked to Alric. If he seemed the least bit concerned, we were out of there. But he still was too relaxed to be worried.

"We all work for her, to be honest, not as diggers, but site security, jobs around her house, etc. Pretty much anything her houseboys won't do." Grillion rolled his eyes. "So, you going to come down with us and save the world? Qianru seems to think you're good at it."

"We have things going on here," I said, "and I'm not sure that leaving on a really long trip would be the best thing right now." There was nothing happening right now, and I wanted to keep it that way.

"We protect!" I heard the faery yells before I saw the actual faeries. Garbage whooped as she led her troop right at Grillion and the other two. So much for our escape. The faeries couldn't have made it to Beccia and back in this time—they'd turned around.

Grillion turned white as a sheet, rolled off his horse, and dove under the large animal. "Keep them away!"

Hass and Fealk didn't look comfortable about the attacking faeries, but they weren't on the edge of a nervous breakdown like Alric's friend.

I looked to Alric, but he was having a hard time keeping his laughter in check.

"Girls! Settle down. We don't think these men mean us any harm. Pull back but keep an eye on them." I knew this Grillion person was a friend of Alric's but that didn't mean a lot considering who Alric used to run with. If the faeries scared him, I was all for it.

The two men with him continued watching the girls as they pulled back but kept circling. Both men seemed calm but had their hands on their swords. If they had some crazy idea of forcing us to go to Qianru, maybe they'd rethink it now. Knowing my former patron, she might have offered them a lot of money to *encourage* us to come back. It wouldn't dawn on her that they might go to extremes to make it happen.

"Not that your timing isn't great, but why aren't you all on your way to Beccia?"

"We hear these. Bad men." Garbage flew up to Hass and Fealk and gave them her glare. But she ignored Grillion.

I knew Grillion probably thought hiding under the horse protected him. I also knew the faeries were aware of where he was, and Crusty in particular was watching him closely. That was interesting. The faeries were watching Grillion but with just an interest. Garbage, Leaf Grub, and the rest of the clump were glaring at Hass and Fealk and looking pissed.

Alric watched them all as well and his eyes narrowed. His sword also reappeared. "Grillion? How well do you know your two friends?"

"You're questioning us based on some crazy butterflies?" Hass started to ride forward, but Garbage buzzed in his face and pushed him to move his horse back.

Fealk's hand stayed on his sword, and the other hand moved toward his waistband. A knife would be my guess, or if they had such things in the south, a spell packet. I didn't sense that any of them were magic users, but this magic-sensing thing was new to me.

A moment later my sword decided to show up. In my hand this time, which was nice. I hadn't consciously called it, though, so either it knew something I didn't, or deep inside I knew something. I backed my horse down the trail a bit to give us more space.

Alric leaned forward. "Grillion?"

Grillion was still under his horse. His friends were on one side; we were on the other. He crawled out on our side, so his horse was between him and the other two.

"Not well, really. They were both newer hires but willing to make the trip. Qianru wanted more than one to make sure the note got to you. Hass? I don't know much about these faeries; what I do know I'd like to forget. Why do they dislike you two but not me?" Grillion had a short sword out and his other hand was near his dagger.

"We're workers-for-hire just like you. These things don't

know nothing." Hass only slightly swung at Garbage, not a real attempt to hit her, more of frustration. He obviously didn't realize what a threat she was.

CHAPTER THREE

———◆———

THAT WAS ENOUGH FOR MY maniacal orange faery. Her war stick was back in her hand, and the dozen faeries closest to her armed themselves as well. She charged forward and stabbed Hass in the offending hand with her stick.

It was just one, and I didn't think she'd been trying. But it was enough to make him swear and pull back his hand in pain.

"What in the hell? I didn't do anything."

"You swung at her. Trust me, those little sticks might look cute, but you won't be getting up if they all go after you." I turned to Fealk. "Either of you."

Grillion had now moved next to Alric. "You know I'm not with them, right?" He shook his head, but his eyes were focused on Hass and Fealk now, not the faeries. "I came up here with them. But I have no idea what they're up to."

Hass threw both hands in the air but kept them far from the faeries. "This is stupid. Your flying bugs don't like us. That's not our fault. We haven't threatened anyone."

Alric had been unnerved by the faeries when he first met them, but he trusted them now. "Both of you roll up your sleeves."

Damn. I hadn't even noticed that both Hass and Fealk had long sleeves. Grillion didn't and it was a warm day.

"Have they always worn long sleeves?" I asked Grillion while Alric had a stare-down with the other two.

He scratched the side of his head and watched them. "Yup. Never thought of it, but regardless of the weather—always long sleeves."

Neither of them were elves, but the elven followers of the Dark all had stylized circle and dagger tattoos on the underside of their right wrist. I hadn't heard of the Dark going beyond elven kind, but Alric might know more about them. Not to mention, they'd lost a lot of their followers up here in the recent months. Recruiting other species might be their current plan to regain their strength. Or, they just used them as disposable flunkies.

"First these things hate us for no reason, now you care about our clothes? No, we're not rolling our sleeves up." Hass folded his arms and Fealk followed.

"Just what did Qianru tell you about me? Or Alric?" I created a spell ball, a nice little bundle of annoyance that would hurt, possibly stun, but wouldn't leave any long-term damage. Mostly it was just a showy way to remind them I was a magic user. They didn't need to know I was still getting the hang of my new/old powers. Who I was had come back to me. What I could do and how to do it was taking a bit longer.

"Just told us to bring you back."

Both men made their horses move back a few steps. The trail wasn't wide, and they were already standing outside of it.

"I really don't want to deal with this right now." Alric flung his hand and his sword vanished. But then so did the right sleeve on both men. Unfortunately, both kept their arms down.

"Raise your arms or I release this." I held up the spell ball and ignored the wide-eyed look Grillion was giving us.

Hass did. There was the tattoo. The circle and dagger

were there on a human wrist.

"They're recruiting non-elves now?" It was what I'd guessed but seeing it didn't make me happy.

Hass threw a dagger. Luckily, he was a bad shot and it flew harmlessly between us, and both he and Fealk spun their horses to run into the forest.

The faeries tore after them.

"Are you going after them? And what is that tattoo? I have more than a few myself, not that I'd do anything to harm any of you." Grillion watched both Alric and me carefully. Alric had never mentioned Grillion, but then he didn't talk much about his time as a relic thief, so I wasn't that surprised.

Alric sat back on his horse. "No. I've learned a lot about those faeries in the last two years, and those two are in worse trouble than they'd be with us."

"So, Grillion, you're one of Alric's relic hunter friends?" I had met a few of Alric's friends; to be honest, sneaking around for years as he had, he didn't have many. His closest friend, Padraig, almost killed him when they first found each other in the elven enclave because a mage wearing Alric's face had murdered Padraig's wife and two friends. Once they'd realized what had really happened, they were fine again. Padraig had gone back to help rebuild their elven hometown—and reconstruct the shield that hid it for a thousand years.

But Grillion seemed extremely interesting.

"Yeah, we were friends, right?" He kept staring at Alric's hair and ears. "Damn should have known you were an elf—too sneaky for a human. We did a few jobs. After that run-in with that Cirocco, I ran all the way down to the southern lands." He shuddered. "He's really not around here, is he? I deliberately made sure to avoid Beccia on our way to find you."

I lifted an eyebrow toward Alric. "Was that what he sent me after you for?"

"Yes, and it was worth it." He laughed and nodded toward Grillion. "After you left, those faeries came back and took their statue from Cirocco. They were not happy, and he had a rough time."

I was going to ask for more detail, but a loud crashing came through the woods at us. Fealk was in the lead and on foot. Hass was right behind him, also without a horse. The faeries—and it looked like they'd added some to their numbers—were forming a curve on the sides and back, cheering the running men on with whoops. Occasionally, a single faery would dive in, poke one of the men with her war stick, then go back into the flying crowd.

Alric was right; they brought the men back to us. Unfortunately, they showed no sign of stopping.

"Girls! Stop chasing them!" I yelled, but the faeries were having too much fun to hear me.

I held out my hands. I could do this, a spell to freeze both men. I sent it out. And nothing happened. "But I felt the spell!"

"I know," Alric said softly. "We'll figure it out later." He flung what I should have been flinging and both men crashed to a stop. Of course, it was just their feet, so they quickly tumbled over.

The faeries, realizing their prey was now behind them, all swung in wide arcs to fly back and contain their prisoners. Crusty smacked into a tree as she turned, giggled, shook her shoulders, and then followed the others.

"Are you sure we're okay with them? The faeries won't hurt us?" If Grillion's eyes got any larger, they were going to come out of his head.

Hass and Fealk both stayed on the ground with the faeries flying low to keep them there.

"The faeries are on our side," Alric said. He swung off his horse and patted down the two men, removing the weapons he found, and then tying them up. Neither one moved. Clearly, while they had been planning something, the faeries made them rethink it.

"Bad men! We keep!" Garbage was in full warrior faery mode right now. She didn't have her war feathers on, but her scowl would rattle any sober person.

"I guess we have to take them into town now?" I was really tempted to send a small annoying itch spell at both men just for ruining our getaway.

"We take!" Garbage flew in closer to Hass and poked him in the shoulder.

"Don't let them!" Hass curled into a fetal position. "We'll tell you what we know."

I shared a look with Alric. The Dark were getting extremely desperate if they were recruiting people like these two. Fealk hadn't said anything yet, but he followed what Hass did.

"Garbage, you and the faeries can have them if they make one move to hurt us or get away on the way into town."

Garbage flew up in front of my face. She was scowling at first, then a small smile appeared. "Pub?"

"Fine. *After* we turn these over." I looked over to Alric. Law enforcement in Beccia had never been active. And I didn't think most of them would care about thieves that belonged to an elven death cult. But they might if these two tried to rob two heroes of the town.

Alric's face said he was thinking the same thing. Or so I hoped.

"Yes, we'll have to take them in, and then our fighting flyers deserve a trip to the pub." He held up his hand as the faeries started cheering. "Once we get these two behind bars."

Grillion watched everyone but still looked confused. "I'm not going to jail?"

"Do you want to?" He'd almost sounded disappointed. I'd rather not lock up one of Alric's friends if he were innocent.

"No, no, no. Just making sure." He turned to Alric. "Lead

on, boss." He got back on his horse.

"Where are their horses?"

"That way." Twenty-three faeries all pointed in different directions.

Grillion looked out into the woods. "I can find their horses and meet you somewhere. Cirocco won't be a problem, for sure?" The longer we were out here, the more worried he'd become about the crime lord.

"Not unless he comes back as a ghost. He came across people worse than him and lost his head." Alric tied a short lead to the ropes he'd secured the men with. Neither would be comfortable jogging along the horses, but that wasn't a concern.

"Good," Grillion said, then froze. "Wait, worse than him?"

"They're dead, too. I made sure of that." I flashed a smile when he got the terrified deer look again. "They were far worse than him, but they're gone. I think meeting us at the Shimmering Dewdrop would be a good idea."

Grillion laughed at Alric. "You still like that place?" He turned to me. "I told him about that pub, went there my last night here."

"And that's where I picked him up. Alric was my bounty."

"Oh! Going for the beautiful magic-using bounty hunter, now, are ya?" He flashed Alric a grin and a wink.

"Yes." Alric got back on his horse and nudged the two men to start walking. "See you at the pub." He was abrupt. Most likely he was afraid Grillion was going to tell me some mystery of his past. I wasn't worried. I was sure I could get all the good stories out of Grillion later. Shyness didn't seem to be one of his problems.

Grillion nodded, got back on his horse, and went deeper into the forest. Those horses could have gone anywhere, but he seemed to have a solid direction.

Alric waited a few minutes, then turned to the other two. "Start talking. We have at least a half hour to get to town. We want to hear all about what you two were doing here and what the Dark is up to."

Hass turned as they slowly went down the trail. "The who?"

"The Dark. What are those marks on your arms?" I'd seen enough of them. There was no doubt that those tattoos were from the Dark.

"These were for a gang. Small-time hoods, but we joined just because it's better to be with folks than not, ya know? Never heard of the Dark. Sort of a weak name for a bad guy, isn't it?"

Alric gave a light tug on the ropes. "They use that mark, and they've been around for over a thousand years. Want to try answering the question again?"

"Jab now?" This time it was Leaf who wanted to go after them, but the surrounding faeries all looked ready to assist. Whether we wanted it or not.

"If we don't start getting some answers soon, yes, jab away." Granted, until we were faced with them, I'd never heard of the Dark. But the odds were a little high that some random gang picked up the exact same tattoo in the exact same location as them.

"Look, we joined this gang. We're thieves, okay? They wanted us to get in with your friend, Qianru. She has something the leader wants. Then she asks for folks to come up and bring you two back. Our boss gets interested and tells us to take the job."

"Fealk? You stand by his words? Are you willing to die if he's lying? Those faery sticks can kill and it's not pretty." With Alric's rope being short, both men had to jog to keep up.

Fealk had appeared to be following Hass on everything. Strong, silent, and willing to let Hass take the lead. But I caught the side of his face as he turned to answer. There was a calculating darkness there. It vanished immediately, but I knew what I saw. I revised who I thought was in charge between the two.

"Yeah, what Hass said."

I shook my head when Alric glanced my way, but I wasn't going to call Fealk out on it right now. If he wasn't what he was pretending to be, letting him think he'd fooled us would be the best way to catch him.

Or so I hoped.

CHAPTER FOUR

BECCIA HADN'T BEEN THE CENTER of fighting during that last battle. That one took place in a huge field a few days ride from us and finished up over the ocean. But it had still been under some duress in the past two years, including a now former tree goddess setting up a massive, magical hedge around it. The town was no longer enclosed, but she'd left sections of the hedge up. Since, as far as I knew, her goddess powers were completely gone now, Amara must have decided the new plant life was staying.

This left Beccia looking pretty much as ragged as usual, but with more green touches. The town's only real claim to fame were the elven ruins. Finding out that the elves were still alive had eased up the demand for dig space a bit, but now more folks were going deeper—trying to find the relics of the Ancients—aka my people. After the events of the last battle, and my discovery of my true self, my friends and I all agreed that would be a secret we'd keep. Myths and rumors were spread around, even among the elven knights who had joined us in battle, to hide what had really happened when I'd transformed. It was easier to hide a difficult-to-believe reality among a bunch of even more outrageous lies.

The main road through the town was also the road that had the most pubs. Foxy happened to be outside sweeping in front of the Shimmering Dewdrop as we rode by.

"Taryn! Alric! Thought we wouldn't be seeing you two for a bit longer yet." He scowled as he saw our tied-up friends. "You're bringing in prisoners? Did they try to attack you?" Foxy was about seven feet tall, with tusks that rose from his lower jaw, long floppy ears, and kind, wide eyes. Unless he was angry. Right now, the way they were lowered and the grip on his broom didn't bode well for either the broom or Hass and Fealk,

"They did, but we're taking them to let the guards deal with them." I looked at both. Hass started to say something, most likely that they hadn't attacked us, but closed his mouth when I motioned for the faeries to come in closer. "Yes, either they go to be locked up or the girls get them."

Technically, neither had attacked us, but since what they were possibly guilty of was too complicated to try to explain to anyone in town, claiming that they attacked us would work for now. We needed them locked up until we could figure out what they were up to.

"Ya coming back for a drink?" It was still early in the day, but that wouldn't stop most Beccians.

"Amara still making the food?" I'd enjoyed my hideaway with Alric, there was no doubt about that. But neither of us were great cooks. Along with being a former tree goddess, Foxy's wife was an amazing cook.

"Every day! She does love it so." Foxy's eyes went dreamy. He loved his tiny tree nymph wife to distraction. He never knew she'd been the last tree goddess, and she'd wanted it that way.

"We'll be back after we escort these two down to the jail." Alric started moving down the road.

The faeries drifted farther behind us. I turned my horse toward them. Yup, they were looking at the pub. "Not until these two are locked up. That was our deal."

"Aye, ladies, I can't be serving ya until you finish your

task." Foxy looked sad but had a little smirk. He adored the faeries but knew I was trying to get them to follow instructions better.

Garbage's sigh was loud enough that they probably heard it miles away. "Is fine. Have job." She darted forward and poked Fealk in the arm. "We jab."

The jab did get him to move faster, so I didn't say anything.

I did, however, drop farther back so they were all ahead of me. Hass appeared to be trudging along. He clearly wasn't happy but looked resigned. Fealk looked edgy. There was something else going on. My hunch that he was up to something became stronger.

We got down to the jail without being stopped or having either of our prisoners cause a scene. We also had gathered about forty more extra faeries from who knew where. That was one of a list of things my girls never told me. How they could just pull in extra faeries for specific jobs. Ones who weren't anywhere near us as far as I could tell and who vanished afterward.

"State the reason for your visit." The bored guard at the entrance to the jail didn't even look up from his counter as we approached on foot with our captives behind us.

"We were attacked in the forest and want these two locked up," Alric said.

"We have to know the entire story before we can lock any—"

"Bad men. Lock up. Now." Garbage cut him off and flew right into his face. I loved my orange faery, but I wouldn't want her an inch from my nose. Even to me she looked like she was thinking of biting it.

The guard screamed, flailed his arms, and tumbled off the stool he'd been sitting on. Hass flinched, but Fealk stood perfectly still. I stepped closer to him. I couldn't put my finger on it, but there was something beyond just a common thug about him.

Two more guards came running into the front, one helping the first one to his feet, the other looking at us. He blanched at the pack of pissed-off faeries, then started nodding. "Alric and Taryn. Nice to see you. Have some prisoners, do you? We can take them right off your hands." He looked like he was going to fall over himself, but it was nerves. I knew we'd become a little famous, but I didn't think we were enough so to make a guard nervous about us. Probably the gang of faeries was doing it.

He didn't wait, just came around the counter, and held his hand out for the rope that lead to both.

"Don't you want to know what they did?" Alric held onto the rope.

"Oh. Yes, we should do that." He went back to the counter where the first guard was cowering away from a still visibly annoyed Garbage Blossom and came back with a pad. "What did they do?"

Alric still didn't look satisfied but shrugged. "They attacked us out in the forest and demanded our money." Technically, Grillion had done that in jest. Hopefully, the Beccian court was still moving as slowly as normal and could keep these two locked up until we figured out what was really going on.

I sighed as the guards took both men into the building to be processed. So much for my romantic trip into the wilds. The faeries circled the building once, then took off.

"You might want to keep them in separate cells," I added as we turned away. I didn't trust Fealk, but as I couldn't say why, I had to keep things vague.

"Will do, thank you again!" Our cheerful, nervous, and far-too-helpful guard nodded and smiled until he and the prisoners were out of sight.

"What was that about?"

"I don't know, but there's something odd about Fealk."

Alric looked thoughtful on the trip back to the pub. "I am sorry we didn't get away. We can try again in a day or two. Maybe get some more information out of Grillion."

"Maybe." I didn't have that optimism, but one could hope.

Foxy wasn't outside the pub when we approached, but Grillion's horse and two more were tied up out front.

The Shimmering Dewdrop would never be called fancy, but since Amara had joined the crew, first as waitress and then as wife and chef, it had a clean, homey feel to it.

Not a lot of people inside yet, most diggers would be working right now, and it was too late for the overnight drunks. The smell of fresh roasted chicken with herbs almost made me climb over the counter to get to the food.

"Ah! You've made it back. I assumed the villains were locked up as the ladies just appeared a few moments ago." Foxy came out from the back before I noticed an entire flock of faeries lining the bar. Sometimes they took over a table, but the bar had a nice rim to it to keep them from falling off too many times. They had a bottle of ale for every three or four faeries and were getting gloriously tipsy.

"You know, I'd kind of thought that maybe once Mathilda found them again, the drinking would stop." Mathilda had been the woman who found me fifteen plus years ago when I'd flung myself into this time from twenty-five hundred years ago. She'd also been taking care of some faeries—three to be exact. Once she decided I could survive on my own, she abandoned me with Garbage, Leaf, and Crusty and took off in her walking house.

While the faeries were drinking steadily, they were being subdued about it.

"They've been this calm lately?" While we'd been on our retreat, the faeries had been in the care of assorted friends. Mostly, as long as my house down the road was open to them, they'd been on their own even though I knew Irving and Bunky would be watching the faeries as much as my house. The tiny faery door above the main door had been reinstalled so they could come and go.

"Yes. Amara had a talk with them, and they've been very good."

I wasn't sure that was a good sign, as they could be storing things up for a wild time down the line. But I'd take it for now. "I think we'll sit away from them anyway." I pointed to a table near the back that Grillion had already staked out and Alric was heading toward. "Odd question, but have there been any visitors from the south? Like way south?" I was now curious as to where the faeries got their idea about us having to go south. Even though they'd backed off on the urgency, it had still been something they were sure of.

"Not really, at least none that stood out. But, come to think of it, there were a group of faeries that your bunch was excited to see. Just after the big war ended. Your bunch even left half-finished ale bottles after talking to them. Very upset about something."

Damn it. Those could have been the faeries we sent with Qianru, reporting in. I shoved that thought aside for now. Getting answers out of my girls was time consuming and difficult in the best of times. Hitting them up after they'd started drinking wasn't a good idea. "Thanks, Foxy. Can we get three lunch specials and ales?"

"Right away." He nodded. "Good to have you both back, by the way. Since all the mayhem is over, I'm thinking you two will be staying in town?"

"Not sure, but probably." I flashed him a big grin that I didn't feel and went to join Alric and Grillion. Truth was, I really hadn't thought past having more time with Alric. I didn't have a digger patron, and as far as I knew, Alric didn't have a job. We'd have to do something, I supposed. He'd briefly mentioned maybe going back to live with his people, but never really pushed it. I'd loved their town, but somehow Beccia felt more like my type of home. And Alric had spent most of the last few years outside of the elven enclave as well.

Alric was standing as he spoke to Grillion and pulled out a chair for me. "I think we have an issue." He nodded to Grillion. "Tell her what you just told me."

Grillion had an ale already and took a long sip before starting. He didn't look happy. "Now maybe I should have said something earlier, but it wouldn't have mattered really, and then they might have been more difficult to get to jail." He gave a weak smile, then continued. "To be honest, I only remembered after you had all left. But Fealk was wanted for murder a year or so ago. I was working with another crew but recalled the case. Got caught in the act. Everyone was sure he was going to hang. Then got a last-minute reprieve and the witnesses all said they'd been wrong." He paused again and looked at his ale before he spoke. "Funny thing, he wore long-sleeved shirts then, and it was one of the hottest weeks in the year."

It was a good thing Foxy hadn't brought my drink out yet; I would have choked. "He was with the Dark that long ago?"

Grillion shrugged. "Since I never heard of these Dark before today, no idea. I know he did hang out with some elves, and they were the ones who got him off the murder charge."

I looked to Alric. "What can we do? We can't let them let him go. Hass might just be a thug who joined a group, but there is something else going on with Fealk."

"I don't know. My people won't step in since he's not an elf. And there's no way we can explain to the forces here what he is."

"Why such heavy looks?" Amara smiled as she came toward our table with a platter. Lehua, the half-giant waitress that came behind her, carried two platters that probably outweighed Amara.

"Just tired and awaiting your lovely self and your healing food." Grillion smiled quickly. "I am Grillion, by the way."

I hid my laugh. He was determined, but he kept hitting up the wrong women. But he took the focus off Alric and me. I got to my feet as soon as Amara put down the food and hugged her.

"I didn't get a chance for a proper thank you for what you did. Actually, no thank you could be enough for what you did." I glanced over her head to Alric. In that last battle, I'd lost him. I'd freed him, but he died. Amara had used the last of her Goddess abilities to bring him back. There was no way to repay that.

Amara squeezed me tightly, then pulled back with a gentle smile. "I'd always wondered why I survived for so long when none of my sisters did. I believe it was to help save him…and you." Her face grew serious. "Things could have ended a far different way."

I nodded but couldn't say anything. Thousands of years ago, in a fit of fear, pain, and anger, I'd thrown my own people so far into the future that they still hadn't reappeared. I could feel them, they were alive. But no idea where they were. Or rather *when*. I'd almost repeated my actions when I lost Alric.

Her green eyes went cloudy for a moment. "There will be other challenges down the line, ones you will have to face." Amara gave me another quick squeeze as her eyes cleared. "Everything is fine now, yet it won't be if you let those two eat all the food."

Grillion and Alric had been blissfully unaware of the conversation and were busy wolfing down the food.

I gave Amara another hug and sat down to eat. Once she was satisfied that we were all eating, she and Lehua went back to the kitchen.

"She made this?" Grillion got out between bites. "Is she married?"

Alric hooked his thumb over to the bar. "To the bartender, Foxy."

Grillion might not have paid much attention to Foxy

when he came in, but he did now. His eyes grew larger than the massive, and mostly empty, platter in front of him. "Oh." His face fell.

"You can still enjoy her cooking," I said. The chicken was golden and seasoned perfectly. The day might not have gone anywhere near where I'd expected it to, but this was almost as good as running away with Alric for a few more days. Almost.

"So, what do we do? Qianru's note really doesn't give much information. She's not my patroness anymore, and she can't force me to do anything." I looked down; somehow, I'd finished everything on my plate.

"No, but if the Dark is rising again? We have no idea how many of them came north. I need to speak to the king and queen." Alric frowned.

"You're friends with the royals around here?" Grillion's eyes were huge again.

"The elven royals, not the ones of this kingdom. But yes, I suppose we're friends."

He didn't look happy and I had to agree. Nothing against the royals or the rest of those in charge of repairing the formerly hidden elven city, many of which I did count as friends. But they could force Alric to go, or not go, depending on their response. Alric came across like a free soul, but before me, everything he'd done for most of his life had been to try to help his people.

Alric watched Grillion's reaction, then turned to me. "You should come with me, and we need to ask your faeries if they know what happened to the ones we sent with Qianru. But Grillion, I need you to stay here in town. Someone has to keep an eye on your two friends."

I could tell he liked his friend more than trusted him, and from the crooked smile, Grillion knew that as well.

"I can do that. Got a place I can stay here in town? I've been living in a tent and a bed roll for the past few weeks."

Alric looked over to me; it was my house after all. Alric

usually stayed in hidden caves, traveling houses, or just rented a seedy dump. He was without a dump right now.

I sighed. "Yes, you can stay in my house." I held up a hand. "The faeries and two constructs live there too, so watch how you treat things." I'd have to make sure to explain things clearly to Bunky and Irving.

Grillion looked over to the bar where my little friends were sitting, chatting, and swimming in ale. "They really aren't as scary as those other ones, are they?"

"They really aren't," Alric said and turned toward me. "We ran into a batch of faeries before you and I met—wild ones. It wasn't a fun experience."

That explained Grillion's initial terror. As well as Alric's fear when he first met them. Hopefully, some caution would remain, and he'd tread lightly in my house.

"Was there anything else you can think of?" Alric asked Grillion as he chased the last bits of food off his plate. "Anything that Qianru might have said? Changes in town?"

Grillion puffed up his cheeks and looked upward. Then he let loose his breath and shook his head. "Not really. I'm afraid I don't notice a lot. That's why I hang around folks like you. Wait, she was concerned about some artifacts. Some that were missing, or some that shouldn't be down there?" He shrugged. "Possibly both."

I pulled out Qianru's letter again. Maybe I was missing something. Nope, still just a vague "get down here now" note. I handed it to Alric.

He read it again but shrugged. "She's really non-specific, aside from mentioning the Dark."

I couldn't believe I was going to say this. I really, really didn't want to say this. "I think we have to go down there." I knew any relics down there weren't from my people. The ones I'd created and that had caused problems were ground magically and physically into dust. But I knew better than most what horrible damage magical relics could cause. Even worse, anything created by the Dark.

Alric nodded but watched me carefully.

"What? We don't really have a choice. I agree we need to talk to your people; the Dark are their issue more than mine. But we sort of have to go."

"I'm just surprised but I agree. I think we need to make a plan."

A rumbling explosion rocked the pub windows before I could respond. Strong enough to knock Grillion, who had been halfway out of his seat flirting with Lehua, to the ground.

Alric beat me to his feet but only by a hair. I turned to the faeries at the bar. "Girls! I need you to follow us." Their drinking had been a bit lighter than usual, so I thought most would be sober enough to help. But they flew up, then sat back down. Those faeries weren't going anywhere soon. Explosions of any type were not a good thing, but especially in Beccia. I'd hoped the town was past them. I was wrong, apparently.

Everyone in the pub ran out into the street. A thin waft of smoke came from the southern end of town.

"The jail," Alric and I said at pretty much the same instant. *Crap*, I'd misjudged Fealk worse than I thought.

CHAPTER FIVE

FOXY WAS RIGHT NEXT TO us, holding a large club. Normally, he controlled escalating situations by size and strength alone, saving weapons for dire circumstances. It said a lot about how things had changed in the past two years that his go-to was now a piece of wood the size of my leg.

"Who were those two that ye brought in?" He nodded toward the smoke.

"People that I shouldn't have been riding with, that's for damn sure," Grillion said from behind us. He looked a bit sick. "I swear, I had no idea what those two were up to." He quickly turned between Alric and me. Then he started nodding at Foxy as well.

Alric kept watching the smoke but waved to Grillion. "I believe you. We need to go down there. It's doubtful that whatever that is, those two are not involved."

We both went for our horses, but Grillion stayed where he was. Alric turned to him as he got on his horse "You too this time, Grillion. Foxy, can you watch those extra horses? They may try for them."

I looked at the closed pub door. "The faeries seem pretty out of it, but if they come out tell them to come after us."

Lehua the barmaid stepped forward with her massive pike. "I'll watch." The grin on her face said she was really hoping someone would try for the horses. Too bad Dogmaela the troll barmaid wasn't on right now. She'd be even more excited than Lehua. Of course, she might also go and hunt the culprits down on her own before they tried for a horse. Needless to say, Foxy never had a problem with customers harassing his staff.

The three of us rode toward the jail. I didn't own a horse before this all started but I had to admit, getting from one end of town to the other on horseback was a lot faster than walking.

Grillion kept drifting behind until Alric turned to him. "If you keep doing that, we're going to think you *are* involved with them."

Grillion didn't say anything but nudged his horse to keep up.

People were moving away from the jail, but no one was running in terror or covered in blood, so that was a promising start.

The guard we'd handed Hass and Fealk over to came running out, looking around frantically. He had his sword held up, but as of yet, there was no sight of whom he had been chasing.

"Did you see them? Four men, running this way. Tried to destroy the jail." He stopped jumping around long enough to recognize Alric and me. "Oh, sorry. Um, those two you brought in seem to have escaped."

"But you said there were four?"

"Yes, well, they appeared to have some friends, or at least someone they knew. They had hidden spell bombs and blew out the back wall. Then all four left together."

Grillion immediately started in. "I swear, they never said anything about—"

"We know." Alric and I both responded at the same time. If we had to travel with Grillion for any length of time, I was going to have to gag him. Or see if there was a silencing spell I could rummage up.

There were no other guards coming out this way, and

the smoke had diminished to a thin wisp. I looked over to the guard. "Where are the rest of your people?"

"Oh, they all went to the forest behind the ruins. The wall that blew out was on that side, so that's where the escapees would have gone."

I narrowed my eyes at him, then turned to Alric and Grillion. "Maybe I'm wrong, but if you were planning a jail break, wouldn't you stay silent, so no would go looking for you?" They were both thieves, or at least had been in the past. Odds were good they'd been locked up a few times.

"Damn it, it would," Alric said and got off his horse. "Who's inside with your other prisoners?"

"I am, er, was. I heard people riding up, you three as it turns out." He looked confused. "But they aren't going anywhere."

Alric's sword appeared in his hand and he jogged toward the jail. I kept an eye on Grillion, the guard, and the area around us. Something was making the hairs on the back of my neck stand on end.

As Alric stepped into the jail, I'd almost expected something to happen. An explosion. Something. But nothing happened. The other guards could be heard yelling to each other in the distance. If Hass and Fealk had been stupid enough to go that way, avoiding the guards wouldn't have been a problem. The explosion had been a distraction, I just had no idea for what. My own sword appeared, which was always nerve-racking when I had no idea why it did that.

I was just about to tell the guard to go check on Alric when a smoking fabric bag flew in between the three of us. The guard was closest, and he crumbled almost immediately. Grillion had time to try to pull back his horse, when both he and it collapsed. I threw up a spell bubble around myself and my horse. It was automatic. The time spent with Alric hadn't been just relaxation—we'd been working on my spells.

The spell bubble hadn't been one I'd known from before, but he was adamant that I repeat it until I could do it in my sleep. Extending it over the horse was harder but I did it.

I felt a little groggy as a whiff of the contents of the bag got in before I could shut the bubble, but that was all. I spun my horse in the direction the spell bundle had come from. Whoever threw it had planned on it knocking all of us out, not killing us. I could see that the guard, Grillion, and even his horse were breathing—just not moving.

The bushes in that direction moved, and I heard at least two people running away. Riding through the shrubs on horseback wasn't a good idea, so I jumped off my horse. The horse seemed fine even as my spell bubble moved with me. That was a really short-term spell. "Okay, horse, stay here." I never knew if they really understood me or not, but Alric whispered to the horses all the time and they listened. I figured it couldn't hurt. I ran to the bushes. They were dense enough that I could be running into a trap. I looked down the street. This would be the perfect time for my faeries to have recovered and be winging their way to my rescue. Or not. Nothing was flying my way. And I had no way to call my constructs, Bunky and Irving. With a glance back at the others—still out cold—I raised my sword and ran into the bushes.

Whoever I was chasing hadn't expected a need to run, or so I assumed, judging by the area they'd attacked me from. Good to hide in, not to move in. I heard rustling as they were getting away. Not if I could help it.

I kept moving forward. We were going deeper into the ruins, but the dig sites were closed on this end, so there was no one else around. I picked up speed, but the trail here was extremely overgrown.

A dark shape ducked around a pile of rocks. Hass, if I had to guess, not tall enough for Fealk. I ignored whoever the third and fourth persons could be. I ran wide of the rock formation, close enough to keep following them, but not so close that they could ambush me.

Four men vanished on the other side of a large dig site. One that was well cleared. Definitely Fealk and Hass, but the other two were in the lead and I couldn't see them well enough. I ran into the clearing and was hit with another spell bomb. This one must have been planted in the ground as it hit me in the face, but no one threw it.

I stumbled and fell to one knee. It hit too fast for me to get up the spell bubble, and my brain and eyes were scrambled. My sword vanished as I dropped to my hands and knees.

"She's still awake!" That was Hass and looking up, I could see three people edging my way. They looked to have a net or ropes with them.

I shook my head to clear it and managed to push aside the fog, but it crept back in. I had no idea what they intended to do with me, but I wasn't letting it happen. It took far too much focus, but I got to my feet as the men closed in.

"Give up, honey, you're going to bring us a hell of a lot of gold down south." It was Fealk and his grin was evil.

"I am not your honey." I got up and forced the change. Forced wasn't really the right word. I was pissed, scared, and drugged so my body sort of did it on its own. Changing into my dragon shape was still odd. Up until a few months ago I hadn't done it for over twenty-five hundred years. But it felt right this time and the change pushed out the fog from my brain.

The four of them didn't react at first. But once I completely changed into my full dragon self—they did. Running and screaming was certainly a reaction. I reached out with a claw to grab Fealk, but he managed to get away and I just got his cape. I stomped to the edge of the clearing, gnashed my teeth at them a few times, and then sat back on my haunches. The spell bomb was even affecting me in this larger form. I wanted to change back, but I was afraid if I was groggy right now, I might have inhaled enough to knock me out if I changed back.

Someone was running toward me from behind. Now I was stuck. Stay as I was and risk someone spotting a real dragon or change back and pass out possibly in front of the men who had tried to grab me.

Alric solved that quandary by bursting into the clearing.

"Why are you sitting like that?"

I sighed and changed back to human form. "I found the escapees. Hass and Fealk have two others with them." I fought a yawn and briefly there were two Alrics in front of me. "They used spell bombs. Knocked out the others. Got me too." I was still awake, but really felt like I needed to sleep for a week or so. "Tried to grab me. Went that way." I pointed where Fealk's cape lay.

Alric dropped to his knees in front of me and tipped my head up to look into my eyes. "Focus on me." There were words, but they sounded more in my head than from outside of it. The worst of the fatigue shoved off.

I blinked and everything came back into focus. "Thank you. Did you see Grillion and the guard?"

He helped me to my feet as I was still a bit unstable. "No, I came out this way since those damn guards were making so much noise the other way. Four cells were busted open and a weapons locker was broken into. Whatever the guards had been keeping in there is gone now."

I walked to where the remains of the spell bomb were. I wasn't going to touch it; the contents could still be active, but there might be a clue. Taking a stick, I lifted the shredded fabric. Flowery shredded fabric. "Would the guards be using tablecloths to contain spell bombs?" I knew that Beccia's guards weren't the best funded in the kingdom, but I wouldn't have thought this would belong to them.

Alric took the stick, then held a hand out toward the fabric. "I doubt it. This looks homemade, one of them probably had it stashed somewhere."

We walked back toward the jail. Chasing them now would be pointless and while less fuzzy than I had been, I wasn't up to running for anything.

"They were trying to grab me, or at least they were when they came back. They had ropes and said something about gold being involved."

Alric spun at that. "What? Damn it, that's not good."

We reached the edge of the road and climbed through the bushes. Grillion and the guard were just getting to their feet, and my horse and Grillion's were watching them. Horses must recover faster than humans.

"We help!" A flock of faeries came zipping up to us. Excellent timing on their part. They must have stopped by the house, as two familiar constructs came flying up as well. Bunky was a chimera, a construct created by my people eons ago. About the size of a large cat, he was all black with tiny wings, a goat face, a tiny fishlike tail, and a round body. All in all, not something that appeared to be designed to fly on its own. There were more of his kind flying free now, but he'd adopted the faeries and us and stuck around. Irving was a gargoyle construct created by an elf named Siabiane. He'd joined us and shown a love for eating the relics I'd created in the past. Both gronked at us as they flew overhead.

"Thanks, girls, Bunky, and Irving. We've got it under control." I stopped. "Actually, you know those two men you were guarding for us? The ones you could jab?"

Garbage nodded. "Bad mens."

"Yes, the bad mens, they got away. Do you think you could find them? Take Irving and Bunky with you and send them back if you find the bad mens." I knew we couldn't hope to follow the faeries in flight, but if they could at least harass Fealk and the others, it might make them do something stupid.

"Do!" She raised her war stick high and tore off into the ruins. It would have been nice if they had shown up when

I was first heading into the ruins myself, but maybe they could still do some good.

"What hit me?" Grillion's eyes were still unfocused.

"I'll stop them!" The guard waved his sword but was facing the jail. He was also rocking on his feet.

"Does your jail normally stock spell bombs wrapped in old fabric?"

The guard spun toward me; his eyes were as unfocused as Grillion's. "What? No. Ours are standard issue with paper wrappers. Fabric can muddle the spell." He paused. "Is that what hit me?"

I nodded to the remains of the spell bomb and the fabric flapping in the light breeze. "Looks like. I got a spell bubble up around me and my horse, but you two dropped fast. They ran off into the ruins."

The guard started to head where I indicated, but Alric put his hand out. "Your jail is missing four people and whatever was in your lockup. Can you tell me who they were and what they took? Pretty clear that the explosion was a decoy."

Grillion rubbed the side of his head. "Wait, so Hass and Fealk found new friends who just happened to be escaping?"

"Depends who they went with," Alric said and started walking toward the jail. "Maybe this entire thing was a setup."

I followed but shook my head. "Where'd that come from? I know my brains are still scrambled, but you think Hass and Fealk wanted us to throw them in jail? They hadn't seemed too happy about it at the time."

"Who knows? They suddenly picked up two buddies? The cells weren't even near each other. The remaining prisoners are pissed they were left behind, but all claim to have seen nothing."

The rest of the guards were coming back from the direction they'd taken off.

Our guard nodded at them, then turned to us. "Please wait out here, let me see who and what is missing."

We waited, but if he was embarrassed that they'd had a breakout and robbery it was pointless. We already knew and Alric had seen it all.

He came back a few minutes later. At first, I thought he was angry, then I realized it was fear. "We had two prisoners that were being transferred to the capital for war crimes. They'd been brought in by a bounty hunter four weeks ago. They'd been part of the forces that captured a good part of this town and locked us in those damn caves last year."

That's where the fear came from. He must have been taken along with about a third of the town by my late and extremely unlamented ex-boyfriend, Glorinal.

"Damn it. What was in the locker they broke open?" Alric looked ready to push past the guard and look again for himself but didn't.

"The items that had been on those first two when they were brought in weeks ago." He shook his head. "The captain is not going to be happy when he gets back."

"Where is he?"

"Went away this morning. Family emergency in Lachi."

I shared a look with Alric. That could be coincidence or not. I turned to Grillion. "You mentioned that you avoided going through town when you all got here, but was there any time that Fealk or Hass came near town alone?"

He started to shake his head, then stopped. "Last night. We'd stopped out of town a bit. I woke up during Fealk's watch and didn't see him. Hass woke up too and said Fealk wasn't feeling good, so he took himself off a ways. Hass took his watch, so I went back to sleep and didn't think much about it. We were close enough to this end of Beccia that he could have made it on foot and back before morning." He chewed the edge of his thumb, appearing to be trying to figure out what else he had missed.

Or how close he could have come to being killed if things had gone wrong.

"Who could those other two be that someone would bring up Hass and Fealk to free them?" Glorinal and his mentor, Jovan, had been elves, but the people they had working for them hadn't been. Maybe having non-elves be part of the Dark wasn't as unique as I thought. We'd figured the people working with Glorinal and Jovan were just hired thugs.

"You do a full search before anyone goes into lockup, right?"

The guard pulled himself up and looked offended. "Of course we do."

"Then you'd see any markings or tattoos?"

"Oh. Yes." He turned back toward the jail and motioned for us to follow.

The other guards were milling around. Ostensibly looking for clues, but they seemed aimless. "Who is in charge with your captain away?"

Our guard looked up from where he was digging through notes. "I am. I am sorry, never did introduce myself, did I? Sargent Kahlies, nice to meet you both officially." He went back to digging through the papers, oblivious to the mild mayhem around him. "Ha! Yes. Prisoner two-two-zero-eight, one Larkspur Johanes. Brought in for war crimes. Has tattoos of snakes, rats, flowers on right leg, also a small dagger in a circle on right wrist." He looked up, nodded to make sure we'd heard, then went back to digging.

"What is Larkspur? Human? Troll?" The ones I'd seen working with Jovan and Glorinal were mostly trolls, humans, or mixed breeds. None of the ones I saw would have willingly gone by the name Larkspur.

Kahlies looked up and blinked. "Oh, he's a troll. One of the Claron gang out of the north." Again, back into his search.

Alric looked as concerned as I felt. If this troll had escaped when we fought back against Glorinal and his people over a year ago, what was he still doing around here? Especially with a bounty on his head? The kingdom of Lindor, which for the most part ignored Beccia, wasn't large or powerful, but it did get cranky when people tried to take it over. Even a small, unassuming portion of it like Beccia. Why would they hang around knowing there was a bounty on their heads?

Kahlies waved another paper around. "Now, this one, I knew he was going to be a problem the minute they brought him in." He put the paper on the counter and stabbed it with his finger. "One Merthas Clenth, or so he said. Magic user of a deadly type, some sort of troll cross. Also wanted for that attack on our fair town." He shuddered. "Surprised we kept him as long as we did, to be honest. Yup, he only had one mark, that daggery thing that the other one had."

Two members of the Dark, rescued by two members. None that seemed to be elves. There was no way this was good.

"Do we know what's missing?" Alric nodded to the busted-open locker.

"That's going to be harder." Kahlies looked embarrassed. "We actually lost the key right after those two were brought in and their things locked up."

Alric sighed and rubbed the back of his neck, and I felt the same. Who knew what those Dark followers had on them when they were grabbed? Not us apparently. Usually the incompetence of the Beccian guards was simply something to joke about at the pub. This time it was a problem.

"Okay, then," I said. "How did they get out?"

Kahlies put aside his papers. "Of their cells or the prison?"

Alric stepped forward. "Both. I looked at those busted cells, and all of them had their locks blown from the outside. And the fact your remaining prisoners collectively blacked out and have no recall of anything that happened?

Those four didn't break out, someone got them out."

"Well, now." Kahlies looked around for someone else to step in, but the rest of his guards were all busily inspecting things further inside the jail.

I noticed a small room on this side of the counter. One with a distinctly singed door frame. "What's that room?" It didn't face the section of the woods that the guards had been searching.

"That's a storage closet. Which shouldn't be open." He stomped over with the air of finding something he could solve. The door had been partially open, but it was dark so nothing could be seen inside. He shoved the door open, hit a glow light near the door, swore weakly, and then passed out.

Alric and I beat the rest of the guards to him, so we got to see inside before any of them could get in the way.

The back section of the wall was cut away, not with a loud explosion like the distraction they'd done on the other side, but quietly cut away. That was bad. The magic involved in something so subtle was huge. What made me turn away and run outside was the body also in the room. He'd been tied to a chair, the gag still on what was left of his face. But someone had painfully pulled a lot of magic off him as he died. Necromancy could pull magic from the dying—whether the dying had magic to begin with or not. The remains of the uniform told me we'd found the missing guard captain.

CHAPTER SIX

—◆—

I GOT OUTSIDE AND ALMOST KNOCKED Grillion down. He'd been hovering near the doorway but must have had mixed feelings about going into a jail voluntarily. He grabbed my shoulders to steady me, then stepped back when he saw my face.

"If you're going to get sick, please go that way?" He pointed to some straggly bushes to the side of us.

I took a few deep breaths and let them out slowly. "I think I'm okay. Someone used some nasty magic to kill a guard."

"Hass and Fealk?" He looked about as green as I felt.

"No idea. Alric might be able to tell, but he might not. It was either one of them or the two people with them." I kept my voice low, but I quickly told him about the locks and what we knew.

"Damn. All I wanted was some extra coin and a chance to come up and get some more of those gold pieces. Now look what's happened." He folded his arms and scowled.

I started to feel less prone to be violently sick and if we were dealing with necromancers, I needed to get a better feel of their magic. "Can you stay here, near the door? Unless it looks dire, don't let anyone in aside from the guards. Tell them there was a magic leak." That would keep most sane people away.

Of course, right after I got him to agree, I marched back

into the building.

Alric was arguing with two of the guards. Three more were huddling in a corner. And our buddy Kahlies was shoved off to the side, slowly waking up. I went to help him.

"Are you okay?" I gently pulled him to a sitting position. If he was going to throw up, I could move away faster if he was still sitting down.

"I believe so," he said. "That is Captain Cleri, or was. So, he never left yesterday? He told me he was leaving clearly and loudly. He was gone when we locked things up last night. We spell the building but none of us stay here."

I looked over my shoulder where Alric was still arguing with the guards. "It looks like he was the intended sacrifice. But he looks recently killed, so he might have been in that closet the entire time. Someone killed him to get magic to get them out silently." Saying it out loud made me realize that made no sense. Yes, cutting through brick like that would have been insanely difficult. But why do it at all? If someone had that much power, they could get out another way. I patted Kahlies' knee. "Get up when you can. I'm sure the mage council will send someone to sort things out."

The mage council pretty much stuck to the Hill where they lived, but in this case, I figured they'd be down here the minute they heard about it. Necromancy was the only forbidden magic, and there were so few practitioners who lived beyond their first attempt that enforcing it wasn't a problem.

Until now.

I stood by Alric for a full minute, listening to him repeating that he needed to examine the body. I knew he could have just moved the guards, forced his way through with magic or muscle, but he was aware that everyone knew who he was now. His days of being a mysterious entity were gone.

"Can I talk to you for a minute?" I kept my voice low and made sure to give a slight smile to the freaked-out guards.

Alric glared at them, then stepped back with me. His glare dropped immediately.

"You were getting what you needed to find out while you were standing there arguing with them about why you should go inside." Sneaky.

"I was, but it would have been faster if I had been closer. I was running out of arguments to keep me standing there. What did you find out?"

"Nothing, really. I was thinking about this entire escape. Someone had that much power and they used it to get out of jail? Wouldn't there have been something easier? Whoever it was escaped then busted the locks. Blocked the memories of the other prisoners. Then used necromancy? That's pretty extreme."

"Good points, but I'm back to thinking it was Hass or Fealk who broke them all out. The locks have spell residue on them." Alric watched as the guards bickered over their next action. Even though they'd been arguing with Alric concerning bringing in the mages off the Hill, they now appeared to be rethinking it. No one wanted to deal with those mages; even the mages didn't like each other. The haughty pseudo rulers of Beccia, they stayed out of things as much as possible.

If any of them were as powerful as they acted, they'd be living in a much nicer town than Beccia.

"Neither Fealk nor Hass were magic users, at least not that I could tell. Not to mention that their initial reaction to being attacked by the faeries was real fear. Any magic user would have defended themselves automatically."

"No, but I think they smuggled in spells." Grillion had snuck up behind us. We were standing close enough to the door that he must have felt safe.

"How?" Alric kept his voice low. "I saw them being

searched when we dropped them off."

Grillion kept his hand low, but he held up the fabric from the spell bomb that had knocked him out. "I finally recognized this fabric. Hass wore it as shirt." He looked around and then held it a bit higher. "See these tiny pockets? They had something in them. Something that when triggered became a spell bomb is my thinking. You know how ineffective these places can be when it comes to searching people. If he layered his clothes, they'd never know about this."

"Then they did want to get caught. There's no way they could have known we'd drag them in. Technically they didn't really do anything to be arrested for."

"Yet." Grillion's look was grim. "They really wanted to live it up tonight, after we found you two. I have a feeling we would've all end up locked up one way or another. You two just sped it up." He folded his arms and glared around the jail. "And guess who would have been left behind? Damn it, I need to work with a better class of people." He nodded to Alric. "No offense to you, obviously. You usually kept me out of trouble."

I glanced up and noticed that while Kahlies had gotten to his feet and joined the others, more looks were coming our way. "We might want to leave. Especially if there's no additional information we can gather."

Alric glanced over as well. "I think we probably want to go to your house and lie low for a bit."

We made our way out of the jail, gathered our horses, and went to my house. I still really didn't have a place for the horses but putting them in the public stables might be a problem if we had to leave quickly. It was sad that my mind was already reverting to those types of scenarios again.

We made a bit of a shelter around the side of the house and Alric told the horses to stay.

The faeries and the constructs had been living here on

their own for the past week. Covey was supposed to check in on them every few days, but if she got caught up in an academic mystery of some sort, that wouldn't have happened. Covey was my best friend and one of the smartest people I knew, but she could get distracted for weeks at a time if she was working on a project.

Surprisingly, the house looked to be in good shape. Someone had cleaned up the minor damage caused when my house went a bit airborne a few months ago. I patted the walls and sighed. It wasn't much of a house, not fancy or large. But it was mine and I found that I really missed it. I had a bad feeling that we weren't going to be staying here long.

Grillion looked around and nodded. "Sweet little place you have here. Doesn't look like Alric, though."

"Alric prefers to live in caves or shady apartments. This belongs to me and the faeries. And the constructs." I pointed toward a table where the faeries' doll castle sat. The original one had been lost, but Harlan had found another one. It was larger than the first one, but still not big enough for the twenty-three or so faeries who regularly hung out in my flock. I looked over and noticed the girls had brought in additional doll houses to line the table. I really hoped I wasn't going to have a bunch of pissed-off diggers or parents coming after me for their additions. The girls rarely paid for things unless forced to.

"He did the same when I ran with him." Grillion turned to Alric. "Isn't it sort of odd for an elf to live like that? I figured you people would all have palaces."

Alric rolled his eyes. "Most elves live in houses. I was staying where I had to in order keep my disguise up. I wasn't doing it because I liked it."

"Okay, fair." Grillion turned back to me. "You have a spare room that I can dump my stuff in? Or your sofa works too. After three weeks on the road just being inside somewhere is great."

"You can have the guest room." I led him down the hall. The room looked clean, so it was probably safe to have him there. "There's a bathroom next door over."

"Thanks." He dropped his bags and flopped onto the bed. "It's been a long day already."

I went back to the living room. "Guess he's staying in the room for a bit."

Alric was sitting on the sofa and studying the bit of fabric the smoke bomb had been made of. "This was well planned. Scarily well planned. I can tell which pockets contained which spell component. Separate, they do nothing, mix them and they knock people out. Sneaky."

From the tone in his voice, Alric was as much annoyed with, as impressed by, the ingenuity behind it.

"So Fealk and Hass used Qianru to come up here and rescue their people? Larkspur and Merthas would've just been locked up by the time they would have had to start up here. And why couldn't they have just come up on their own?"

"Ah, that's the rub." Grillion's rest didn't last long as he came down the hall. "You need to have proper passage to cross the channel. Just came into being a year ago. Some of the smaller towns got concerned with strange things going on up here from what I gather. You have papers or you row your own boat." He patted his pockets and then went back down the hall. "Hold on."

He came back out with another dusty-looking letter and handed it to Alric. "We had to show this when we got on the ship to cross and when we got off. This side isn't trusting anyone either." He tilted his head as he looked at me while Alric read the note. "Hass and Fealk had been with Qianru only a short time when she decided on this emergency trip. No offense, but I don't know how you're going to help whatever it is she has an issue with. Magic user or not, you don't look terribly fierce."

"You never know with Qianru, she might have needed

something dug up." I really wished she'd been clearer on why we needed to go down there. I wasn't seeing a good reason yet. And I was re-thinking my earlier statement that we needed to go south. Things were messed up enough here—I didn't need to make things worse by traveling to another continent.

"I'm sure she has some obscure reason." Alric unfolded the document Grillion handed him. He scowled as he read. "These are required?" He handed it to me.

This was where Qianru shined. The level of thees and thous involved in allowing passage for her servants was extremely overdone. It was a flowery letter with a bunch of official stamps on it to let the three of them pass heading north and through the channel.

Grillion settled into one of the chairs. "Yep. It wasn't like that when I went down there a few years ago."

I read it and Qianru's letter to me again. "Just how were we supposed to go south if you need a letter like this each way? It's pretty specific to you three."

"Oh, there's a second letter…oh crud." Grillion's face fell. "Hass kept it with him. It allows passage for the original three and you two."

"Kind of ironic, that most likely these checkpoints on the ships are to stop the movement of the Dark even if the people behind them aren't sure who they are trying to stop. Yet we'll have a group, which includes a necromancer, traveling down without a problem."

Alric stayed lost in thought for a few moments. "I still need to talk to my people."

I wasn't sure I liked the emphasis on "I" in his comment. I'd like to see the elven city again as well as Padraig, Lorcan, and Siabiane, but I wasn't up to dealing with elven politics. But I also didn't want to be excluded.

A heavy thud at the door made all of us jump. Well, it made Grillion and me jump. Alric just looked up calmly.

A second thud hit, this one much louder. Alric got to his

feet, and with his sword in his hand stood to the right of the door. "Open it slowly." He kept his voice low.

I went over and pulled open the door, staying behind it. Alric stepped forward with his sword raised. Then he shook his head, stepped back, and fully opened the door. He might have been laughing, but he appeared to be hiding it.

Hass was surrounded by a cloud of faeries. He was also wrapped in plant life, string, rope, and random bits of fabric that might have come from what he had been wearing. There were red welts all over his face and arms. He looked completely beaten.

Considering I had seen the faeries kill with those sticks, they clearly were trying to capture and bring him to me. Bunky and Irving flew in the back of the faery mob.

Garbage flew into my face. "Others run. Catch this one." For emphasis she jabbed her war stick backward and nicked his cheek.

"Please! Tell them to stop! I'll do anything you ask!" Hass was almost crying.

Alric stepped aside and I walked up to the mass of faeries. "Great job, girls, and thank you, Bunky and Irving, for assisting the faeries. I'll need you to wait while we question him. But you might get him back if we don't like the answers." The faeries were starting to look bored. They'd captured him, but now that was done, they clearly wanted to move on to something else. My offer of further options got their attention. Bunky and Irving flew through the door and settled on my kitchen counter. If I did ever get a chance to come back in here to stay, I was going to need to have some rafters built for them.

The new attention from the faeries and the close pass by the constructs made Hass look ready to throw up. I almost felt bad for him. I wasn't one for torture. But then I recalled the guard captain. Whether he'd been working with the Dark followers or not, he didn't deserve to end up that way. Hass might not have killed him, but he'd been involved in releasing the one who did.

Alric led Hass to one of the hard dining table chairs and pushed him into it but didn't touch the ropes and other fabrics that tied him up.

Garbage, Leaf, and Crusty flew into the house as well, after some chattered directions from Garbage to the remaining faeries. I shut the door as they looked to be setting up a perimeter around my house. That would make the neighbors happy.

"We stay." Garbage announced her intentions. Of course, she and the two others were already perched on top of their castle when she said it.

Bunky and Irving gronked.

"They stay too," Leaf translated.

Hass tried to squirm away. "Keep them back. They tried to kill me."

Alric's sword had vanished again, but the menace in his face was still there as he pulled up another chair to face Hass. "Oh no, had they wanted to kill you, you would be dead. Probably within minutes of them catching you. The only reason you're not is that Taryn asked them to bring you to us alive."

"Jab." Leaf wasn't usually the violent one, but she looked seriously annoyed as she waved her stick at him. They didn't leave the top of their castle, but they didn't want him to forget they were there.

Hass glanced around the room.

Grillion folded his arms and glared back. "You were going to leave me here, weren't you? Or was I going to end up like that guard captain? What the hell, Hass?" They might not have been friends, at least according to Grillion, but traveling with someone for a few weeks would make you think you knew them a little.

Hass swallowed a few times and was turning green again. "That wasn't me. It was just a job, Grillion. You would have been safe up here." He turned to Alric and me. "I had no idea he was a necromancer. No reason either. The captain was on our side. What he did to him…"

I got up and brought out a bucket. I really didn't want him being sick all over the floor.

Hass swallowed a few times but no longer appeared ready to be sick. "Actually, could I have some water?"

I looked to Alric; he was more accustomed to interrogations. He gave a slight nod. I got a glass of water and brought it back. Hass seemed weary and nervous of everyone in that room, except me. I'd turned into a dragon in front of him and he was more afraid of Grillion?

This was odd. I'd told Alric what happened, but I didn't want to bring it up in front of Grillion. Alric had been watching us both. I doubted he'd missed Hass's dismissal of a dragon.

"You were telling us about the necromancer?" Alric leaned back in his chair.

"I can't…he'd kill me. The bastard even wiped out some memories. Fealk said he didn't, but I remember seeing you in the forest, we set a spell bomb trap for you. We ran toward you, then suddenly we were half a mile away and being chased by those faeries."

Alric and I shared a look. Why would the necromancer hide the memories? I'd seen four men for sure, so if there had been only four, he was part of that grouping. He saw me, but hid it from the rest of them?

"Did the others recall anything?" Alric asked but Hass looked to me.

He shook his head and nodded toward me. "Does *she* recall anything?"

"I remember a failed spell and you all running away. You were too far for me to catch up, so I sent the faeries to find you." I made sure to keep my face as neutral as possible. There was no way to know if the memory loss was something I did, or the necromancer did. I really hoped it was somehow something I did. The idea that a necromancer knew what I was and blocked his companions from knowing scared the hell out of me.

Hass narrowed his eyes for a moment, then shook it off. "I don't know what happened then. But none of the others did either. Even him."

"What's his real name? How did you know to get him? Who was the other one you got out?" I had sort of figured that the names given were not their real ones. Obviously, Alric shared that belief. He was also losing his patience. I was about to let the faeries at Hass again just to scare him into responding.

"The troll was a miner named Theria. He was involved in something big up here, and our bosses wanted him and the other one rescued and brought back. Didn't know the other one was a death mage." He was back to looking sick.

"What was his name?" Alric held up his hand. "The necromancer. What is his real name?" Names could have power in some magic sects. Jovan had gained control over Alric by the use of his full family name.

Hass tried to answer, but nothing came out. He tried again and he started choking and turning blue.

Alric rushed over and started pounding his back. "Stop thinking about it. The spell will choke you."

Hass started pulling at his neck to remove invisible cords that were strangling him. Eventually, he passed out, but his breathing eased up. Alric put him on the couch.

"So that guy, the one I would have been involved with trying to rescue, although not really because I would have been left behind, but still I would have been connected to in some way—that guy can kill people just for saying his name? From a distance?" Grillion looked ready to pass out as well.

"Yes, I think he will survive," Alric said and shook his head at Grillion's lack of concern. "But as for your questions, necromancers can place dangerous spells around their names if need be." He turned to me. "I don't understand, though, if there was one this strong in the battle with Glorinal and Jovan, why didn't he show himself then? I figured the people Jovan had with him were hired."

"I would have thought so too. Unless he ran when Glorinal killed Jovan." That was one of many days that haunted me, and I tried my best to pretend never happened.

"Could be. Okay, no more questions about the necromancer to Hass. We need to figure out what to do with him. I don't know that locking him up would be a good idea right now."

Grillion still looked green but stayed silent.

"Does Foxy still have that area in the back of the pub? With some spells on it that should hold him." I looked over to Hass. I believed that he wasn't aware of what was really going on. It could be an act, but the fact was he was really a bit too stupid to be that sneaky. Then I noticed that the way he was tied his tattoo showed. "Or should we take him to your people and let them keep him? He's not an elf, and possibly has no idea what that tattoo means, but he still has it."

"Taking him to my people might be a good idea. People like Padraig and Lorcan can get information out of him without triggering the necromancer behind the spells." Alric got up and adjusted the faeries' improvised rope. "Do you have any real rope?"

"Clothesline? It's in the kitchen in the broom closet." If things were going to start messing up my life again, I was going to make a list of items to carry with me. A few good ropes would be on that list.

Alric found the rope, after only having to move out half of the broom closet, then came back and securely tied up Hass. He peered down at him. "We can't ride to my people with him fighting the entire way. Nor would having an unconscious body on a horse for a few days look good."

A spell from before, long before, came drifting through

my mind. They'd done that a few times in the last few weeks since I had realized my true self. But most of them were way beyond my ability. I might have known how to do them before, but not all the pieces connected now.

This time it was a sleepwalking spell. The person stayed asleep if nothing rattled them too much, but they appeared awake. And could be posed.

"I think I know of a way." I quickly described the spell.

At first Alric looked doubtful, but then he nodded. "That might work. Your people had a different way of seeing magic than mine." He looked ready to say more but Grillion was leaning forward to catch everything.

"So, you're just going to let me stay here?" Grillion was far too pleased about the concept.

"I think that might be best." Alric waved the faeries over. "I need you to select half of your group to stay here, along with the constructs, and keep an eye on Grillion plus whatever is happening in town. The rest of us are going to visit the elves."

Garbage and Leaf looked upset at first, until they realized they'd be going to see the elves. The elves weren't completely sure what to think of the faeries. They'd been myths before the elves went into hiding.

On the other hand, the faeries *loved* the elves.

"We do!" Garbage yelled, and she and Leaf flew out through the tiny faery door above the main door. Crusty hadn't appeared to be paying attention, but slowly spun to Grillion. She flew forward and patted his cheek. "You be good." Her tone was extremely serious for her. She shook a finger at him. "Good."

Then she flew up to me. "Could go bad. Could not." With a nod that said she had clearly explained everything, she flew out the tiny door.

"What does she mean?" Grillion was back to looking freaked out about the faeries.

I'd never seen Crusty do something like that. But faking it worked. "She knows things that others don't. She'll tell the faeries who remain to make sure you stay good." I leaned forward. "Be extremely good while we're gone. Those constructs can do even worse things than the faeries." I had an odd feeling Crusty hadn't been talking about the few days of our trip, but something deeper. Wasn't going to share that with Grillion either.

"You know, I should check in with Harlan and Covey. They could keep an eye on things too." Not to mention both would be annoyed if I didn't see them now that I was back in town. My two best friends both knew what I was and still put up with me. The least I could do was say hello before taking off again.

Alric watched Grillion with an odd look. One I thought might be related to Crusty's odd comments. "That's a good idea. I think Grillion and I should catch up on things as well. I can make sure Hass stays out until we're ready to try that spell. Or at least until you get back."

I left them to it, not sure what Alric had planned, but there was more than just catching up on his mind.

The question was where to start on my visits. Both would be upset they weren't sought out the moment I got back in town, so whichever one was second would probably be cranky.

My way of thinking was which one I could get to first.

"Where you go?" Crusty broke off from the faery discussion taking over my small lawn and flew next to me as I walked down the street.

"I'm going to talk to Covey and Harlan." I knew as soon as I said his name out loud it was a mistake. The faeries liked Covey; mostly they gave her respect, something they didn't even give me. But they loved Uncle Harlan.

Long before I'd found out there were so many more faeries beyond my three, he became their uncle and spoiled them with abandon.

I now had all the faeries from my flock plus a few more

swarming around and behind me. I'd better find Harlan first. Covey would slam the door on my face if I showed up with this ravenous horde at my back.

Harlan was married to multiple wives. Or had been. He was a Chataling, large, bipedal cat-like beings who were polygamous. Unfortunately, a few months ago his wives collectively threw him out for his outlandish ways. Although Chatalings looked cat-like, they were supposed to keep their curiosity to themselves. Something Harlan was horrible at.

He now lived in a cute cottage on the edge of town with his current girlfriend, the elf Orenda. The cottage was entirely her idea. He preferred places he could slink in and out of if he was on one of his capers. Not something bright and cheery with a low white fence.

The constant chatter of the faeries buzzing around me was distracting. It was also attracting too many annoyed glares from people we passed. "Girls, settle down, or I'll tell Uncle Harlan not to give you any treats." That shut them up so quickly I wished I could use that threat more often.

Harlan was in front of his cottage, sitting on the ground near some flowers. It wasn't completely clear if he was planting them or pulling them out. He looked happy, though.

"Taryn!" He scrambled to his feet, dusting his tail and rear end off as he did so. "I didn't expect you and Alric to be back for a while yet." He automatically reached into his pockets and pulled out two handfuls of rock sugar. The faeries swarmed him with kisses, shoved the sugar into their mouths, and flew up into a nearby tree. At least they would be quiet for a bit.

Faeries dispatched, he engulfed me in a hug.

"We weren't planning on coming back so soon. But the girls showed up babbling about danger to the south, and they needed us to join them and their war cats. Then we had an issue."

He shook his head at the happy faeries in his tree but looked back sharply at my last sentence. "Please tell me none of you were involved in the explosion at the jail?"

I sighed. "Would love to, but it would be a lie."

He held out his arm toward the cottage. "I think this tale requires tea. Orenda is back in her homeland, so it will just be us."

Orenda was an elf from a different enclave than Alric's group. They'd come out when she went searching for what was rumored to be a major religious icon for her people. That it had actually been a dangerous, mind-controlling relic was another matter. She originally fell for Alric while he was disguised and had to spell her, but once free she fell hard for Harlan.

"Anything wrong?" Some of Orenda's people had come down for the battle over the relics a few weeks ago, but there were still some harsh feelings between her elves and the rest of the elven kingdom.

"Not really, she's just picking up some things and wanted to check in. She just left two days ago. Now, about the jail break?" He'd timed his question perfectly as he placed a cup of tea and a plate of my favorite biscuits in front of me.

I told him everything except about one of the people being a necromancer. Until we had a better idea of who he was and what his plans were, inciting panic wasn't a good idea. Like our guard friend, Harlan had been captured by Glorinal and Jovan and told me in secret that he still had nightmares about it.

"The Dark? But not elves? I'm sorry, I'd really hoped that you and Alric could settle down, raise a batch of wee ones and live normal lives." He added another lump of sugar to my tea.

"I was hoping to just settle down at least. And maybe we still can. Alric and I are taking Hass to the elves. See what they think. Which brings me to my favor."

He sat up and his eyes went wide. "You want me to join

you? I can be ready in mere minutes. Always ready for an emergency jaunt now, you know."

"I'm sorry, this will be short. We're leaving behind that friend of Alric's, Grillion. He's going to stay at my house with some of the faeries and the constructs, but I'd appreciate it if you could keep an eye on him and them."

Harlan deflated a bit. "Probably for the best. Orenda would be most annoyed if I left on an adventure without her—even a short one. After fighting for our lives, life seems dull without the threats."

I took another sip of my tea, then peered at him over the cup. "Really? You liked being in constant danger?" Harlan was smart, and he loved his friends, but he was not a fighter.

"Well…no. I liked the adventuring part. Just not the people trying to kill us part. Say, couldn't you just change and fly all of you up to the elves?"

That was a horrifying thought. I wasn't even great at flying alone—there would be no way I'd carry anyone with me. "And let the entire area see a real dragon? Something that hasn't existed for twenty-five hundred years and everyone thinks are myths? No thank you. We managed to ensure that those rumors died down, and that needed a lot of magic from Mathilda, Lorcan, and Siabiane. No way would I risk opening that up again." I carefully ignored the fact that I'd gone dragon when Hass and his friends attacked me. I hadn't told Harlan about that either.

"I understand." He patted my shoulder. "Never fear, I will keep an eye on this thief."

"Thank you. Like I said, we shouldn't be gone long, maybe two weeks at the most."

"That's a fairly fast trip." Harlan studied me as if I had some secrets to share.

"Alric knows the fastest routes." I shrugged. Alric and I had time to talk of things on our retreat. One was how the elven knights had moved a huge number of troops to the final battle. I'd just figured they'd made the decision to come and fight in enough time for the weeklong trip. Alric said they had finalized their plans two days before.

Some elven secrets concerned hidden magical paths. He'd never been able to use them when he'd been out before because they were tied to the enclave. And they took a lot of magic to travel on. If Alric wanted to tell others about them, he could. But I doubted we'd be using them in this case.

"Very well," Harlan said as he finished another biscuit. "If I don't see you in three weeks, we will come search for you. I assume you told Covey?"

The twinkle in his eye told me he was hoping he was first. "Not yet. Since they insisted on joining me, I thought it might be better to get the faeries their sweets before moving forward."

"Ah, then I shall coordinate our watching with her after you've left."

The rest of the visit was just catching up. A lot had happened before the battle that we never really talked about, so chatting about world-annihilating relics, which were now safely destroyed, was a nice way to spend some time.

I finished my third cup of tea and got to my feet. "I hate to eat and run, but I do want to catch Covey while she's still in her office." She was a professor of elven and Ancient studies at the local university. I knew where her house was, but the university was a ten-minute walk, and her house was more like a half hour. I'd spent a half hour here already.

"Understood. We will catch up more when you get back." He gave me another engulfing hug and sent me on my way.

The faeries all waved me on from their sugar hangovers in their tree. They liked Covey, but she didn't spoil them, so they'd stay here until they were ready to fly again.

We hadn't said when we were leaving, but the day was getting too short to be traveling today. Evening would be upon us soon, but there were still several college students roaming about the halls.

Covey's office door was shut, but a light came from underneath the door. I normally knocked before entering, and I did so this time as well, there just wasn't much time between the knocking and the opening. Granted, things were hopefully settling down, but there were too many times in the recent past where someone who shouldn't be in her office was.

I flung open the door, but it was just Covey tossing maps and scrolls around. "What!" she yelled without looking up. Then she aimed her glare at the door. "Taryn? Why are you back so soon?"

"Good to see you too." She'd mellowed out from her extreme academic focus while we'd been running around saving the world. That obviously had snapped back into place when she got back to campus.

She shook her head and put down the papers she had in her hand. "I am sorry, it is good to see you. We'd expected that you two would stay away for at least another week or so. Foxy believed you'd come back before then, however. Guess he won the betting pool."

"Foxy? Since when have you been hanging out at the pub?"

"Just for the camaraderie with Orenda and Harlan. I'm not drinking, nor am I sure I approve of a bar. But Amara has made it homey. We've also been working on rumor control. Making sure no one started talking about seeing a you-know-what ten days ago."

She added that last part with a serious face. As if that were the true reason for socializing and not that she'd gotten used to being around people on a regular basis. She wouldn't want to contradict that tough academic exterior. Even though I knew better.

"Well, to be fair, we were planning on coming back later." I ran down the entire story all the way from the faeries to the capture of Hass. I included that one of the men was a necromancer. Covey had also been captured by Jovan and Glorinal as Harlan had been. But she was of much sterner stuff. I needed someone to know about this creature. Harlan would have freaked out, but Covey just looked pissed.

Covey's face tightened and a pencil she had in her hand snapped. "Is he still in town?" That wasn't a good voice. Covey's people were Trellians. A species who had left behind eons of berserker rages. Mostly left behind. Covey found out she was susceptible to them two years ago. She kept them under control now. But right now, she was looking for a reason to let it out.

I certainly agreed.

"We don't know. They took off and we got Hass. Apparently, the southern continent is requiring documents to travel to or from; hopefully, Hass still has the one they were going to use." I swore in my head. We forgot to check. Grillion said it had been with him, but he could have handed it off. As much as I would like the world to be short one necromancer, I'd settle for him going far away from here. Unless Qianru had something secret in her message that was more motivating than, "*I need you to come down here.*" I was not planning on traveling any time soon. Beyond the trip to see the elves.

Covey slid a paper and charcoal stick over. "Can you do a rough drawing of the culprits? Not just the necromancer, all of them."

"I only saw them for a few moments." I sighed and took the stick. I'd start with Fealk since I saw him more than the other two. And if they were staying together, he'd be easy to spot. "Let me see what I can do, but you can't go after him, Covey. I just wanted you to be aware."

Covey folded her arms but still looked mad enough to break a few dozen chairs. "I'm not planning on it. I just want to know who I'm looking for…not to follow, just to avoid."

I tilted my head. That lie wasn't even good enough to fool Harlan. "Fine, but I really didn't see the other two." I continued sketching. Most diggers could sketch since patrons were often less interested in coming down to the dig site than they were obtaining trinkets to make their friends envious. Being able to sketch was a requirement so they could determine if it was worth coming to the dig site or not.

I finished drawing Fealk, turned the page to Covey, and grabbed another sheet. "He's the one who came north with Alric's friend. But I really didn't get a good look at the other two."

Covey studied the drawing and nodded. "Actually, I've been deciphering more scrolls on your people. When in your original form, you have amazing recollection. At least supposedly. You were in your original form when you saw them, right?"

"Yes, but I've never noticed any powers of recollection when in either form." Honestly, I seemed to be less likely to recall things in my dragon form. Of course, even though I now knew that was who I was, part of me still panicked whenever I changed. Fear made it hard to recall my own name.

"Focus. Look at me but keep your hand on the charcoal." Covey's people were reptilian, so focusing on her eyes could be hypnotic.

I did what she said, feeling only slightly stupid.

"Now focus on that moment when you ran into the clearing. You got hit with the spell bomb and dropped down. The men ran at you and you changed. What did they look like?"

I pushed back to that memory; the spell bomb wasn't helping, as while it didn't knock me out as intended, it did make me woozy. "I don't know, Covey. I just don't..." Images hit me: Fealk and Hass in front; another man, the troll Hass mentioned; and then the fourth.

He was wearing a long dark cloak with a hood, but I had one clear shot. Long white hair and pointed ears. "He's an elf?" I said more to myself than Covey, but she caught it. Kahlies had said his name had been Merthas but not an elf. Wrong on both counts—there was no way a necromancer let anyone have his real name. Interesting that whoever he was he'd been able to keep up a glamour when inside a spelled cell. That was one thing I had to make sure to tell Alric.

"He's an elf? That would fit more with him being a true member of the Dark. But if he were involved with Jovan and Glorinal, wouldn't we have noticed another elf? And look, it worked." She tapped the paper.

There was a decent rendering of the scene in the meadow. At least of the two who had been broken out of jail. The angle was a bit odd, but I was also almost as tall as the top of the trees at that point. Both faces were tilted upward toward me.

"At the least, Alric should have noticed. But maybe this necromancer stayed hidden. I don't know that either Jovan or Glorinal would have liked to share power with another of their kind." I kept looking at the drawing I'd made. The troll didn't look familiar, but there was something more than just the fact that the necromancer was an elf that was making my skin crawl.

"I've seen him before. Or someone like him." I didn't have a huge list of elves that I knew, so I should be able to sort it out. It just started giving me a headache. "I need to make another one of these for Alric."

"It's okay, I saw enough. I'd know them if I see them." Covey slid back the drawings.

"Will you be okay with keeping an eye on Grillion while we're gone? He seems mostly harmless but should be watched. And it was odd but Crusty told him to be good."

"Crusty?" Covey narrowed her eyes. She'd become fond of the faeries to a point, and for some reason liked Crusty the best. Like me, she realized that wasn't normal behavior.

"Yeah, none of the other faeries said anything, but she was actually serious for a moment."

"That's good enough reason. Between Harlan and me we'll keep an eye out." She paused. "One thing you have to promise, if you do go adventuring, you'll take me with you." She didn't look as deadly as she had earlier, but there was no doubt what my answer needed to be.

"Aren't you ready to go back to the academic world? Living in a house? With a bathroom of your own?" I knew what my choice would be, at least for a while. We'd only been done with action, adventure, and deadly threats for a short time, yet both Harlan and Covey were jumping at the chance to go back out again.

I liked sleeping in a real bed. And not having evil people trying to capture or kill me. Simple things.

"I believe my adventures will do nothing but increase my academic fortitude." She said it with a snooty look that dropped a moment later. "Or maybe not. But as odd as this sounds, I felt more alive when we were fighting for our lives than I ever have." She leaned over the desk. "Don't leave without me. I'll just find you. And things could get ugly."

I waited until she leaned back and smiled before responding. I knew she would never hurt me, but I still believed her threat. "I promise to drag you along on any death-facing and general mayhem-inducing adventure we get led to. Although hopefully not for a while."

She stared me down and then nodded. "Very good. Okay, so be off, show Alric that sketch. And do report back when you return from the elves. I'd go on this trip, but it doesn't sound terribly important, plus we do have finals."

She went back to scowling at scrolls and I took that as my sign to leave.

There were fewer students around right now, but still enough to keep the halls lively. That made me feel good as I felt an odd chill as I left Covey's office. I took a slightly different route back home than I normally would as the chill turned into a strong feeling of someone following me. I stayed on the busier streets and paid more attention to my surroundings. I certainly couldn't turn dragon in the middle of town, but hopefully my sword would show up and I did have magic. The sword would be an issue if there were a lot of people around since most normal weapons don't pop out of thin air.

The feeling of being followed grew worse, so I detoured completely and went to the Shimmering Dewdrop.

CHAPTER SEVEN

IT WAS EARLY DINNER TIME and while Amara's food was becoming renowned, the pub still acted like a pub from time to time. This being one of the times. The only folks in it were the early evening drinkers. Mostly older men from the gnome, brownie, and pixie tribes.

I nodded to the one or two I recognized, and they poked the rest to all turn and stare at me. It was hard to tell if the looks were admiring, annoyed, or fearful. I couldn't blame anyone in Beccia for seeing me as a bringer of troubles. If it weren't for me and those damn relics, they probably wouldn't have had any problems.

The odd looks turned to smiles. Of course, they didn't realize the relics were my fault, so maybe they thought I saved them.

"Ach, Taryn, ya coming in for dinner alone?" Foxy came out from the back kitchen and went behind the bar.

I went to the far end of the bar, away from the gnome contingent, and shook my head. "Maybe in a bit with Alric." I dropped my voice as he came closer. "I think someone was following me. I didn't see anyone, but just got an odd feeling as I came back from the university."

He immediately looked toward the door as if undead hordes would be pounding it down any second. "Nothing coming in." He nodded slowly to himself. "You've got senses the rest of us don't know of. If you thought you were followed, you had reason. I'll send Dogmaela to walk you home."

I started to shake him off, but that chill from before was still messing with my insides. "Maybe that would be a good idea. It would be nice to catch up with her also." Dogmaela was a troll, a full-grown troll woman who could probably take on every one of the guards in that jail, and the private services as well, and win. She was the head waitress here and was fiercer than Foxy about defending her friends and patrons.

He nodded and went back into the kitchen. A moment later he came back with Dogmaela and Amara.

"Are you okay?" Amara might not be a goddess anymore, but she had the motherly thing down. Her tiny face peered up at mine and she put her arm around my waist.

"I think so, just an odd feeling." I laughed. "With all we've been through, I don't really ignore those anymore." I didn't mention I had planned to do just that, but the feeling was too strong to ignore. Even for me, the queen of denying. Someone with some serious mojo was out there, and I didn't want to think about who it might be.

"I'll protect." Dogmaela gave me a comforting pat on the shoulder. One that almost sent me flying across the room. If there were any physical attacks, she would stop them. My fear was how we would face the magical ones. Trolls were more impervious to magic than the other species, but I didn't want to endanger her.

If it was the necromancer I was sensing, we were both at risk.

But from the look on her face even if I told Dogmaela never mind, I knew she would follow me anyway. I mentally pulled up my still most reliable spell, "push", and nodded. "Thank you. We should be off, Alric is waiting."

Dogmaela grinned. She liked Alric.

I didn't feel anything as we left the pub and Dogmaela started telling me about her trip back to her homeland. We were halfway home when she froze. Completely stuck in place, one foot starting to lift froze. The chill from before was around, but unfortunately no one else was. Not that it would have mattered. Had the others been here, they probably would be doing statue impersonations too. I pulled up my push spell and called up my sword as well. It behaved this time, which was nice. Keeping my back to the frozen Dogmaela, I slowly walked around her. That spell would need line of sight no matter how powerful the mage.

A cloaked shape was just to the side of one building, hiding in the shadows, but thanks to training from Alric, I knew what to look for. The necromancer. I took a deep breath. He might be more powerful than me—his magic was certainly more vicious than mine—but even a death mage wouldn't want to be hit with a push spell.

I waited until he stepped forward a bit more. I wanted to push him, not the building he was hiding against. Then I released the spell at him. At the same time, I snapped a spell bubble over Dogmaela and me.

I'd managed to catch the necromancer unprepared and he flew backward and over the house behind him. Too much to hope for that I seriously hurt him, but hopefully it slowed him down. I turned to Dogmaela. At first, I thought that we were still in trouble. That mage could come back at any time and if she were frozen, I wasn't going to leave her.

But she gave an odd groaning noise and her foot slowly went down. "What happened?" Her speech became closer to normal with the last word.

"You were spelled. But I chased him off, and we need to get to my house." I dropped the spell bubble and started walking toward my house, but she was standing still and glaring around searching for the one who spelled her.

"Dogmaela, we can't risk trying to find him." I'd managed to push him away once; I wasn't sure I would be able to do it again. We needed to get out of here fast.

"No one attacks my friends."

"And I appreciate that, but we need to leave." Also, technically, he had attacked her. Most likely to get to me, but still.

She took a deep breath and gave a bull-like snort. "Okay, get you home." She started striding away, and I had to jog to keep up.

The faeries had reconvened in the tree and lawn in front of my house when we walked up. They swarmed down to greet Dogmaela and chittered at her in native troll. At least that was what it sounded like. I didn't know they spoke native troll, but Dogmaela seemed pleased.

I walked around the swarm and went into my house. Hass was still tied up and knocked out on my sofa, but Alric and Grillion were nowhere to be seen.

Had the necromancer come here first? Alric was far stronger than me magically, at least currently, but I'd seen him lose against two necromancers.

A rustling sound came from the hall leading to the bedrooms. I'd put away my sword when I'd sent the mage flying, but I called it back now. Two calls and two appearances in such a short time. It might be setting me up for a massive failure to appear at a later time, but I appreciated it being here now.

The noises were coming from the guest room and the door was mostly shut.

I eased my way down the hall, listening for anything that would give me a clue as to what was going on. I'd just reached the door itself, still unable to figure out what the noise was, when Crusty and two other faeries came flying in behind me, whooping and yelling.

"What do?" Crusty yelled as she executed an amazing spin, then slammed the door open. The other two were right behind her.

"No!" I ran after them. To find them flying around Alric and Grillion as they were looking at a collection of scrolls and maps. The rustling had been from them working in a small space and the scrolls kept rolling up. Crusty and her crew did a full circle of the room, shrugged collectively, and flew back out to find something more interesting.

"Taryn! Good, you're back safe and sound." Grillion smiled as he waved a scroll at me.

Alric took one look at my face and ran to me. "We thought it best not to discuss these in front of Hass, even though he's unconscious." He paused. "What's wrong?"

I still wasn't sure how much to trust Grillion, but this concerned him as well. If I was being stalked, we might all be. I briefly told them about my feelings, the detour to the pub, and Dogmaela being spelled.

"Who is Dogmaela and why did you go pale at her being magicked?" Grillion had remained silent when I was talking but watched Alric carefully.

Alric ran his hand through his hair. "She's a troll who works at the pub. It would have taken a lot of magic to spell her like that." He looked at me closely. "You're sure you're okay?"

I made my sword vanish and nodded. "Yeah, but that was scary and in daylight. Oh!" I reached into my cloak and pulled out the drawings I'd done. "Covey had some tricks up her sleeve and got me to recall what I saw of our friends. Fealk we already know." I handed the papers to Alric. "But these are the other two."

Alric glanced at Fealk first. He started shaking his head and muttering under his breath when he got to the drawing of the mage. "You're certain this was who you saw?"

"As much as I can be drawing from memory like that, but he looked familiar for some reason."

Alric kept staring at the drawing. "You're picking up the family resemblance. He's Siabiane and Mathilda's brother. He was kicked out of the enclave long ago and tried to get back in once when I was young and training with Siabiane. The shield stopped him, but it was a near thing. His name is Domniall."

"Who are they? And why is the picture odd? Where you standing in a tree?" Grillion hadn't picked up on the tension in Alric at realizing who our mage was, but it was hard to miss. I had a feeling Grillion missed a lot of things.

Alric was still swearing under his breath at the drawing, so I responded. "The women he named are two strong elven magic users, sisters, who originally came up here from the south. As for the angle"—I shrugged and thought quickly—"just an odd side effect of how I was drawing them from memory." I might trust him with some things, if Alric kept feeling it was okay, but not with everything.

"This has to be him." Alric shook his head. "He was locked up because he'd been involved with Jovan and Glorinal? There is no way I would have missed him if he'd been in that cave. We have to find out who in the hell turned him in on made-up charges and why." He looked up. That was a scary thought. There was someone even more dangerous out there? If someone locked these two up, for whatever reason, they probably weren't bad. But I wasn't going to count on it.

Grillion tilted his head and peered at the troll drawing. "I can't answer any of those questions, but I might know this gent." He chewed his thumb as he looked closer. "Yup, in Kenithworth. Met him back a year or so before Alric and I became acquainted. He was running one of the gangs. From the north. Mean as all get out, but he wasn't using the name Theria, if that's what Hass called him." He tapped the page. "But that's him."

"Again, probably not likely to have been working with Jovan and Glorinal a year ago here in Beccia. Neither of these sound like followers." I was now becoming far more concerned about who was powerful enough to lock those two up than their reasons for doing so. Proving or disproving that some bad mage and gang lord had been involved in one of the scariest times in Beccia's history would be almost impossible. But like us locking up Hass and Fealk for crimes they didn't commit, someone claimed that's what they did. And was able to get them in jail.

Alric kept looking at my drawing and shaking his head. "Domniall should have been nowhere near here. He's banished from this continent. We have to get word to my people." He looked up. "Now."

"But it's already almost nightfall, and this Domniall showed no fear of coming after me in the daylight." I knew how powerful Siabiane and Mathilda were. The idea of a necromancer with their strength made me want to hide under my bed and not come out for a few months.

Alric rolled up the scrolls he and Grillion had been studying and handed them to Grillion. Whatever they were, they weren't related to our current problem. "I know, I'd rather not start at night either. But we need to get this information up there and as you said, Domniall went after you in the daylight. The sooner we leave the better."

We walked out to the hall, and I turned toward the bedroom. "Let me freshen up my pack." I'd pretty much been on the move for over a year and had been looking forward to living out of a house instead of a pack. Guess that wasn't going to be happening just yet.

Alric and Grillion continued out to the living room.

I'd dumped my pack in here before I went out to find Harlan and Covey. Without ceremony, I emptied it out on my bed and sorted things, then re-stuffed the bag. I was about to walk out of my room when an odd glint caught my eye from the things I'd left on the bed. It was small and mostly buried, but a stick pin, like one used to hold a cloak closed, was laying there. One I'd never seen before. I poked it, but when nothing happened, I picked it up. The letter from Qianru was loosely wrapped around it.

It had a swirling design engraved on it, so small it was almost invisible. I squinted closer. Something was there; I just needed to look closer. A moment later a bolt hit me and flung me across the room on my ass.

Alric came running down the hall with Grillion a foot behind. "What happened? You yelled." He had his sword out and was looking around the small room. My encounter with Domniall had left all of us on edge.

"I have no idea." He helped me to my feet. "I didn't yell. This weird pin was in my pack. I was looking at it and it shocked me."

"You did yell, and if you were standing near your bed looking at your pack things, it managed to send you across the room." He looked at the pin in my hand but didn't touch it. "Do you feel anything from it now?"

I figured he meant magically. Non-magical things usually didn't fling people around unless they were exploding. I shook my head. I couldn't make out the scrolled markings anymore.

"It's a pin?" Grillion stayed in the doorway.

"Yeah, but there had been markings on it. Tiny ones that I couldn't see well." I held it up. "They're gone now."

Alric peered at the pin more closely, then scowled. "Can you put it on the bed?"

I did. But his scowl deepened. "Can you open that hand?" He pointed to my right hand.

I held it up, completely open, facing him. "It didn't hurt me if that's what you're thinking."

"Look at your palm." Alric didn't move closer but looked like he wanted to.

I held my hand up to my face. At first, I couldn't see anything, but elves had sharper eyes than just about anyone. Slowly words appeared on my palm. Tiny, and there were a lot of them, but clearly they were words. "What kind of spell is this?" The words stopped when they reached the sides of my hand and fingers. I shook my hand, but they stayed put.

Grillion maintained a safe distance, but he was leaning in closer. "Does it hurt?"

"No." My hand felt like normal, it just didn't look it.

Alric came closer. He held up my hand, turning it different ways to see the words. Scowling the entire time. Never a good thing. "This looks like a lock spell. An old one. I've only heard about them, even Siabiane couldn't show how they were done. She just told me what to look for and the possible effects." He held my hand and kept tilting it but his frown etched deeper.

"Couldn't or wouldn't?" I liked Siabiane, but both she and her sister had a bad tendency of not being forthcoming about certain things. If she felt this kind of spell would be something the younger Alric shouldn't know, aside from how to identify it, she would have held back what she told him.

Alric looked ready to argue the point, then shrugged. "Probably wouldn't. I was a bit wild in my youth. What I do know is that these are compulsive spells. It's impossible to read this. Siabiane might be able to, but I can't. It is a way to control the actions of another in a delayed form."

"Oooo so they could just take over Taryn at some predetermined time and make her do what they want? That's not good." Grillion was exceptional at stating the obvious.

I glared at my hand. "How do we stop it?"

"No idea," Alric said. "But it's another reason to get to my people as soon as possible. I can put a spell on you that should slow it down, but without knowing what it's designed to do or when. We're stuck."

"So, it's like a geas." We didn't have a good history with those.

"Extremely so, only less aggressive and with less serious results. They don't have the strength a geas would." Alric picked up my pack and started for the door, then turned. "Something about the way they work just struck me. It looks like you'd dumped everything out; was anything unusual near the pin when you found it?"

"Just that letter from Qianru. The pin was sticking out

of it. Must have gotten wrapped up in the jumble of my pack." Which didn't answer who put it there or when. I hadn't completely dumped out my pack when Alric and I were at the cottage, so it could have been put in by anyone.

"These take a while to work. It takes time to take over your will, so I'd say you're safe until we can get to my people and have Lorcan or Padraig look at it." He looked at the wrinkled letter. "We should bring it and the pin too. Hold on." He left the room with Grillion trailing behind, then came back with a small black bag. A familiar one.

"I borrowed this bag from Leaf, as mine has things in it I'd rather not expose to that pin." He held out the impossibly tiny faery bag.

Grillion had followed him back but now it was his turn to scowl. "That pin is small, but it's not that small. And that note really won't fit in there."

I held up the bag and slipped the pin in, and then added Qianru's letter. "These are faery bags. They don't work the same way our reality does." I saw his eyes get huge and could see calculations going on in his head. "And they are protective of their bags. Don't get any ideas, you saw what they did to Hass." I handed the bag to Alric to put in my pack. A quick look at my hand told me the writings had almost completely vanished again, but there was no doubt that they were still there.

Grillion sighed and went back to the living room with Alric and I following him out.

"Is he going to stay like that traveling?" I pointed to Hass on my sofa. I still had the spell in my head for him to sleepwalk, or in this case, ride, but no idea how to execute it.

"I wasn't planning on it, but I don't think we have time to test that spell of yours. We'll just avoid being seen." He gave me a pointed look. "By *anyone*."

Damn. Harlan had been right. Judging by his emphasis on that last bit, Alric was planning on taking the secret routes. My only real exposure to that way of travel was the vortex he and Padraig had taken when we were chasing Nivinal at the Spheres. And what he'd mentioned when telling me about magical things I should stay away from. It was risky, and the amount of magic used was high. That Alric was willing to do it said a lot about how much trouble he thought we were in.

Lovely.

"Girls?" I looked around the living room; the front door was still open, and Dogmaela and the faeries were still out there.

"Taryn! Alric! I will go now." Dogmaela broke away from the faeries and came over to give us both hugs. Alric's was a bit more forceful, and she lifted him a foot in the air, but he was laughing when she put him down.

"Thank you for protecting Taryn." He clasped Dogmaela's massive forearm.

"Watch her. Lots of dangers." She shot a glare at Grillion, who was hovering just outside the front door.

"It's okay," I said. "He's with us."

Dogmaela watched him for a moment, then gave a sharp nod. "You need me, come to pub." That was good. I had no idea what Grillion would get into, but this way Dogmaela would be on his side. She nodded to all of us, said a few words in troll to the faeries, a joke, I gathered by the mad laughter that rippled through the squad of faeries, and took herself back to the pub.

I motioned for the faeries to follow us inside, as well as Bunky and Irving who were just coming back from whatever patrol they'd left on. "Girls, we're leaving now. We need the ones who remain behind to be careful and stay here tonight. I want Bunky and Irving to stay here too. Keep an eye on everyone, please." I raised my hand at the grumbles from the faeries that followed my announcement. Bunky and Irving seemed pleased, buzzed through the house once, then settled back on the counter. "I know, but I was attacked on the way home, so was Dogmaela. We don't know if they will try for Grillion or you." I wasn't too worried about anyone going after the faeries, even a necromancer. But I wanted them to stay in tonight.

Grillion blanched at that, but Garbage looked torn.

"Should stay. But need go." Her lower lip stuck out as she decided which would be more interesting, staying here and fighting if someone attacked, or going with us to see the elves.

"We could also be attacked along the way." I doubted it, especially since we were using the secret paths, but anything could happen. And it might be best if Garbage was with us. There were enough of her faeries trained to fight off bad guys now, but she might go looking for trouble if left behind.

That helped her make up her mind.

"Yes, I go with." She started chittering in native faery, and half of the faeries flew farther into the house while the other half stayed near her. "You watch him. Protect well." She waved to ones near her. "We protect." She folded her arms and gave an imperious nod. All was settled in her mind.

Grillion was back to looking a little pale, but fear of his faery guardians might keep him from doing something stupid.

"Okay, then. I guess we get the horses and head out?" Even using the secret travel path, I wasn't sure about leaving at night. Alric and the faeries could see better at night than I could by far. I'd hoped that my natural form was more equipped for night vision, but not by much—from what I'd noticed, and I wasn't going to change just to test it.

Alric handed me my pack and picked up Hass. I knew he was far stronger than he looked, but it couldn't be easy to lift someone like that. I ran out and brought Hass's horse around to the front. Draping him over the horse wasn't pretty and would raise a lot of questions if anyone saw us. But he was secure. Alric touched Hass's head once to keep him unconscious.

We got on our horses and our half of the faeries flew out to join us.

Grillion stood a few feet back from the open door, still cautiously watching his half of the faeries. "Good luck." It wasn't clear whether he was aiming that comment at us or himself.

Alric led the way down the road.

"So, where do we catch it?" I was riding behind Alric with Hass's horse tied behind mine.

"I want to get out of town a bit before I open the way. But let's stick to side routes; there are still too many people out."

My stomach gave a grumble, reminding me it was dinner time.

"I put some bread and meat in the small bag looped on your saddle. Might as well have some. It won't be a long trip, but I'll need your magic as well as mine. You don't work well when you're hungry."

I would have argued, but I was too busy making a meat and bread snack. Magic can burn through a lot of fuel, both magically and the more mundane food kind.

I snacked, Alric led, and Hass began to snore. The faeries flew around us.

Eventually we got out past the edge of town and Alric stopped. "I'll hold the way open, but if there is anything that interferes, you'll need to take care of it."

"If this is a secret path, how can anything interfere?"

Alric turned and tilted his head. "It is possible for other elves to access this."

He didn't have to remind me that the necromancer who had followed me was an elf. "Okay, with our luck we'll be found. I'll be prepared." I called up my sword—this made three times it had appeared without problem. Maybe it liked that I now knew what I really was? Or it was setting me up. We'd never really figured out why the odd spirit sword had latched onto me. None in the history of the elves had gone to anyone not elven. Once I started regaining my lost memories of who and what I was, I realized that my people never had them either.

"Anything that I need to know about this? Or that the faeries need to know?" They were all still buzzing around expectantly.

"Just be aware of your surroundings. Things will look odd, but if something appears to be a danger, push it out of the path. That spell of yours would come in handy in here. Enough of a nudge will toss them out." He looked up to the faeries. "We'll take the Chawsia paths. Are you all ready?"

I didn't recognize the word, but the girls did. Crusty was clapping and doing flips in the air. Even Garbage looked happier than before. "We ready!"

Alric said a spell, his hands moving away from each other in increasingly larger arcs. The air in front of him shimmered slightly. I don't think I'd have noticed it unless I had been standing right behind him. He started to ride in, but the faeries burst in first.

I followed as closely as I could on my horse and Hass's horse stuck close behind mine. Now I could see a difference in the air around us. We were still on the path through the forest that we'd started on, but it was as if I was looking at the trees from underwater. Light-filled, swirling water. That the faeries loved.

As soon as they flew in, they started bouncing along the edges of the tunnel. They were flying, but most of the energy pushing them along was coming from the magical pulses of the path.

"Should they be doing that?" I didn't want to interrupt Alric as he held the path open, but if I could magically push someone out, I didn't want the faeries to accidentally fall out because they were goofing around.

Alric didn't look back but laughed. "They're fine. They feel these paths even more than elves do; they can't fall out."

I shrugged and watched the girls having fun. It was better than watching the nebulous woods ghosting alongside from the trail we'd been on. We'd started picking up speed and now the trees were blurring by. Just a bit disturbing and the movement didn't settle well with my earlier snacking.

We'd been in the path for about an hour when I noticed a growing dark patch hovering to the right side at about knee level to my horse. It looked to be outside of the tunnel we were in, but unlike the blurring scenery, it was keeping up with us. From the stiffness of his back, Alric was focused on the path, and I didn't want to disturb him.

"Garbage? Can you come here?" The girls seemed familiar with the path so maybe she'd have an idea.

"Is yes?" She really liked riding those energy waves or whatever the tunnel gave off. I couldn't recall the last time I'd seen her grinning like that.

"Do you know what that is?" The dark shape was lower than they had been, so they might not have noticed it.

Her eyes went wide. "Bad!" She had her war stick out and was calling her troops before I could get a word out. Then they all dove through the tunnel wall.

Damn it. That wasn't what I'd wanted them to do; I just needed to know if she knew what it was. Alric was still focusing. As far as I could tell from his back, he hadn't even noticed the faeries' departure. I called up my push spell.

The dark spot vanished moments after the faeries dove out of the tunnel. We were moving faster, and it felt like we'd slightly changed direction, but still no spot nor the faeries. I knew the girls were fairly indestructible, but I was still worried about them.

My horse followed behind Alric. None of the animals

seemed to notice they were moving far faster than they were walking, so I called up my sword and kept one hand open for my spell. Eventually we started slowing down, and the areas outside of the tunnel became visible. Still no return of the faeries, nor the dark spot.

The tunnel around us dropped completely and we returned to a normal pace. We were closer to the elven town than the first time we'd gone there when they still had a shield. But farther out than I expected.

"Alric? Shouldn't we be closer?"

Alric tumbled off his horse.

I banished my push spell and jumped off my horse to run to him. "Alric!" I rolled him onto his back. There were no wounds that I could see, but his skin was so pale that it was almost blue, and his eyes were locked open. My heart stopped as I thought he was dead.

Then I heard his heart. He was breathing shallowly, but not moving, nor appearing conscious even with his eyes open.

I looked around for help, but while I could see the elven town, it was still a good mile or so away. A burst of air near me caused me to jump and spin.

It was the faeries. They were laughing when they appeared out of nowhere.

"Garbage, go get help. Something is wrong with Alric." I heard a grunt and looked to Hass. Alric's spell was gone now, so he was waking up. He was still tied, and I wouldn't be gentle if he tried to get away, but I needed help for Alric.

Garbage buzzed close to Alric and a worried look crossed her face. "Get!" She and the rest of the faeries took off in a multicolored swarm toward the town.

I really hoped Hass was still too groggy to move. I put down my sword but didn't banish it. I didn't think Alric had been attacked by something out here, but there was no way to tell. I threw a spell bubble over him. Mine weren't nearly as strong as his but it should at least slow down anything trying to get through. I walked over to Hass. He was moving more now, but still solidly gagged, tied, and secured to his horse. That last part made me nervous. If he thought he had a chance of getting loose and freeing himself, he might try to get the horse to run.

I brought out one of the stakes we kept in the saddle packs and tied his horse to it, then with magical assistance stuck it hard into the ground. Then I walked around to where he was hanging upside down and pulled his head up so he could see me.

"Here's the deal, there are deadly elven assassins all around us. Right now, it is extremely important that you hold perfectly still unless you really want to see if your necromancer friend can bring you back from the dead."

I assumed there were such things as elven assassins. I'd just never heard of them. But from the look in his eyes, accompanied by frantic nodding, Hass was willing to believe in them.

I gave him another glare, one Garbage would have been proud of, then let go of his head, and went back to Alric. I didn't want to disturb the spell bubble, nor did I want to get trapped if Hass changed his mind. So, I picked up my sword and stood between the two, looking for anything coming our way.

The faeries came into view first, a cloud of bright colors flying toward us. Well, flying forward then turning back, most likely to chastise the three horses and riders following them. Then they flew back toward me again.

The riders were recognizable in a short while. I wasn't too surprised to see Flarinen, the leader of the elven knights. Padraig was behind him, and an unknown female elf was behind Padraig.

"They fix." Garbage hovered over my spell bubble and shook her head. "How gets broken?"

"I don't know, sweetie, that's why I need help." I turned

to Hass behind us. "Can you and your girls keep a close eye on him for me? He shouldn't move at all." I'd raised my voice loud enough for him to hear. His head went still.

The faeries swarmed him, and I dropped my spell bubble from around Alric.

"Thank you for coming. We were riding the secret path, he seemed fine, but then the path stopped, and he collapsed."

Flarinen nodded formally, but Padraig came forward to give me a hug. "I'm happy to see you, but not in these circumstances."

Flarinen dropped down to look at Alric and then glared. "It's dangerous to use those paths."

"We had reason," I said with my coldest tone. Flarinen could be a major pompous ass, and I wasn't in the mood for it right now. "One that would be better discussed inside somewhere. By the way, there was some sort of odd dark shape keeping pace with us outside the path. The faeries chased it off, but maybe whatever it was attacked him?"

Padraig stepped over to Alric and the female elf joined him. She had lovely dark skin and thick black hair. Like all elves, her beauty was ageless, but there was a wisdom in her eyes that said she was far older than she looked.

"This is Ceithera. She is a healer," Padraig said. "You didn't see anything else beyond a shadow? Girls? What was it?"

I shook my head, but the faeries all started jabbering at once. I held up my hand. "Garbage? What did you see?"

She flew up to us. "It was a bad. All smoky. Thought it hidden." Her grin was vicious. "We see. We push out."

Padraig nodded sagely. "Thank you for that. You saved them."

Garbage bowed and flew back to guarding Hass.

I dropped down next to Padraig and Ceithera. "That made sense to you? We had been dealing with a necromancer in Beccia. Could that have been what they fought off?" I'd kept my voice low, but the scowl on Flarinen's face as he watched the surrounding woods said he'd heard me.

"I have a feeling that this mysterious necromancer, or another strong magic user, was latching onto the tunnel." Padraig's voice was equally low. "We need to stabilize Alric and get back into town. The faeries would have damaged whoever it was, but we'll need more protections before we start looking into things."

I nodded. I knew who it probably was, but this wasn't the place to discuss it.

Ceithera had been checking Alric's pulse and breathing, then closed her eyes and held her hand over his chest. "He has taken damage, but he can be moved now." She rose to her feet and held out her hand. "I have heard of you, Lady Taryn. I saw you briefly during the final battle of the relics." She gave a crooked smile. "I believe you were heading toward open water."

Which meant she fully knew who and what I was. I'd been flying in my dragon form when I headed for the ocean. I shook her hand. "I'm pleased to meet you. Thank you for helping Alric."

Ceithera looked down at him. "He is a favored one of my people, whether he likes to acknowledge it or not." She turned to Flarinen. "Will you help get him to his horse?"

Flarinen nodded with none of the mild annoyance he normally flung around himself like a cloak. Whoever Ceithera was she was high up the pecking order among the elves. He moved Alric onto his horse and stepped back. Padraig threw a spell on Alric, and his back went rigid and he stayed on the horse.

I'd have to ask Padraig later how he did that.

I removed the stake keeping Hass's horse in place, then retied the horse to my saddle.

"Do we want to know why this *person* is in this condition?" Flarinen looked over to Hass but didn't appear to really care about my answer.

"It's part of what we need to discuss inside, would be my guess," Padraig said as he and Ceithera got on their horses.

I shrugged and got on mine as well.

Flarinen glared, just because it was his thing more than for any real reason, and turned to lead us back.

The faeries had been locked in a discussion but broke free when I called for them. "Keep an eye out for any more bads, and make sure our friend doesn't make any moves." I nodded to Hass still hanging upside down on his horse behind me.

"Do!" Crusty flew out from the mass of faeries and flew up to Flarinen. "Hi!" She kissed his cheek and then flew back to join the others.

He turned slightly as she flew off, a look of utter confusion replacing his usual hauteur. Then he shrugged and kept riding.

I had no idea where that came from. He'd tolerated the faeries before when we'd been all stuck together, but he'd sort of sold them out at one point. Apparently, Crusty at least forgave him.

I'd have to watch my little blue faery and see what she was up to.

The elven town looked far better than it had a few months ago. At that time, its protective shielding had been destroyed by a megalomaniac mage who then let evil rakasa and sceanra anam attack the populace. We'd won, but the city had taken some serious damage, most of which was repaired now, and it looked like new buildings were going up as well.

"New houses?"

Padraig turned as we rode. "Yes, many of the elves from the other enclaves wanted to relocate. Almost half of the ones from your friend Orenda's town have come over. So, we have a housing boom."

"No new shield?" When I'd left all those months ago,

they'd been working on building a new one. But we were now approaching the outer streets, and there was no barrier that I could see.

"Not anymore." Ceithera responded this time. She was closer and riding alongside Alric's horse. "We worked on it, but hopefully with fewer threats we don't need it." Her scowl was fierce and while she might be a healer, there was no doubt she could inflict damage as well. "We have other ways to protect ourselves."

We went a few streets in and then turned to the left. The road was older and wider here and eventually we stopped in front of the building of healing. It was so gorgeous it could have been a mansion somewhere else.

"Flarinen? If you would be so good?" Ceithera got off her horse in one fluid movement and started up the steps without even looking to see that her request was being followed.

Padraig hid his smile as Flarinen removed Alric from his horse and carried him inside.

"I take it we want that one inside as well?" He tipped his head toward Hass.

"Yes, he's part of the problem. Is Alric going to be okay?" I'd distracted myself from worrying by focusing on getting help for Alric. He was now in good hands so the full-on worrying could commence. It was taking all my willpower to not run after him.

"I need to look at him closer, but I am confident that between Ceithera and myself, we can revive him. I am worried about the person who might have latched onto that tunnel however." He had picked up Hass and carried him to the door. I pushed it open as far as I could. The faeries managed to hold the other side open without even being asked. Then they looped around the inside and tore out the door and into town. I thought I heard a yelled "back later," but I wasn't sure.

The inside was even more ornate than the outside, and

again, didn't look like any healer house I'd ever seen. Of course, the ones in Beccia looked about like the bars, so it wasn't too surprising.

"This place is amazing." I walked out into the center of the front room, and the ceiling soared high above me.

"Ceithera has been here a long time. She was one of the healers who saved our people after the battle against the Dark."

"She doesn't look it at all." That put her at more than a thousand years old. I was still having trouble with the ageless elves.

Padraig went down into a large room with beds and put Hass down on it. "I wouldn't recommend trying to get away. You are still tied, and my people will not be helpful to you." He patted Hass on the cheek, then turned back to me. "Yes, she and I are the same age, but she wasn't locked in a chamber for five hundred years. Some elves have all the genes."

Ceithera stuck her head out of another room. "If you two have settled our prisoner, I could use some help with Alric."

Flarinen walked out of the room as she spoke. "I will tell the council about this new threat."

"We're not even sure what it is." I was pretty sure it was Domniall the necromancer. But I wanted to talk to Padraig about it before I said anything.

"It was still too close to our city." He gave a tight nod and left the building.

"He has not changed." I shook my head.

Padraig laughed as we went to the other room. "And never will. I sensed there was something you wanted to tell me but not in front of him? Good judgement. But anything you wish to say can be said in front of Ceithera."

"Please tell us your tale. Healing Alric will not be hard, but it will take time. I am running the healing spell through him as we speak. The one who attacked him was draining his magic, and since he was already using a lot to hold open the tunnel, he collapsed."

Alric looked a bit less blue, so whatever she was doing was helping. I smiled at the healer. I'd figured she was one of the good ones, but it was good to have it confirmed. Especially since I couldn't ask Alric. I quickly ran over what had happened, including the doubts we had that the necromancer had been involved in the battle with Jovan and Glorinal.

Both Ceithera and Padraig looked more serious as my tale went on.

"Did Alric mention the name of the necromancer?" Padraig's face was grim.

"Yes. I did a sketch of what I recalled, and he recognized him immediately." I dug in my pack and brought out the page. I didn't want to say the name, but if they said the same one, we'd know for certain that was who it was.

Padraig's face went pale and he handed the page to Ceithera. Her eyes narrowed, and she looked like she needed to break something. Or someone.

"Domniall. That bastard. I knew the wards keeping him banished to the southern lands wouldn't hold." She looked up from the sketch. "That's who Alric thought it was as well, wasn't it?"

I nodded. "He wanted to tell your people and make sure Siabiane knew. He said that person was her brother."

"He was. Who knows what he is now." Padraig folded up the page and started to hand it back but held it. "Would you mind if I took this to Lorcan and Siabiane? And the royals, of course. It's one thing to hear a rumor that a monster has come back, but it hits stronger when faced with proof."

"Sure. But how did your people banish him all the way to the southern continent? You were still hiding then, weren't you?" Alric and a few other scouts had been secretly traveling around, waiting for the time their people could come out again. But I knew Alric wouldn't have been able to banish someone that strong. And all the way to another continent.

Ceithera put one hand on Alric's chest and nodded. Whatever she felt was good. She looked up. "For the most part, only the scouts went out. But Domniall murdered a nearby village to gain power to break our shields. He failed, so myself, Padraig, Lorcan, and a few others overwhelmed him and banished him. Banishing works better if there is a physical component. Like the water between this continent and the southern one."

I must have looked pale. Padraig led me back to a chair and all but pushed me into it. "And that's who tried to capture me. And who rode along in the tunnel Alric made to get here." They weren't questions, and I didn't really mean to even say them out loud.

"I would say it was. We should have known when he broke the banishment spell, however," Padraig said with a look to Ceithera. "There were serious alarms tied to it."

Alric twitched and Ceithera was all healer now. "This is good, but things might get difficult in the healing process right now. He's fighting to come back. I'll ask you both to go to the waiting area, if you would."

We got up and left. Padraig shut the door and he and I went to the huge entryway.

"He will be all right? I'm sorry, I just… He doesn't do well against necromancers."

Padraig leaned over to hug me. "He will be fine. Domniall threw a dark spell into the tunnel. Since Alric was tied directly to it, it pulled out some of his energy. It's not like what happened with Jovan."

"That was terrifying." I rubbed my arms. "Alric couldn't fight back. None of us could."

"I won't lie, Domniall was a nasty piece of work. That he was able to get back here without us knowing he broke the spell is concerning. But he doesn't have the will to become as strong as Jovan." He nodded. "I knew Jovan before the battle with the Dark. I have theories that he might have been the one who sent me into that coma. Jovan fooled our entire kingdom." He shook his head. "But we still need to remove Domniall on a more permanent basis. I know his sisters would be first in line to help with that."

"I'll help in any way I can."

He peered over at me. "How are you doing, by the way? I have to say, seeing who and what you really are shocked a lot of old elves. Lorcan and I did some fast moving to convince them to leave you alone."

I gave a small chuckle. "Think how I felt. Those memories, the real ones of my past, hit hard when they came through. There are still large gaps, and while I can sense more of what my magic was then, I can't do as much. It's like I can tell something is missing, but I'm not sure what."

"Give yourself time. It took me a while to regain my abilities when I woke up, and I'd only been unconscious for five hundred years, not flung across twenty-five hundred years." He lowered his voice. "There are other healers who use this building, and while good people, we have worked to keep your secret away from the general populace. But have you noticed anything different when you've changed? Do your memories become stronger?"

It was reassuring that they were trying to keep my status concealed. I knew I didn't want anyone in Beccia knowing, and the old me would have trusted the elves implicitly. That wasn't true anymore. I was the last Ancient, at least until we figured out what I did with the rest of my people. I would be a valuable commodity to many.

"Somewhat. But I haven't really had a safe place to explore that concept. I am sort of noticeable when I change." In theory, with Alric and I having had a few more weeks of alone time, I was thinking of reaching out to Padraig, Lorcan, and Siabiane in hopes they could help me get in touch with my inner dragon. That was sort of shot to hell right now.

"True. But I have to say, your wingspan was quite impressive. I wonder what this world was like when your people were in power."

An emotion hit my gut along with a flood of images. I was young and wandering down one of the primary streets in my hometown long ago. "It was gorgeous. Our landscaping and buildings were so beautiful."

He leaned forward. "You're seeing them?"

"Yes. My parents were with me as we went to market. We flew many places but walked through the market. The dragon form was dominant, but our human forms were handy for doing smaller things. Our buildings were built for both sizes as some of our people stayed in human form." I closed my eyes to focus, but everything swirled around me. Sights. Sounds. Feelings. "It was beautiful." I opened my eyes as the feelings and images faded.

"You're crying." Padraig handed me a handkerchief. "I'm sorry, I shouldn't have prodded."

I wiped away the tears that I hadn't even known I'd shed. "No, it's good. I haven't really talked about it much since everything happened. Alric wanted to give me space and I encouraged it." I looked up with a smile. "It might be good to talk about it some." Maybe I could convince Alric to stay in town for a bit once he recovered. Remembering that scene from when I was young had felt good. Sad, but good.

A young elf came jogging through the foyer on his way to the front door. He wore the colors of the royal court.

Padraig got to his feet. "Page? Could I bother you for a moment?"

The page ran over and gave a bow to Padraig. He looked to me but being unknown and human confused him, so he gave a brief nod.

"Can you find Chancellor Lorcan and tell him that Taryn and I are here in the healing house? We'd like to speak to him as soon as he can get away." He looked outside, as if he'd just noticed how late it was. It had been dark when we arrived, it might be close to midnight now. "Actually, ask him to meet us here first thing in the morning."

The page nodded as Padraig spoke, then gave a final nod. "Yes, sir." Padraig handed him a coin and the boy ran out.

"Shouldn't we get Siabiane as well?"

"They'll both come if she's in town. She still goes back to her own place occasionally."

I leaned back against the wall. Worry and running and more worry and no sleep were slamming into me.

"Another reason to wait until daybreak, you're probably exhausted."

"It's been a really long day." I couldn't believe that it had started back in the cabin where my biggest concern was getting away from the faeries.

"I only heard part of it, but it sounded extremely long. I'd say I can find you quarters, but I have a feeling you won't leave until Alric has recovered."

"She'll stay here." Ceithera came out of the room, looking tired but happy. "You both can say hello, but he needs to rest. Regardless of what he says, he is staying in that room tonight even if I must lock him up. Taryn, I have smaller rooms upstairs that you can use as long as you need." She glanced over to Hass and scowled. "I'd like him removed as soon as possible however."

I nodded my thanks and followed her into the room.

"Lorcan will be here in the morning, but I'll take that one with me when I leave this evening," Padraig said as he followed us in. "He can spend the night in the knights' jail."

Alric was pale but not blue as he was when we came in. He tried to roll to his shoulder and sit up but Ceithera was at his side in a blink. "I wasn't kidding. I will leave you tied to the bed all night if I must. You're safe. It was a lot closer of a call than it should have been in part because you are too stubborn. Now say something nice to the woman who saved you."

I came around and Alric smiled. "Can I at least sit up? I won't leave the bed."

Ceithera narrowed her eyes, then nodded.

He sat up and I ran into his arms. "You scared the hell out of me. Don't do that again."

Alric pulled back and looked at my face. "I promise to try." He nodded to Padraig. "Good to see you, my friend. Thanks to all of you for saving me." His smile fell. "I assume Taryn told you about Domniall?"

Ceithera pushed him back down into the bed. "Yes, she did. And no, you're not discussing it until morning. You're exhausted, Taryn's exhausted. Sleep. The problem will be there in the morning."

Padraig clasped Alric's shoulder. "I wouldn't argue. We'll talk in the morning."

He and Ceithera left, with one long, narrow-eyed look from the healer.

"Are you really okay? I thought that…thing in the tunnel had killed you."

He leaned up again and gave me a soft kiss. "I'll always come back to you. I'm fine. Only tired and embarrassed. I should have realized what was going on before I did." One more kiss, then he went back to his pillow. "You'd better go out there or she *will* chain me to this bed."

I gave him a quick kiss on the forehead. "She's given me a room upstairs, Padraig is taking Hass, and we'll all sort this out in the morning."

He reached up to brush my face, but he was fading fast. Sneaky Ceithera, like all healers, she must have slipped something to him to help him sleep.

I left the room and found Ceithera and Padraig talking softly in the foyer. They dropped the conversation, and both looked to me with smiles. Good way to make me suspicious.

"What's wrong?" I looked around but no one was in sight. I kept my voice down.

"Nothing, we were catching up." Ceithera's smile was too bright.

I glanced to Padraig and tilted my head.

"She doesn't believe you. Sorry, Ceithera. It's easier to tell her what she wants to know." He bowed.

"I was telling him that the attack on Alric was specific, far more so than I originally believed. To be honest, I thought Domniall would have been after you, but since Alric was the one behind the tunnel, the draining spell hit him instead." She frowned. "I don't believe that now. Domniall was trying to destroy Alric specifically. While I do still blame that boy for being extremely stubborn and plowing through when he should have stopped, he probably would have fallen anyway."

"Why would Domniall be after Alric? He said he was only a kid when Domniall was banished." I knew he was okay, or so I told myself. If he weren't, Ceithera wouldn't be out here.

"That is a good question and one we will figure out in the morning. This building is shielded, so even if Domniall continues his attack, he won't get through." Padraig used magic to lift Hass up, pulled him over to them, and held him there. "Until we can question him with Lorcan, might you make him rest?"

Hass's eyes went wide over his gag. If he were as innocent in the real purpose of their visit to the north as he claimed, he'd be more careful what jobs he took in the future. I didn't think he'd been that innocent—he knew they were going to do something—but I had a feeling he hadn't counted on Domniall being a necromancer.

"A sleep spell," Ceithera said as she peered down at him. "For now."

If Hass's eyes could have gotten any larger, they would have. Ceithera muttered a few soft words, then his eyes closed, and his breathing slowed.

"Good night, ladies." Padraig nodded his thanks, then motioned toward Hass's body to follow him and they went to the door. "I'll return in the morning. Once Alric is okay to leave, we can work on our prisoner at my place."

Ceithera turned and led me up a delicate set of stairs. "These rooms are used for families of the injured, but Alric is our only visitor at the moment." She held open the first door we came to. "Please rest. I will come get you for the morning meal."

"Thank you, for everything." The room was small but had a bed and bathroom, and that was good enough for me. The door was closing when another thought hit me. "Oh, my faeries are out and about; they might stay out or try to come back in." That would be great, a mass of drunken faeries trying to bash their way into a healing house.

Ceithera smiled. "I have a special doorway open for them. Never fear." With that she shut the door. I managed to drop my pack to the floor before I tumbled into the bed.

CHAPTER EIGHT

I'D FALLEN ASLEEP QUICKLY, BUT that didn't last long, as nightmares jolted me awake more than once. Mostly they involved an encroaching darkness that came forward with a roar. First it took Alric, then the faeries and the rest of my friends—then nothing was left but me and the rumbling void.

That wasn't too surprising, based on what had happened, but it still didn't make me happy. Nor did it leave me with much rest.

I gave up trying to go back to sleep and rolled over as I stretched…to find the entire side of my bed covered in snoring faeries. They'd obviously found their way back inside and made themselves at home. At least I knew where the noise factor from my nightmares had come from. It was amazing how loud four-inch-tall beings could be when they were dead asleep. There was no way to easily get out of bed without disturbing them since they were lining the side of the bed that wasn't facing the wall.

I was cranky from my nightmares, so I might have shaken the blankets to get them off a bit harder than needed. All the faeries tumbled to the ground. One or two woke up as they fell; the rest did when they hit the ground. I wasn't worried about damaging them. It would take more than that to do anything to them. But I did step over them as I got out of bed.

I'd fallen asleep in my clothes and they didn't look so great, so I quickly showered and put on fresh ones from my pack. By the time I finished, the faeries were more or less awake and stumbling around on the floor. A few had crawled back up on the bed.

Garbage looked the most coherent.

"Did you find anything last night? Oh, and Padraig and Lorcan might want to talk to all of you about when you chased out the bad." The girls had come back laughing, so whatever Domniall had done to Alric, he hadn't been a threat to them. I hoped that they could give Padraig and Lorcan enough information to help.

Garbage snapped to attention at that, and even a few of the faeries on the bed perked up. "Nothing goods last night. Hims both good, we help." The faeries didn't often use names for other beings, but they understood them.

"Good. I'm going downstairs; see if you can wake up the rest of your friends." Although they'd briefly perked up from their fall to the floor, about half of the faeries were sliding back into sleep. They must have been out extremely late.

Leaf was one of the awake ones even though she'd gone back on the bed. "We do!" she yelled, then started rolling the sleeping faeries back off the bed.

I nodded and went downstairs.

There were more people coming and going in the foyer now than last night, but I didn't see anyone I knew. The door to Alric's room was shut so I went there first and knocked softly.

Ceithera opened the door and smiled. "Excellent, I was about to come get you. I am having food brought here and Lorcan and Padraig should arrive soon, I believe Siabiane will be joining us shortly." There were five chairs around the room, making it seem even smaller than it appeared. "We'll be a bit close, but I thought privacy was more important."

Alric had been leaning back on the bed but sat up as I came in. "I agree. I'm not sure why, but Domniall seems to be places he shouldn't." He looked much better than last night, and I moved one of the chairs a bit closer to his bed before I sat.

"I can sit in a chair, you know," he said to Ceithera.

"You have recovered far better than I'd hoped. But I can't fit another chair in here." She turned to me. "Are your friends coming? I heard a report by the night watchman that we were briefly invaded last night. I figured it was your faeries."

"They had a rough night out at the local pubs looking for clues. But Garbage and Leaf are waking them up."

A knock came from the door. It was a pair of elves laden down with food and beverages. They set things up the best they could in the cramped space, then nodded and left. Ceithera had returned to her seat when another knock came.

I was expecting Padraig and Lorcan; I was not expecting how annoyed they both looked.

"Taryn and Alric, it's good to see you." Lorcan dropped his frown long enough for a quick hug and smile. Then he took a seat, and the frown came back. "I'm afraid there is bad news."

Padraig shook his head. "Your prisoner was freed."

"What? Where did you have him?" Alric was angrier than I was, but he'd also recently been fighting for his life thanks to someone connected to Hass.

"He was secured by the knights. There should have been no way he'd get out. But someone spelled both knights on watch and broke him out. The knights will recover in a few days, but Flarinen is ready to start ripping people apart."

"So Domniall came into town last night?" He was the only one I could think of who might not want Hass alive and talking to anyone. Although, Hass kept saying he'd no idea who Domniall had been other than a job.

"I don't think it was Domniall." Padraig shook his head slowly. "Or if it was, he's massively changed his magic signature. The lingering traces weren't of anyone I knew."

"Could he have sent one of the other two? Fealk or that troll, Theria?"

Alric shook his head. "Neither were magic users that I could tell. At least I know for certain that Fealk wasn't. The troll might be, but he didn't appear to be from what I sensed in the jail after they escaped."

"And why break him out? Hass wasn't the brightest bulb, and I seriously doubt anyone told him anything important." I didn't see a nasty necromancer sharing his diabolical plans with a two-bit thief.

"The pass to cross the channel? If Grillion was correct, they wouldn't be able to cross without it."

Lorcan had started putting a plate of food together but turned. "A what?"

Alric quickly explained what we'd been told. "I have the pass now, though; I took it off Hass before we came up here."

"But how can they close off an entire continent? I know I haven't been down there in a long time, but that still seems extreme." Ceithera brought over food and tea for both Alric and me. "Ships used to travel freely."

"They could have done it, if they limited what ports ships can use," Lorcan said. "There were some strong magic users amongst the southern elves. It wouldn't be that hard for powerful magic users to limit crossings with dire consequences if disobeyed. I don't see why they would, though."

"Grillion believed it had to do with the battles and troubles going on up here with the relics." Alric shook his head. "I doubt Fealk or Domniall would have thought we'd leave the pass with Hass, though."

"Nor that it would be worth the amount of magic spent getting him out," Padraig said. "There are always ways around things that need paper to get into if you're a good enough magic user. And as much of a bastard as Domniall is, there is no questioning his magical ability."

"Then what?" I had no idea what else was going on; this entire thing was a mess. Before I could share more of my total confusion a series of sharp knocks hit the door.

Ceithera jumped, her hands curled in the manner of a spell fighter.

I motioned her to relax and got to my feet. "Let me get the door. I have a feeling this is a demonstration of life with faeries."

I opened the door slowly in case I was wrong, but got pushed back by the swarm of faeries as they flew in.

"We help!" Garbage yelled and flew up to Lorcan, smacking into the side of his face. Okay, she might have been hugging the side of his face, but it was a little hard to tell the difference.

Lorcan grinned and patted her tiny orange head. "It hasn't been that long, but I am glad to see you, too." He looked up to the rest of the mob buzzing around. "All of you."

"Faeries, I'd like you to meet healer Ceithera. She saved Alric from that bad you chased out of the travel tunnel." I motioned toward Ceithera.

"Nice lady!" They all swarmed to her but didn't fling themselves at her. So that was good.

"These are the tiny warriors who dispatched the bad in the tunnel? You deserve sweets." Ceithera took the lid off the sugar jar and poured the crystals on a large plate. "Before that, could you tell me how you stopped him? The bad?" She covered the plate with a napkin. The faeries were looking back and forth between her and the covered sugar frantically.

Garbage nodded. "We tell. Bad was stupid. Not tied to tunnel. We jabbed. He fall. Boom!" All the faeries joined in on "boom" and laughed hysterically.

Ceithera removed the napkin. "Thank you, ladies."

The faeries all yelled and dove for the sugar.

"For someone not around them much, you certainly know how to get to them." I watched as they all stuffed their faces until their cheeks bulged.

"There are a number of documents about the faeries, many by our own Lorcan. That is interesting, though; Domniall is well trained. He would have known what would happen if he wasn't tied to the tunnel correctly."

Alric ran his hand through his hair. "I should have noticed that he wasn't tied in. I felt the attack but thought I could get us here before I had to deal with it."

"Which wasn't your brightest move," Padraig said with a smirk. The two were hundreds of years apart in age, but Alric had been a boy when Padraig was brought out of a few-hundred-year coma. They'd grown up together as Padraig was re-taught how to be an elf.

"Yeah, I realized that when I woke up in here," Alric said. "Thank you for coming, by the way."

Padraig smiled.

"I don't get it, though." I wolfed down my food and then went for more tea. "Why would he be sloppy? The girls were laughing when they came back from dislodging him. He hadn't been a threat to them." He'd been a threat to Alric, that was clear, but the faeries weren't even concerned about him.

"I agree that something is odd about that," Lorcan said. "Domniall was too smart to do something that stupid. Are we certain it was Domniall?"

Alric and I looked at each other. I reached over and handed Lorcan the sketch. "Here's what I saw in the clearing and who I'm sure came after Dogmaela and me. He didn't throw a spell at me but froze Dogmaela in place before we saw him."

Lorcan studied the sketch and then handed it to Padraig. "That does look like Domniall, but something is off about him."

Padraig looked closely, shaking his head. "It's got to be him."

Alric shrugged. "The magic I felt in the jail was positively death magic, but I do admit, his carelessness with the tunnel doesn't sound like the Domniall I heard stories about."

"With Taryn, he might have been testing your abilities—he took your friend out to see what you would do," Padraig said. "Your unusual spell of simply flinging him away probably caught him off guard."

"What was his goal? To grab me or test me?" Neither was a great option, but I'd like to know what he'd been planning.

"I thought grab, since he saw what you turned into. But there might have been something else in mind." Alric adjusted himself in his bed.

A soft rap at the door startled all of us. Lorcan was the closest, and his smile told me who it was before she came in.

Siabiane smiled and made her way over to Alric and me. "I am so glad to see you two, but not given the circumstances." She hugged us both and then took some tea and sat. "Now, we are certain it was Domniall who attacked Alric?"

Padraig handed her the sketch. "There's some confusion. This looks like him, but he's not acting like him." He quickly filled her in.

The faeries had still been stuffing their faces, but they all looked up, then ran across the table to Siabiane.

"Nice lady!" At least it sounded like that. Their mouths were too full, and they looked like deranged, brightly colored chipmunks.

Leaf managed to swallow her sugar first and flew to Siabiane's lap. "We beat him up. Jab, jab, jab!" She motioned to reenact the jabbing portion.

"You beat him up?" They hadn't claimed that before.

Garbage now flew up. "Yes. He get angry. But didn't fight us. Curl away. Jab!" Her reenactment involved swinging so hard she spun in a circle.

Lorcan and Siabiane both shared a frown before she spoke. "Domniall is a vicious, nasty creature. But he is powerful, yet he didn't fight them? Girls, I have no doubt of your ability, but he didn't fight at all?"

"Nos!" All the faeries who could open their mouths yelled at once. They seemed quite sure of it.

"And someone broke our prisoner out of the knights' jail last night, but it didn't feel like Domniall," Padraig added.

A memory crossed my mind. "It couldn't be a changeling, could it?" Alric had been replaced by changelings a while ago. At first, they really seemed like him, but there were gaps in their knowledge. They also didn't have access to Alric's magic. It would be terrifying if there were a way to copy more than just the semblance of a person.

"No, they can't copy the magic, nor can they do magic on their own. They are magic beings so doing spells won't work for them," Alric said but the others were silent. "What?" He had spent the past few years off trying to find relics and ways for his people to rejoin the rest of the world. Which meant he wasn't up on the newest research, but he was clearly annoyed about this one. "You're implying changelings can now use magic?"

Siabiane waved him off. "Not as such, and not regular changelings. But for a few years now, there have been studies of their abilities. Studies not followed by any of us in the north, as they were not clear on how the changelings were brought in for study or what happened to them." Her scowl stated they'd feared that the changelings were being used poorly.

Siabiane, Lorcan, Padraig, and two of our other friends, Dueble and Nasif, were all researchers. But they had ethics.

"Could someone down south have experimented on

normal changelings and created super ones able to work magic?" The food I'd wolfed down wasn't so happy now.

All of them shared looks that went right over my head. Even Ceithera looked concerned. The faeries didn't, but that wasn't unusual.

"They might have?" Siabiane shook her head. "We should have paid more attention to what they were doing down there. But to be honest, we've had a rough couple of years."

"While we were fighting to keep the relics away from people who would have destroyed the world, the mages in the south were creating necromancer changelings? How many can they make? Will they all have different powers? I felt the strength of the one that attacked Dogmaela and me—he wasn't weak." From the looks on the faces around me, the hysteria building in my head was coming out quite nicely in my face and words. Good. That was a disturbing concept in a disturbing world.

Alric reached over and took my hand. "I'm sure there are limits, especially if this has only been going on for a few years."

"I agree," Lorcan said with his trying-to-soothe-a-freaked-out-wild-animal voice. "I seriously doubt they were able to duplicate a full necromancer's abilities. But I want to see the area where the death magic was used to verify."

"They would have cleaned it by now. I did feel some death magic there. Although it was oddly diffused." Alric sat up higher on the bed. "That is another issue to look at. It appears this Domniall and the troll Theria were captured and brought into jail under the statute that they had been working with Jovan when he attacked Beccia. Something we seriously doubt. Then Hass, Fealk, and my friend Grillion were sent up here to get them free. Rather, the other two were under the guise of bringing Taryn back to the south. Grillion thought that was what they really were doing."

"And the letter from Qianru seemed legitimate." I briefly explained about her vague, *come south I need you* letter.

"That does sound like Qianru. She was helping us as reconnect with the Alioth elves in the south, but she was a bit imperious." Lorcan shook his head. "I can't see what the purpose of this is. He used death magic to get out of the cell in the Beccian jail?"

"No, more oddness," Alric said. "It looks like Hass had strapped prepackaged spells to himself. Once inside his own cell, he used them to get everyone out. They used one as a distraction, but then still killed the captain with death magic. Purposeless death magic. Not to mention, Hass said the captain had been on their side."

Siabiane shook her head. "There's no way that Domniall would have wasted magic like that. Also, I agree, had he been here when Jovan attacked your people, we would have known. When the shield was still up, the alarms would have been unavoidable. Whatever is out there, it wants someone to think it's Domniall. However, it's a fake."

"And we're back to wondering why. This entire thing makes no sense." I threw my hands up in exasperation. Siabiane and Padraig, the two facing me more directly, leaned forward immediately with worried looks.

"Can you hold up your right hand for us?"

I couldn't figure out what they were talking about. Then I recalled the weird pin. I glanced at my palm before I held it up, but I couldn't see anything.

"A lock spell?" Padraig looked like he wanted to jump forward and grab my hand but held back.

I tilted my hand and could see the faintest of words. Those elves had really good eyes.

"I'd say so," Siabiane said as she came forward. "Do you mind?" At my shrug she lifted my hand up, turning it slightly as Alric had when it first happened.

"It was a pin, one someone managed to slip in her pack."

Alric reached into his pocket and pulled out the faery bag. He dumped it on the bed, careful not to touch it. Qianru's letter came out as well.

Lorcan took a napkin and picked up the pin. "Oh my, this might even be as old as Taryn here." He looked up with a warm smile. "Sorry, there are not a lot of beings older than me. But this is exceptionally old."

"So, it's not elven?" I briefly had a panicked vision of more charmed Ancient relics floating around.

"Oh, it's elven." Padraig came forward and peered at the pin but kept his hands locked behind his back. "Just extremely old. What's that paper?"

"It's Qianru's letter to me. It was sort of wrapped around the pin when I found it in my pack." I reached to grab it to hand it to him, but a chorus of no's filled the room. Another napkin was taken from the food table and Padraig used that to pick up the letter.

"You are all now really worrying me." Even the faeries had come over to see what was going on. And Ceithera was peering over Siabiane's shoulder. "What does it say, what has it to do with Qianru's letter, and what does it mean?" My concern about the magic-wielding change-lings was now switched over to my hand and a stick pin. But I had plenty of worry to go around. One thing that I'd learned in the past two years—what could be worried about, should be worried about, because it will probably try to kill you.

"It is a lock spell, an old one that has been reused many times," Lorcan said. "But not for at least a few hundred years."

Siabiane held up my hand. "This writing is a crafted spell that will affect you. However, these spells can't be used for evil, or really much of anything as they aren't that strong. Because it's not a serious one, I think trying to break it would cause more problems than following it through. We can mitigate what it does once it becomes active. It also has a lot of other information beside the spell. Things that are only a month or two old but are so layered upon each other it will take a while to sort."

"As for the letter," Padraig said as he held it through the napkin. "That's actually where the pin came from. Some-how, somewhere, Qianru got a hold of that pin, then had someone in the south spell it into this letter. It probably appeared the moment you put it in your pack."

CHAPTER NINE

———◆———

THAT WAS EXTREMELY UNEXPECTED. "SHE did what now?"

Padraig shook his head in admiration. "She needed to get you the information you needed but knew she couldn't trust the ones carrying the letter, so she went covert with the old ways. Really ingenious when you think about it. She must have at least one powerful magic user on her side down there. Your reading the letter activated the release spell for the pin."

"Yeah, great." I briefly looked at my palm, but the writing was a size the faeries could read. "So, this is going to make me do something? Like follow her orders to go south?"

"That would be my guess," Alric said as he too looked over my hand.

"Why is no one upset about this besides me?" I looked around, but the prior concern about Domniall had given way to full scientific inquiry. Covey would feel right at home here.

"Oh, we are, child," Siabiane said. "We are all fascinated by this use of such an old spell artifact. Never fear, I don't believe Qianru means harm, but we do need to figure out what she is up to. I did run into her a few times when she stayed in the enclave a few years ago. She's a bit odd, but I never got a feeling of evil from her." She started pushing my fingers apart and holding my hand vertically. "Can someone get me a blank scroll?"

"I have a blank fabric napkin," Ceithera said. "Unused and of the finest cloth."

Siabiane nodded. "We'll work with that." She took the napkin and spread it out on a flat part of Alric's bed. "I'm going to transfer a copy of the markings. The original will still be there, but once I stop poking at it, the writing should go back to a dormant state until it is called upon to act. This way we can work on figuring it out without you losing all feeling in your hand."

"I'm good with that." I let her move my hand around until she had it as she wanted on top of the napkin. Then she pushed it down and said a few soft spell words. I didn't feel anything, but a glow peeked out from the edges of my hand, then vanished.

"There we go." Siabiane released my hand and picked up her cloth. "This will be much easier."

"What do we do now?" I closed my hand a bit self-consciously.

Alric shrugged. "We have to find Hass and whoever is pretending to be Domniall."

"Not to mention now we have to find out who made a changeling into Domniall and why," Siabiane said.

Padraig folded up Qianru's letter and handed it back to Alric—napkin and all. "I'd say he was sent up as a test. I do wish we knew how long ago. The changeling didn't set off our alarms, which means it's not close enough to the real Domniall, but definitely far stronger than we want to deal with roaming around."

Alric tucked the letter back into the tiny faery bag. "I'll agree on that. I might have been able to fight him off when he attacked the tunnel if I had stopped instead of pushing forward. But there was still a lot of magic behind his attack."

"Big oomph running low. He no fight." Crusty settled down next to us while the rest went off pillaging the food table.

"What do you mean, sweetie?" They'd already said he didn't fight back, which was odd and according those who knew Domniall not like him. But this felt like more than that.

Crusty scrunched up her face, trying to sort it out. "Magic oomph. You had, then didn't, then did. He didn't, then did, now didn't." She shrugged. "No oomph, no fight." With a bright, lopsided smile she nodded and then flew over to the food table and joined the others.

I watched the faeries as I thought. "Maybe the abilities they gave the changeling were limited? Sort of like a pre-packaged spell, they look like real magic, but they aren't and are limited."

The heavy magic users had already started discussing things, but my observation brought them all back.

"Since we really have no idea of the parameters of infusing a changeling with magic, there's a good chance that there would be limits." Lorcan was still studying the pin but had obviously still been listening to things.

"We need to find him before he gets away. If his borrowed magic is depleted, this would be the time to grab him." Padraig got to his feet.

While I was happy to hear that the person who had attacked Dogmaela and me wasn't really a necromancer, I was afraid they were all getting ahead of themselves. "Isn't this all speculation?" I waited for the angry response from the others; "speculation" was a fighting word for Covey. But none of them looked upset in the least.

"I'd like to keep this if you don't mind?" Lorcan held up the pin. At our nods he put it into his own tiny black bag and continued. "There is a lot of evidence leading to this speculation, but you are correct. It could be wishful thinking; we're afraid if our spells didn't keep such a monster out, what else have they failed at?"

"Which means it's even more important that we catch

him," Alric said. "I'm fine, and the longer we wait the harder it will be to track who grabbed Hass. Hopefully, it will lead to our Domniall changeling—if it is a changeling," he added with a nod to me.

"Flarinen has people on it," Lorcan said.

Alric rolled his eyes. "And who is a better tracker?"

"You have a valid point," Lorcan said. "If Ceithera doesn't object, I believe we should make haste and let our tracker track, and the rest of us will see what we can find out on the more magical side."

Ceithera had been silent but finally nodded. "He's healed, but that was a serious magic drain. I'll release you but try not to throw any spells for a few days. Let Taryn handle the magic end of things." She turned to me. "He'd probably sleep in the woods if need be, but do you have a place to stay?"

I opened my mouth to say no, but Siabiane beat me to it. "They can both stay with me in my cottage here in town. I'll be sticking around for a few days, and it would be nice to chat without worrying about the end of the world coming upon us."

I looked to Alric, but he shrugged. "That would be lovely, thank you." I turned to Ceithera. "And thank you for the offer and for fixing him." I patted Alric's shoulder as we all got up.

"We play!" The faeries had finished all the food off and were flying, a bit lower than usual in my opinion, toward the closed door.

Lorcan got there first and opened it. "Don't forget to come to the palace for a visit, ladies!" He smiled as they flew off. "I'd really quite gotten used to being around them on a regular basis. The world seems less colorful without them nearby."

"It's probably quieter, though." I walked out with him. I'd still need to gather my things from the guest room upstairs.

"That is true. Still, I do hope more of them will come to visit us here now that the shield is gone for good."

I nodded and went upstairs to get my things. Luckily, I hadn't had made much of a mess, but I fixed what I could, grabbed my pack, and headed down the stairs.

Only to smack into an invisible wall halfway down. One that had a freaked-out, semitransparent Qianru in the middle of it.

"Taryn? I hope you can see me. Oh dear. Things have gone extremely wrong. You must not—" And then the entire image collapsed, leaving me stunned and still sitting on the stairs.

"Taryn?" Alric came running up the stairs with the rest not too far behind. "What happened?"

"I'm not sure." I let him pull me to my feet. "What did you see?"

He tilted his head and then shrugged. "You came down the stairs, then you froze, fell back, a shimmering wall partially blocked you, then it vanished."

"Yup, that's what I saw too. Only it was Qianru. She was more disturbed than I'd ever seen her. Said things had gone wrong, and I must not do something."

"What?"

"I have no idea. She was talking to me and it cut off right then."

"She sent a visage? Those are extremely difficult spells. I'm one of the few who can do them here, and we have many powerful magic users," Siabiane said. The first time I'd met Siabiane she'd been a transparent vision like Qianru. Since she lived on the far outskirts of the city, it was helpful for her to have the ability to connect and speak that way.

"Qianru has that ability?" There was no way that was possible. I *needed* for there to be no way for that to be possible. Being hounded by her wherever I went? The shudder that thought caused echoed through my soul.

"No, whoever is helping her does." Siabiane frowned. "And that's even more difficult. I might be able to do that to one of you since you'd all be able to help me on a magic level. But a non-magic user? That's something I would have said was impossible if you hadn't just seen it. I desperately wish we knew who was helping her."

"And what the rest of her message was. She obviously wanted me to come down, and then whatever else she included on my hand." I nodded to the napkin Siabiane still held. "But what if she was saying don't come? Or don't pick up the pin? Or don't not come?"

Siabiane frowned. "That's an issue. I would try to reach out to her, but unlike whoever is helping her, I need to know where I'm trying to appear."

"Are they tying the appearance to Taryn herself instead of the place and the person? The magic user most likely had never met her and would be going off Qianru's memories." Alric shook his head. He might not be able to do this, but clearly, he understood some of how it worked.

I held up my hand with the spell on it. "Maybe this?" That was a disturbing thought. What if the spelled information on my hand was enabling Qianru's magic user to track me? Better than Qianru being able to do it on her own, but still not good.

Lorcan started to shake his head, then shrugged. "Since we're not sure exactly what is in there, I'd say we can't exclude any possibilities."

"Where does that leave us?" My relaxing back into my former life was looking less and less likely.

"Same as before," Padraig said. "We find that Hass person, hopefully find Domniall or whoever is pretending to be him, and Siabiane figures out what's on your hand. Be prepared if Qianru pops up again."

Alric and I came down the rest of the stairs, and we all left the healing house. Lorcan and Padraig went to the palace to work on the pin itself and any more information they could find on the magic signatures involved with it.

Siabiane went with us toward the knights' jail. The elves had their own more formal prison system, but this was for people who'd specifically pissed off a knight. Most eventually got transferred over to the main prison or released. While not used often, Alric had assured me it was pretty hard to break out of.

The knights stationed outside of the building looked as stoic as Flarinen. But one smiled once he saw us.

"Kelm! Good to see you." Alric stepped forward and extended his hand. The red-haired knight shifted his pike and shook Alric's hand. He smiled at me and bowed to Siabiane.

"How have you been? Both of you?" Kelm had ridden out as Flarinen's second when we were still trying to find the relics. He'd left after my attack at the Spheres when he and Flarinen had come back here to report the updates to the elves. "Still have the faeries and your constructs?"

I smiled. If anything, he looked younger than when he'd been out with us on the road; of course, we weren't fighting soul-stealing mages right now. It had taken him a bit at first, but he'd come to like my flying friends. "They are still with me. Well, Bunky and Irving are back in Beccia, along with some of the faeries. The rest are flying around here somewhere."

"That's good to know." He straightened stiffly. "Might I inquire as to the company's business here at the station of the knights?"

Siabiane stepped forward and inclined her head. "Thank you, good knight. We are here to examine the place that the prisoner brought in by Sir Flarinen had been kept in. There appears to be foul magic afoot."

Flarinen was the captain of the knights, and not fond of magic. He reinforced that mindset with the rest of the knights. Both Kelm and the other knight, a tall, deadly-looking woman, nodded and held open the doors.

Neither looked comfortable, even though Kelm had been around a lot of magic when he traveled with us.

Kelm probably still would have let us in without Siabiane but having her did speed things along. She technically had an official status, one she'd had for hundreds of years, as advisor to the king and queen. That covered a lot of ground.

The knights' house was far less decorated than the healing house. It also didn't encourage one to sit and stay long. The entry was small, and the rest was guarded by a long counter—not unlike the one at the Beccia jail. There was far more to this place than only their jail, but obviously they didn't encourage visitors.

The knight standing there took one look at Siabiane leading us in, bowed, and opened the way to go farther back. "Is there anything we can do for you?" He paused, normally there would be a title of some kind; there wasn't, yet obviously he didn't feel it was proper to only say her name.

"Not as of now, thank you, good knight." She regally led the way down the corridor, and we followed.

"Are you sensing anything, Alric?" She didn't turn, but as she spoke, I felt something magical flow from her.

I reached out magically the best I could and felt Alric do the same.

"Not yet, but it's a good thing most knights aren't magic users. Whoever broke him out was a magic user. They will be easier to trace without the knights mudding it up."

Siabiane slowed a bit—perhaps sensing something—then nodded and walked faster. "Agreed."

The hallway was empty, but we soon turned down a small corridor. I could see the bars of the cells, but there was no one watching them. "They trust the building that much?"

Alric shook his head as he stepped forward. "They don't have anyone else here. Padraig mentioned that he'd been told Hass had been the only prisoner."

When I stepped forward, it was clear which cell Hass had been in; the bars around the door were singed and melty-looking. The door itself was gone. There was fresh straw on the floor, and it looked clean aside from the bits around the entry which were burnt. Hot enough to melt metal, but didn't start a fire in the straw? "How did the entire city not hear it?" Yes, they'd used some heavy magic on the knights, but this would have been loud.

Alric held his hand up over the edges of the melted bars and closed his eyes. "There was serious power behind this. They could have added dampening spells as well. Even if they hadn't knocked out the two knights on duty, they might not have heard it."

I watched as Siabiane and Alric prowled around the damaged cell, into the hall, and back into the cell. That both elven faces were locked in scowls didn't bode well. Personally, I felt like one of the faeries. I felt the power that had been used. But if asked, my response would only be that there was a boom. I couldn't separate out the threads of magic as the other two were trying to do.

I briefly wondered if I'd been able to in my former life.

"Question, if these are bad guys, and there is no doubt of that, why didn't they kill the two knights instead of only temporarily disabling them? Wouldn't killing them have been faster?" I was glad the two knights were going to recover, but that seemed more than a bit odd. Particularly if that was Domniall or a changeling pretending to be Domniall out there.

Siabiane turned slowly. "That is a good observation, my child. And a clue. Whoever took Hass values life to some degree, which is definitely not Domniall."

"How do changelings feel about life?" My run-ins with them had been annoying and frustrating because I wanted to find out where the real Alric was, but never deadly.

"They aren't killers," Siabiane said. "There are few of

them around anymore, haven't been for hundreds of years. But they aren't violent by nature."

"So, if the person we thought was Domniall is really a changeling, then they might be following their own normal behavior as much or more so than whoever created them." I was proud I was sorting some part of this out.

Alric shook his head. "Good points, but someone killed the captain of the guard with death magic. If Domniall isn't the necromancer in that group, one of the others is." He looked about as thrilled about that thought as I was.

"I'd bet that troll, Theria. It wouldn't make sense for Fealk to have been it. He wouldn't have even been there if we hadn't brought him in. They couldn't count on us doing that."

Siabiane continued to walk about the cell slowly. "Could it have been this Grillion?"

Alric immediately shook his head. "No. He's a con man, and not completely trustworthy, but he's not even remotely a magic user. Not to mention he was with us when the death happened."

"What if one of the others killed the captain, and then Domniall's changeling threw some death magic at it to make it look like it was him?" It was a bit odd, but things weren't matching up.

Alric stopped his prowling around the cell. "That's twisted thinking, but I guess it could be. I felt a necromancer's power on the body, but obviously wasn't going to try and force the guards to let me see if that's what killed him."

"I would think if the entire point was to make the elves think Domniall had broken back into this land, through our alarms, they would have brought him closer to the enclave." Siabiane stopped in one corner of the cell near the small cot and froze. "Interesting, not magic related but fear. Your prisoner was terrified of whoever broke him out. Extremely so."

I didn't want to interfere with their searching, but I felt

an odd pull to the far corner of the cell. I stepped inside slowly. "If someone overpowered the changeling and the troll, and locked them up on fictitious charges, they might have been captured on their way to this city. Grillion recognized Theria the troll from a few years ago in Kenithworth, but that doesn't mean he'd been up there all this time." Whatever was pulling at me in the cell got stronger, and I stepped around the other two.

"Good point," Siabiane said. "Do you see something?" She saw me heading for the corner.

Alric turned toward me as well. I felt silly saying it was a feeling, but it was now a feeling that was becoming insistent.

"No, but there's something in that corner." The smart thing would be to stand back and let one of them see what it was. But my right hand was tingling with wanting to get whatever this was. "I think I have to grab it." I tried to pull back, but my hand seemed to be on a mission whether I wanted to be or not. I stumbled forward as it dragged me to the corner.

Alric tried to stop me, but while the cell wasn't huge it was large enough that my hand, and the rest of me, got there first. Without my say so, my hand dove into the straw piled in the corner. I felt cool metal, then was flung across the cell. I missed Siabiane, but Alric did manage to cushion my landing.

I rolled off him, but my fist was clenched around whatever I had grabbed and wouldn't open. "Are you okay?" I reached down with my other hand to help him up.

"I should be asking you that. I'm not the one who went flying across the cell." He dusted himself off. "What's in your hand?"

I looked down at my closed fist. "Yeah, not sure. It's metal, I feel that. Kind of like a certain pin I found, only wider."

Siabiane stepped forward. "Can we see it?"

I held my hand up and tried to force my fingers open.

"I'd love to show you, but it's locked up my hand."

"That's the hand the lock spell went on, isn't it?" Siabiane took my hand and gently tried tugging my fingers open.

"Yup. It pulled me over there. Did Qianru stash a bunch of spelled jewelry around?" Alric had patted down Hass and Fealk before we took them to the jail in Beccia and again when the faeries brought Hass to us. But something this small wouldn't have been noticed as a weapon—or it wasn't on him when Alric searched him.

"I want to cast a spell to try and get your hand to unclench." Siabiane gave me a far too reassuring smile. "Alric? It might be a good idea to hold on to her."

Now that was not reassuring at all.

Alric came behind me and put one arm across my shoulders and supported the closed hand with his other. "Anything else I should be prepared for?"

Siabiane looked up from her study of my hand. "Just hang on to her. And grab this thing if it decides to take off once I release her grip." She gave me a nod, then started chanting. Not all magic users said words with their spells, and she only did sometimes—this must have been an older spell.

My hand tightened at her words until I yelped. "Hurts!"

Siabiane immediately pulled back and my hand relaxed a bit. "Let me try a different one. You are all right, yes?"

"I want my hand back at this point." I held my arm out to her.

The spell this time was different, still some words, but they were almost like a lullaby. My hand popped open, and Alric used the edge of his cloak to grab the bit of metal resting in my palm.

My hand tingled, but I had a feeling it was as much from being locked closed as from whatever had been inside it.

"What is it?" Siabiane didn't grab it out of his hand but she looked ready to.

"I have no idea." Alric held it up gingerly with the tips of two fingers. It was about the length of the pin—maybe a bit longer—with two raised holes on either end and about an inch wide.

"The base for that pin?" It looked like would fit it perfectly. "And look—more writing too." I pointed at but didn't touch the tiny, elegant scrollwork on the piece. As far as I could tell, there hadn't been anything new added to my hand, and I wanted to keep it that way.

"Do you feel anything from holding it?" Siabiane was still peering closely but not touching it.

"No," Alric said. "I'd like to put it in the bag the pin had been in. If they are connected, and I think we can believe they are, that won't be a problem?" He was watching it closely. My guess was he didn't want to be spell locked either.

"It should be fine to put it in there. Taryn, can you get the bag?"

They were both being so cautious that they were making me more concerned. "Sure." I got it out of his pocket and held it up to him. I didn't touch it. Not at all.

The damn piece of metal leapt for me.

CHAPTER TEN

NOW, I'D NEVER HAD TINY pieces of spelled jewelry come after me before, so screaming and running backward, forgetting I was in a not-so-huge cell, was to be excused. I hit the bars, went down, grabbed some hay, used that to grab the jewelry trying to get back into my other hand, and shoved it and the hay into the tiny faery bag.

An army of flying blurs came tearing into the cell as soon as I tied the bag closed. The yelling outside indicated the knights hadn't been pleased with the faery invasion.

Siabiane quickly stepped out into the main hall and calmed the knights down. Then she came back into the cell.

"Attack!" Garbage had her war stick out and buzzed around the cell with the rest waving their sticks as they followed her. After the third loop, she flew down to me still sitting on the cell floor.

"Where go?" She rattled her war stick, but it was in general, not at me specifically.

"Where did who go, sweetie?"

"Bad! Boom…here boom!"

I seriously wondered if any of my ancestors ever understood boom. My people had been friends with the faeries, but my memories of that time were still scattered. "There's no one here but us."

Garbage narrowed her eyes and glared at the tiny bag

still in my hand. "Boom." She pointed to it with her stick but didn't come closer. "Not enough." She handed her war stick to Leaf, then started fishing around in the tiny front pocket of her overalls and pulled out another small bag. This one was a dark tarnished silver color. I'd seen a lot of the small black bags, but this was the first one of a different color.

"Is in. Now." She waved the new bag at me. "*Now.*"

I took the bag. "You want me to put this bag in that one?" The faeries hadn't even noticed the pin when I'd been zapped by it, but they'd come in from wherever they'd been off to, totally worried about this new piece.

"Yes. In. Now." The glare that followed motivated me to drop the black bag into the silvery one and tie it closed.

"Now give to nice lady." Garbage was still upset but the agitation was dying down from the faeries around us.

Siabiane stepped forward and I handed her the bag. Alric helped me to my feet.

Siabiane gave a huge smile to the faeries. "Thank you, Garbage Blossom. Do you know what it is?"

I almost laughed out loud. Asking a faery for an explanation of anything was a pointless exercise.

Garbage looked serious, nodding her head as if she were thinking. "Is boom."

Crusty flew up closer to Siabiane. "Bad magic. Hurt peoples. In there." She too was serious, but at least she said something other than boom.

Siabiane waited for a moment in case there was more, then smiled. "Thank you, ladies. This new bag will protect us?"

"Yes. No boom. Keep in bag." Leaf had to join in. The rest of the faeries nodded along.

"That will make it difficult to examine." Siabiane slipped it into the small pouch she carried. The faeries seemed unmoved, but I knew if anyone could find a way around this problem, Siabiane could.

My hand started tingling again, not good since it had been feeling less tingly up until a second ago. "We may have a problem." I held up my arm. The words from before appeared on my palm again, and new ones went up the underside of my arm from wrist to elbow. "What are these things doing?"

Both Siabiane and Alric stepped closer and looked at the writing. "It's another part of a lock spell. When we get to my cottage, I'll try and do a transfer of this one as well. The flare up should go away in a bit."

As they both stepped back, Garbage, Leaf, and Crusty flew forward and looked at my arm. "You bad. Go away now." Garbage shook her finger at the writing.

"Thank you, sweetie, but I don't think that will make a difference." My last word faded as the writing and itching started to vanish. I twisted my hand around but couldn't see anything. "How did you do that?"

All three looked extremely smug. "We magic," Crusty said with a winsome smile that quickly turned unhinged. "Need ale!"

Within two seconds all the faeries had flown off.

"Okay, all of that was odd." I looked around the cell. "Do you two need to be here anymore? I think I'd like to settle down with a nice cup of tea. It's been a far too interesting morning." Truth was, I was exhausted. I'd felt a bit tired earlier but whatever power that lock spell had, it was wiping me out.

Alric glanced around the cell. "I think I've gathered what information I can. There is only a faint trace of who took him, but enough that I should be able to follow it out of town. From there I should be able to track them in the woods."

"Why don't you go track, and Taryn and I will relax and chat about some spells and markings back in my cottage. We will meet you there once you're done."

Alric leaned over and gave me a quick kiss. "If they went

far, I may be gone longer. I'll get a message to you, though."

I grabbed his hand. "Be careful." I was too tired to be helpful tracking someone and really wouldn't have been even if I weren't exhausted. But he'd just recovered.

He smiled. "I promise." With a nod to Siabiane, he left the cell.

She and I walked out of the cell and left the knights' house.

"Now that was good to see." Siabiane smiled as we went toward her home.

"Which part? Me being attacked by another piece of old jewelry? Or the fact there was a lot of power used on that cell?" Since the writing had faded, the itching was gone, but there was still a faint tingling as if the spell didn't want me to forget it was there.

"That kiss. Alric has never been demonstrative emotionally. That might have been nothing for some people, but for him that was huge. He is extremely attached to you."

"It was a kiss." I wasn't sure what to make of her reaction. He was the love of my life—he better be attached to me.

Siabiane laughed. "I meant he felt comfortable enough to kiss you in front of me. It was more his attitude than what he did—he was totally relaxed. I am glad you two found each other."

"So am I. Maybe I had to fling myself so far in the future to find him." I was joking; I didn't believe in fated loves.

Siabiane looked serious. "It could be. One never knows." She stopped in front of a charming two-story cottage. Larger than most of the ones around it but done in such a way that it didn't stand out. It was much smaller than her sprawling place outside of the city.

Siabiane led the way up the path and I followed, enjoying the gardens as we passed. Until a pair of small red caps came darting out into the path, and were quickly followed by the two brownies under those caps.

"Stand back! They can be dangerous." I held up my hand

for a spell, but my sword didn't feel like coming back.

Siabiane turned and looked down at them with a smile. "Taryn, meet Welsy and Delsy, a pair of reformed brownies now in my employ as gardeners."

Both nodded and bowed with huge grins. Extremely different from my other run-ins with their people. One time they had created a golem to attack me in the woods, and another time they took over Covey's house. They were not a nice group of people.

"We are reformed."

"It is much nicer living here with all the food we need and lovely plants than being out there."

"Destroying things."

The way they tagged on each other's sentences was cute, but I still didn't trust them. Judging by the continued smile on Siabiane's face, she did.

I forced a smile. "It is nice to meet you. I'm Taryn."

"We know." They both smiled even larger, then doffed their caps to Siabiane and vanished into the garden.

Siabiane went up the stairs and held open the door. I shot another look to where the brownies had gone, then went inside.

The inside reminded me of a larger and far more organized version of Siabiane's sister Mathilda's cottage. Of course, Mathilda's cottage could walk, and I didn't think this one could. But it was cozy and spacious at the same time. And honestly, neater than Mathilda's place. Siabiane went to the kitchen but pointed to the lavish sofas on her way.

"Please sit anywhere. I believe some tea is in order?"

"Yes please," I picked the softer-looking of the two sofas and collapsed into it. "Could these lock spells be draining my energy? I've been exhausted all morning."

Siabiane popped her head out of the kitchen. "They could be. Those are extremely old spells. Let me grab some tea and biscuits, then we'll see if we can sort you out."

I nodded and leaned back into the warm, comfy sofa.

"Taryn? Taryn?" The voice was close and concerned but sleeping felt good. I tried to roll over but found that someone was holding my arms. Shaking them even.

I opened a bleary eye to see who was in my bedroom. Then saw Siabiane's concerned face and her living room behind her. "Oh my…what happened?" I had slid down and was crumpled into a corner of the sofa.

"You gave me a serious scare, that's what happened. I came out here ten minutes ago and couldn't wake you. I was about to resort to magical means, but as I didn't know what knocked you out, I had my concerns." Siabiane grabbed some pillows and put them behind me. She also pulled my legs out flat on the sofa.

"I'm fine." I started to get up but then flopped back down. It was like I hadn't slept in weeks. My eyes felt so heavy.

"You're not fine." She got me propped up enough to put a teacup in my hand. "Drink this and see how you feel. You look a bit wan."

I took a sip and tried to hand it back. That was some strong tea. Small rodents could probably walk across it and not sink.

"Nope, all of it. I need to get you awake so we can see what's happening."

While I worked on my tea, Siabiane held out my spelled hand and slowly brought the words back up. It gave a slight tingle, but a lot less than before.

She scowled and shook her head. "I don't see how this spell could be doing it, even not really being as familiar with it as I could have been. The lock spell is dormant now. I'll need to make a copy when it flares again."

She lifted an eyebrow until I finished the last of my tea. "Right then, let's stand you up. You can stand up, correct?" She started to pull me to my feet, then paused and carefully watched my face.

"Yes," I said with more force than I felt. But I was proud I stood on my own. Not to say that if someone gave me a big fluffy bed right now, I would say no.

"Then I need you to stand still. I'm going to use a wand and see if it picks up anything that magically shouldn't be there. Then we'll work on more mundane things that could be causing it."

I'd never seen any magic user with a wand, and this was more of a small narrow sword, minus the sharp edge and stabby point. She held it up directly in front of her fore-head, then waved it an inch or two from my body all along the side and over the top of my head.

Just like a doctor, she did the obligatory "hmms" and "ohs." Then she stepped back with a satisfied nod, and the wand vanished. "Someone started to put a latch spell on you. It got cut off, but it's still draining you. I think we know who our real or fake Domniall was after when he attacked the tunnel."

I flopped back onto the sofa. "Wait, that spell on the tunnel was directed at me? I thought it was decided it was an attack against Alric. What cut it off?"

"Alric was running the spell for the tunnel, so he was drained when Domniall's changeling jumped on. I think you can thank your faeries for breaking it off. When they attacked him and threw him out of the tunnel, they broke his spell. That was why you didn't notice it."

"That's twice that someone around me has been spelled because of this guy. And wait, so now you do think it's a changeling for sure?"

"That is something we need to look at—his first attack was aimed at your friend, and probably he had taken her out of the situation to go after you. But this time he was after you, this was specifically directed. His spell took Alric out as well since most of the magic was from Alric. And yes, the spell placed on you feels a bit like Domniall, but not really. It's different enough that I feel it is not my brother."

"Excellent. Not Domniall but wants us to think he's Domniall and he's after me, but not really, just kinda. And this spell is making me want to climb into a bed for a month." I rubbed my face, willing the tea to kick in faster. "I wish I could recall more of the magic I knew in my time. If I had the abilities to create that weapon, and the individual parts, I probably had some power." I leaned back into the sofa, but the tea was helping. It was frustrating to know that powerful magic had been part of my life but was out of reach now when I needed it.

Siabiane went to the kitchen and came back with her own cup of tea, the pot, and a plate of custard cream biscuits. "I was wondering about that. Nothing has come back of your abilities from before?"

She handed me the plate and I took three biscuits. Sugar could help perk me up too. "Not really. Sometimes I can feel a spell that could be used, but I can't make it work. Like I have the memory of doing something, but no instructions were left."

"You have to admit that what you did was fairly remarkable." She raised her hand to stop me. "Not the weapon, although that really was impressive. But the fact you flung yourself this far into the future and are recalling any of it."

"Do you think I'll gain more of it back?" I wanted the magic, I thought. Part of me hated that me who sent all her people somewhere lost in time, but another part understood the grief and fear that motivated her to try and save them. Even as my magic came back, I would be questioning every action. Alric had stopped me from doing something stupid during that battle, but I couldn't count on him to be there to do that all the time.

"It is hard to say. I know there are many magic researchers who, if they knew exactly who and what you are, would be extremely happy to help you find out."

I had a biscuit in my mouth so I violently shook my head before I could swallow. "I don't want others to know.

They can't. I'd never get my life back." I wanted to know who I had been, but not at the cost of whom I currently was.

"Never fear, none of us will tell. But maybe you could work with Nasir and Dueble when they come back from their travels. They are exceptional researchers and already know you."

I nodded. Those two I would feel safe around, like I did around Siabiane, Lorcan, and Padraig. Alric and I had met Nasir and Dueble a thousand years in the past, before the Breaking, which was what the elves called the massive battle with the Dark that launched a thousand years of hiding. Nasir and Dueble had helped us get back to our time, but in the process, they'd been changed in their own time. They were both more or less immortal.

"Any idea where they are now?" The tea she refilled my cup with wasn't as strong as the one she'd hit me with before. However, I was feeling less out of sorts so the first cup must have done its job.

"Interestingly, they are down south. At the tip of the southern continent researching some old elven and syclarion finds." Nasir was an elf and Dueble was a syclarion—but a good one. That type of dig site would be perfect for them.

The fact they were already in the south got my attention. "How far from Qianru? Do you have any idea where the real Domniall is?"

"Not close, but if you do end up going south to Qianru, your faeries can probably find them. As for Domniall, who knows? Hopefully, he's rotting in a dark cave somewhere." The anger that flashed across her face could probably reduce a tree to splinters. She shook it off with a smile. "The tea seems to have helped. The rest of the aftereffects from that aborted spell will fade."

"Thank you, I am feelin—" My words were cut off when yelling exploded right outside the window.

CHAPTER ELEVEN

A MOMENT LATER I REALIZED THAT the yelling was familiar. I put my cup down and got to my feet. Didn't jump to them, but I was steady.

I flung open the door with Siabiane right behind me. "Damn it, girls, what are you doing?" Yup—faeries in war feathers with their sticks, yelling, and dive-bombing a bunch of bushes.

"Bad little men!" Leaf yelled right before she dove down again.

"Sorry, we've all had some bad experiences with brownies," I said to Siabiane. "Girls, stand down! Those brownies are friends of Siabiane—of the nice lady." I had to repeat myself twice mostly to be heard over their yelling. Finally, all of them flew up to us.

"Is real?" Garbage looked extremely doubtful. And torn. Brownies were their enemies, but she liked Siabiane.

"Yes, my dears. Welsy and Delsy are in my employ. You may come out now."

The two brownies I'd seen before, or I presumed they were the same, came out from the bushes, but they were each holding two of their kind by their ears. The ones they were holding were clearly angry but not moving. It was as if their entire bodies were controlled by their ears.

"The faeries were right."

"These tried to invade."

"The garden."

The one on the left waggled the two he held. "Want give to faeries?"

I was impressed that they each had two.

Siabiane narrowed her eyes as she watched them, then shook her head. "Not yet. The girls might still get them, but I want to talk to these personally. Thank you for catching them." She held out her hands, and all four of the outsider brownies floated. Welsy and Delsy eventually let go of their ears, but they held on long enough to hurt.

I'd have to recall that ear trick if I were ever attacked by a band of brownies in the wild. And if I was close enough to grab their ears.

Siabiane turned and went back into her cottage with the floating brownies and all the faeries right behind her.

"We find." Garbage was looking far too smug again.

"Yes, you did find them, but I need you ladies to settle down while you're in here."

"Fine." Garbage nodded, but I noticed that none of the faeries put away their war sticks.

Siabiane went to the large dining table and set the brownies on it. One tried to run but was bounced back into the center by whatever spell she had on them.

"Now, I know for a fact we do not have any local brownie families within city limits, or anywhere within a plausible distance around the city." Siabiane brought her fingers together and the brownies clumped closer together.

"Not talk." One of them stepped forward, folded his arms, and glared at Siabiane.

Now these were more like the brownies I knew. More like what the faeries knew as well. Garbage and one of her gang, a lapis blue-colored faery named Tangle Morning Glory flew closer to the table.

"We make talk," Garbage said.

Tangle Morning Glory gave a wide grin. "Yes." She landed on the table and started stalking the brownies.

The brownie tried to maintain his glare, but while he didn't appear afraid of Siabiane, he was nervous around the faeries. "Nothing to say. We were talking to our friends." He hooked a thumb behind him. "Out there."

Siabiane laughed. "You mean the two who caught you? Welsy and Delsy are my friends, not yours. Why are you here?" An edge of steel crept into her voice.

Garbage and Tangle sat down outside of the brownies' reach. Both looked ready to charge forward given any opportunity.

The leader looked around and folded into a sitting position, looking like a two-year-old who had eaten something he shouldn't have but was refusing to open his mouth.

"Well, if they aren't afraid enough of the faeries or you to talk, we do have those extremely hungry rakasas still caged in your back room. They liked eating brownies last time I saw." I gave an evil grin and leaned forward. "And you really only need one of these to talk, right?" As far as we knew, and I desperately hoped, the last of the rakasas had been destroyed in the battle of the Spheres. Nasty subterranean creatures only about three feet high with mouths filled with sharp teeth, they made sure I would never take the ground rumbling as something natural again.

The brownies tried to pretend like they hadn't heard, or at least didn't care. The trickle of sweat running down all their faces revealed I'd hit a few nerves. These might never have run into a rakasa, but they knew of those who had.

"What say we save the first one who talks?" Siabiane looked over the brownies. "You are correct, the rakasas are getting hungry, and we really don't need all four of these."

It took less than three seconds before all four were talking so fast that nothing could be understood. Garbage stomped over and smacked all four brownies in the head. "Stop." She rose and hovered over the table, glaring at them until they all shut up.

"Since you are all now willing to speak, I will hold off

feeding you to our rakasas—for now. One of you start speaking. The others step in if he's missed anything, but only after raising your hand." Siabiane looked like an imperious schoolteacher—one you would never talk back to.

The other three brownies sat down where they stood, and the first one started speaking quickly.

"We were paid to come here and find some missing items for an employer. Then we saw your two brownies and feared you had captured them. We were trying to get them to come with us when the damn faeries showed up." He glared at Garbage and Tangle. All the faeries stuck their tongues out.

"What were you supposed to find?"

The first brownie bit his lip, so the one to his left raised his hand.

"Yes?" Siabiane nodded to the second brownie.

"Some valuable jewelry stolen by a gang of thieves and brought here."

"Here to my house?"

"No…well, maybe."

A third brownie raised his hand. "We lost the trail. Four pieces, all old silver. Valuable if we bring them back."

"You have nothing to go on beyond that? Four random pieces of old jewelry? You do realize that you're in a large elven town. Everything we have is old."

The fourth brownie practically jumped to his feet with his hand waving. Siabiane nodded to him. "We use this thing! But it stopped working." He scowled as he fumbled in his vest pocket and pulled out a small compass. "It pointed to our prizes." He shook it. "Not working now."

Siabiane held out her hand for the gizmo and kept it up in such a way they wouldn't be able to see it start going toward me, then her, then spin around and stop with the arrow facing outside.

"It does in fact appear to be broken. However, I will be keeping it. Who hired you and where did you come from?" She tucked the compass inside her dress pocket without another look.

"In Hobin, man find us, give us milk and honey, old ways. Say pay us if we bring them back. They are hidden and we had to wait until they appeared, then grab them." The first one held up a small scrap of paper to Siabiane.

The writing and images were too small for me to get a good look at, peering as I was over her shoulder. But I did note a slight intake of breath from her right before she put it away. I had a bad feeling we knew what two of those pieces were. The faeries' silver bag might have blocked the brownies' gizmo from seeing the most recent piece, and Lorcan was most likely in a protected place studying the first one. I was worried that there might be two more, but glad that thing hadn't detected them. We probably would need to find them; I wasn't sure I liked the way they kept finding me.

"Where were you to meet to give the man the trinkets?"

All four brownies looked at each other and fear crept across their faces. That they looked to be seriously considering not speaking and facing the rakasas was disturbing.

"In Beccia. In pub."

"Shimmering Dewdrop," the second one provided.

Siabiane and I shared a look this time. The pin and its mate were likely to have come from Qianru, so who knew about them and would be hanging around the Dewdrop?

Damn it. Alric's friend Grillion might be more involved than we thought. The likelihood of the brownies working with the Domniall changeling were slim. But it was also a bit odd that the spelled silver pieces were obviously smuggled up from Qianru with Grillion or his two traveling companions, yet one of them hired the brownies to get them back. Of course, if I was what triggered the appearance of the pieces, they might have wanted to make sure they got them even if they didn't get me.

"Wait, was this man from Hobin also? Did you travel

with him?" I couldn't imagine anyone wanting to travel with the cantankerous, murderous little brownies, but I also doubted the two situations were not connected.

"No. They pass through Hobin. Tried to rob, but he offer us a job."

"We hide on way up."

Siabiane tilted her head at the brownies' wording. "Hide?"

"Yeah, he had way to keep us hidden. We get to Beccia and wait. Then the compass went spinning and we had to race here. Now lost it."

The faeries were chattering idly, a sure sign they were starting to get bored. Bored faeries were a bad thing.

I stepped over to them. "Girls, thank you for capturing these brownies. The rest of this will be dull, I'm afraid. If we do decide that they will be given to you for punishment, Siabiane can keep them in a magic cage and we'll call for you."

They looked torn. They clearly were bored, but also didn't want to miss out on some brownie harassment.

Siabiane smiled. "I promise, ladies. We will save them for you."

They took Siabiane's word over mine and raced for the door. I managed to get there first and opened it. More faeries than Crusty had smashed into closed doors before.

Once the faeries had flown off, with much hooting and hollering, we turned back to the brownies.

"I will have to figure out what to do with you, but as of now, we have other pressing issues."

Siabiane turned to me. "Keep an eye on them. If they try to escape, use your push spell. It'll tighten my spell and crush them." At my nod she went into the kitchen.

"She really has rakasas?" the first one asked quietly.

"In the back room, locked in a rock lined cage so they can't get out." I folded my arms and tried to look fierce. They might not fear me like this, but they would if they saw me change.

I rocked back at that thought. I couldn't be thinking about changing into my dragon form for shock value. Letting people know who and what I was could be annoying if not fatal. It was bad enough I did it in front of Hass and the others, but I'd been drugged. Thinking about it, even without the intention to do it simply to cow four brownies was stupid and reckless.

Siabiane came out from the kitchen with a large wooden box. "I've used this for trapping and releasing wild animals when they get too far into town. It will also work for four brownies. It's spelled so don't think to try anything." She set it on the table and opened the door.

"We're not going in there." The first brownie put his foot down. Literally.

"I have things to do. In there or in the rakasas' cage, I don't care at this point."

The brownies grumbled but walked in. Siabiane shut and locked the door, then hit all four with a sleep spell. She shoved the box in a corner of the dining room.

"You could have put them to sleep and then put them inside."

Siabiane shuddered. "Touch wild brownies? Do you know where they've been? Because I don't. This way they put themselves in, which will strengthen the cage spell if they work through the sleep spell. If you're feeling up to it, I think we should go see Lorcan about this update."

I shrugged but followed her. I wasn't as sleepy as before, but still a bit out of sorts.

The path we followed was less direct than the way we'd come in and took what felt like to me a much more serpentine route to the palace. Granted, I'd only been here once, but the palace was easy to see from most places in the city. And we zigged and zagged like Crusty on a two-day bender. Siabiane also kept looking up as if watching for something.

"Are we trying to avoid something or someone?" I finally asked after she went three blocks the other direction before turning back.

"Hmmm? No, well, possibly. I don't want the faeries to join us on this. They cause a lot of excitement, and I would like to keep this visit quiet."

That explained the looking up part. "But faeries don't follow streets."

"Yes, well, there might be something else that either followed the brownies or was working with them. I added a layer of protection on my cottage as we left. I hadn't noticed it until we stepped outside to leave, nor can I describe it." She shrugged. "Just a feeling really."

"Is this a feeling that might require a sword?" The elven city seemed too calm to be worrying about attackers in broad daylight. But I'd rather be prepared.

"I don't think so." She gave a shiver which discounted her words. "It's only a sense, not even of wrongness necessarily, but something odd."

That was enough for me, I thought about my sword, and it played nice and showed up in my hand—belt, sheath, and all. I buckled the belt on but kept the sword in the sheath. I kept my hand on the hilt, though. If something was giving Siabiane a weird feeling, that was something I wanted to be prepared for.

She shifted direction once more, then made a direct line for the palace. Lorcan was the primary royal advisor and lived in the palace. He had extensive laboratories there as well. So did Padraig.

"You didn't notice anything before? When we left the knights' place?"

"No, I did not. I thought it would be nice to chat without the rest around, but now I am questioning that." She started walking faster. "Something is following us."

There still was nothing I could see, nor was I feeling anything. Then again, she was a far stronger magic user—at least until I figured mine out. I didn't think my magic was stronger than the elves, but it worked differently.

Maybe because I was extremely focused, but I swore I felt a rumble under my feet as we traveled the last block. If those were rakasas, I was going to allow myself to change and stomp them all so far into the ground it would take thousands of diggers to put together enough to figure out what they were. The risk to my daily life if the elves knew what I was be damned. Those little monsters needed to be gone.

I tightened the grip on the hilt of my sword. If we were attacked, it would be sword and magic first, then life-changing transformation.

We'd reached the steps of the palace when the rumble became a roar.

CHAPTER TWELVE

NONE OF THE ELVES PASSING by had reacted to the prior rumblings, but this got their attention. It knocked about half of them off their feet. Even the royal knights standing guard outside the palace tipped a bit, but they didn't fall. Probably would be against regulation.

I grabbed my sword. I didn't feel weird as anyone around us with a weapon also had theirs out. Most of the magic users were easy to spot by their raised hands, looking for something to strike down. For a people who had spent a thousand years secure in their hidden pocket of the world, they'd adapted quickly to the potential dangers of not having a shield anymore.

Of course, these people had also survived the rakasa attack that took down their shield.

"I thought Padraig said there was another defense mechanism in place?" I stood close to Siabiane, watching for any holes in the ground that could start erupting short, bitey monsters at any moment.

"There is, something less obtrusive than the shields. And something that should stop any new dangers." She was watching the sky as well as the ground. "Where are the faeries?"

"I thought we wanted to avoid them?"

"I did, but whatever caused that should have brought them to the source."

I watched as the elves eventually put away their weapons and spells and continued on. "Which means the source wasn't here. I know those hooligans. They would be right in the middle of something like that. Whatever that was."

"And the source not being near here, or even within city grounds, could explain why the defenses didn't kick in. We should still get Padraig and Lorcan. I want to tell them of the new piece of spelled jewelry and the brownies. But after that, see if you can call the faeries to you. They can lead us back to whatever just happened."

I sheathed my sword with a shrug. "I can try. It depends how interesting whatever just happened was," I didn't add *and if we can get them to accurately lead us back.*

Siabiane was still scanning the street in front of us but turned, nodded, and went into the palace.

I pointed to her retreating back as I fell under the watchful eyes of the guard-knights at the front door. "I'm with her." They both soberly nodded. They didn't try to stop me, which was good, but they were almost respectful, which was a bit disturbing.

It was busy inside the palace, but no one looked panicked. Either the building itself insulated them from feeling the shake, or they trusted that others would take care of it. A dangerous thought, in my opinion.

Siabiane was stopped by a court functionary who was trying to talk to her, so I looked around. Most of the original palace had been destroyed a year ago. You'd never know it from looking inside now. The interior looked almost exactly like it had the first time I'd been here. They'd even aged the murals painted on the walls. Very impressive.

"Come along. Lorcan and Padraig are in Lorcan's suite." Siabiane started striding for the winding stairway. The palace was a long warren type building, and I hadn't been certain if Lorcan's rooms had been in the section that had been destroyed. But I wondered if I'd be able to tell if they were.

I recognized where we were going, or at least it looked familiar to me. Not all my travels through this place had been good—nor of my own volition. I'd been locked in a tower while Alric had been in a prison cell the first time I came here. I hadn't thought of it in months, but I really hoped we didn't see any of the kitchen staff. During our escape Garbage, Leaf, Crusty, and myself had done a fair amount of damage to the kitchen.

We went up a much smaller staircase, and I realized that Lorcan's area must not have been destroyed before. It would be hard to replicate thousand-year-old rocks and stone.

Lorcan opened the door right as Siabiane was raising her hand to knock.

"You old conjurer you, you have a spying ball on the stairs."

He grinned. "That's how I've lived to be an old conjurer, thank you." He stepped back. "Come in, ladies. What news? We didn't expect to see you for a while yet."

We followed him into a tidy front room. He'd already set out some tea and sandwiches.

"We thought it would be a bit longer as well. It would have been nice to engage in a conversation without things trying to kill us." Siabiane took a cup of tea and sat in a large red chair.

Padraig had been in the next room, a laboratory of sorts. He stuck his head out at that. "What happened? Someone tried to kill you?" He watched us both, looking for injuries.

"Not directly," Siabiane said, and then looked to me. "But another piece of spelled jewelry showed up."

I had my tea and sandwiches and was settling down but glanced up when she spoke. "Yes, Siabiane has it, but it appears to be the mate of the stick pin." I held up my arm with the underside of my hand and forearm facing both. Again, I couldn't see anything, but Siabiane muttered a spell word and the print appeared.

Lorcan and Padraig came over and peered at my new markings. "Oh my. Did you make a copy of this as well?"

Siabiane laughed. "I was going to but held off. We were accosted by brownies. No, not the ones who live with me. And Taryn showed some magic draining from the Domniall changeling going after her. He tried to attach a latch spell on her when she was in the tunnel with Alric. He failed but it was still pulling on her. I broke the connection with some special tea." She explained a bit more and told them how I found the other part to the pin. Then about whatever she felt following us and the rumbling. She was vague even to them, but both seemed extremely concerned. She pulled out the small silvery bag and handed it to Lorcan.

"You didn't feel the rumbling at all?" I asked them. Neither had reacted like they'd felt anything.

Padraig shook his head. "We were both in the lab running studies on the pin. But this part of the palace is solid rock all the way down. It would take a lot for us to even notice it."

"None of the alarms went off," Lorcan said as he untied the silver bag and pulled out the black one. "You say the faeries gave you this special bag? I wonder if they would give me one for study."

Siabiane laughed. "Have you been able to figure anything out from their regular bags?"

His face fell. "Not at all. Very well then." He pulled the flat metal piece out of the black bag. "Yes, that pin would fit here. It's odd that Qianru had access to such things. We assume Hass had it hidden on him and left it in the cell?"

Siabiane watched him examine the pin. "He was frightened of whoever came to get him. He must have thrown it. There's no way it would have accidentally been dropped that far from him or the door."

"It was well buried in the straw floor of the cell when I found it." I got up for a third small sandwich. "And I think the piece was referred to in the document the brownies who invaded Siabiane's cottage had. The one that mentioned two more pieces."

"Two of the images do look like rough versions of the pin and this new piece." Siabiane filled them in more on the brownie confessions, then brought out the note they'd given over.

Padraig took the paper and sat down.

Lorcan focused on the new piece of jewelry. "I believe these might be Robukian."

The others nodded and looked like they knew what he said.

"Robukian?"

Lorcan looked up and blinked. "I am sorry. Robukian are a class of spelled items, jewelry mostly. They carried simple spells. I haven't seen one since before the Breaking. They usually came as a set. Fascinating really." He went back to his study.

After a few minutes I had another sandwich and offered Siabiane some.

"No thank you, dear. But you should eat more. It might help with the latch spell."

That wouldn't be hard to do, like when I overused my magic, I was ravenous. "What exactly would it have done?"

"It's a basic spell but one that can snap back on the caster—as it might have done in this case. Had it worked perfectly, you would have passed out and dropped out of the tunnel. He could have grabbed you before Alric would have known."

"The faeries said the bad man had no fight left, so it snapped back at him? But he recovered enough to grab Hass?"

"I don't think he did. Yes, from what you and Alric said, Hass might not have realized who he was freeing, so he might not be comfortable with a necromancer, but the terror I felt was more than that. Whoever got him out had their full powers."

Padraig looked up from the tiny scribbles. "According to this, your brownie prisoners were actually working against Hass and Fealk. The brownies had known they were going north when they pretended to rob them, had they not been invited along, they would have followed them. This note describes Hass fairly well."

"Hass and his people didn't plant that pin on me?" I was still having trouble imagining that Qianru's letter was spelled to release the pin. But everything was pointing to that being the case.

"I don't think he knew the pin was there, but the person who told the brownies to bring the pieces back wasn't working with Hass or his people. Hass and Fealk are flunkies, hired to do a job."

"Free Domniall and this troll Theria." And bring me back if they could.

Padraig nodded. "Yes, and I think Domniall and Theria had their own job. I'd say their imprisonment in Beccia was real and it stopped their goal. How long had they been in jail?"

I shrugged, then recalled something Alric mentioned. "Around three or four weeks? Not that long before our final battle with Nivinal and Edana."

"Maybe whatever they were really supposed to do would have hindered Nivinal and Edana." Lorcan nodded.

"Either of those two could have easily overpowered the real Domniall, let alone his changeling copy," Siabiane said.

"So, before our battle, Nivinal and Edana were hanging around Beccia and locking these two up? Why not kill them if they were in their way? They did enough of that." That was weird. Those two added what bad folks they could to their fight. If not, they killed them. Locking them up didn't fit their normal behavior.

"I'm afraid we can't confirm if that's what happened, but it makes sense with those two being strong enough to lock up a necromancer." Lorcan looked up from the metal as he spoke.

I rubbed my head. I liked puzzles, but this one was twisted.

"Let's see how these go together." He took the two pieces and put the stick pin in the first loop. Nothing.

"Maybe you should do that in the lab?" Padraig watched, but sat back away from Lorcan.

"This is close enough. I think these are simple spell tools." Lorcan slipped the end through the second loop.

We held our breaths collectively, but nothing.

"Okay, so I was right, and these were meant to—" His words were cut off as the pieces burst into flame. Or at least smoke. Lots of smoke.

Padraig ran to the lab, and I heard a loud whirring noise, and the smoke started being pulled out of the room. He came back out. "Sometimes he forgets he doesn't have windows to remove things like smoke. I always have windows in my labs."

Lorcan waved his hand to help move the smoke along. Neither seemed worried about it, so I assumed it wasn't dangerous.

Then the smoked cleared.

"Um, why are there now four?" The pin and back piece had been joined by the remaining two pieces on the original page the brownies had shown. I stuck my hands behind my back to stop any urge I felt to touch them. One of the two new pieces looked like a small brooch with a stylized but unrealistic elven face in it. The second looked like a simple ring.

Padraig let out a low whistle. "Whoever Qianru is working with has some seriously old tricks up their sleeves. Hass didn't carry them, nor put the first one in your pack."

I looked at him blankly and the other two might have covered better, but from the looks on their faces, they still weren't sure where he was going.

"It's a flunten spell," Padraig said. "Extremely old and rarely used—the mage who set this up linked the pieces to the letter. Or rather the first piece to the letter. The second piece was linked to the spell on your hand. Most likely it hadn't been there when Hass was in the cell, and these two came in when the spells on your arm, the other pieces, and the letter were all in the same room."

"All of these pieces were triggered by the letter?" I kept my hands behind my back.

"Yes, isn't it amazing? These types of spells were used by the first of the elves. The Alioth who stayed south." Lorcan was far too excited about this.

"What are they supposed to do, put more spell-charged writing on me?"

"I honestly don't know, but at this point I'd say don't touch them," Lorcan said.

"I had no intention of doing so." I took a few more steps back. I didn't think they would jump but it was hard to say. That second piece had been able to jump.

"They would all be part of the same spell. We might want to lock them up separately for a bit while we deal with other things." Siabiane got to her feet. "There was something going on outside of town."

I'd almost forgotten about the shaking and Siabiane's odd feeling before it had happened.

"You are right," Lorcan said. "I get caught up in these things." He and Padraig took the pieces to the lab, and I heard sounds of tiny cells being bolted. Hopefully, those sneaky pieces of spelled jewelry would be trapped in those cells. I'd never been much for jewelry; those pieces were going to make me swear off it forever.

"Let's go see what can be found. I was going to have Taryn call the faeries, but I think that might be better when we're not in the palace." Siabiane went to the door we came in, tapped twice in the center, and it swung open.

There were more people in the main entrance hall of the

palace than when we came in, but none looked agitated as if something horrible had happened—that was good.

I waited until we got a few feet away from the entrance and mentally tried to call my faeries. As before, it took several tries, and I had to mentally create a large collection of ale bottles before they came swooping down the street.

"Where?" Leaf looked around the bushes in case the ale was hiding from her.

"You not have." Garbage put her hands on her hips, but there was a little smirk on her face. She heard me when I first called but made me keep trying until I offered ale. And she knew there probably wouldn't be any.

Faeries were weird.

"No, I don't. Did you girls notice anything a little while ago? The ground rumbling, odd things?"

Leaf, Crusty, and a few of the others were still looking for ale in the shrubbery. Garbage watched them for a moment, then turned back to me with a shrug.

"Ground ramblers. They go now."

I waited for more clarification, but Padraig stepped forward. "What are ground ramblers? Rakasa?"

Garbage pulled back with a look of revulsion. "Is no! *They is ramblers*. They ramble. Came close to this place, then he chased off. They go away. He went with."

I closed my eyes and counted to ten. They needed to start using names.

"Which he, honey?

"The he you come here with."

"Alric?" He was tracking Hass and would have gone out of the city if needed.

"No, silly, he not he." She glared at me. "The he we caught."

The two "he's" sounded the same to me. "Hass? He chased off these things?"

"Yup—jumped on one too. Other he not happy."

I took a deep breath and turned to Lorcan with a pleading look.

He smiled and then turned to Garbage. "This second he, was that Alric?"

"No. He was not here, but this he took *Hass* from elves." By the way she enunciated the names I could tell she was really trying. "*Alric* tie up in trees."

"What?"

She nodded. "Yes, can't get down. Magicked." She wiggled her fingers. "You come get."

The others could probably tell I was going to strangle her soon.

Siabiane stepped in this time. "Sweetie? Can you take us to where he is?"

"Follow!" Garbage spun in a circle, then took off down the road. She came back when no one was behind her as the other faeries were now playing ring around the bushes. "Is go!"

"We'll follow and so will they, but you can't lose us, okay?" Siabiane said as the mass of faeries rose out of the bushes. We were moving quickly, but while I wanted to run, doing so in the middle of town might cause issues. I had no idea how or why Alric was stuck in a tree, but I held out hope that he was fine. Just stuck.

"Fine." Garbage slowly flew ahead of us, then sped up, dropped back, and finally settled on flying close enough to us that we could still follow, but far enough in the front of everything that everyone would know she was the leader.

I found myself walking quickly alongside Padraig. Lorcan and Siabiane were in front of us. "Do you have the slightest idea what ground ramblers are?" I kept my voice low; the faeries could have great hearing when the need called for it, and I didn't want to go through another round with them.

Padraig shook his head. "I was hoping you might. It sounds like horses, especially if your prisoner ran off riding one. I suppose one could ride cattle too, but neither horses nor cattle should be roaming around the woods outside our city. And I can't imagine anywhere around here having enough to make the ground shake."

"Go faster." Garbage had flown around behind us. She hadn't pulled out her war stick yet, but I wouldn't put it past her.

The faeries flew faster with the rest of us almost jogging to keep up. We would have looked odd, but we were at the edge of the city at this point, and there weren't a lot of people around. Besides, the other three still looked refined and elegant even at this pace. I felt like a clod. Garbage swooped around us and retook the lead.

The edge of the city tapered off to thin woods that grew thicker quickly. The faeries picked up speed, but I wasn't running through a bunch of exposed tree roots and low-hanging branches.

We came to a clearing with an oddly squirming bundle in the tree directly across from us. With the amount of vines covering him, I almost couldn't tell it was Alric, but his light hair and the steady stream of muffled cursing told me who was up there.

Way up there. He was easily three stories up and tied solidly to the tree. Probably a good thing considering the height.

"Alric? What happened?" Okay dumb thing to ask when someone was gagged, but it came out automatically. "Never mind, we'll get you down."

Siabiane waved Garbage and the faeries over. "Ladies? Can you start working on the vines? Remove them gently. The gag first, though."

Garbage nodded and then led her faeries up to Alric.

"Hold still, the faeries are going to get you down." I hoped. If I transformed, I could easily reach him, but I wouldn't have any hands. Not to mention I really didn't want to be switching back and forth. At least not if I wanted to keep my secret.

Leaf and Crusty pulled free the gag. Garbage was busy supervising the removal of the other vines.

"Watch out, he still could be here." Alric had stopped trying to break free but was watching the faeries carefully.

"Who?" *Great.* Was referring to everyone as *he* or *she* now contagious?

"Domniall, or rather his changeling. It is without a doubt a changeling. It put me up here."

Padraig rocked back to take in the size of the tree. "That's some pretty serious climbing."

"And serious tying." Siabiane nodded appreciatively.

"That's great that you're admiring its work—please get me down?" He nodded to one of the faeries as she loosened a vine near his throat. Which then tightened a vine around his arm. "Maybe someone else could help?"

Siabiane closed her eyes and then levitated. Only it wasn't her, her body stayed on the ground. It was a partially transparent projection that rose, a visage, if it was the same as what they called Qianru's earlier trick. "I can give them better directions, but you're higher than most of us can climb."

With her talking them through it, and the faeries more or less doing as they were told, they got the vines loose enough for him to pull off the rest off and climb down.

I was impressed. I doubted I could climb down from that far. Alric looked a bit roughed up, but not injured as he dropped to the ground.

"Thank you. That changeling is a seriously messed-up piece of work. He ambushed me as I was following Hass's trail. I don't think the changeling took Hass. The foot tracks were a lot larger—troll-sized larger. I think the changeling was trailing Theria and Hass like I was and took me out of the equation."

"Did you see Hass?"

"That's the fun part. I never actually saw him until he rode through this clearing strapped on a licten beast. The troll, Theria, was on one as well and leading Hass's beast behind him. They even had a few extra beasts running alongside."

Damn. Licten beasts would make a rumbling noise even if only two were running. They were massive, thick-skinned animals favored by trolls for riding into battle—they did not live this far south. Judging by what we heard, they also did something else. That last shake was loud and final sounding.

Siabiane clearly had the same thought as well. "Explains the rumbling that we felt. But there was a final shake, knocking down people in the middle of town."

"I felt that too. I'd say Theria is a magic user and opened a tunnel. If he closed it at this end quickly, it would cause that boom backlash." Alric stretched and rubbed his arms.

"Boom!" Crusty yelled. Most of the faeries were buzzing around, but Crusty was staying near us and appeared to be listening.

"Yes, sweetie, there was a boom." I looked through the forest and saw damaged and broken trees. Licten beasts weren't fans of heavy forests, or more importantly, heavy forests weren't fans of them. Their natural environment was so far north, it was beyond the tree line. The trail led away from the clearing and in the opposite direction from town. "Crusty? Did you see the creatures who went boom? Could you show us where?"

Padraig nodded. "Yes, if we can find this end, we might be able to learn where they went. Closing it like that would leave broken bits."

"We go!" Crusty wasn't used to leading, so she looped back a few times. Then Garbage and the others realized what was going on and they all raced to be first.

"Slow down!" Luckily, it was a clear path due to the destruction, because the girls were flying like someone had given them each a cup of tea. Luckily, that wasn't the case, and no one splatted into any trees that I saw.

We caught up to them near a burned clump of trees.

Alric ran to them and dropped to a crouch, sifting the burnt parts through his fingers. "Not only did Theria slam it closed, but he also pulled in magic from around him to create his tunnel. They went far."

"North? Maybe back home?"

He shook his head. "I can't get an exact location, but he was aiming for the south, way south. It would take a huge amount of magic to get them to the southern continent and not drop them into the ocean."

I looked around for clues, but I wasn't sure what I was looking for. "We were watching this Domniall changeling, but the real power was from Theria?"

"It looks like. Not that we can discount the Domniall changeling. He might be low on magic, but he didn't need much to overwhelm me. And he has spell packets." Alric held up a piece of what I'd thought had been paper trapped in the vines that had been wrapped around him. "Didn't any of you wonder why I couldn't magic my way out?"

"I thought maybe you forgot, so didn't want to say anything." Padraig gave a smirk as he shifted through the burned grass and tree branches that marked where the tunnel had been magically closed. Before our final battle, Alric and Padraig had spent a few weeks retraining as knights. It brought back their old friendship even stronger.

I was a little embarrassed that I hadn't asked about Alric's magic, but it had been disconcerting seeing him tied up like that so I would just claim stress. "What spell?" I had used a fair amount of the pre-packaged spells when I had been a bounty hunter. Back before any of my own magic had come back. Before I even knew I'd ever had magic that needed to come back.

"A pretty expensive one. Shuts down all magic for at least an hour." Alric carefully handed the wrapper to me. "Whoever that changeling is working for, they were willing to send them off with expensive trinkets."

The others spent the next half hour going over the immediate area where the tunnel had been, back to the clearing, and Lorcan even stopped at a small pile of licten beast dung. The faeries had been following along up until that part. They drew the line at poop. I agreed on that.

"Actually, you can learn a lot from animal droppings." Lorcan chastised us as we stood back.

"And what did you learn?" I'd take his word for it, but I didn't need to get any closer.

"Not as much as one would hope in this case." He continued to poke around with a long stick. "However, it doesn't look as if they'd been eating our plants for long. There are bits of the scraggly pine, a slow-growing shrub found only in the far north."

That was interesting, and maybe once we figured out more about Theria, might be even useful. Not enough for me to start poking around dung, though.

I got the eerie feeling of someone watching me. The others were all talking and investigating, and the faeries had flown off as things got boring. But I felt someone behind me. I was closest to Lorcan, so I made it look as if I was fascinated by what he was looking at, then swirled around as fast as I could.

Which would have looked stupid if I hadn't seen Domniall staring at me from the bushes. He took off a second before I yelled and ran after him.

I heard my friends behind me, but this one was mine. He stumbled at one point, and I misjudged my leap over a bush and landed solidly on his back. Might have heard a few cracks, but those could have been from plant life that he smashed down on.

"Taryn! You scared me!" Alric reached me first, but the others weren't far behind.

Domniall tried squirming but I hit him in the head. "Hold still, you. I'm not in a good mood." I looked up to Alric. "Sorry, but he was watching us, and I've about had it with him skulking around me." He gave a twitch and I smacked him again. "Seriously. Stop moving." I called for the faeries. They hadn't gone far and quickly returned.

"Girls, if this person so much as moves, I'm giving you full rights to jab the hell out of him. He only moves where and when we tell him, or you jab him."

"We do!" All of them yelled as they pulled out their war sticks.

"Can one of you heavy-duty spell users do something to keep him from escaping so that I can get up?" My adrenaline was a little high, so I didn't want to try spelling him. He'd be of no use to us if I pushed him thirty feet into the ground.

Lorcan stepped forward, muttered a few words, and the changeling under me froze. Lorcan squatted down and pushed the changeling's long hair aside. "I think that will do. Changelings have a different physiology that other beings, so I had to be careful which spell I used." He nodded to me. "You can get up now. He won't be moving anything for a while. And he knows it, doesn't he?" He'd turned back to the changeling. Judging from the look in his eyes, there was full awareness of the situation.

Alric leaned forward and pulled me to my feet. I turned quickly in case the spell hadn't worked, but the changeling stayed where he was.

Siabiane looked around. "I'm not sure what else we can find out here, and I would like to get this one locked up. I suppose we can't talk to him for a while?"

Lorcan, Padraig, and Alric got the changeling on his feet. There was no movement but he glared at us. "You can talk to him all you'd like, there won't be a response for a few hours. Possibly tomorrow, I put the spell on a bit heavily."

"And how are we getting him back?" The changeling tipped forward a bit but Padraig caught him. Stiff as a board.

"Ah, this spell should work." Lorcan muttered words, again under his breath, and stepped back. He motioned for

Alric and Padraig to do so as well.

The changeling tilted back, and I moved to catch him, but Lorcan shook his head. The movement continued until the changeling was floating flat on his back a few feet off the ground.

"Isn't this wonderful? Mathilda modified a floater spell, helps me move things around."

We started our return through the forest. Siabiane and I were in the front, Lorcan and the floating changeling in the middle, and Padraig and Alric in the rear. The faeries were flying around us, finding it hilariously funny to see who could fly around the floating body the fastest. Their humor came from odd sources, but at least it kept them occupied.

As we began to spot the city up ahead, Lorcan called for us to pull back. "I'd rather this not be noticeable to the general public." He released another spell; this one blurred the floating form until it was invisible. He nodded for us to start again, but Siabiane held up her hand.

"And you think no one will notice the large empty space between us? What if someone tries to pass through? Details, Lorcan, you are too honest and forthright some-times and forget that deception is all about the details." With a flick of her hand, the place where the changeling floated was now filled with a large mule. An ornery look-ing one at that.

Lorcan gave a short bow. "Thank you for watching out for us. You've done an exceptional job as always." The mule turned its head to Lorcan and snorted. He laughed. "An exceptionally exceptional job, in fact."

We started off again with Lorcan now leading a difficult mule who glared at everyone we passed.

"Are we walking the mule up the front steps of the palace?" I had no idea where one should put a frozen changeling, but I figured they'd want it to be secure.

"That won't work either. How secure is your cottage?"

he asked Siabiane.

"For the brownies I'm holding, very. For this? Not enough. My country home would hold him, but I fear my cottage is more on the cute, and less on the jail, side of things."

Padraig looked around. It was later in the day, but there were still a lot of people in the street in front of the palace. "We can go through the back. Once we get there, I'll remove everything except the floating spell, stand the changeling upright, and escort him up the stairs."

Lorcan nodded. "We shall meet you in my chambers. The more of us going that way, the more noticeable it will be." The two strolled toward the front as if they'd been out for a walk.

I looked to the changeling-mule as they left. "How does she make this so real?" Unless I ran a hand through it, which I did through part of the tail, there was no way to know this wasn't real.

"Eons of practice," Padraig said as we rounded a corner of the palace. "I don't know that anyone can match her."

We stopped as we came around to an extremely non-glamourous and neglected part of the palace. No part of this section of the palace faced any of the roads, so it mostly was left to fend for itself. Three steps led to a heavy wooden door crossed with thick black metal bars. And no noticeable handle.

The mule vanished first, then our floating changeling reappeared. His eyes were closed now, so either Lorcan's freeze spell went deeper and knocked him out eventually, or he decided to take a nap.

"How do we get into your super sneaky and not pleasant secret entrance?" I looked around but didn't see any secret lever or button.

"Ah, you have to look beyond what is there." Padraig closed his eyes and held out his right hand like one of those fake mystics who would wander through Beccia from time to time.

Alric snorted and tapped twice in the center of the door and a latch unlocked. "Or you know where it is." We pushed open the door, and Padraig and Alric got the changeling upright and moving forward. He was still about a foot above the ground, but from what I could see this entrance was not only rarely used, it was rarely lit. Padraig released a few glows to drift up into the dark ceiling. The magical spheres of light went more or less where you wanted them. The faeries had taken off again, which was good as sometimes Crusty became hypnotized by the glows and I didn't want to deal with her right now. The mysterious door quickly closed behind us.

We went into the narrow hallway, then up a long flight of equally narrow stairs. Padraig led, Alric followed with the changeling, and I came up last. I knew we were technically in the palace and therefore probably safe, but I couldn't help thinking I really needed my sword.

"Couldn't bad guys get in this way? I mean, Nivinal did pretty much destroy the palace."

Alric looked back over his shoulder. "Even he didn't come in this way, nor did his flunkies. It's only known by a few. Padraig knows because he works with Lorcan, I did because of Padraig, and now you do because of all of us. Honestly, it would probably be harder to force that particular door than to blow a hole in the wall."

I wanted to trust him. I did trust him. But I kept my hand cupped for a spell the entire way up the stairs.

Chapter Thirteen

———◆———

MY CONCERN WAS UNFOUNDED, BUT better to be paranoid than dead. A doorway at the top of the stairs blocked the forward flying glows, and they gathered around it like pack dogs awaiting their hunter. Padraig sent them back to wherever they came from and cracked open the door. I wasn't the only one being a bit wary.

Padraig paused with the door only slightly open, seeing with more than his eyes if there was anyone waiting for us.

We stayed quiet as we went into the much wider and normally lit hallway and toward Lorcan's rooms.

"Here or in the lab?" Alric paused with the changeling bobbing next to him.

"The lab, we can shut that room off if Lorcan gets any official visitors." Padraig stood back and Alric led the changeling in and put him on a table. "I'm going to go see what's holding up Lorcan and Siabiane."

Alric and I nodded, and Padraig went through the door in the back. I looked down at the changeling. "He doesn't look like he did before." The face was sort of the same, but not as angular as when I'd first seen him. The hair seemed darker and shorter too.

Alric peered down. "This changeling was made to look like Domniall at least a few months ago, and without reinforcement he'll change back to what he naturally looked like. At least we know that means this was planned a while ago."

"He'd been in jail three or four weeks, so while we were getting ready for the final fight? What was he doing? Grillion said he knew Theria, and he'd been around up north a few years ago, but if Domniall was more recent, what was his plan?" I'd looked over to Alric but was still partially leaning over the table. I screamed when the changeling's eyes popped open.

I backed up, but Alric moved forward. "I think the spell is wearing off." He quickly bound the changeling's hands and feet, then stepped back. "If you can't talk yet, you will be able to soon. The more you tell us now, the less hard stuff we have to hit you with when the rest of our people show up."

The changeling didn't open his mouth, but a movement along his jaw told me he probably could.

"Why do you look like that? Why were you in Beccia? Why did you try to grab me?" The bindings that Alric used were good, but I wasn't taking any chances. I stayed a few feet from the table as I spoke.

The changeling looked like he wasn't going to talk, then won or lost a battle with himself. "I was captured and made to look like this. I was supposed to make the elves think I was someone they'd feared. I was also supposed to bring you back at any cost."

"And how did that work? Who is behind this?" Alric was closer to the table than me but still a few feet back.

"We were stupid. Theria was stupid. Made the wrong mage mad and she locked us up. Took them three weeks to send someone to get us out."

"Why me?"

"Because they want you. I don't care why. I bring you back and I get released with a spell bond not to capture me again."

Voices, and the sound of a door opening ended our questioning. Lorcan, Padraig, and Siabiane all came into the lab.

Whatever they had been talking about was dropped.

Siabiane came forward. "You don't look so much like Domniall now. Did you know Domniall is my brother? Do you know I've sworn to kill him when I see him? The only question will be if I get to him first or my sister does. Why did you come to the party disguised like a future dead elf?"

"You haven't figured it out?" The changeling gave a rough laugh. "I heard these two talking about timing; they were almost there. The timing was off because we were locked up. But I was sent from the south to work with that idiot troll. The people behind me counted on you and your sister going after me." He twisted his head to look at everyone except me. "All of you and more. They wanted all the magic users except you out of the final fight. We could have changed everything." He glared my way with the last line.

Padraig and Lorcan looked annoyed. Siabiane and Alric looked pissed. I'm sure I just looked confused.

"I thought Nivinal or Edana put you in jail?" I was guessing, but from the snarl I was right.

"Those idiots. They didn't understand what the plan was. Nivinal thought the Dark worked for him. They didn't." He looked at the faces around him and then back to me. "You still don't get it? If your magic-using friends weren't in the battle, you would have lost. I'm not sure how you created that illusion when we tried to grab you in that clearing, but you would have lost without your friends. Nivinal and Edana would have claimed the relic weapon, but we could destroy them. They would be weakened from fighting your forces. We would win."

I caught his change of words and tone a moment after Siabiane did. At least I assumed that's what her sudden grin was.

"You said we, not they. You weren't captured, you are part of the Dark." I almost stepped forward in my excitement but held back.

He focused on me. "Where are the relics? I know that Nivinal and Edana didn't survive, but where are the relics? You are tied to them; my people know that."

"Where did Theria tunnel off to? And why did he want Hass?" Alric did step forward as he spoke, his stance and closeness daring the changeling to move. Even bound as he was, that was risky; changelings could shift things and get out of bindings. Alric looked like he really wanted to punch something, so I understood why he was doing it.

That was a bit chilling, that someone, or most likely someones, had orchestrated distracting my magic friends so the battle would fall against us. But they weren't on Nivinal's side. This was not good.

"He probably went back to our Masters, leaving me behind to clean up his mess. Hass was a flunky to get us out, not sure why he took him unless he wanted a snack. Probably already killed the other one."

"Theria is the necromancer." Alric took a step back but was still close.

"You are brighter than they claim," the changeling shot back and then turned to me. "Where are the relics?"

My skin started to crawl. Changelings weren't supposed to have magic; that's why they had to use spell packets. But something spell-like was hitting me hard. I needed to tell him everything.

"Taryn!" Alric grabbed my arm as I stepped closer to the changeling.

"The relics are destroyed," I said it against my will, but the words still came out. Alric blocked the line of sight between the changeling and me. I shook my head as the feeling vanished. "He's using magic somehow."

Alric spun and dropped a spell bubble over the change-ling right as he burst free of his bonds.

The spell bubble flared and shook, but it held.

"I will get out; you can't stop me. I will get the relics

and her and take them to my Masters." He was frothing a bit now.

I held on to Alric's shoulder as I leaned forward. "The relics are gone. I destroyed them. Like I destroyed Nivinal and Edana. Like I will destroy your Masters. And you." I wasn't sure where the feeling came from, but I had an overwhelming urge to run him through with my sword. Or stomp on him.

"They can't be gone. My people would know." There was confusion there and his eyes focused on things not in the room.

"When was the last you saw your Masters? Before the battle you were supposed to hinder?" Lorcan asked. "The relics were still around then, hidden, but intact. I felt the spell you threw at Taryn. Somehow you had a truth spell available to you. I'd guess embedded under your skin. It worked. She told the truth—she destroyed them."

The changeling looked at all of us and panic took over his face. "No. That can't be true." The cockiness that had been there was quickly dissolving into terror. "They were to bring about our new world. How could you…" His voice dropped as he saw something in my face. I was still pissed about him, but less than before. Whatever he saw there was far worse than any face I could make. "You. You are more than they knew—you will consume them all!" His pupils expanded, taking up his entire irises. Then his face started to bulge around his mouth.

Alric grabbed me and Siabiane since we were closest to him. "Get out now! He's got an exploding spell in his mouth!"

Padraig dragged Lorcan and we all dove for the front room. Padraig kicked a panel as they went past, and the lab door slid shut behind us. Then rattled and buckled as an explosion hit it.

CHAPTER FOURTEEN

———◆———

"WHAT IN THE HELL WAS that?" I pulled myself up. Alric had pretty much thrown Siabiane and me as far across the room as he could. I was grateful he had to toss two of us; had it only been me, I might have ended up splattered against the wall. I was reminded again that elves were a lot stronger than they looked.

"He bit down right before his eyes changed." Lorcan got to his feet and dusted himself off. "Someone really equipped him well on the spell front. Suicide with a side dish of 'kill as many as possible.'"

"He said he was supposed to bring me to his people. Wouldn't blowing us all up kind of gone against what they wanted?" I patted myself down in case some body part hadn't made the trip. I was shaking but still whole.

"Thank you for pulling us out, Alric," Siabiane said as she dusted herself off. "Something changed when he really looked at you, Taryn. I was watching you as well as him, but I didn't see whatever he saw."

"Could he have realized what I really was?" I nodded to the door. "He threw a truth spell at me, right? Could that have shown him I'm an Ancient? He might not have recognized a dragon when he saw one, but he would know I was something different and dangerous. He said something about me consuming them all?"

"It's hard to say, and no way we'll ever know now."

Padraig put his hand on the door to the lab. I had no idea what it was made of, but it withheld a strong explosion.

Alric went to the door and together they slowly opened it.

The lab survived well overall. Because of Alric's spell bubble the blast was contained to the table, and some items a few feet out had scorch marks. There was nothing left of the changeling.

"I told you making your door blast-proof was a good idea." Padraig stalked around the table remains.

Lorcan rolled his eyes. "I hate it when he's right. Padraig is far more paranoid than even me, but it served us well this time." He went to a far corner, collected a glass jar and a wide dull knife, and then came back to the table. "Might as well see if there was anything different about our friend. I hadn't known that changelings were taking interest in solids' politics, but he sounded like he was a member of the Dark."

"Solids?" I glanced around but it appeared to me like Lorcan was scraping up table ash.

"That's what they call anyone who isn't a changeling."

That made sense. "Where does this leave us? We might have Fealk roaming around, or as the changeling suggested, he might have been killed by Theria. I guess this adventure is over?" I didn't try too hard to keep the hopefulness out of my voice.

"Aside from whatever Qianru was upset about, and those magically charged trinkets she sent." Lorcan finished scraping up what he could from the table. He then locked the smaller jar inside a larger one and disposed of the blade he had been using.

"And what those brownies were after." Siabiane led the way back out to the front room. "Qianru might have sent them up here to keep them safe."

That was something I hadn't thought of. Of course, I'd been busy dealing with other things—including what two of those items had done to my hand. "Qianru is obsessed with old things, that is certainly true. But do any of you recognize anything about them? Yes, they pack a nasty punch, at least two of them did. Aside from being old, is there anything unique about them?"

Lorcan sighed. "I didn't notice anything before I locked them up. I will need to study them further. But those marks they gave you need to be examined. While I don't know of any dangerous jewelry of that sort, we can't be too careful."

"I think we need to talk more with those brownies," Alric said. "Fealk could be anywhere if he's still alive and Grillion will be pretty useless. Unless Qianru manages to pop up again, the brownies are our only source for getting more information."

Alric wasn't against research; he used it when he needed to. But if he could get some answers out of something living, he always started there. I couldn't blame him, but I wasn't sure what those brownies would tell us.

"Talking to brownies isn't always useful," Padraig said.

"They might talk to mine, though." Siabiane gave a sly smile.

"Do you think your two are ready for a full interrogation on their own?" Lorcan didn't look confident.

"They passed on the first interaction. Those southern brownies had no idea that mine weren't flesh-and-blood brownies. They can get around the capture issue. Brownies turn on each other fairly regularly, I understand."

The rest of us watched the debate with growing confusion. Then Padraig's eyes went wide, and he started laughing. "Welsy and Delsy are constructs? They seem so real!"

Siabiane bowed from her seat. "Thank you. It took me quite a while to get them to that state. Well, and I did have to stop fussing with them when we had to work on saving the world. I actually had started on them long before Irving the gargoyle."

I thought about Irving's odd talent for swallowing extremely dangerous things and hiding them somewhere inside of him. "Can they swallow things like Irving can?"

"Sadly, no," Siabiane said. "That was a special trick for him only. I wasn't sure why I did it at the time, but I'm glad I did. It's difficult to create something like that. The brownies are meant to look, act, and behave like regular brownies. Within certain parameters that removed the nasty behavior of real brownies. They are also self-aware that they are constructs."

"Really? I have to sit in on one of your projects sometime." Padraig turned to me. "Siabiane is the first elf to be able to make a construct. Your people took the secret with them."

Lorcan leaned back in his chair. "Well, it's believed the first elves were able to make them back in Arlienia, our ancient homeland, maybe even when our people first migrated up here. But not since then."

Padraig turned to me. "You don't happen to recall how to make them? Those chimeras came in handy during the fighting."

As far as I knew, the chimeras had mostly survived the final battle, but then had taken off again. Aside from Bunky, they were all wild constructs, if that could be said. "Nope, sorry. I'm not sure I knew how to make them then either. I do think that's why I can't touch Bunky directly. Though they were made to store memories, and the ones in him flood me. But I don't get the idea that I could make them even in the past." Part of me wanted my skills, abilities, and full memories to come back. The other part of me was fine with things as they were.

Alric watched me, then turned to the others. "What say we go find out some brownie gossip?" He reached over and squeezed my hand, but kept looking to the others.

"I think that is our next step." Siabiane got to her feet. "And I believe a nice meal might be in order. Nothing against living in the palace, but unless there is a formal event the food is mediocre."

Lorcan followed her to the door. "Siabiane is a food snob, but also a fine cook."

"I'm perfectly fine with all of the above. And once we're back at your place, I can call and check in on the faeries." I often didn't see them for hours at a time. But there were too many problems they could cause here. Having a good idea where they were from time to time was safer.

Alric and I were the last to leave, and he pulled me back before following the others down the stairs. "Are you okay? You turned really pale when Padraig asked you about building constructs."

"I'm fine." I shook my head and shrugged. "I don't know. I guess I need to start dealing with things from my past, but I'm not sure I'm ready."

He squeezed my hand again. "No one will force you; things will come back when you're ready."

"Thanks." The others were busy chatting, so hadn't noticed us falling behind. Alric and I hurried to catch up.

Evening was now falling and if anything, the city was more beautiful at night. Last night I hadn't really noticed as I was worrying about Alric. But tiny glows grouped into beautiful light structures, and each one was spaced out enough to keep the darkness at bay.

"I know there was a lot going on when I was here before, but I don't recall those." I pointed up to a particularly beautiful flower made entirely of glows blooming on a corner as we crossed.

"We didn't have them then." Lorcan waved to the brightly colored lights. "The shield took a lot of energy and things like these lights would have been frivolous. In the months that we've been without the shield, we've been allowed to go back to some of our old ways."

I remembered about calling the faeries as we turned down the street to Siabiane's cottage. I sent out my usual mental call. By the time we got to the door, I'd added a mountain of ale bottles and a massive pile of sugar. Still nary a fluttering wing in sight. There were also no sounds of people being attacked or things being destroyed, so maybe they were being good for once.

Siabiane gave a light whistle, and two red caps popped out of the well-tended shrubs. Both brownie constructs came forward with massive smiles.

Even knowing they were constructs, they still made me edgy. Brownies overall had not been my favorite creatures. They hadn't been dangerous so much as massively annoying.

Siabiane crouched down to both, her voice low as she explained what she wanted them to do.

"We have it," Welsy said, and the two jumped up the stairs and ran inside.

"Let's give them a bit of time to wake the brownies up and get some answers. Brownies have a speech they use that is far faster than our speech. It shouldn't be too long." She looked around. "Where are the faeries?"

I scowled at the sky. "I'm not sure. I've tried calling but they aren't responding."

Lorcan patted my arm. "I'm sure they are fine. Most likely they found something to annoy and are off causing trouble."

"Or they found a pub," Alric said.

"You have pubs?"

"Why wouldn't we have pubs?"

"I don't know, this is such a nice, clean, lovely city. Nothing against pubs, I am all for them, but the ones I know don't fit that description." Which was true, and another thing I hadn't noticed my first time here.

"We have lovely pubs." Siabiane tilted her head at something inside her cottage. "And it appears that this may take longer than I expected. What say we take Taryn to the Oak and Lion?"

Lorcan nodded. "I will never say no to that."

The pub was a few streets over and looked like no pub I had ever seen. Huge windows with metal-crossed glass showed a nice fire and comfy dark furniture. There was no way any pub in Beccia ever looked like this, even when they were first built.

"Maybe we should bring Amara up here," I said more to myself than to anyone. But Alric nodded in agreement. Amara was slowly changing the Shimmering Dewdrop into something more respectable. While her tiny sandwiches and outdoor dining weren't the hit she'd hoped for, this might work. I sent another call to the faeries. Not that I really thought the owner of the pub would appreciate them, but maybe I could buy them some ale and send them somewhere else to drink it. But still no response.

The widest elf that I had ever seen stood behind the bar. "Ah, fair met, Siabiane and friends. The table in the back is open."

Siabiane smiled, then led us to a large round table. "Please sit, friends, I'll go order for all of us." Before anyone could stop her, she'd gone back to the bar and we sat.

"This is lovely. Not saying anything bad against your palace, but I'd probably eat here every night if I lived in the city." Heavy drapes that were currently pulled back could obviously provide some privacy for this table. Like many of the furnishings they were crimson red.

"It is one of my favorite haunts." Lorcan leaned back as an elven waitress came in balancing four glass tankards of ale and one tall glass of red wine. That she held the tray in one hand, perfectly balanced while she set them down, made me rethink showing Amara this place. The thought of Dogmaela choosing to do that made me almost burst out laughing. And glass tankards? A recipe for disaster in a town where bar fights were a nightly occurrence. You might knock someone out with a good hit from a metal tankard, but broken glass could kill.

I had to admit after taking my first sip, that this was a damn good ale.

"Padraig, how are the new guardians working?" Alric leaned back. He noticed me looking at him with a questioning look. "The replacement for the shield. They're called the guardians and act as individual shields that can lock together if needed. Instead of a shield running all the time, these only expend energy when triggered. They were working on them before the last battle."

He and Padraig had come back here before the final battle to work with their people—and to set up new defenses, it sounded like.

"I thought the king and queen had already started on a new shield?" Granted, that had been months ago, but they'd seemed determined.

"They did and we were." Lorcan took a long sip of his ale. His voice dropped and he leaned forward. "To be honest, we as a people don't have the magical strength we had a thousand years ago when the shield was first built. I haven't studied it as much as I'd like, but I believe our locking ourselves up has hurt the elven species. At least in terms of magical abilities."

That was a shocker, not only their belief that it had happened but that they were admitting it. Granted, these people were like family now, but still disclosing this had to be hard. Elves were a proud people.

"How long have you known?" I kept my voice low as well. Obviously, while this might be known to the group I was with, and most likely all the top mages and academics, it wasn't common knowledge.

"Only recently, sadly." He shook his head. "It was meeting up with Mathilda a few months ago that brought it to light. Unlike all the elves up here, she didn't shelter under the shield. Her powers feel different than ours. She is comparatively more powerful than she had been."

Siabiane leaned forward. "I was always the stronger of

the two of us, but not anymore. Although since much of my time was spent outside of the main shield, but still within another, I appear to be less impacted than the rest."

"What about Nasif?" I asked. "He was away from the shield."

"Like Mathilda, he's another outlier," Padraig said. "As am I, technically, since I was stuck in time in that state Nivinal locked me into. Once Nasif comes back up from the south, we'll run tests, but for now we really only have Mathilda as a good example."

"How bad is it?"

"We don't know for sure and won't for a while. But things like the shield are beyond us for the time being. We were able to maintain it, but creating it anew was impossible."

Silence filled the group until the waitress came back with plates of assorted foods. It was family style and we each took our plates.

The food and drink made me think of the faeries. I tried calling for them again. This time a stabbing pain slammed into my skull. My vision blurred and I found myself tipping over. Then everything went dark.

CHAPTER FIFTEEN

M Y HEAD WAS A DULL echoing drum, and some sicko was pounding on it. I slowly opened my eyes to find Siabiane rubbing my cheek, Alric brushing back my hair, and no one pounding on my head. At least from the outside. Inside, there was still a steady beat.

"Taryn? Are you all right?" Alric had his speaking-to-skittish-horses voice on, and Siabiane's face reflected the same mindset. I must look as bad as I felt.

"I don't know." I rubbed my eyes. "It's really bright in here." Padraig dropped the curtains without a word and Lorcan dimmed the glows. That helped, but everything still hurt.

"What were you doing before you collapsed?" Lorcan leaned forward.

"I was trying to call the faeries. I reached out for them again and then darkness crashed into me. Everything hurts."

"Have you ever had this happen before?"

"No? Yes? Sort of? My magic has caused some weird situations before, but I wasn't even sure if my ability to call them was magic or something they let me do." Siabiane was now trying to get me to drink some water, so I sat up more.

And almost threw up. "Down, down, down." They quickly moved me to a bench against the window. I heard whispers, then a cold cloth came to rest on my forehead.

"The faeries always answer when she calls?" Siabiane was talking to Alric and that was fine by me. I pulled the cool cloth lower, so it covered most of my eyes.

"Usually. I know she's been trying for a while, but they've come every other time since we've been here."

"I'm feeling a block of some kind." Lorcan also was whispering and not to me, but I could still hear him. "I can't tell if it's her or the faeries."

That got me to try and roll to my elbow at least. While keeping the cloth on my face even though I moved it from my eyes. "What? You think something has happened to the faeries?" I didn't yell it, but it was only because I figured my head might explode if I did. The faeries were pretty indestructible, but as I'd seen over the past few years, things could still hurt them.

Lorcan gently pushed me to lie back again. "Now, now, we don't know. It could be something has shut down the connection you have with them for right now. Can you do any magic?"

"Like what?" I held my hand up and tried to magic a glow. A tiny one that might light three inches of space around it formed, then vanished. "Okay, probably that's a no."

"I think we need to get back to my cottage, someplace less public." Siabiane rose to her feet and left through the curtain.

"So, the faeries might be fine, I just can't call to them?" That made me feel a little better. Not that I wanted something wrong with me, but it would be easier than something wrong with them.

Lorcan patted my hand. "I'm sure that's the case and it's a temporary issue. You have had some serious changes in the past few months, you know."

I gave a small smile; that was the king of understatements. I knew Lorcan kept things positive until he had enough information. At this point, I appreciated it.

Siabiane came back with the waitress right behind. "Jacobin insists on sending the food with us. I explained that Taryn had fallen ill. Shey will box it up and bring it over."

Padraig smiled. "I'll stay, help her, and then I can bring it over." His smile was warm, and I knew Siabiane trusted these people, but I had an odd feeling that he was also being cautious. After everything that had happened to him, I couldn't blame him for being paranoid.

"Will you need a stretcher?" the elf Shey asked, as she glanced my way. Again, I was glad I didn't have a mirror based on the worried and sympathetic look on her face.

"I can carry her. Thank you, though." Alric helped me sit up slowly, then picked me up. "Are you okay like this?"

I started to nod, then thought better of it as I wrapped my arms around his neck. "I will be."

"Alric and I will see to getting Taryn set up in my cottage. We'll see you two once you've packed up the food." Siabiane gave Lorcan and Padraig a nod and led us out.

I found burying my face in Alric's neck was not only pleasant and comfortable, but it kept me from having to see the questioning stares of the other patrons as we left. I tried not to think about the faeries, but it was hard. I focused instead on why Siabiane had Lorcan stay behind as well. Paranoia was a big thing with my group of friends.

We made it back in minutes. Although it hadn't felt like he was running, both Alric and Siabiane must have been moving extremely fast to make it in that time.

I felt us going up the few steps and Siabiane opened her door. The sound of chatter interrupted made me look up.

The brownies, both real and construct, were sitting on the table. The real ones were tied up and there were now six of them. There was a smaller tied-up bundle in the middle of the table.

An orange bundle.

"Garbage?" I tried to scramble out of Alric's arms but

didn't make it and ended up crashing both of us to the floor.

Siabiane beat me to the table and grabbed Garbage. She was extremely tied up, including her mouth, but from the look in her eyes she was going to kill whoever did this.

I started to crawl over there, but Alric got to his feet and helped me up.

"Take her to the sofa," Siabiane said as she worked on releasing Garbage, then turned to the brownies. "I've just saved your lives. Talk quickly or I will let her at you."

Her two brownie constructs rose to their feet and bowed. "We were afraid to try and liberate her."

"Kill you! What you do!"

Siabiane had gotten Garbage's gag off first. I would have said that wasn't a great idea.

"Garbage? Honey? Are you okay?" I called over to her but wasn't up to standing yet.

She turned to glare at me, saw how bad I obviously looked, and squirmed to be free of Siabiane's hand.

"I am trying to untie you. Do you want to keep your wings or not?" Siabiane's glare matched Garbage's but it wasn't directed at her. "Who tied up this faery?" No one responded, but it had clearly been the brownies.

As soon as the last string fell, Garbage flew over to me. "We get back."

"Get what back?"

Garbage walked across my lap and patted my hand. "My people."

"The rest of the faeries have been taken?" I tried to force myself to my feet, but Garbage herself was able to push me back before Alric could.

"We were trying to save it," one of the brownies said. "They were being sucked into a tree. We grabbed it. Tying it up was the only option."

"Reward?" another brownie said.

Siabiane looked at the six. "You *saved* her?" Her glare

managed to reach each of them at the same moment. Six rattled brownies.

"We might have thought to negotiate…?"

One of the construct brownies gave the other brownies a narrow-eyed glare, then turned to face Siabiane. "Those two attacked the house with the faery restrained in their hands. We tied them up, but the faery didn't want us touching her either, so we couldn't release her. They were trying to negotiate their release by offering us the rest of the faeries."

"They know where the rest of my faeries are?" I still felt out of sorts, but there was no way I was going to sit here if my faeries were in danger.

"I do too. Would have said, but stuff in mouth." Garbage was upset, but not freaked out the way she'd been the time Crusty and Leaf had been kidnapped.

"You can still hear them, can't you?" What had upset Garbage the most the last time they'd been taken, was that she couldn't sense them.

"Yes. Not getting out."

If I already didn't have a headache from whatever had hit me in the pub, I would now. "Why don't we go get them then?"

"You look bad. Head wrong." Garbage stayed on my lap but took a few steps backward and shook her head. "Lady fix?" She pointed to me as if I were one of her broken playthings.

Siabiane came over and kneeled before me. "That's what we were planning on doing, sweetie. Are you sure your friends will be okay? This might take a while."

She didn't add, *because we have no idea what's wrong with Taryn*, but that thought was crashing around my mind.

Garbage tilted her head and mostly closed her eyes. Then she shrugged. "They okay, stuck, but okay. Fix?" She pointed to me again.

I was touched by Garbage's actual concern at my current

situation. And disturbed. She wasn't normally a compassionate individual.

Alric got up and pulled a chair over for Siabiane so she wouldn't have to crouch in front of me. Then he stood to the side to watch.

"You can relax, my boy, I'm not going to hurt her."

"Oh, I didn't think that. I simply wanted to see what you'll do."

Garbage flew to him and landed on his shoulder. "Me too." She folded her arms and stared at me.

I sighed, ignored them as best that I could, and focused on Siabiane.

"First, I need you to relax, don't think about anything. Lean back."

Of course, the first thing I do when someone tells me to relax is the opposite, but I knew she was trying to help me, so I took a deep breath and leaned back against the sofa.

Siabiane started chanting softly and I felt my eyes growing heavy. The magic words she was chanting were old. I didn't know where I'd heard them before, but I had. I wasn't sure if what she was doing was fixing the problem, but the pressure in my head eased up and I was possibly more relaxed than I'd been in years—without the aid of ale, that was.

The opening of the door made me jump and I almost slid off the sofa.

"Oh, I am sorry, we were trying to be quiet," Lorcan said, as he and Padraig came in with the food. They quickly took everything to the kitchen.

"It's my fault. I didn't think I'd have to go that deep. I should have set her up on the bed in the guest room." She turned to me. "Do you feel any better?"

I nodded. "I'm not feeling the pain from before, but I still feel like something is missing. But I can't say what it is."

"You look better—less pale, and sickly." Alric smiled.

Garbage flew over to me to investigate. "Is better. Still broken."

"Can you tell what's broken, sweetie?" Siabiane leaned down a bit.

Again, Garbage was looking at me with her hooded stare. I didn't know what she could tell. The new look might be like her crazy one-eye stare—something she thought looked cool.

"Missing. Something here." She flew up to me and lightly tapped my head. "And here." She tapped my heart.

Like that wasn't cryptic.

Siabiane nodded slowly as if Garbage had clarified everything for her. "I hate to ask this, so only try for something small, extremely small. But can you do any magic?"

I tried for the glow again; they were extremely easy to call up once you knew how. This time nothing at all. I couldn't even make a small, dysfunctional glow. I tried harder and the stabbing pain sliced into the side of my skull, and I fell over onto the sofa.

Alric was at my side in a second. "Drop the spell, stop it."

"Gone now." I sounded like the faeries but that was about as much as I could formulate. My attempt at a simple spell had really scrambled my head. I tried to reach where I normally felt my magic. It wasn't a place so much as a feeling. It wasn't there. Not that I should be surprised after what I just felt. But it was still painful. "I don't have any magic. There is nothing."

Alric wiped away a tear before I fully realized I was crying.

"Now, now," Lorcan said as he and Padraig came out of the kitchen minus their boxes. "I missed most of what just happened, but lost magic can come back. There could be any number of reasons. You could have caught a cold, or something you reached for was too far, and your magic shut down to protect you. Whatever the reason, we will fix it."

Padraig nodded to the brownies still tied up on the table. "Do we need them here?"

Siabiane looked at her two constructs who were standing behind the real brownies. Both smiled and gave slight shakes of their heads. Whatever useful information the brownies had, Welsy and Delsy had already gotten it out of them.

"No, we do not." She turned to Garbage. "As the wronged party, do you wish to have first shot?"

Garbage flew over to the six and scowled. "No. But I better no see again. No troubles!" Then she flew back to me.

Padraig picked them up but they squirmed so he could only grab three.

"I can help," Alric said, and then turned to me. "You are okay?"

I waved him on. I wasn't okay, but there appeared to be nothing we could do about it right now.

Alric grabbed the other three. "I will knock you out and leave you near a bear's den if you don't stop twitching." His three and the ones being held by Padraig immediately went limp. Brownies were good at annoying people and rabblerousing, but actual fighting wasn't their thing.

Garbage flew over them, nodding in agreement. Whether Alric and Padraig wanted her along or not, she was joining them to make sure the brownies were properly disposed of.

They left and Siabiane nodded to her two brownie constructs. "Thank you for questioning them. I will get a full report later. Right now, we are going to have dinner. Would you like to join us?"

I had two constructs of my own, one created by Siabiane, but neither ever ate. Well, Irving seemed to like relics, but that was more an obsession than a need to eat.

"Thank you most graciously, however we would like to patrol the garden." They hopped down from the table and showed themselves out.

"They actually eat?" Lorcan got out before I did.

"They don't need to, but they can. Part of my making them brownie-like. Still working on them and doilies, though."

I'd forgotten about the brownie and doily invasion of Covey's house a few months ago. A troop had broken in and were settling in for a week-long hibernation. Somehow that involved a lot of doilies. "Why do they like dollies so much?"

"That is a question for the ages." Siabiane rolled her eyes and shook her head. "Okay, maybe not the ages, but no one aside from the brownies appear to know why they have that obsession, and they won't talk."

Lorcan came over to help me to the table.

"I'm fine, really." But I still let him help me. The missing magic was disturbing, even more so was the big hole it seemed to have left. And I felt like I had been running for a week—absolutely nothing was left energy-wise.

Siabiane brought out the food from the pub and the three of us dug in. I wanted to wait for the others, but both Lorcan and Siabiane kept shoving food my way.

"Let me guess, whatever is wrong with me is related to not eating enough?" The pub food was far and above any food to be found in Beccia, even the high-end places. But I could still only eat so much.

"We're not sure what's wrong, but before we start testing, we want you fueled up. You'd already been exhausted from that spell in that tunnel—this new issue couldn't have helped." Siabiane passed the bread plate to me.

The door opened and Alric and Padraig came back in. Garbage flew over their heads and landed on the table. Siabiane had taken a saucer from a teacup and made up a plate for her. I really hoped Garbage didn't think I'd be doing that regularly.

"I changed mind. But they no let me punish." Garbage

seemed only mildly annoyed, but the food seemed to help ease her annoyance.

"They did save you," Padraig said. "They were telling some truths that didn't set off any lie spells. The faeries got sucked into a vortex in a tree, and Garbage would have gone in with the rest had they not grabbed her."

I really felt that words like "vortex" and "sucked into" should be more concerning, but the fact that no one looked worried, including Garbage, kept me from saying anything about it.

"But not good." Garbage had finished her plate and started to stalk more food. It was amazing how much the tiny faeries could eat when they wanted to.

I smiled at my little malcontent faery. "True, it seemed they grabbed you to trade for their friends. But if they hadn't grabbed you, we wouldn't know where all of you had gone."

Garbage started to give me a glare—reason wasn't often her friend—then shrugged and went back to eating. "Guess okay."

"Speaking of which, shouldn't we go after the faeries now? And what did you do with the brownies?"

"We loosened their ties and dumped them a bit out of town, past the guardians. I told them they would be fried if they came back," Alric said.

Padraig laughed. "And then he fired a zap spell at them when they weren't looking. They ran into the woods at that point."

"If the faeries aren't in danger..." Siabiane paused as Garbage, Alric, and Padraig all shook their heads. "Then let's see if we can get Taryn up and running first. I'm not sure if going out at night looking for a vortex in a tree is a good idea."

"They can wait. Just stuck. Not hurt." Garbage leaned back on a napkin.

"Okay, let's try and fix me."

Lorcan helped me up and then Siabiane motioned both Alric and Padraig back down. "Finish eating. We're going into the guest room. When you're done, come in, but I have a feeling this will take a while."

Alric looked ready to argue, then something in Siabiane's face made him sit back in his seat. "If you need anything, say so."

"She'll be fine." Siabiane led Lorcan and me to the back bedroom, obviously guest quarters but still about the size of my entire front room in Beccia. "Okay, sit on the bed and both Lorcan and I will do a scan."

"What should I do?" Sitting on the bed was easy. It was keeping from falling back on it that was hard. I was still unnaturally tired and now full—not a good combination.

"Just sit." Siabiane closed her eyes and waved her hands slowly around me. Lorcan also closed his eyes but muttered soft spell words.

I felt a weak tingle in my hands, like they'd been asleep. But then it vanished. Both Siabiane and Lorcan frowned, then repeated their spells.

Not even a tingle this time. The only way I knew they finished was when they opened their eyes. Padraig and Alric might have been waiting in the hall, as they both came in a second later.

"Nothing?" I asked. I had no idea what the spells they were casting were supposed to do, but their looks weren't good.

"I have to be honest with you, you are showing no magic ability at all." Lorcan came closer and sat next to me. "Didn't I hear that you were magic numb when you first came to Beccia?"

"Yes, I have no idea what triggered my magic to come back, but I was a serious magic sink for most of my time in Beccia."

"I can verify, there was nothing there magically when we first met." Alric nodded. "Until we found the gargoyle, which given your connection to all of the relics most likely did start things. I also think that your reactions to dragon bane triggered it."

Lorcan got up and stepped back. "You knew her then; can you tell if she feels the same now?"

That chilled my soul. I'd been a magic sink, yes, someone who couldn't work magic but who also was hard to work magic on. I'd been fine with it. But that was before I got my magic back and found out whom I really was. Now I knew that magic was a part of me, of whom I was now and whom I'd been long ago—the idea that it might be gone again was terrifying.

Alric took the place next to me and took both of my hands. "It will be okay; we can get through this. We have gotten through far worse." He waited until I took a deep breath and smiled.

Then his magic punched me in the face. I fell backward on the bed, and I saw stars swimming everywhere.

"Taryn!" Alric yelled and tried to pull me upright, but the magic pouring off him hurt.

"Please, just let go." Even I could barely hear my voice.

Alric's horrified face was replaced by Lorcan's calm and soothing one. I barely recalled my parents, and I had no memory of any grandparents. But I'd like to think they would have been like Lorcan and Siabiane. Only Ancients instead of elven.

"I need you to focus on me and my voice. Slowly come back. You're on a trail through a forest, my voice is guiding you back to us. Don't pay attention to anything but my voice. The trees are cool and soothing. Keep following my voice."

At first, I tried to shake him off. Back where they were was dark and scary. Here was nice. Then the idea of the forest sounded good. And Lorcan did make sense about the trees. Eventually I found myself back in Siabiane's guest room. I was still on my back, and there were four worried people watching me.

"What happened to me?"

"Something that shouldn't," Lorcan said. "I should have been more suspicious of that jewelry when I first saw what the pin did. Damn it."

Padraig shook his head. "You had no idea, no one has even seen one of those since before the Breaking. None of us had any idea what they really were."

I looked from one to the other; they all looked like I was dying, and they were debating if they should have known it was coming. "Okay, things are bad. How bad? How do we fix it? And can someone help me up?" I wasn't as out of it as I'd been before Lorcan called me back from wherever I was, but I still could have been pushed over by a newborn kitten right now.

Alric started to pull me forward but that weird blackout thing started again. I flinched.

"Let me help her, your magic is hurting her." Lorcan gently pulled me forward.

"I am so sorry." Alric took a few steps back. "Why is it only me?"

"It might be your magic; I think the two pieces of jewelry worked as a team. One is blocking her magic, and the other is trying to destroy any magical connections she has. You were her teacher of magic, yes?"

"Yes, but I still don't understand. I've never heard of a spell that can do this."

"Because we're only seeing one part of it, but by teaching her you infused some of your magic into hers. That's being compounded by the fact that Taryn has existed in some form for over twenty-five hundred years, as she passed through time to get here. It might have appeared like she zapped into our time frame, but she did touch those years albeit fleetingly. This spell is attacking her on all those levels."

I was sitting up now and getting mad. After all we'd gone

through to save the world, now I was having some sneaky spell take me down? "But I didn't stop and live all of those years, I sort of threw myself across them." Mad was good, my voice was stronger.

"But you still touched them as you passed. While Qianru sent them to you, I know she couldn't have done this, nor do I believe she would have intended this result. Whoever set this spell knew who and what you were."

Chapter Sixteen

"HOW CAN THAT BE? TARYN didn't even know who she was until a few weeks ago. Those thugs were sent up here before that." Alric was mad, too. Good.

Siabiane looked like she was afraid I was going to break apart. "I think Lorcan is right. You may not have known who you were, Taryn, but someone in the southern continent did."

I was still sitting, but I doubted that I had the energy to jump to my feet—I would have liked to, though. "Qianru? She knew a lot more than I thought, but not enough to realize that Jovan and Glorinal were homicidal maniacs. Are you saying *she* knew what I was?" That was impossible to believe.

Lorcan shook his head, but there was a brief pause before he spoke. "I doubt it. I would say not at all, but she is more resourceful than any of us knew. But I seriously doubt it. If she knew what you were, she never would have gone south without you in tow. She isn't a mage, but she works as the advisor for the Emperor Fian, the largest empire in the southern continent. Bringing back a living Ancient would have been her biggest coup."

"Could she be trying to do that now?" Padraig looked thoughtful. "Perhaps she found something that made her realize what Taryn is and is using this spell to get her to come to her?"

I watched them and pondered my own interactions with Qianru. She was pushy, imperious, and sneaky about not sharing information. I just didn't think she was evil. "This sounds weird, but I don't think she's up to anything evil. I think if she knew what I was, she would have been up here herself, not sent hired flunkies. And I really think she was terrified in whatever that message was. I wish I'd seen all of it—but she was really rattled. Trust me, it takes a lot to do that."

Siabiane nodded, but it seemed like it was more to herself. "I know it's late, but if Welsy and Delsy are done with their patrols, I'd like to have them come in and tell us what they found. I would have asked them at dinner, but they get edgy if they can't do their patrols. We should go back to the front room."

Alric started to reach forward to help me up, then stepped back. "Maybe I shouldn't be near her?"

"Might be a good idea until we get a better handle on the spell attacking her." Padraig stepped forward and helped me up. I felt a slight twinge, but not like from Alric.

"Yup, I forgot you helped with teaching me a few spells too. Not a lot, so I only felt it slightly." I looked back to Lorcan and Siabiane behind us. "I hope you can solve this spell issue and give me back my magic. I think I need to go pummel somebody."

"I think we should be able to find a way to modify the effects at least. I need to find out more about the Robukian. They were never common even back in the old days." Lorcan helped Padraig settle me on the sofa, Alric took a chair at the dining table, and Siabiane called to her brownie constructs. Garbage had been watching things in the window, so she quietly buzzed over to sit next to me.

Nice. But a bit nerve-wracking. She could be resting or thinking of some way to single-handedly destroy the world as we knew it.

Welsy and Delsy came in within a few moments, both

looking pleased with themselves.

"The yard is secure."

"We have confirmed it."

That made me feel a bit better. Not that I really thought someone was going to sneak in and grab us all, but you never knew.

I turned to Lorcan and Padraig. "Hey, how come these guardians of yours didn't stop the Domniall changeling or Theria from getting into town? And Theria was able to break into the knights' station, free Hass, and yet nothing happened with the guardians?"

Lorcan shrugged. "Unlike the shield, the guardians have to rely on perceived threats. A bunch of rakasas from underground or sceanra anam from the skies would trigger them. An individual or even a pair of magic users wouldn't." He looked to Siabiane. "The real Domniall would, though. Certain people have been coded. As for the knights' station breach, they do have a mage or two who will be looking into it, I'm sure. They get touchy about help."

I wasn't sure that was a great answer, and my faith in these guardians dropped even lower. But they obviously were dealing with their own problems.

Welsy and Delsy stepped forward like two young children about to recite one of the epic poems in school.

Siabiane smiled. "Thank you for protecting. Now if you could tell us what you learned from the other brownies?"

One of them nodded to the other; unless they started wearing name tags there was no way I could tell them apart—nor probably even tell them apart from real brownies.

"I will begin." The brownie stood proudly and stepped forward. "The others were hired to follow the group heading north, to join them if possible, if not then to follow. There had been a group of ten originally, but four vanished while they were waiting for the northern-heading rapscallions. The belief is they were killed. They had the full description of the items—a set of four Robukian of old—and were supposed to get them before anyone touched them. That was a critical point apparently." He stopped and looked right at me. "They are aware somehow that two of the Robukian have been exposed to you and had debated taking you back to the one who hired them along with all of the Robukian once they found them."

That was nice. I had no belief that a trip south with them would have been good for my health.

"They were going to kill you to make getting you down there easier."

That answered that.

The second brownie stepped forward. "We pointed out that they had already violated the command and therefore returning to the one who hired them would result in their own deaths. We advised going north. Extremely north. As a means to escape."

There wasn't much information, but at least the brownies hopefully were running for their lives.

"Thank you, Welsy and Delsy. You did exemplary. Please return to the garden."

Both brownies beamed at Siabiane, bowed to us, and left.

A huge yawn escaped against my will.

"I think that's our cue to head back to the palace." Lorcan stood and walked toward the door. "We can meet to report what we've found and get the faeries back from their tree in the morning."

Garbage had also been getting sleepy. "Yes, is good." She gave a yawn. "Sleep near you. Protect." She nodded to me.

"That's a good idea. Taryn and Garbage take the guest room. Alric, this sofa does make a nice bed, if you don't mind." Siabiane seemed a bit awkward, but it really wasn't a good idea to have the two of us in the same bed right now.

Alric nodded. "I've slept in worse."

Padraig and Lorcan left, Siabiane got Alric some blankets

and pillows, and Garbage and I went to the guest room.

"Are you okay?" I'd rarely seen her like this. She wasn't mad or somber; but she was contemplative as she flew into the room.

"I is. Thinking. Bad people set trap for us." She gave me a huge evil smile. "Will find and hurt."

That was more like the Garbage I knew. I settled into bed, feeling a bit better but still exhausted. Garbage took the other pillow, punched a spot a few times, then turned in a circle and went to sleep.

I tried. And considering how tired I was, I should have been able to go to sleep immediately. But I kept thinking about the fact that someone knew what I was before I did. Edana didn't even recognize me until I'd changed—and she'd known me twenty-five hundred years ago.

Who knew me enough to want to destroy my power? I doubted that whoever the brownies were working for was behind the mess. But they'd need to be on this list.

I missed Covey right now. She was perfect for organizing these types of things. Not that I doubted Lorcan and the others; they'd been dealing with mysteries longer than Covey had been alive. But she was more single-minded.

The door cracked open and a shaft of light fell across my bed. "I thought you might be awake." Siabiane came in and put a glass on the table next to my bed. "Just some milk to help you sleep. That spell is taking your energy."

"Thank you, I'll drink it."

Garbage had been curled in a tight ball but opened one eye, watched Siabiane, and then leapt to her feet. "No! Not right." She flew forward, knocking the glass off the side table. Then flew right through Siabiane's face.

The thing I thought was Siabiane cackled and dropped in height to reveal a short, hairy creature. Ghostlike images of tall, skinny beings drifted behind her, but weren't touching the floor. Garbage started growling, of all things, at the wafting forms behind her and they vanished. The creature's eyes glowed red as it watched Garbage turn around to come back at it. "You shouldn't have been here. Next time." Then it vanished.

I yelled. Obviously, that was another visage, and just as obvious, this time it had been able to move things and carry things. They weren't supposed to be able to do that. The glass and its milky-gray contents were still on the floor pointing out that they could.

Siabiane got there first, but Alric was right behind.

"What happened?"

Garbage flew up and aggressively sniffed both. "Is okay. These right."

"Something just came in. She looked and sounded like you, tried to give me a drink. When Garbage attacked her, she turned into…something else. There were some other tall, skinny dark, ghosts behind her. I couldn't see much of them. Garbage knocked the glass to the floor, and she vanished." I still felt wiped out, but I was alert now. Nothing like an incorporeal being trying to kill you in bed to really wake you up.

Alric went to the glass. He started to pick it up, then pulled back his hand, shaking it and swearing. "There's an acid of some sort in that."

Siabiane said a few words and the glass, contents, and the rug that it had been dumped on all vanished. "I would have liked to see what it was exactly, but acids are not to be trifled with."

"How can someone who isn't here be moving things that are here?"

Alric and Siabiane shared a look.

"Could it be a hilstrike mage?" Alric's voice was low as he checked the rest of the room.

"I don't think so. They were mostly destroyed in the mage wars even before the Breaking." But Siabiane's face belied her words.

"You think that's what that was." I wasn't asking a question. "I've never heard that term, but you are both freaked out about it."

Garbage flew back to me. "I protect." She sat back down on her pillow.

I smiled at her and nodded to the others. "She did, and whoever that was, they weren't expecting her. They were probably behind sending the rest of the faeries away." The look on that creature's face as it saw Garbage made me shudder. It wasn't happy, and it was surprised to see Garbage, but not angry. More like that was another battle to be won later.

"I'm calling Welsy and Delsy in to stay in the front room, and I'm also putting up a full shield around the cottage." Siabiane was already setting up some spells, judging by the way she was muttering under her breath.

Alric stepped back toward the door. "Does my being this close bother you?"

"No, but I don't want you to stand there all night."

"I can sleep fine here; I'll relocate the pillows and blankets." He gave a smile and went into the hall.

Siabiane finished whatever spell casting she'd pre-set and turned to Garbage and myself. "Do you think either one of you could sketch what the fake me turned into?"

I looked to Garbage and she nodded. "I supervise." Considering most writing implements would be a bit taller than her, that would probably be for the best.

Siabiane came back with a pile of paper and two charcoal pencils. Good thinking—even if we knew Garbage wasn't going to use them, it was better to offer.

Alric came back with his bedding and piled it near the still open door. He and Siabiane watched as I drew the thing I'd seen. Garbage had me redo the face at least four times, but she'd been closer to it than I'd been. Much closer.

After much scowling and tilting of her head, she pronounced it finished.

"This is about as good as we got, looks almost familiar

now that Garbage had me change the face." I started to hand it to Siabiane.

"We make one go boom." Garbage looked matter-of-fact about it as she nodded.

I pulled the paper back. "Boom? Oh, crap. That weird thing that exploded in my old apartment two years ago. Zirtha." That had seemed so long ago that I didn't even recognize the likeness when I saw it in my room. I did now, though. "That's not her come back from the dead, is it?"

Siabiane looked at it and handed the paper to Alric. "I don't believe I know that story, but it does look like a Grimarian troll. They haven't been in this land in centuries. Well, in your land. The elves never let them cross our border. They are from the far south if any still exist."

Alric shook his head and gave her back the drawing. "One at least came this far north, almost two years ago in Beccia. She was hunting Taryn, but the faeries destroyed her."

"This is not good. That thing could have been sending a visage from not far away, which means she's too close. Or she's killed enough magic users to be able to translocate items when she sends herself at a distance. Neither are good." She walked to the outer wall and put her hand on it. "I can't sense her essence, but I wouldn't have been spelling for one of those." She dusted off her hands and looked between Alric and Garbage. "You protect her." Then to me. "I know it's hard but sleeping will help you recover. Welsy and Delsy will guard inside and I'm now adding even more layers of spells upon the cottage. Good night." Muttering spells to herself, Siabiane closed the door.

"I wish I could hug you." I watched Alric set up his bed across the door. I hadn't meant for that to come out as pathetic as it sounded.

He looked up and his smile almost made me run to him regardless of what pain it might cause. "I wish you could too. But until we figure out how someone hit you with this spell, and what it's doing, me keeping a safe distance is a good idea."

"We no let icky thing get." Garbage was still sitting on her pillow but looked extremely awake.

"Thank you both. I'll try to sleep." I turned out the glows and went back to laying in the dark, thinking. Zirtha had been working for Thaddeus, my evil former patron, trying to take over the world. But the faeries, a bunch of them, not only my three, including their Queen Mungoosey had destroyed her. I wondered if somehow the information of how she had died had gotten to the others of her kind. This one likely tricked the rest of the faeries into being "stuck" and would have gotten Garbage as well if not for some mercenary brownies.

I might have to find those brownies and thank them after all. Except for the whole going to kill me so I'd be easier to carry back part. But I hated to think what would have happened if Garbage had gone with the rest of her flock.

I was sure I wouldn't be able to sleep, but Garbage bouncing on my pillow right next to my head told me I had done so and that she was ready to get up.

"Let her sleep," Alric whispered from the door. The sun was just rising, but there was enough light to see that he was sitting with his back against the door and his sword across his knees.

"Too late." I stretched and Garbage grabbed my hand.

"Get others. All protect."

She hadn't been worried about getting the rest of her team until now.

"Are they okay? Can you feel them?"

"Yes. But need you."

Alric rose to his feet and gathered his bedding. "Let me go see if Siabiane is awake."

He left and I quickly showered and dressed. I had no idea if we were staying here, going back to Beccia, or moving into the palace. While I hadn't been sure what would happen after the last battle, this hadn't even crossed my mind. I neatened my things and left them in the room.

Siabiane and Alric were talking quietly in the kitchen. Welsy and Delsy were watching the front door with an intensity I usually only found among faeries waiting for an ale to be opened.

"Hello?" I didn't want to startle them, but both turned around as if they knew where I was.

"We watch the door."

"Keep you safe."

"Thank you, Welsy and Delsy, you can go back to your gardens now." Siabiane stuck her head out from the kitchen. The brownies bowed and then left.

I felt an odd popping sound as the door shut behind them.

"The warding is still on the cottage. I didn't notice anything triggered during the night but who knows what a hilstrike mage could do." She pointed me to the table and indicated I needed to eat.

"I thought you said it was a troll thing, like the one that the faeries destroyed." I started to tuck in; the food was good, and I was seriously hungry.

Siabiane came out and joined me with Alric right behind her. "A Grimarian troll, yes. But sadly, the two are not mutually exclusive. I have no idea if this Zirtha from your past was a hilstrike mage, but they are often one and the same. Hilstrike magic is a quite old, and vile form of magic. Usually only the extremely nasty and desperate fall into that way of life."

"And that covers Grimarian trolls." Alric sat down as well. "I'd guess Zirtha wasn't a hilstrike; I don't see one of them actually working for someone less powerful than them. Thaddeus was dangerous, but when I fought him, he wasn't stronger than a hilstrike."

"What makes hilstrikes deadly? I've heard of the Grimarians even before one tried to kill me. But I've never heard of these mages."

"They practice dark arts that make necromancers like my brother seem tame. Luckily, their magic is even more likely to turn on them. One of the reasons they are so rare."

Garbage flew around the entire cottage doing her own inspection, but she finally settled on the table. Again, Siabiane had put out a saucer of food for her. Garbage sat down and started eating. Then looked at our teacups. "Me?"

I covered my cup with my hand and moved it away from her. "No, you do not get tea."

Siabiane had been in the act of getting another cup for her but stopped. "Is there something wrong with her having tea?"

"Yes!" Both Alric and I shouted at the same time.

"Sorry, tea makes the faeries extremely hyper." I looked down at Garbage. "And more than a little insane. She once caught and brought back a bird for Harlan to eat while on a tea high. Her reasoning was that he is a cat."

Siabiane laughed. "Oh dear."

Garbage gave a massive sigh and went back to eating her food. "Could help. Might need." She said it loud enough for us to hear, but trying to appear as if she wasn't talking to us.

"How could the tea help?" I kept my cup as far from her I as could.

"Is make fast. I go fast get friends out. Tree slow."

"Trees usually are slow, so if they are slow, you don't need to go fast to beat them."

"Better if faster."

I was trying to decide if it was really something she knew about where her friends were, or she was angling for some tea. She was being too artful with eating her food and not looking at us. I looked to the others and slightly shook my head. Ignoring Garbage would probably be the best option right now.

"How do I stop that Grimarian troll from doing what she did again? How did she do what she did in the first place?"

"We can make amulets that will help keep her eye off you. I can teach Alric how to make them in case something happens, and you need more." Siabiane held up her hand before Alric could swallow and speak. "Yes, I know, you are a strong magic user and fighter, and you can defend her. But different magic needs different tricks, and these will work better. The best way to avoid a Grimarian is to not be seen by one."

CHAPTER SEVENTEEN

IN THE END GARBAGE DIDN'T get her tea, Alric got a quick jewelry-making lesson on amulets, and he and I got sparkling new pendants to wear. I couldn't help making them, as my magic was still not around. The amulets were small, no larger than a copper coin, with tiny magical engravings all over them, and thin. But they would supposedly keep the evil eye off us.

Siabiane stepped back and inspected her work, or rather, that no one could see her work. The chains they were on were extremely thin and the amulets hung under our clothes. She assured us that although thin, the chains were exceptionally strong. "Excellent." She tilted her head, and gave me a questioning look. "How do you feel right now, Taryn?"

"Okay, still a bit sore, but better."

"Even now?" Alric said, right next to me.

I knew he'd been near me as they worked on the amulets, but I hadn't realized how close he was. I wrapped my arms around his waist and hung on to see if the pain would hit. Nope. I released his waist but stayed close. "I give up, so why isn't being close to him bothering me anymore? Not that I'm complaining."

Siabiane narrowed her eyes as she tried to look beyond the visual, and then shook her head. "I can't see anything different, but I'd guess it's because of the amulet. I think we know who is behind that attack on you at the pub."

"That Grimarian troll? Is there a way to destroy those things without an army of pissed-off faeries? Is she how I lost my magic too?"

"I'd gather yes, she is behind all of that, but she's clearly not here. I should have noticed last night but I think she was far away when she cast her spells. Hopefully, the amount of magic she expended in a relatively short amount of time should slow her down. As for the killing, they are extremely difficult to kill."

"Maybe Taryn's magic is back now?" Alric sounded more like he was being nice, but I liked that thought.

"Let me see." I held up my hand and tried pushing the chair two feet in front of me. I thought I felt something, but the chair didn't move. "Nope."

Siabiane put her arm around my shoulders. "Don't worry, we will fix it. And that amulet should help slow down anything else she tries. I have to talk with Lorcan and Padraig, figure out how she is spreading this drain across decades you weren't even in."

"And that she didn't have magic in," Alric added.

"True. I was magicless when I got here, which would mean the self I sent forward in time when the relics did their thing was magicless too." The entire idea that someone could track me through time when I was passing through that fast was freaking me out more than the recent attack. Okay, almost more.

"Get friends." Garbage had been patiently watching us— well, patiently for her. Unless they were asleep or passed out, faeries didn't sit around doing nothing for long. At least not when it was only one faery.

"Okay, Garbage, we needed to get ready. Is there anything we should bring?" I might not have access to my magic, something I thought I was handling extremely well, but I had other weapons if needed.

"Honey." She nodded as if that needed no explanation.

"Are you calling me honey, or you want us to bring honey?" Not really what I had been expecting in either case.

"Bring. Honey. And stick. Big stick." She looked like she was making things up, but we had to get what she asked for just in case.

Siabiane went into her kitchen and came back with two small jars of golden honey. "Will this be enough?"

Garbage walked over like a general inspecting her troops and nodded her approval of the jars.

"We can get a stick on the way." Alric looked as doubtful as I did, but Garbage would be the one most focused on her friends.

Garbage nodded and flew to the door. "I lead."

We all followed her out and down the garden path.

Siabiane paused as we turned toward the road that would lead out of the city. "Garbage? I think I need to go talk to Lorcan about that creature you chased off last night. Can you do this without me?" She handed me the two jars of honey.

"You go tell. I won." Garbage smiled and then flew down the road.

Siabiane smiled as Garbage turned into a distant orange speck. "I didn't want her to think I was abandoning her. But I don't think you'll need me, and I do think Lorcan and Padraig need to be made aware." She started to turn the other way but turned around. "I've set the locks on my cottage to recognize both of you if you need to come back here but meet back at the palace once you've freed the faeries."

"Will do." Alric and I started after Garbage. "Do you know what we would need honey and a stick for?"

Alric shrugged. "Not a clue. But does anyone understand how they think?"

Garbage had gotten too far ahead and was buzzing back toward us. She'd been fine with her friends being trapped last night, but now she couldn't wait.

"Come now!" She circled around our heads, then tore down the road.

I walked faster, but I was not running with two jars of honey down one of the main roads in an elven city.

After a few more loops of her urging us forward, we reached the tree line. Alric had to go through four sticks before Garbage agreed on one. The one she settled on was as long as my leg and as thick as Alric's wrist.

We caught up to her in front of a huge old oak tree, the kind that looked like it might have been full grown when the elves first came to this part of the world.

The trunk had what first appeared to be a large crack a bit taller than Alric and almost as wide right in the middle. But when we got closer it was clear that it was only a stain and the tree was solid.

"Okay, so what do we do now?" I walked a bit around the tree, but there was no entrance anywhere. I even looked up in case it had been higher, and the faeries had flown in. Nothing.

"Now, tie stick and me with this." Garbage held out some of the rope vine that the brownies had used on her. She flew to the middle of the stick and pointed.

"You want me to tie you here?"

Garbage took one end of the rope, circled her waist, and then handed the end to me. "Stick."

I looked to Alric, but he shrugged and held up the stick. I tied her to it. But it was more like a leash, as she could fly about a foot away.

"Now what?"

"Honey. Dump on tree. There." She pointed right in the middle of the dark spot. "Move fast."

That was a bit disturbing. But I walked closer and poured the honey on the tree. I was halfway through the second jar when I heard groaning from the branches above us.

"You move close. Hold ends." Garbage got Alric to move

closer right as the dark area popped open. A leafy tendril grabbed the second honey jar out of my hand, and Garbage darted inside. Alric and the stick were pulled closer and he pushed me free of the tree. The stick was too wide for the gap in the tree, so he stayed braced outside of it.

Garbage started yelling and then dozens of faeries, far more than we'd had with us, all flew out from the tree. Alric was almost smashed against the tree as she flew farther in, but the rope vines didn't break. Garbage was flying against a bright light in an impossibly cavernous tree interior, still yelling at a few straggling faeries. Once they'd all flown past, she turned and tried coming back but something was pulling her in. Alric snarled and pulled back on the stick with all his might.

He, the stick, Garbage, and a half-empty jar of honey all flew backward, and we all crashed to the ground. The tree slammed shut and we were soon covered in dozens of faeries.

The faeries were kissing all of us, including the stick that was still in Alric's hands. Garbage flew above them all, dragging the stick into the air as she did so.

"Is good now. I save. Go homes. Not mine, though."

Most of the ones not part of Garbage's troop were wearing leaves, a sure sign of wild faeries. I wondered how they'd gotten pulled into the tree, and when.

The wild ones circled, yelled native faery things that sounded nice, then took off. We were left with Garbage, Crusty, Leaf and the other fourteen or so who'd come up with us from Beccia.

Alric got off my legs, untied Garbage, and tossed the honey-coated stick away. Actually, he and I were a bit honey-coated too.

"I think they were licking the honey off." I took his hand as he helped me up. Some of the faeries had honey on them as well. "What is that tree? I saw inside, it was huge!"

"Something I'd bet my people didn't know was out here. This is past where the shield had been, so we'd not be aware of it. Lorcan will be fascinated."

I waited as he admired the tree for a few moments, and the faeries buzzed around chattering and swinging their arms about. "And what is it?"

"Sorry." He turned around with a sheepish look. "These can be tricky to be around. Let's head back into town, I'd like to get this honey off me."

We started walking, but the faeries flew a different direction as soon as we were out of the trees.

"Back later!" Leaf yelled as they flew away.

"That tree is a sycubian. They were far more populous in your time, at least in theory. There were never a lot, as they hunt and maintain large territories."

I was annoyed that there was yet one more item from my past that I'd not recalled. "Wait, hunting? So that tree was trying to eat the faeries?"

"Not so much. They mostly eat bugs and wouldn't have harmed the faeries." He scowled. "I'd say our Grimarian friend tricked the tree into pulling in the faeries to get them out of her way. And from the look of the number of ones wearing leaves that I saw, pulling in any faery it could reach." He led us back to Siabiane's cottage. I agreed, the honey was getting itchy even if there wasn't a lot of it.

CHAPTER EIGHTEEN

———

I DIDN'T SEE THE BROWNIES, BEYOND a brief peek of two red cap tips. They paused in the plants near us, then went back to their patrols.

We quickly showered and changed.

When Alric came out, he paused in front of me in the front room and took my hands. "How are you doing? I know you wanted to relax, and we have been doing anything but that."

"And my magic is gone." I wrapped my arms around his neck and enjoyed a nice long kiss. "At least I can be near you again. To be honest, I'd be more worried if I didn't have some of the smartest elves in the world working on the problem." That was true. What was also true, and I wasn't going to mention, was that I was afraid if I thought about losing my magic for good too much, I would probably curl into a ball and stay there. My magic wasn't great, or as under my control as it should be. But it was mine. And a connection to who I was. Having it blocked right now emotionally hurt.

"I promise we'll get this sorted out and you and I will go somewhere alone that even the faeries can't find." His grin was sincere.

I smiled back, but I was doubtful. I knew those flying maniacs too well.

We left the cottage and headed back to the palace.

I paused as we started toward the main entrance. "Shouldn't we be sneaking in the other way?" The palace still overwhelmed me with its formality. Sneaking in made it less scary.

"We have legitimate business, and believe it or not, they do let me in the front door most of the times."

We walked up and the two knights standing near the door stood at attention.

"Your grandmother has been looking for you, Alric," the older one said as they stood back to let us enter.

His grandmother raised Alric after his parents died when he was young. She was a high-ranking official in the royal palace and sort of scared the hell out of me.

"Thank you, Mithon. I'll make a point of finding her. We have a meeting with Lorcan right now, though."

"Of course." He gave a slight bow, flashed me a smile, and then resumed his guardian stance.

I watched the grand foyer carefully, keeping an eye out for the fierce woman who raised the love of my life. I let out a sigh when we reached the stairway that led to Lorcan's rooms.

"She's not that bad you know." Alric nodded toward the foyer and the people buzzing about on important missions.

"I thought you didn't notice." Trying to deny what I'd been doing would be pointless with him.

"I would have been blind to miss it—not to mention you started radiating terror once we crossed the doorway. Seriously, she's really not as fierce as she appears in front of the palace flunkies."

I said nothing but followed him up the stairs. We'd debate that later.

This was the only path that I knew to get to Lorcan's quarters, although if I had to, I might be able to find my way in the back sneaky route we came up yesterday. But I knew this wasn't the "official" way to his room, and the fact that Alric took this one instead told me he didn't completely trust some of the palace residents.

Alric gave a sharp rap on the door and it was pulled open by Padraig. He stood back to let us in. "Good of you to join us. We were about to go searching. I presume that you found the rest of the faeries?"

Siabiane and Lorcan were all the way in the lab so we went through the front room.

"Yes, they were caught in a sycubian not far outside the former shield area. And far more than only Garbage's little army were in there."

Between us we quickly explained the adventure, including the honey. "We had to leave our clothes at your place to soak."

Siabiane nodded. "I did wonder about the change of clothing. Don't worry, most likely Welsy and Delsy have gone in and washed them. They take their duties a bit to the extreme."

Lorcan shook his head. "I can't believe there was a sycubian tree nearby all this time. They are fascinating." He turned to Alric. "It's probably not hungry right now, is it?" There was a lot of hopefulness there.

"It ate a jar and a half of honey, so probably not." Alric nodded to where the four Robukian were placed on a metal sheet. "Any luck with them? I take it Siabiane filled you in on our visitor."

"No luck on the pieces yet, but we're getting closer." Lorcan came to me. "Yes, she did. How are you feeling? Still no magic?"

I shook my head. "Aside from that I feel fine. Whatever she hit me with is gone now, along with my magic." I knew they were trying to help but it was going to be difficult to ignore the loss of magic issue if they kept bringing it up. Staying in denial took effort.

"Do we have any other wards to keep her away? She was a nasty bit and if Garbage hadn't been there, she would have succeeded in whatever she was planning on doing to me." That was another thing I was trying not to think about, but this time I only had myself to blame for bringing it up. Zirtha had been trying to kill me. Not sure if this one had the same plan. But the glass of a liquid that could burn through a rug was a good hint.

Padraig pointed to a pile of books and scrolls taking over one of the tables in the back. "I'm working on it. There really isn't much about hilstrike mages or Grimarian trolls so the search will take a while. Until Siabiane told us that you'd had one run in with a Grimarian already, I would have said they haven't been on this continent in a few thousand years. But our people did run into them before we came north."

"Yes, but even then, rarely. Mathilda and I were young when we came up here, and I don't ever recall seeing one."

"But how did she project like that? Is Qianru working with her?" That was an unhappy thought. Qianru wasn't a friend per se, but for the most part a well-thought-of-acquaintance. Life-and-death situations seemed to tie people together.

Lorcan frowned. "There's no way to know, but I doubt it. Even Qianru wouldn't go that far." The discussion pretty much broke down into topics far over my head, and from what I could tell more academic, than fight to save the world stuff. Even Alric joined in as the discussion veered into the tree we'd gotten the faeries out of. Lorcan was far too interested in it.

I walked over to the table holding the Robukian collection. The two newer pieces, the ring, and the brooch, didn't call to me the way the second piece had, but I kept my hands behind my back and didn't move too close.

They didn't seem familiar, and if the others were right, they were of elven origin, not of my people. But they were almost soothing to look at. The brooch was lovely, and without thinking I reached forward to pick it up.

Alric grabbed my hand. "Probably not a good idea."

"Thank you." I rocked back a few steps. "It didn't drag me in the way the pin back did, but it still almost got me." I already was having enough problems with the marks from two of the pieces; I didn't want to see what would happen with more. "Can we make an amulet against these things?" I pulled out my amulet and waved it to the others.

"Oh, nice work." Lorcan came forward to look at the amulet. "That should slow down that Grimarian a bit. But I'm not sure what we would use to get you free of the Robukian influence. I did find out that we were right: the letter was spelled for you. Once you read it, it triggered the pin, which triggered the backing, then when they were together it brought up the other two."

I took another step back as the brooch was looking appealing again. "How do we know there are only four? And how do we stop them? And aside from messing up my life, and possibly giving that damn Grimarian a focus to cast spells on, what are they doing?"

"Good questions, but while you and Alric were playing with that tree, we found some answers." Padraig went back into the lab and brought back two old leather-bound books. The covers weren't stiff, like newer books, but simply a soft leather covering. That and the yellowed pages made me think they might even be as old as me.

He set them on the front room table and flipped open to some drawings in both. "Now this one is from Arlienia, our ancient homeland that's been lost for eons. Not many books survived the collapse, but we do have a few. The Ali-oth elves still in the south probably have more."

Siabiane nodded. "We did when Mathilda and I came north, but that was a long time ago."

The differences between Siabiane, her sister, and the rest of the elves that I'd seen were subtle. "So, if there are two types of elves, what are you three?" I'd only ever heard them called elves, nothing to make me think there were different types.

"There are only slight genetic differences between us, and we rarely use the names ourselves. But Padraig, Alric, and I are Mcallini elves. Our people left Arlienia long before the collapse and lived in the northern part of the southern continent, until we moved to this land a few thousand years ago. There hadn't been any animosity between the two groups in thousands of years and we are genetically compatible." He shrugged. "We just went different ways."

They all looked fine about it, but something bugged me. "So, these Dark, they were Mcallini elves, even though they came from the south?"

"There are still many Mcallini elves in the northern part of the south; the Dark were our issue, not the Alioth's." Lorcan sounded extremely sure, but I wondered if they'd really thought things through. The battle against the Dark had caught them ill-prepared.

Siabiane frowned. "Or not. I think we got so used to all just being elves, but there were some extreme groups among my people when Mathilda and I came north. My brother was not alone. We look enough alike that they could have been living around us up here for years and neither Mathilda nor I wouldn't have noticed the difference unless we knew to look."

"So then who made the Robukian?" It was sort of surprising that none of them had seen the possible connection. But I guessed that thinking of themselves as one people for a few thousand years might do it.

"The Mcallini." Lorcan spoke a second faster.

"The Alioth." Siabiane was right behind him.

They both looked at each other and laughed. "They are old enough that they could have come from either race," Lorcan said.

I wasn't sure if that resolved things or not, but a lot could have changed for those southern elves while their northern cousins were in hiding for a thousand years.

"She's thinking something through." Alric was still

standing close enough that he could grab me again if I went after that damn brooch. Good thinking on his part.

"What? Well, yeah, I am. You guys were driven into hiding by the Dark, who you thought were just your people gone bad."

"They were our people gone bad."

"But what if they weren't from this land? Jovan was one of your advisors before it all went to hell, and he turned out to be from the Dark and had come up here from the south."

Alric shook his head. "He fled to the south, all of the survivors did. He came back up with Qianru."

"But you don't know if he or the rest of his people didn't start down there. How free was the traveling between the groups before the Breaking?"

"I see what you're getting at." Siabiane's voice was soft. "We indeed had cut off contact. Nothing bad that I can recall, just distance. We really have no idea who or what the elves to the south are now."

Lorcan frowned. "The entire group of Alioth elves are bad? I don't believe it."

"Maybe not all, but some of them. Glorinal was from them as well and he made no pretense of not being from the south." I wasn't sure if knowing the Dark were local elves trying to take over the world was better or worse than elves from elsewhere wanting to take over the world. In my mind, them coming from the south, with a potentially much larger base still living there, was worse. I didn't care which race they were.

Everyone dropped into their own thoughts at that point. I gave them a few minutes to ponder the origin of their almost demise a thousand years ago had come from within or without. Then coughed to get their attention.

"I wasn't trying to start a major think-fest, only trying to sort a few things out, like what are those Robukian pieces trying to do and how do we stop them?"

"Well, you brought up some heavy points that we really never thought of." Lorcan got up and paged through one of the books Padraig had brought out. "We haven't been in contact with any of the elves in the south since our shields came down—none of the enclaves have."

"You have been sort of busy since you came out of hiding." The elves who had survived the Breaking had broken into smaller enclaves, thrown up heavy shields around them, and gone into hiding. They hadn't even known the other enclaves existed.

"True." Lorcan looked up and smiled. "And we need to get this spell off you first before we go searching beyond it. Someone, Alioth or Mcallini, set this spell for you. Whether Qianru was a willing and knowing participant or not, we'll sort out later as well."

Padraig opened his book. "So back to our original issue." He tapped a page. "I believe this set is the one we're facing. Believe it or not, it was originally designed to woo a wayward lover."

I went to go look. They looked a bit different, mostly because they were brand new in the drawings and they were showing their age now. "A wayward lover?" Seriously? That did almost sound like something Qianru would try. Never mind that I wasn't her lover, nor wayward.

"That was the original intention." Padraig turned the page. "There were four pieces for this set, so there should be no more popping up. They could be spell hidden in a love note triggered to the lover."

"Where is the letter?" Siabiane read over the section Padraig pointed to. I glanced at it, but it was in a language I couldn't even tell which direction it was going.

Alric took his faery bag out. "I still have it." He started to take it out, then instead handed the entire bag to Siabiane.

She reached inside and pulled out the letter and the napkin they'd used to grab it. With a deep breath, she dropped the napkin and held it.

We watched but nothing happened.

"It was triggered only to you, it would seem. These pieces could be used repeatedly. They would be spell cleansed, then reset." She walked over to a set of candles at the edge of the desk. At first it looked like she was going to burn the note, but instead she held the letter over the flame—not touching but extremely close.

"Now, the Robukian might have been triggered through the spell placed on this letter, but there was more to this letter than that." She held the letter over the flame for a few more seconds, then pulled it back and held it up.

A series of elaborate words appeared. Not really a list, but they didn't look like a letter either.

"Hmmm, still missing something." Siabiane lowered the letter again. I really thought it was going to catch fire. But she finally held it up. More words and a small map had appeared.

"I can't read it at this distance, but that sure looks like Qianru's writing." Even if she'd not been involved with the Grimarian troll, she was going to have a hell of a lot to answer for.

"This is actually addressed to Alric." Siabiane handed it to him.

Alric raised an eyebrow at Qianru sending him something but took the page. "She was involved with the Robukian, but was misled on what they would do. She doesn't want us to come down and sent her faeries to warn us." He looked up at that and shook his head. "There is something unique about these pieces, and she allowed them to be spelled to smuggle them out of the country. Things are dangerous, but she's being watched. It's more elaborate than that, she likes flowery words, but that's the gist." He held it up. "This is a map of something, but she doesn't say anything about it."

CHAPTER NINETEEN

"CAN I SEE? IT MIGHT be somewhere up here," Lorcan said. "Qianru did have a fascination with maps."

Alric gave it to him with a shrug. "It doesn't look familiar; it also doesn't appear to be drawn by Qianru."

Lorcan turned it over and then back again. "The map is another spell. She might have known it was there or not. But the magic user or users who set up her second note, along with the triggering of the Robukian, would have known it was there."

I looked over Lorcan's shoulder. "How many spells can a single paper have?" It was useful in the sense that one page had many spells; cut down on wasted paper. But three seemed a bit extreme.

"It's rare to have three unrelated spells. Even though the same spell caster might have set them all up, they function individually." Padraig left for the lab, then came back with a small canister. "I think we should try to lock all of the spells on it. We need to study that map. Who knows if they added more."

He uncapped the lid and sprinkled a light gray powder over the page. It settled into the paper. Then the Robukian pieces, all of which were at the other end of the table, flew together. I was glad I wasn't the only one seeing them jump, but I stumbled back the moment they moved.

Padraig stayed near the note and the others went after the pieces. They flopped off the table and seemed to be jumping around with no direction. "Someone knew we'd use that. Damn, another spell. I'd stand back from the Robukian."

He didn't have to tell me; I was trying to keep as far away from the floating and bouncing piece of metal as I could. Was seriously considering running into the hall. The others all stepped back as well, and the pieces started slowing down.

"Any idea what they are doing?" Lorcan watched the pieces.

Padraig wasn't taking his eyes off of them either. "Not a clue."

The pieces stopped, hung in midair, then all came shooting at me.

I screamed and ran for the door. I'd gotten it open only a bit when something hit the door frame right next to my head.

I'd shut my eyes, waiting for the rest of the pieces to hit, but nothing followed.

"Where did that come from?" Alric was right behind me, so I opened my eyes.

A dagger was still vibrating from being thrown into the door frame. It was less than six inches from my head.

I ducked and ran into the lab and slammed the door. "Where in the hell did that come from?"

"I think Padraig using the fixing spell powder triggered it. Whoever spelled it knew what we'd probably do." Lorcan's voice was a bit muffled, he was probably still near the other door. "Although, there could have been a number of triggers for this."

"Triggers that made a dagger come out of nowhere and try to kill me?" My voice only went up a bit at the end— that made me proud.

"It didn't come from nowhere." Siabiane sounded like

she was right on the other side of the lab door. "And I think it was excited to see you. You can come out now."

I cracked open the door, but that was as far as I was going at the moment. "Where did it come from?"

"It was a spell on the Robukian. Or rather, it is the Robukian." Lorcan came into view with the dagger in his hands. He looked like a kid with a new toy. "They all came together to make this. Can you believe it? I've never seen a reference to anything like this." He held it up to show me, but the dagger twitched.

I slammed the door shut again. "Keep it away from me."

"I really think it was spelled *for* you, not to hurt you." Lorcan was obviously staying right at the door.

"A relic set of spelled jewelry turned into a dagger that can move on its own and has a thing for me. No thank you. I already have one unexplainable possessed weapon." I looked around in case my sword came back. It had vanished once we came into the room, but if it showed up when I felt threatened, this would be a good time.

Not that I wasn't sure the two weapons might just make friends and decide they didn't need me.

Yelling came through the door and I almost flung it open to save my friends. Then realized that the yelling was from outside of Lorcan's rooms. Considering these walls were solid rock and stone, that was some serious yelling. Pounding followed the yelling, and I heard the front room door open.

"Girls! Settle down!" Alric was yelling, but his tone was more faery caused annoyance than fear or concern.

"We save!" Garbage's yell was the clearest. The rest of the faeries were still whooping but there were other non-faery voices as well. They weren't yelling.

"Lorcan, what is the meaning of this?" At first, I thought it was Flarinen, but it sounded older, and I knew Flarinen would never speak to Lorcan that way. Maybe a relative of his from higher up the food chain.

"I do apologize, Chancellor Sealia; they are excitable things, and they often act without thinking." Lorcan might have said he was sorry, but his face didn't indicate it.

"They do most things without thinking." Alric's voice was low, but I clearly heard him so most likely he was right by my door.

"Yes, yes, lots of excitement. Nothing to see here. Take your lovely guards and go about your day." Lorcan sounded like he was pushing people toward the door.

"See that they behave next time." The chancellor was the only one who spoke, but I'd guess about four or five people had come in with the faeries.

After some more low-level muttering I couldn't hear, the door in the front room shut. And the pounding of tiny fists on the door I was hiding behind started.

"Taryn, you may wish to come out; that door was designed to hold against explosions, not faery invasions." Padraig sounded like he was trying to be serious but was laughing.

I thought about ignoring Padraig and the faeries, but I couldn't stay here forever. The faeries were getting more insistent in their pounding too.

I cracked open the door and a flood of faeries hit me. They also pushed the door farther and Alric opened it the rest of the way.

"We save!" Leaf flew to me and gave me a big kiss on my forehead. Then I noticed that not only did all of them have their war sticks out, but they were in their war feathers. Well, most of them. Crusty must have misplaced hers as she was still wearing her overalls, but had a few random, and fresh-looking feathers tucked on her. There were probably a few annoyed birds outside the palace, was my guess.

"Girls, settle down, now what are you saving me from?"

"Don't know."

"But we save!"

"You flew in here, fully geared up, but you don't know

why?" Maybe their little tree adventure had addled their brains more than before.

"You in trouble." Garbage had been chatting with her troop, but she flew over to me. "We make it stop."

Crusty spun in a circle. "It stop!"

I glanced over to my friends, but they all looked about as confused as I was. Then I saw the dagger. And I have no idea how it did it without eyes or facial features, but it saw me. And freed itself from Lorcan's grasp, flying right for me as if someone had thrown it.

I ducked but couldn't do much more than that this time.

Garbage, Crusty, and Leaf all flew up between me and the blade.

"You no!" Garbage yelled as she held out her war stick. The other two did the same, and soon we were surrounded by angry faeries yelling at a dagger.

That hovered in midair.

"Girls, can you tell the dagger to drop to the ground, please?" Lorcan was slowly moving closer. The rest of my friends were holding back but all appeared to be ready to cast nasty spells if needed.

Garbage nodded to Lorcan, flew to the dagger, and smacked the blade near the point. "You been bad. Sit." She sounded like she was talking to one of her war cats during training.

Luckily for us, the blade responded better than the cats usually did and immediately dropped to the carpet.

"We save!" Garbage shouted again and all the faeries whooped and raised their sticks.

"Garbage? How do you talk to that dagger?" I wanted to ask more questions about the now still dagger, but I knew I'd never get solid answers from her.

"It alive. Hears. Sees. Like us." She sounded like I'd asked her how she spoke to the other faeries.

"But you don't talk to my sword? Or any other weapons?"

"Sword snotty, no talk. Other weapons not alive." She peered closer as if gauging my sanity. "You think they are?"

I looked past her to my friends for help.

"So, this one is alive and speaks to you, but the others are not alive?" Lorcan came forward first and held out his own dagger.

"That not alive. Metal dead." Leaf was closest and flew to Lorcan.

"But that metal is alive?" Alric came forward with the other two trailing. "Could you sense it before?"

Good question; they'd reacted to the pin back, and not favorably, but they hadn't indicated that it was alive.

"Could tell bad," Leaf said.

"Not sure what bad," Garbage added.

"Is pretty." Crusty drifted down to the dagger and was petting it.

"Yes, it's pretty. But it tried to kill me."

Crusty flew up to me. "Is no! He says need you."

Again, looking to my friends for help brought nothing but the same confusion that was probably on my face.

"Needs her how?" Lorcan was still the closest and he exuded calm. I was still in the freaked-out-and-might-still-run-for-the-door stage.

Crusty shrugged and flew back down to the dagger. Garbage and Leaf followed, but the rest of the pack stayed in the air. Crusty might trust it but the rest of the faeries weren't sure.

"How is you?" Then she tilted her head to something only she could hear. Rather she, Garbage, and Leaf. Both had the same reaction as she did.

Garbage flew up to Lorcan. "Dagger say meant help her. Says not bad."

"Do you think it's bad?" Lorcan was putting a lot of faith in those faeries.

"Is not meaning." Garbage flew over to me. "You pick up."

"I don't know if that's a great idea, sweetie." The dagger hadn't moved since they told it to drop, but it was made from some pieces that had set a spell into my skin. Who knew what touching all of them together and transformed might do?

Padraig had gone over to one of the books and was furiously flipping pages. "Hold on, I found it." He looked at the dagger, then back at the book. "I think I did. One of the Robukian sets, one like this one, but with a larger ring, and a full necklace instead of the brooch, reportedly could be locked into form. A permanent lock. The drawing is close to that dagger, but not exactly."

"And this helps how? Can it spell me like the pieces could?" It was great he found a reference, and I think I liked the locked idea, no more changing around things. But there were more important issues.

"No. That was part of the original spells on the individual pieces. This is a different thing entirely." He shrugged. "I'd say pick it up."

"I felt nothing from it when I was holding it. Until it took off after you, anyway." Lorcan had been squatting down and looking at the dagger.

"We bring." Crusty and the rest of the faeries all flew down to the dagger and lifted it up.

Alric and Siabiane moved next to me, both appearing to have spells at the ready.

I took a deep breath and held out my hands.

The faeries dropped the dagger into my hands.

Nothing happened.

Then I started laughing as tingling sensations shot through my hands and up my arms. "Stop it!"

"Is it hurting you?" Alric was ready to rip the dagger out of my hands.

"No, it's tickling!" The dagger stopped and stayed still. "Thank you." I thought I felt a rumble from it but wasn't sure it wasn't a remnant from the tickling.

My original three faeries all flew up to the blade and patted it. "Good."

"Okay, so do we know why the jewelry turned into a dagger is now my friend? Or how it turned into a dagger?"

Padraig was still looking through the book and Siabiane joined him.

"Go south. Faeries say bad. This help."

Alric held out his hand for Garbage to land on. "The faeries you sent with Qianru said it's bad in the south?" At no point during the faeries' harassment of Alric and me in our retreat had they mentioned the other faeries.

"Yes. Bad. Need us. She need that."

"Glad it here." Crusty had gone back to petting the dagger.

I felt silly holding it. "Does anyone have a sheath for a dagger that I can borrow? I don't know that I want it to be out and about. Whether we go south or not, it looks like this thing is here to stay."

"Him." Crusty patted the blade. "Is him."

"Fine, can I find a sheath for him?" I looked down to Crusty. Names were dicey with faeries, but she seemed extremely attached to the dagger. "Does he have a name?"

Crusty's face grew serious as she leaned into the dagger, then pulled back to look at me, still with a serious expression. "Is no. You name. Later."

"Name come in battle!" Garbage yelled as she buzzed around the room. "We go south now?"

South did seem to be where a lot of the problems were coming from, but I still wasn't convinced going there was the best option.

"Can you have the faeries that were with Qianru come up here? We'd like to talk to them if we could." Lorcan turned away from the faeries and scowled at the door that led to the rest of the palace. "We may want to move our operation to your cottage, Siabiane. Chancellor Sealia is an annoying functionary, but he can rally the others to poke and see what the faeries were doing. I want to keep most of this unknown at the moment." He glanced to me.

"You think this is happening because of what I am?" That wasn't a good thought, probably true considering the way my life went, but still not a happy thought.

"I'm not sure. We can't be certain that all these elements were working together. I do think that Grimarian troll does appear to be behind the spells on you, and the fact that Siabiane felt a time ripple means she knows what you are. Or at the least, that you came from a distant time. We've no idea what triggered the Robukian changing into the dagger. Lastly, the Domniall changeling was after you, but he was set on your path before the final battle."

"Either way, we don't need Flarinen's great uncle suspecting something." Alric moved back closer to me. He also kept an eye on the dagger in my hand.

"Ha! I knew that voice reminded me of Flarinen. Yes, if it means staying away from people like him, can we please relocate?" Everything that was happening was already too much to deal with. I didn't need to be questioned by any relative of Flarinen's.

Siabiane nodded. "I do have a large workshop in the back of the cottage; we can use it as a laboratory. Garbage? Can you call the other faeries? Get them to come up here from Beccia?"

"All?" There was an unhealthy gleam in those tiny faery eyes.

I stepped in front of Siabiane to make sure I was closest to Garbage. "Only the ones who left with Qianru, the bird lady. Leave the rest where they are, including the ones watching Grillion." I could imagine every faery, wild or not, invading Siabiane's cottage. Not to mention, Grillion most likely still needed to be watched, and we had no idea when we'd be heading back to Beccia.

Garbage tried to stare me down, then sighed. "Fine. Only bird lady faeries. Tell come to nice lady house."

Siabiane smiled at her moniker. "I want all of you to fly out calmly as we leave. We need to be quiet and make sure no one sees you."

"Like this?" Crusty held her breath and started flashing.

If the faeries focused and held their breath, they could flash like mini colored glows. I had no idea what the purpose of it was, but the faeries liked that they could do it again.

"That's great, Crusty, sweetie, but you are noticeable like that."

"Or maybe that would work." Alric darted into Lorcan's lab and came out with a large piece of loosely woven black cloth. "Toss this over them, hang onto the corners tied together, and it's just another one of Loran and Padraig's experiments being taken to Siabiane's for a tune up." He looked to the others. "The chancellor was extremely upset. I don't think flying the faeries out will work."

"That is actually quite brilliant." Padraig came over and held up part of the fabric. The girls darted underneath, and a few started glowing. It did look like a weird floating experiment.

Lorcan laughed and shook his head. "And no one will doubt that it's one of our dangerous creations. They'll probably be extremely happy that we're taking it elsewhere."

They got all the faeries under the fabric, after telling the faeries they needed to keep glowing until we told them to stop. The glowing bit wasn't as important as them not flying around yelling was.

Alric held the "experiment" and Lorcan and Padraig gathered the books they'd brought out, plus a few more. Lorcan came out with a folded piece of black leather.

"This is the only thing I have that might work for your dagger friend." He unwrapped it as he handed it to me: a small sheath—well, smaller than my sword's but a bit larger than the dagger.

I held it up to the dagger. "Nothing personal, but it

might be better for all if you traveled this way." I felt a little odd speaking to a piece of metal, but the faeries did it. I felt a slight tingle in the hand that held the dagger, which I took as acceptance, then put the blade in the sheath. It didn't fly back out, so I buckled the belt around my waist. "I guess he likes it, thank you."

"You and he are most welcome." Lorcan went out the door and the rest of us followed.

Alric really did look like he was escorting an odd flying experiment. Occasionally, a color light would flash off, then pop back on again. The faeries could hold their breath for hours if need be, but I think sometimes they forgot.

We were starting across the great foyer when a voice called out. "Alric? Could I have a word?"

The voice was female and came from a bit behind us. I froze as I thought it was his grandmother. But a quick glance told me it wasn't. A younger elf woman was striding toward us. She wore an elaborate outfit of the royal colors, but it still looked almost uniform-like.

"Well met, Lashia." Alric took the woman's extended hand after handing over the faery experiment to me.

"Your grandmother really does need to speak to you." Lashia nodded and smiled to everyone, although she looked confused when she got to me. She recovered quickly and flashed a smile. A very political one.

"I'm right in the middle of something important. Tell her I promise that I won't leave town without seeing her." He went to take the flying faery bag from me, but she stopped him.

"I hate to insist. But either you come with me, or I go with you. I'm sorry, she demands it."

Alric gave a long sigh, then turned to the rest of us. "Get started, I'll meet you as soon as I can." He started walking but Lashia stopped him.

"And one other thing." She looked to me and this time the smile was real, small, but real. "I assume you are Taryn?

Since I know the others. Lady Delphina would like you to join us. Insists, actually."

I looked to Lorcan and the others, but each gave a shrug and a slight nod. The woman I really didn't want to meet was calling for a private audience. I'd almost rather meet that Grimarian troll again. I handed the flying faery bag to Padraig and tried not to look like I was being dragged to the gallows.

Alric stepped back and took my hand almost fiercely. It could be love or it could be a fear that I would bolt. Probably a combination of the two.

Satisfied that she'd captured both of us and completed her sworn duty, Lashia turned and marched to a far more delicate stairwell. It was the one I'd seen Alric's grandmother come down a year ago. Now, granted, she had been dealing with determining if her grandson was a killer and a spy, but she'd seemed tough to me.

"It will be all right, I promise. She probably wants to check in. She might have heard about my dying in the battle after all."

I forced a smile as the stairs led to a small walkway and a pair of ornate doors. I also kept reminding myself that the king and queen liked me and that I'd helped save this enclave a year ago.

Delphina was even more impressive when relaxed and in her domain. She was standing near a window larger than the entire wall in my front room that looked out over the city. She turned as we came in. As she completed her turn she smiled, but I caught an odd look on her face as she turned. I was closer to that side of her, so I doubted that Alric saw it.

She came forward with both hands extended. Alric dropped my hand and hugged his grandmother. There was real happiness on her face, but an odd sorrow also. "I heard that you had some trouble in the battle. Padraig was circumspect, but I gather we almost lost you."

"To be blunt, I died." Alric took a deep breath. "That geas the old woman put on me, the family one, almost destroyed me. I chose to fight Nivinal to the death, both of ours, as it turned out. Taryn and the last remaining tree goddess saved me." He stepped back to include me, but his grandmother didn't move forward.

"I have heard tales, dark ones. That it was not a goddess who brought you back, but some dark arts from your lover." The look she gave me was neutral, but the words were not.

I was seriously weighing what my chances were if I bolted for the door. Being afraid of his grandmother was one thing. Having her think I was some sort of necromancer? That was terrifying.

"What? Grandmother, it was a tree goddess along with Taryn's powers that saved me. Who is spreading lies?" Since his grandmother wouldn't step forward to me, he stepped further back and took my hand. "Do you doubt what I say?"

"You were dead. It would be hard for you to know who saved you." Her voice was soft. "Yes, I knew you died before I heard any tales. I felt your heart stop." She narrowed her eyes. "Then it started again. I would like to know how that was done without death magic." She was testing us, but the longer we stood there the less aggressive she seemed.

I kept holding Alric's hand but took a half step forward. "I agree, Alric was dead, so he didn't know what happened. *But I was there*. He died. Trapped in a spell bubble of his own making so that geas didn't make him try to kill me. He died fighting against Nivinal. I tried to save him but couldn't. I killed Nivinal and destroyed the relics, but I couldn't save him." I was crying now but it was half from sorrow and half from guilt. "Our friend Amara is now a normal dryad, but she was a goddess. The last tree goddess, and I'm sure if you spoke to her you'd believe her. She gave up all her powers, her immortality, to save Alric.

There was no death magic, and you insult what was given by believing there was." I snapped my mouth shut. I hadn't meant to say all of that, but it felt good that I did.

Delphina tilted her head and slowly walked around Alric and me, pausing directly in front of me. "You are not human." It wasn't a question.

"No." I lifted my chin as she was taller than me. "I am human in one form. My people are known as the Ancients." I caught a glint in her eye. "You already knew that."

"I had been told that by people of high station here in the city. I had also been told that your friends were practicing the dark arts by persons of low station. One should never be complacent about who one listens to. Truth can sometimes come from strange places."

"Which do you believe?" Alric's voice was low and he was subtly trying to move me behind him.

"You would protect her, even from me." Delphina watched us both and slowly smiled. "Good. Of course, I believe Lorcan, Padraig, and Siabiane. Those three would never have let dark powers run anywhere near them. But it is concerning that a few knights did come back with rumors." She walked into the sitting area and motioned for us to sit. "Do come in and be comfortable. Had someone come see me when he first arrived here, I wouldn't have had to go dramatic on you both."

"I had a rough arrival, and yes, Taryn saved me again." He was laughing but he was also making sure we were close to each other as we sat. "Domniall has a changeling or had."

Delphina hadn't heard about that yet. If she was friends with the others, then it was a matter of time before she heard. But we shared what we knew.

She shook her head as we finished our tale and flexed her right hand. Magic clearly ran strong in their family and she wanted to blow someone up. "I am sorry that I didn't get a chance to interrogate the changeling myself. But we do have to believe that the real Domniall was involved in this. It smacks of his trickery." She leaned forward. "I am also sorry that I made you defend yourself, my dear. I had to be certain, not only for my grandson, but for our kingdom. The king and queen would love to meet you again."

"How many people know what I am?" I had been ready to change right here in the palace if needed to get Alric and myself out, but since that wasn't needed, the idea of too many people knowing what I was made me ill.

"Not many, your secret is safe. Your people aren't dead?"

"Just missing in time." I really wasn't up to talking about that right now.

Delphina was wise enough to see how uncomfortable I was and nodded with a warm smile. "That will be for another day. Will you join me in some tea?"

The rest of the visit went smoothly. Delphina seemed happy about Alric and me and no longer believed I was some deranged necromancer. That was a plus.

After a bit of chatting, Alric got to his feet. "I am sorry that I didn't come here once I'd recovered, but things have been happening in the past two days. I promise to come see you before we leave."

Delphina and I got to our feet as well. "Where will you be going after leaving the city?"

"I think I'd like to settle down in Beccia for a bit, see what it's like not to be a thief or agent for the crown." He tugged on my fingers.

"That would be nice, and you have earned it." She smiled to me. "I believe both of you have. And this tree goddess might have saved him, but I know you did as well. Thank you." She stepped forward and kissed me on the cheek.

We turned to go.

"Oh, I almost forgot. This letter was left for you, both of you." She handed Alric an extremely old envelope, complete with a dried wax seal. Her look was neutral again. I might not know her well, but those neutral looks were disturbing.

"From who?" Alric looked at it but didn't open it. I didn't blame him after the trouble that had already been caused by a letter.

"The Lady Nuthaina, she helped create this enclave. She also died before you were born." Delphina gave both of us a questioning look. "Yet, somehow, in her belongings her great-great-granddaughter found that. Since your given birth name was on it, she brought it to me."

I looked at the front. Flowing script spelled out Lord Alricianel Lis Treann and Lady Taryn St. Giles. I knew I'd never told her my full name.

Alric took a deep breath. "That geas I mentioned, she put it on me." He still wasn't opening the letter, and I still couldn't blame him.

Delphina glanced at both of us when he didn't continue. "And how did she do that? It would explain why that was so strong, though, if it had picked up a thousand years of existing."

Clearly, Lorcan and Siabiane had told her some of our adventures but not all. While neither of them had joined us on that trip, they had met us in the past. They'd spelled themselves to forget until much later.

"We got spelled into the past. From what I could tell, we were flung back days before the Breaking began."

Her eyes widened. "And no one felt it pertinent to tell me? Do the royals know?"

"Not unless Siabiane told them." He ran his fingers through his hair. "I know how dangerous time travel is, and trust me, neither of us did it deliberately. It was a trap set by Nivinal. Nasif and Dueble got us back."

"That would explain Nasif and Dueble wandering around the world. They aren't aging, are they? Side effect of a time spell." She waved her hands at us. "You two will age normally, but it sounds like Nasif and Dueble got side spelled when the original spell diverted in the casting. This gives me much to think about."

"I figured the fewer people who knew about it, the better."

She nodded. "And from the way both of you are looking at that letter in terror, I won't make you open it here. Please share anything of importance to the kingdom if you would. Nuthaina was an odd old woman, but while some of her sightings were horribly wrong, others were terrifyingly correct."

Alric nodded and we left her room. He tucked the letter into his shirt. "She was right. I don't think either of us wants to read it here."

"Good point. If we were back in Beccia, I'd suggest a rousing drinking fest at the Shimmering Dewdrop. Sorry, but your fancy pubs just don't do the same for me."

"We'll see what we can find after we check on the others." Alric led us through a few back streets and quickly brought us to Siabiane's cottage.

"Do you think we're being followed?" I knew him well enough to know those streets were chosen on purpose.

"No." He glanced at me. "Possibly. I don't like that there were people spreading rumors, and that they got to her. I don't want people watching us and we should warn the others."

I nodded and we went inside.

There was no sign of anyone inside, and that reminded me that I hadn't seen Siabiane's brownies either. I automatically tried to pull in a spell but stopped when I felt a stab in my head.

Alric motioned toward the back of the cottage but stayed quiet as well.

There were no noises, which could mean they were all really focused or that something bad was happening.

CHAPTER TWENTY

M Y SWORD HADN'T POPPED UP and I wasn't sure calling it right now would be a good idea, so I grabbed my new dagger friend. Luckily, he refrained from tickling me this time.

Alric led the way toward the back to a pair of closed doors. He nodded for me to take one side and he took the other. He didn't have his sword out either, but he was also still able to use magic.

We nudged open the doors to find no one there.

No faeries, no brownies, none of our friends. We looked around the room, but there were no signs that they had been here.

I opened my mouth, but Alric shook his head and led us through the entire house in silence. Then back out into the garden. Then he spoke.

"I don't think they made it here."

"But the brownies are missing too, and they weren't with them. And who could steal three powerful magic users in the middle of the day, in the middle of town?"

Alric scowled at the garden a bit more, then went back up to the door. He froze with his hand above the door handle. "You might be right. I didn't notice when we came up but look at this." He held his hand farther away from the door and small cracks appeared in the wood.

I leaned forward and my dagger started sparking, sending

green arcs toward the door. I didn't scream like I wanted to, but I did drop it and jump back. Little arcs of green light kept shooting from the dagger and hitting the door, almost like it was tasting it.

Then the door crumbled apart.

"Bad dagger! You broke her door." I picked him back up cautiously. The dagger didn't speak, obviously, but it sent a little charge up my arm.

Alric bent down to the door shreds and shook his head. "Your dagger didn't do it, he only removed magic that was holding it together." He went back to the garden path and started sifting through the dirt. "Someone grabbed the brownies over here. And there are recent footsteps to indicate our friends went inside."

I followed behind him and kept my dagger low. He was in tracking form now, more so than when we first came in. There wasn't a lot of room in the cottage, but when his sword appeared, so did mine.

Whatever he was tracking had gone into the work room. The right door collapsed as well once Alric used magic on it and my dagger got close. But nothing was disturbed or broken. Of course, not having been in this room before today there was no way to know if anything besides our friends were missing.

Alric was focusing on one area so I stayed out of his way.

Yelling came from outside, and I went to the front room with both my sword and dagger held up. But it was soon obvious that the yelling was echoed by laughing and familiar voices. The flock of faeries came flying into the house through the shattered door. I stepped into the room to greet them and get them to stay out of the back area until Alric was finished.

"Girls!" I waved them to settle down, not easy with a weapon in each hand. My sword vanished, which I hoped was a good thing. I put the dagger back in its sheath. "Settle down, please. Something has happened."

Crusty was buzzing around near the front door. "Is gone." She nodded sagely.

"Yes, sweetie. Someone bashed the door down. Did any of you come back here with Lorcan and the others?"

Crusty's comment had now made the rest of the faeries swarm the doorframe, all trying to see where the door went.

"Garbage? When did you leave the nice lady?" I figured focusing on one faery and one person they had been with might be easier.

Garbage had been outside looking at the door frame from the porch but flew through her people to get to me.

"We leave big stuffy, then they let us go." She shrugged.

Big stuffy? "Do you mean the palace?" When she nodded, rather half-heartedly because she wanted to make sure no one else found anything interesting about the missing door while she was away, I continued. "Were they coming here?" That was a hard one.

Garbage focused on me, the empty room, and then glanced back to the door. "They taken!" Her words and tone were now different, and the rest of the faeries came and surrounded us. "Who took?"

"I don't know. That's what Alric and I are trying to figure out."

Before I could stop them, the faeries flew into the work room. Judging by the annoyance in Alric's voice, they were being their usual helpful selves. I ran to help.

The faeries were flying everywhere, looking into boxes, under papers, everywhere that our friends couldn't be.

"Girls!" I yelled. "Settle down, you're making things worse." It was always iffy about them listening to me, but they did this time. All of them stopped what they were doing and settled on a large worktable. "Thank you."

Alric nodded. "They didn't mess anything up because there are no clues here. Besides the fact that someone blew apart those two doors, along with the front one, then spelled them back in place, there's nothing to even show something is wrong."

"They went here." Leaf got off the table and flew to the far wall. She put her hand on the wall and nodded. "All go here." The rest of the faeries took that as a sign, and they all flew over as well.

"They went through the wall?" I shared a confused look with Alric. But all of the faeries were touching it and some closed their eyes.

"Is feel." Garbage didn't leave her spot on the wall but motioned for us to come over.

I was closer so I got there first and put my hand on the wall before common sense, or Alric, could stop me. It was extremely warm. I pulled back. "Is it on fire?" I figured we would have noticed if the garden in the back had been burning, but the wall was quite warm.

"No. Doorway." Crusty patted it. "They go."

Alric put his hand on the wall and tilted his head. "How do you know it's a doorway?"

"Feel. They go through. So did bads." Crusty frowned and patted the wall.

Garbage had her war stick out. "We save. Open door." She was about a foot from the wall, looking like she was waiting to fly through it.

"We can't. It's a wall." I knew whatever doorway had been there certainly wasn't now and most likely involved a hell of a lot of magic to open.

"I'm not even sure what spell was used." Alric kept tapping the wall at different locations.

"Someone, or ones, broke the front door down, then one door to this room, grabbed our friends and dragged them through a magic portal? Our heavy magic-using friends?" Yeah, my voice went up at the end. I had no idea who could have done that. Those three were the strongest magic users I knew.

"That's what it looks like. Damn it, there isn't enough

spell residue to get a feel for what spells were used. I'd say they managed to immobilize our friends, probably before they even broke the front door down." He dropped lower, almost to the floor. "It's a lot hotter here."

"Is where he stuck." Garbage drifted down to the ground and marched along the wall. "Is yes, he stuck."

"Who is stuck? And where? In the wall? Wherever the doorway went?" The wall looked the same down there as it did all over—solid.

"In between. Tangle Morning Glory come here, you have feels?" She waved down one of her faeries. I'd seen this one from a distance, a rich lapis blue, lighter delicate wings, with pale yellow hair sticking out from under her flower hat. She had an almost metallic glow to her.

The faery flew down and sat cross-legged on the floor, then put both hands on the wall. She closed her eyes and nodded after a few silent moments. "Is yes. Here. Stuck. No there. No here." Her grin reminded me of Crusty's. "I sees things."

Garbage turned back to me. "Need get out. Break bad magics." Then she flew back up to the others.

"That's great, sweetie, but how?" All the faeries were now looking at me.

Alric stood up and cast a spell where Tangle had been. The wall seemed to waver a bit, or it could be just me focusing too hard on it. He tried again, and then raised his hands.

"Is no. Use friend." Crusty flew over and tapped the hilt of the dagger.

"Use him how?" The answer came as I asked it. Somehow the dagger had broken down both spells cast to reassemble the doors. Maybe he would work here too. "Never mind, let me try."

I bent down to the lower part of the wall and held the dagger next to it.

Nothing.

"Um, it's not working?"

"Need juice." Leaf flew up to Alric and pushed him down toward me. "You. Then you." She pointed to him first, so he shrugged and cast the spell again.

I wasn't sure if this was what the faeries expected, but the moment he sent his spell, the dagger turned green and crackling and flung itself into the wall. Which made the entire wall start popping with green lightning that struck out at everyone.

I was flung across the room, and many of the faeries were as well. Alric hung onto the table but got a lot of wall flung at him for his troubles.

The wall didn't look so good. It was still there but all the inside plaster was gone, and I thought I could see through to the garden in a few places.

"There's a person there." I didn't scream, but there was a dangerously ghostly looking form appearing down at the bottom. It looked almost like smoke, then started to solidify.

"Padraig!" Alric was closer and he recognized the prone shape before I did. He grabbed his friend and snapped a spell bubble over both as the wall collapsed on top of them.

I ran over and started pulling away rubble. Hopefully Alric's bubble was holding; there was so much wall collapsed that I couldn't even see them. "Girls! Help me get to them!"

It had only been Padraig, not Lorcan, or Siabiane, but we'd get the others back once we found out what happened.

The faeries were small, but strong and determined. They worked to pull aside the pieces and eventually I saw the dusty spell bubble. It dropped a moment later.

"Thank you, I almost couldn't hold it." Alric was hunched over an unconscious Padraig and pulled him free of the rubble.

"We might need to hide this somehow." I waved to

the missing wall. The cottage seemed structurally sound, but there was no way an entire missing wall wouldn't go unnoticed for long. Luckily, it was a back wall and Siabiane had high walls around her back garden. But still, leaving it open with everything that was going on didn't seem like a great idea.

Alric looked up and focused, but nothing happened. He even muttered a few spell words and nothing. It took three tries to form a passable glamour of a wall where there was none.

He shook his hands and scowled at the glamour. "That bubble took way more out of me than it should have. Something was draining my magic the moment the wall exploded."

Padraig stirred but didn't open his eyes. "Spell attack. Draining." Then he passed out again.

"Damn it, there's some sort of spell draining magic in here?" Alric looked around. "I don't see any focus, though." He ran his hand through his hair. "It could be hidden as anything, but they are usually large, especially one this strong. Never mind, first we must get Padraig to Ceithera. Get your things together. I don't think we want to be staying here."

I gathered my things and Alric's pack and put them by the empty doorframe. That was another spell he was going to have to cast. Maybe if he stood on the porch to cast it, the drain would be less. I'd never heard of a focus item that could drain magic without the spell caster present. But I'd noticed that Alric and the others had tried to keep some of the more freakish magic things out of my training. Since I'd been kicking around with magic users for two years and never heard of it, it had to be uncommon. And I'd get a full reporting of what they were after we got Padraig looked at.

Alric half-dragged, half-carried, Padraig out of the work-room and put him on the sofa. "It's still too light for us to move him without a lot of unwelcome notice. I'm going to need you to go to the healing house and bring back help."

"Wouldn't they be more likely to listen to you? I can stay here." Even as I spoke, I saw the answer on his face.

"My magic is having some problems, but yours is gone for now. If our attackers come back, I can defend things better."

"Against someone who took out the three of them? This isn't safe for anyone." I tried to imagine dragging an unconscious Padraig through the nice, peaceful elven streets. That wasn't going to fly either.

"Hold on for a moment." I held up my hands and motioned to the faeries. "Girls? Come with me."

If Siabiane had a garden, she probably had a wheelbarrow or something of the sort. "Girls, help me find a cart. But only on Siabiane's land, okay?"

I was still on the side of the cottage when Gracie Twinkleshine, a gorgeous fuchsia faery, flew up. "This way!" She zipped away, then back two times before I got to the other side of the cottage. A small shed sat there. There was a lock on it, but Crusty picked it almost without thinking. That was a scary trait I didn't know she'd picked up.

Inside was an old fashioned and extremely dusty hand cart. It was larger than a wheelbarrow and fancier with railings on three sides. "Good find, girls." It had been there awhile, judging by the webs on it, but it moved well once I got it going. The faeries took one handle, I took the other, and we pulled it around to the front.

Alric was standing right inside the open door.

"Your magic worked?" The door looked solid to me, but I knew if my magic were working, it would sense a spell.

"Yes, but still not well." He nodded to the cart. "That will get us there. I do think we'll cover him up, though. There would still be too much to explain hauling him back in broad daylight." He went inside and came back with Padraig in the half carry, half drag, hold. Elves were strong, but Padraig was taller than him. Not to mention magic drains can physically weaken someone. I didn't think Padraig would mind the short part he was half dragged, though.

The faeries helped us get him into the cart, then Alric brought back a bunch of blankets and our packs and tucked them in around and over Padraig. Once everything was secured, we started pulling the wagon. The faeries kept flying around us, attracting attention.

"Girls, could you all sit on Padraig and protect him for us?"

"We do!" Garbage yelled and they all swarmed to sit in the cart. They were still noticeable, but less so when not flying around.

The healing house was farther than I recalled, but it could be that Padraig was heavier than expected.

Eventually we walked up to the building. Alric let his end of the cart drop. "I'll get help." He jogged up the stairs but still seemed slower than usual. He might not like it, but I was going to ask Ceithera to look him over after she fixed Padraig.

The girls were staying in the cart but getting restless when Alric and Ceithera came down the stairs. Two larger elves came down behind them with a stretcher.

"Hello, Taryn." Ceithera was all business as she went to the back of the cart. The faeries rose at her approach but stayed nearby. "He doesn't look good." She turned to the other two elves. "Take him into the lower room, but keep the lights dim." They gently moved Padraig to the stretcher and then carried him up the stairs. Then she turned back to us. "Are both of you okay?" She scowled at Alric. "You are not. Let go of your side."

I hadn't noticed since I'd been watching them move Padraig, but Alric was now holding his side.

He winced and moved his hand. A patch of blood was

spreading on his shirt. "Something got me when I dropped my spell bubble. Yes, I'll explain what happened once we are inside."

Ceithera didn't look happy, but she nodded to another orderly. "Take their belongings inside, if you would, and move this cart into the stables. Thank you." She motioned to the stairs. "After you."

Once inside she went to the same room Alric had been in, then stopped and pointed to another room next to it. "I'll have my second patient wait here please. I'm going to check the lighting and temperature in Padraig's room. Then you can both explain what happened." She looked up as the faeries drifted in. Unlike their prior visit they weren't buzzing around.

"We wait?" Leaf asked Ceithera. "Is broken."

"As long as you wait quietly. Thank you for helping."

The faeries all smiled and settled down along the benches inside the foyer. Now that was something I'd never thought to see. I shook my head and followed Alric into the second room.

"You might as well show me; you'll have to take it off when she gets here anyway. Why didn't you tell me?"

Alric frowned but pulled out the note his grandmother had given us, and handed it to me. "Hang onto this, it could be important." Then he lifted his shirt. There was a gash under his ribs, but the bleeding was slow, so hopefully it wasn't deep. "I didn't think it was important given what happened to Padraig. But I think I should lie down now." His face had gotten paler as we stood there, so I led him to the cot. He went down without a fight.

His body felt hotter than it should have, and his eyes were closing. "I need you to stay awake." I shook him a little. Passing out wouldn't help. I needed him to tell Ceithera what was going on.

His eyes fluttered and I could tell he was fighting to stay awake. I was about to yell for help—even if Ceithera was with Padraig there had to be more healers here—when Ceithera came in.

"This isn't good." She stuck her head out of the door and called to an orderly to bring some things.

Alric passed out.

She tore off his shirt and ugly black lines radiated from the wound. Where it hadn't looked too bad a few moments before, it now looked nasty and infected.

"It didn't look like that before."

"It's a magic infection. Some magical contaminant got into him. I'm going to bring his fever down, but I need you to tell me exactly what happened."

While she and her assistant worked, I told her about the doors, the missing people, the weird wall, and the faeries finding Padraig in the wall.

"And your dagger did that? Is that normal for it?"

"Well, there was other magic involved and it's sort of a new dagger." I was wary of how much to tell her, but I had to trust someone, and Padraig and Alric trusted her. I told her a brief summary of the Robukian and what they became.

Neither of them stepped back from Alric. His wound looked less ugly and he seemed to be breathing easier.

Ceithera leaned forward. "Can I see the dagger?"

I held it up, but she didn't touch it. "And it shoots green static?"

"Sometimes? I really am afraid we don't know much about it. After all, it's been in existence for only a few hours. That was what we were going to study." I started swearing. "Whoever took Siabiane and Lorcan also took those books." I added an explanation of the types of books Lorcan had on him when he vanished.

"Any books that Lorcan has are probably dangerous in the wrong hands, possibly extremely so." Ceithera glanced at the dagger once more and then shrugged. "I'm afraid arcane relics and totems and the books that dealt with them were never my field of study. But I think Alric should be fine with a bit of rest. He over-taxed his magic and most likely part of the spell from that portal got into his wound. I told him not to overuse his magic for a reason." She shook her head at him, and then led the way into a third room. This was set back from the sick rooms and looked more like her study.

"Please sit. I'll have some refreshments sent to the faeries and bring something in for you." She called in one of the staff, then sent them out with instructions.

"How is Padraig?"

She met my eyes and then shook her head. "Honestly, not good. It's a magical issue and not one I'm familiar with. In any other situation I would call for Lorcan, Siabiane, or Padraig. They are our foremost experts on magic issues."

"Could someone have been after me and they got them instead?" That thought had hit me the moment we realized strong magic had been used. I briefly summed up the prior night's attack.

She scowled but dropped it when the assistant came in and brought in tea and snacks. I heard the faeries giggling softly out in the foyer. Once the door shut again, her frown came back. "Now that is something I am familiar with, Grimarian trolls. I'd venture to say they went after three of the people most likely to be able to protect you. And the biggest threat to them."

"Do you think it's an attack against the enclave?" I knew the troll who had been in my room last night was trying to take me out, but those three were vital to the enclave itself. There could be more than one level of attack going on.

"It might be. There have been some odd illnesses as of late. Ones that seem to vanish on their own, but in each case, it has been a magic user and their magic has been diminished."

That brought another thought to mind. "Lorcan had

mentioned that one of the reasons the shield hadn't been rebuilt was because the magic level overall seemed to be weakened. He said it had been subtle over the thousand years your people have been here."

"That could be. There were changes that we didn't realize during the time here, and not many of us who were around at the start are still alive." She shook her head. "The more I think on it, the more the attack on him and the other two feels like it was aimed at them specifically for their abilities. Unfortunately, I need them to help me fix Padraig so he can figure out what happened to them."

A thought hit me. "Where did Mathilda go? After the battle, Alric and I took off, but does anyone know where she went?"

"That is a good idea. She's even more knowledgeable about the odd magic issues than the other three and might be able to help me with Padraig." She got up and started pacing. "She's hard to find when she doesn't want to be found and that's most of the time. I might have to put Padraig in a controlled coma again. I can't be sure how long it will take to find her."

"Or we can use the faeries." I got up and opened the door where the girls were still sitting politely, more or less, in the remains of their meal. "Girls?" I held open the door and they all flew into the room. "Can you find Mathilda?" I don't know if that simple command would have worked seventeen years ago when she first dumped the faeries on me and ran. But we'd been all working together for the past few months.

"Need her?" Garbage flittered up to my face.

"Yes, we need her to save Padraig."

"We gets!" They yelled in unison and flew for the closed door.

"Wait!" I stood in front of the door. "Please bring her back nicely, with her cottage if she's not too far away." I looked to Ceithera's desk. "Can you write a quick note to Mathilda? Easier than having them ask." I turned back to the faeries. "And no picking her up and carrying her, understood?" I'd been carried against my will by the faeries twice, and it was terrifying both times.

Ceithera handed me a sealed envelope.

I handed the envelope to Garbage. "Now take this to Mathilda, directly to her. No stopping." I hung onto the envelope until she nodded. "Guard it."

"We do!" the other faeries yelled, but Garbage nodded solemnly.

"Okay, good luck!" I opened the door and watched them zip past everyone in the foyer and out the main door.

"Are they always that well behaved?"

"No. And it's a bit worrying. But they should be able to find her quickly. Hopefully, she's not too far away."

Yelling in the foyer made both of us jump. Damn it, had the compliance of the faeries been a ruse? I was closer to the door still, so I flung it open and ran out with Ceithera right behind me.

The yelling wasn't directed at anything flying, but at two blurs at ground-level. They both zipped over to me and stopped. Welsy and Delsy doffed their caps and bowed to Ceithera.

"It is us. We don't mean harm."

"Please tell them so."

I turned to Ceithera. "These are Siabiane's…brownies." I almost said constructs, not a great idea with fifteen people watching us, including two armed knights.

Ceithera nodded to the knights and the rest to stand down. "Won't you please come into my office?" She held out her arm and both constructs marched inside.

Once we were in with the door shut, I faced them both. "How do we know you are Welsy and Delsy?" Those other brownies were hopefully on the run far from here, but they knew Welsy and Delsy. I had a hard time believing that Siabiane had been taken if her two constructs were still around.

"Can she know?" One of them stepped forward slowly and looked toward Ceithera.

"Yes." Hopefully Siabiane wouldn't mind, but we were in a tight spot, and she and Lorcan were in a worse one. This wasn't an issue a bunch of faeries and I could solve alone.

The brownie removed his cap and tapped his head. A nice metal sound was heard. The second one did the same to the same effect.

Ceithera took a step back behind her desk. "What are they?"

"We are constructs."

"Siabiane created us."

They both turned to me. "She is missing."

"We know. I thought they'd taken you two as well. Where were you?"

Both frowned.

"We were lured away. Thought the other brownies had come back and followed them way out into the woods right after you and the Alric person left." The first one spoke. Not being able to tell them apart was going to be annoying.

"Was it the brownies who came to the cottage before?" Alric had been sure they were still running north, but they might not have been as scared as we thought.

"No, they were nothing but wisps. Sent to mislead us," the second one said with an impressive scowl.

"I'm sorry, but I can't tell which of you is which. Can we do something to make you different?" I looked over to Ceithera's desk, but I wasn't sure if ink would work on them.

"Of course." The first one reached into his vest pocket and pulled out a pin. "I'm Welsy." It even said that on the pin. The second one pulled out his tag as well.

"You have name badges?" That was a bit odd. Handy in

this case, but odd.

"When Siabiane first made us, she couldn't tell us apart, so she gave us these." Welsy pinned his on his chest and Delsy did the same.

Ceithera and I looked at each other over their heads, then we shrugged.

"Okay, so something lured you both away, but what led you here?" I was glad they were here. The more information and people involved who knew what was going on the better. But it wasn't like Alric and I had left a note saying where we went.

"We followed your signs." Delsy this time and he smiled at their cleverness.

"Signs? We didn't leave signs."

"The cart you pulled."

"It has unique wheels."

Mystery solved. "Did you two notice anything unusual around Siabiane's cottage before you went to find the brownies?"

They both nodded. "No." And both spoke at the same time.

Ceithera came around her desk to get a closer look at them. "No, you didn't notice anything or yes?"

"No, we didn't notice anything after Taryn and Alric left to go to the palace and join the others." Welsy held up a pair of familiar bags. Tiny ones. One was black, the other silver. "But these we found in the work room when we came back, and everyone was gone."

"Lorcan had those." Welsy handed me the bags. "Where did you find them?" Not only had Alric and I looked all over, but so had the faeries. If anyone would have spotted two of their own bags, it should have been the girls.

"They were deep in the rubble. Possibly on the other side. But we searched all we could." Delsy sighed. "The other side is closed now."

"What other side?" Had there been a chance that Alric

and I could have saved Siabiane and Lorcan and we missed it? There had been nothing that any of us could sense after we got Padraig out.

"It's difficult to explain. But the takers left a way through. A trap. You didn't go for it, so it closed. You saved Padraig, yes?"

The people behind the attack had been expecting Alric and me to go through the wall of our own accord to find our friends. My guess was that the trap was already fading by the time we got there. I was grateful that Alric's grandmother kept us as long as she did. If whatever took them could overcome those three, grabbing Alric and me as well wouldn't have been a problem.

Ceithera nodded but looked worried. "They brought him here and I stabilized him, but he still hasn't woken up." She nodded to the bags. "Those are extremely tiny, but you seem happy to have them."

I didn't want to deal with the silver bag yet; it had held parts of the Robukian, but I had no idea what Lorcan had in there now. I took the black bag over to her desk, opened it up, and pulled out three books. I'd thought he only took two, but he could have had one in there already. "They're faery bags. Impossibly tiny, but they hold a lot. And these are the books I was afraid whoever grabbed Lorcan had gotten." I'd rather have Lorcan and Siabiane back instead of the books, but knowing how he felt about his collection, Lorcan might argue the point.

"That is fascinating. I really should listen to Lorcan more when he speaks of the faeries," Ceithera said. "What's in that one?"

I held up the silver bag but didn't open it. "I'm not sure. There should be another black bag in there, but the faeries gave this one to me when there was something they were worried about. One of the Robukian pieces. I don't have a clue what he has in there now, and I'm not sure we want to check." I wanted a heavy magic user who understood these arcane things around when this bag was opened. Or when more searching was done in the other bag. I'd felt other things in there when I pulled out the books, but I wasn't sure digging was a good idea.

"Thank you for finding these, however you did it." I smiled at both. Never thought I'd be grateful for brownies, but this was the second time. Granted, these were fake brownies.

A soft knocking came at the door. I tucked the books back into their bag, secured the bags inside my vest, and then Ceithera opened the door.

A healer stood there. "I believe the second patient is stirring. I explained to him he still needed to rest. He is exceptionally stubborn." The tall elf man was calm, but clearly not happy with Alric's behavior.

"Thank you, Lwain. I will take care of him." Ceithera headed out the door with me, Welsy, and Delsy trailing behind. The healer Lwain raised an eyebrow at the brownies but didn't say a thing.

Alric was arguing with another healer when we came in. I was beginning to think that if we ever needed him to rest, drugging him was the best option. From the look on Ceithera's face, I wasn't the only one who thought it.

"I'm fine, really. We need to get out there and find the others." He wasn't pushing hard against the healer who kept pushing him back; it was more out of habit in my opinion.

Ceithera waved the healer off. "Thank you. Can you please relieve Saian with our other patient?" Her smile dropped when the healer left. "You are not fine. You always say you're fine when you are clearly not." The words were accented by taps on his chest. "Now stay down or I will medicate you and Taryn will help me."

Alric glanced around Ceithera to me and I shot him a scowl. Yes, I needed to discuss these issues with him, but I needed him to be able to stand up without collapsing.

"Fine. How long?" He flopped back and looked at the ceiling.

"At least until this time tomorrow. Then I will reevaluate. Now do you want updates on the situation or not?"

"Can I at least sit up for them?" His grin told me he was feeling better, but I trusted Ceithera's judgement on this.

"Yes." Ceithera nodded to a pair of chairs as she helped Alric rearrange his pillows.

I brought the chairs over and Welsy, and Delsy brought over a foot-stool for them to sit on.

Alric watched them in surprise. "They didn't get taken? Or is everyone back?"

"They weren't taken, and we were lucky that we weren't grabbed while we were in there looking for the others." I filled him in on what we'd discovered, with a few add-ins from Welsy and Delsy.

"That's good that you sent for Mathilda, something is wrong with my magic still." He lifted one hand, then turned it palm up. A small glow appeared before Ceithera could stop him but vanished a moment later. From the annoyance on his face, vanishing hadn't been part of what he was trying to do.

"That's not good." Ceithera got to her feet and left the room.

"That's how it started with me." It was scary enough that I couldn't access my magic, but if Alric couldn't? And what if it spread across the enclave?

"Hopefully, we can reverse it in both of us."

Ceithera came back in with a small metal tool. It looked like a long pincher, but the two arms were curved and the points were dull. "This will give me an idea if your issue is environmental or internal to the injury you took and the drain that portal caused."

Alric must have recognized it because he held up his bare arm. Ceithera placed it around his bicep and pressed a small knob on the handle.

It didn't look like anything happened, but both smiled. Ceithera removed it and turned to me.

"His magic loss is related to the injury he took. Most likely that portal was still open in some form when you two were there. It should return as he rests and recovers." She held the tool up to me. "This will give us an idea of your loss."

I rolled up my sleeves. The metal was cool as it wrapped around my arm. Moments passed and Ceithera began to frown. Not a full one, but her eyebrows were creeping in on each other. She adjusted the tool. Still nothing.

"I'm not getting anything from you, one way or another. It could be your unique situation; this is designed for elven magic but usually works on the few humans I've tested. But since you are neither, perhaps it can't reach you."

I rolled down my sleeve. I'd gone without magic before; I could do it again. Sure, I could. Hopefully, Mathilda would be able to help me get it back.

Alric wanted to see the books from Lorcan's bag, but Ceithera pulled healer rank and told him not until he was stronger. Good point, those were heavy books.

"Did you read the letter from Lady Nuthaina yet?"

Ceithera had been watching the brownies but turned at that. "Lady Nuthaina died over one hundred years ago. How did you get a letter from her? *Why* did you get a letter from her?"

The time travel issue was tricky and not really related to our current situation, so I wasn't sure about bringing it up. But Alric already had by asking about the letter. I slowly pulled out the envelope and gave it to Alric.

He took it but didn't open it right away. "My grandmother gave it to us. As for why, I have no idea. But had we not stopped to see her, most likely we would be missing too." He opened the envelope and unfolded the letter. Or rather, letters. There were three pages written on front and back in a tiny font. He folded them back and set them down next to him. "This might take a while, and I doubt it has anything to do with the attack at Siabiane's house."

Ceithera nodded and went to the door. "I want to check on Padraig and a few other patients. Please send for me when Mathilda arrives." She narrowed her eyes. "And you'd better rest, young man."

Once she'd shut the door, Alric pulled out the letter again. Then slid over on the bed. "Unless you think I'm reading this long thing out loud to you, come on up."

Welsy and Delsy stayed on the stool but appeared to be waiting.

"Could you stay outside this door and watch for the faeries or anything suspicious?" It wasn't that I thought they shouldn't know what was in a hundred-plus-year-old letter, but I knew they were used to doing something. Having a task worked wonders sometimes.

They both hopped off their foot stool and ran for the door. I got there first to open it, but I had no doubt they would have found a way to reach the handle. "Thank you." They stood outside the door with their backs to it, looking like small guardian statues.

I shut the door and climbed onto the bed next to Alric, who was currently reading the first page and scowling. "What is it?"

He held it up to me briefly, then took it back. "This woman's writing is horrible and almost as confusing as she was when she spoke to us."

Even though he said he wasn't going to read the entire thing out loud to me, that was what he did. Fine by me after one look at that tiny, scratchy-looking handwriting.

"She says she knew when we met who we were, and she is sorry for what the mark did, but it had to be done. It was the reason we were sent back in time." He looked to me at that.

"You went back in time because you are nosy and fell through a trap. I went through to find you. We weren't there for a reason." That was ridiculous. I had heard of truth-sayers and seers, but I never believed in them.

"I wasn't being nosy." He sighed. "Okay, that might have been part of it, but I certainly didn't expect to go back a thousand years. I don't see how Nuthaina could have believed that." He went back to reading. "She claims that there is a chest we have to find." He squinted at the page. "Wait, a chest that we *did* find. That you had when you were not what you are now." Alric looked up. "I don't know if I can read three pages of this."

"A chest? We've come across a few of those. Can she be more specific?" My first thought, which I quickly shoved into a dark corner, was that she meant the Dark chest. The one that almost destroyed me when I found it while being brought in as a prisoner by the elven knights a while ago. Lorcan had put it in one of the faery bags in an attempt to keep anyone from getting it. The chest itself had nasty spells on it, and apparently the books inside it were worse. I was really hoping that by now he'd locked it up somewhere that it could never be found.

"No real clues. Just that it was old before she was born and kept secrets and magic hidden." He looked up. "That one you had the relics in? What happened to that?"

I shook my head. Once the relics, Nivinal, and Edana had been destroyed I wasn't thinking about anything else. "I kinda lost track of it after you died, and I had to fly out into the middle of the ocean to save everyone else." Truth was it probably got picked up by some treasure hunter after all the fighters left. It was an odd chest, blocked magic, but also seemed to have things appear in it. Losing it wasn't a great thing, but I was a bit distracted. "I know I didn't stomp on it when I destroyed the relics."

"You had it when you made the relics the first time, right? Do you recall anything of it from that time? She acts like we know what she's talking about, and it would have been older than her."

"I only know in theory that I had it." I shrugged; my memories weren't that good yet. "I knew I'd kept the relics hidden; my parents were still alive when I started making them." That was odd, I hadn't realized that before, but now that I thought about it, I knew I started making them quite a while before the final battle. "I had that chest to hide them. But beyond that, I have nothing in terms of what it was or where I found it."

"That has to be the chest she's talking about. She goes on to add that 'it belonged to the lost people. Find it and get the key. The war is coming.' Not much else of use after that."

I hit the paper. "Ha! There we go, she was talking about her future, but it's now our past. We did find it, we did use it to hide the relics, and we won the war." My smile crumbed as he kept reading and frowning. "That was it, right? She was telling us about the chest being buried in Beccia, but that's already happened."

"Maybe. But the way she's talking about a key, that doesn't fit anything that happened. The problem is her view of time is different from that of everyone else. And a lot of this I can't read at all. It's an archaic elven script." He read through the remaining pages but at the speed he was going, he was just scanning for words he might know. And not finding many.

"If she was all-knowing, wouldn't she have known we couldn't read this?" I glanced at one of the discarded pages, but it didn't make sense to me either.

"One would think." He shook his head and kept trying to find something that made sense. "Growing up in the enclave there were always stories of her. She had predicted the Breaking, but no one believed her and thought she was a crackpot. She was given a place to live in the palace because she was a distant relation to the king. After the Breaking occurred, opinions of her changed. But she was still viewed as an eccentric even as her memory for helping in the creation of this enclave was honored. And she was a powerful magic user."

"How did she die?"

"I don't know. I never really cared much about history as a kid, and as I grew up, I became focused on getting us out into the rest of the world. But it seems that a lot of the ones who set up the enclave passed on."

With non-elves that would be a fact of life, since it had been a thousand years. But elves were extremely long lived. I thought about two who had been around when this enclave was set up and who hadn't passed away; at least I had to hope that Lorcan and Siabiane were still alive.

A soft rap at the door broke up our thoughts. The door opened before I could roll off the bed and open it.

"Oh dear! I do hope I didn't interrupt anything!" Mathilda looked a bit ragged around the edges as she blushed and started to shut the door.

I got off the bed and laughed. "No, we were reading a letter together and Alric isn't supposed to leave the bed. Ceithera's orders." I ran forward to hug her. "I am so glad you're here." As I pulled back, I removed a twig from her hair. "Is there a story behind this?"

Fifteen faeries must have been quietly waiting, as they took that moment to fly right at us.

"We bring!" Garbage zipped around Alric's room. The healers and patients in the front area didn't look pleased about the faeries.

"That's great." I pushed open the door wider. "How about we all get inside? Quietly?"

Welsy and Delsy stayed at their posts. "We will keep watching." From the way they both cringed as the faeries flew in, I had a feeling they didn't want to be trapped in a small room with the flying hooligans. I didn't blame them at all.

"Probably a good idea, thank you." I shut the door and motioned for Mathilda to take a seat. "Oh, wait a minute."

I opened the door. "Could one of you find someone to get Ceithera? Tell her Mathilda is in Alric's room."

Welsy nodded to both me and Delsy and trotted off.

"Okay, now what did the faeries do to you?" I was still holding the twig I'd removed from her hair, and Mathilda was dusting herself off. She didn't appear injured, but did look a bit rattled.

"They were a bit exuberant when they found me. Unfortunately, I was up an apple tree at the time."

The faeries stopped buzzing and looked a little contrite. Well, some did. Crusty was bouncing on the edge of Alric's bed and not watching anyone.

Leaf flew closer to us. "Is sorry, needed you here."

Mathilda smiled at them. "That's okay, just makes life more exciting." She turned to me. "Now why is Alric in a sickbed, and what was so urgent that you needed me?"

Between us, Alric and I filled her in. Her face darkened at the news of the attack on her sister, Lorcan, and Padraig. "But you got Padraig back? That's something. This is not good news. Those three are exceptionally powerful and should not have been taken easily."

"We find one." Garbage came over and sat on Mathilda's lap.

"I know, dear, and thank you. Now we have to get the others back."

Ceithera cracked open the door, then came in and hugged Mathilda. "Thank you for coming. This is out of my area of study, and whatever is still affecting Padraig is more magical than physical."

Mathilda got to her feet with one final dusting of her clothing. "Can I see the patient now?"

Ceithera opened the door. Mathilda and I followed, and a movement caught my eye. It caught Ceithera's as well, as she turned sharply.

"Not you, Alric. I was serious."

I waved to the faeries. "Girls? Can you make sure Alric

stays in bed? If he tries to get out, sing to him. Loudly."

The look Alric gave me wasn't pretty, but I did what had to be done. The faeries singing was horrific and not a weapon to be used lightly. But he was stubborn.

CHAPTER TWENTY ONE

———————

WELSY AND DELSY NODDED AS we left and assumed what looked like a knight's stance in front of Alric's door. They really needed things to keep them busy. I might have to see if Ceithera could find a long-term job for them until we could get Siabiane back.

Padraig's room was still dark with muted glows and a lightly fragranced mist. The mist was coming from two rock cones near either edge of the room. The scent wasn't one I recognized but relaxed me the moment I smelled it.

"Thank you, Kain. I'll be in here awhile with my guests." Ceithera smiled at her healer and she nodded and left. "I have done what I can to keep him comfortable and soothed. But I'm afraid there really isn't much I know in the way of healing magical illnesses." She raised the lights of the glows a bit, not up to normal levels but enough so we could see how pale Padraig was.

Mathilda immediately went to his side and lifted first one eyelid and then the next. The swearing that followed was more like Alric than her. "Whoever did this was good. They stunned them heavily, opened a damn portal, and then dragged them through. They were sloppy, though, moving faster than they should have which was how Padraig became stuck." She checked his arms, the back of his neck, behind his ears. "Okay, no tracking marks, again, didn't have time. If you're going to do this sort of thing, do it properly. This was sloppy indeed." She folded her arms and glared down at the unconscious Padraig as if by glare alone she could send a message of reprimand to his attackers.

I looked to Ceithera, but she shrugged. "So, knowing it was sloppy helps us how?"

"Because sloppy work can be undone." Mathilda's grin reminded me of Siabiane when she was up to something. "And we can tell more about them than they would want. I can wake him, never you fear. But I would like to get as much information as I can from him before I wake him up." She'd turned to Ceithera as if waiting permission. Afterall, he was her patient.

"Is it going to hurt him?" Ceithera didn't really look like she believed it but had to ask. When Mathilda shook her head, she motioned toward Padraig. "Then go ahead. Besides, if information was missed because we'd woken him up first, he'd probably find a way to knock himself out again."

Mathilda smiled and rubbed her hands together. "Have either of you ever done a spell search?"

"Sadly, no." Ceithera was standing close by to watch everything that was done.

I shook my head. "But it doesn't matter, my magic really is missing right now."

Mathilda's eyes narrowed as she looked at me. "Hmmm, we shall see. But watch closely, both of you. This is a way to find out more about your enemy than you can listening outside his tent during war." She shrugged. "My father used to say that. Anyway. This spell will settle over him and let me see what he was hit with, and who might have done it. It's important for strong magic users to hide their signature when they cast heavy spells. It can come back to get them. That's why being fast and sloppy is bad."

I nodded but wasn't completely sure what Ceithera and I were supposed to be watching for as Mathilda settled into a spell trance.

It didn't look like she was doing anything, but she started at his head, her hands about an inch above him, her head down, and eyes closed. She froze for almost a minute over his heart, then kept going. A few more pauses brought slight nods. And at one point she pinched his hand between the thumb and forefinger before moving down.

Finally, she stepped back. "Yes, I can bring him back, but I will need to get some supplies from either my sister's cottage or Lorcan's lab." Her look was thoughtful as she gazed at Padraig's resting form.

"Could you tell who was behind this? Are they nearby?" I really wasn't looking forward to fighting heavy magic users without magic of my own and most of my magical friends out of action. But we needed to know who to protect against even if we couldn't go after them yet.

"Yes and no. You mentioned that a Grimarian troll had attacked you last night? I'd say she or one of her kind was involved in this. Their magic leaves a foul stench. But she wasn't alone. There were at least five other magic signatures. All strong, all cocky, and all stupid. I should never have been able to see their signatures. I could even trace them back. They shut me down, but not before I got a good idea where they are."

Both Ceithera and I waited. Mathilda was as bad as Lorcan at getting lost in her thoughts.

"And?" Ceithera said before I could.

"I am sorry, I was already putting the healing spell together in my head." Mathilda winced. "Siabiane and I used to say that someday we might like to go home, back to the south. It looks like Siabiane has beat me there."

"Damn it, I was afraid you were going to say south. Everything around has been pointing to me having to go there. First the faeries, then Qianru, now this."

Mathilda shook her head. "I'm not quite certain who will be assembled to get them back, but I don't believe it should be you. There's already a lot of unhealthy interest in getting you down there, which means that would be the last place you should go. We can get a party to go south." She tapped her lips. "Do you think your friend Covey might be up for an adventure? She's not a magic user, but good in a fight and has a lot of knowledge of elves—including my people in the south."

"I'm not staying here while you go and rescue people. Maybe I can turn things around?"

Padraig interrupted everything by sitting up, his eyes wide but not looking at anything. "You're mine." It was not his voice that came from his throat and it sounded like that Grimarian troll. Before anyone could act, a red bolt shot from his right hand directly at me.

My new dagger friend had been in his sheath this entire time but that didn't stop it from crackling out a green charge of its own. The two arcs met in midair and exploded with enough force to knock all three of us down.

I reached down to the sheath, but the dagger was almost too hot to touch. "What was that?"

Mathilda scrambled to her feet first and rushed to Padraig while Ceithera and I were still getting up. His eyes started to close but she grabbed his arms to keep him upright. "Oh no you don't, you sloppy zielian goat. We stopped you and will do so again." She put her hands on either side of his head and closed her eyes. An echo of a scream that didn't come from any of us hit the room, then faded away. Mathilda released Padraig and he fell back into bed looking the same as before. She then tapped the hand the red charge had come out of and stepped back.

"Don't stand too close. I've shielded him. That Grimarian knew they couldn't get all three through, so they dumped him halfway through the portal and left a trap in him." She turned to me. "Nice trick with that dagger. That's the one that formed from the Robukian you mentioned?"

I patted it; the sheath and dagger were cool now, so I

took it out. "Yup, not sure exactly what he is or does, but that arcing green light of his is handy."

"His?"

I should be embarrassed giving a gender to a weapon, but many people did that with swords. "The faeries can speak to him and say he's a he. No name yet, though."

If Mathilda wanted to ask about that last part, she refrained. "Might I see him?"

I felt oddly strange about handing him over but held him up first. "Dagger? She's on our side, okay?" I held my breath as I gave him to her.

"What was he going to do?" Mathilda held him up, looking at all angles.

"No idea, but I'd rather he not go after friends. I can't lose any more right now."

"Is there anything I can do to help Padraig?" Ceithera wasn't interested in my weird dagger but in her friend and patient.

"Right now, resume the dimmer lighting and the Lavilda mist. It'll help until we get back. And keep everyone else except yourself out—that spell I put on him will pack a serious punch if anyone tries to touch him."

"Understood. You might want to update Alric before you head out." Ceithera was already at the door. "Maybe take some flying friends along with you at least to Siabiane's?"

Mathilda handed the dagger back to me, and I put him right back in his sheath. "Good ideas on both fronts. We'll take Siabiane's brownies as well."

I followed Mathilda back to Alric's room. True to their word, the faeries were all sitting on Alric. Since he looked only mildly annoyed, I figured they hadn't gotten a chance to sing at him.

"Thank you, girls," I said, as they all rose to greet us as I opened the door. "Could you go ahead with Welsy and Delsy and secure Siabiane's cottage? Mathilda and I will be there in a bit." I turned to the brownies. "Can you especially look for any evidence of tampering in the cottage or garden? We had a visitation and I'm not sure if they went back there or not." Partially true; I wanted them to have something to do, but who knew where that disembodied Grimarian troll went.

The faeries and brownies took off, to the annoyance of the people they brushed into, but the relief of everyone else in the building.

Mathilda came inside and sat, but I waited until they were out of the building before I shut the door.

"I stayed put, now what's gone on with Padraig? I heard an explosion of some kind. Garbage was taking a deep breath to start singing before I laid back down." Alric turned to me. "That was a nasty trick, by the way."

"You weren't leaving much of a choice. I need you to be healthy to help find our friends and my magic, and you didn't want to do what the healer ordered." I folded my arms. "I'd do it again."

"I wouldn't mess with her, my boy; she may not have access to her magic at the moment, but our Taryn is a formidable woman." Her smile dropped. "We do need you to recover quickly, however. I can bring back our Padraig, but I was also able to find out more about who took the others." She quickly told him about the magic users, the trap in Padraig, and that I really shouldn't go south.

I glared at her for that, but she was focused on Alric and missed it.

He caught my look. "Everything points to someone or multiple ones wanting to get you south—"

"Nope," I cut him off. "I am not staying here. Either I am not in danger going south, in which case my going isn't a threat to myself, or I am in danger which means more friends will be taken until I go south. And I have to go."

"She is also formidably stubborn." Mathilda shook her head, but I saw the small smile she was trying to hide.

Alric, however, was not smiling. "That is the most…no. You don't have magic. We do. We could make you stay here. Or in Beccia. You said you wanted to get back to a normal life."

I glared at him. "With two of my friends missing and the rest of you out trying to find them? I started this without magic, I can damn well hold my own." I had been annoyed before but now I was pissed. And scared. If they really wanted to, they could spell me in such a way that I couldn't follow them. I had to go. I knew the Grimarian troll and her buddies were after me. I also realized that for good or bad, Qianru had been trying to warn me to stay away, even as someone had forced her to send for me.

"Ah, Taryn?"

I had been caught up in my annoyance and fear and missed what Mathilda was saying. She'd gotten to her feet and had moved away from me. She was pointing to my dagger sheath.

"It's glowing." That was a little odd.

"I think it's the dagger." Alric didn't get out of bed, but he did sit up. "When you stopped talking the whole thing started to glow."

I pulled it out of the sheath and the glow faded. "We really need to find out more about this. Preferably before we head south."

The debate went in a few dozen circles, primarily with Alric and I being the adversaries and Mathilda being the guard to break things up. Whenever I got too upset, the dagger glowed. When I was holding it, I could tell it was warmer too. Not as warm as when it blocked the red stuff that came from Padraig, but noticeably warmer.

"I hate to call an end to this lively debate, but we should get over to Siabiane's, then get Ceithera and go to Lorcan's rooms. Nothing is going to be resolved right now as to who, if anyone, should go south." She glared at both of us since obviously neither of us looked agreeable.

"I want to go look over Siabiane's too." Alric made to push himself off the bed.

"And I want to be five hundred years younger. We all want things we can't have. Taryn was right, we need you. You are still pale and while I'm not a healer, I can feel your magic levels are still depleted. I don't have faeries to threaten you with, but trust me, I could find something worse." Her glare reminded me slightly of Garbage's, although Mathilda looked dangerous, not crazy.

Alric sighed and went back to his pillow. "Fine. Keep me updated. And be quick. If I must suffer in bed, I want Padraig awake to suffer as well."

I leaned over him and gave him a quick kiss. "Thank you for worrying about me, but I'm not letting you all go without me. Rest well." I dodged out of the room before he could respond.

Or rather, so I couldn't hear his response. He said something to Mathilda that made her laugh, then she came out and shut the door behind her.

"I would hate to see you two actually in a serious fight. You are both so stubborn it makes my teeth ache. Let's go see what we can find, shall we?"

It was late afternoon, but it seemed to me that there were fewer elves out and about than before. I was going to ask Mathilda, but she had drifted into one of her contemplative looks and I didn't want to take a chance of causing her to lose her thoughts.

Siabiane's cottage looked the same as it had when we left, aside from two noticeable brownies standing on the stoop. While in the past they'd guarded from the hiding spots in the garden, now they wanted people to know they were watching.

"Any signs when you arrived?" Mathilda stopped in front of the stoop to address them.

"Nothing that we could see. We will continue to guard the premises while you are inside." Welsy motioned to the door. Or rather, Alric's illusion of a door. "Your flying friends are doing…things…inside."

"If Alric is magically drained, wouldn't this spell make it worse? Can we get an actual new door?" I walked through. It might have been my awareness of Alric's situation, but it seemed less solid-looking than before.

Mathilda walked through slowly. "It should have vanished when he collapsed." She walked back and forth a few times, finally muttering a spell and the door vanished. "That's not good. This entire cottage might be spelled to draw magic."

I looked out into the garden. "So, we leave it open? What about the wall in the back? That's probably still up too."

"I think we'll fix both the old-fashioned way, with a carpenter. But for now, the brownies will work." She leaned out toward the stoop. "I'm going to have to drop the magic illusion on the back wall. Could one of you stand guard back there until I can bring someone out to fix it?"

Delsy bobbed his head. "I will guard the back." He nodded to Welsy, then trotted around the side of the cottage.

"We find!" I heard Garbage before I saw her. She and all the faeries came flying down the hall. But they weren't coming from the workroom; they were flying in from the guest bedroom I'd used last night.

"What did you find, sweetie?" The faeries were all buzzing around us.

"The key." She looked far too smug, but I knew if it had been an actual key, or anything she could carry, she would have been flinging it about.

"Can you show us?" Pretty clear whatever it was had been in the guest room, but I'd learned that letting Garbage, or any of the faeries, display their finds was safer.

Garbage looped around us both and then she and the rest of the faeries tore back down the hall.

We started down there, but Mathilda stopped at the workroom door. "Go see what they have. I believe this wall is also draining Alric. It might take a few minutes to pull him free of it."

I nodded and went into the guest room. When I'd grabbed my things a few hours ago, the room had been neat and tidy. Now it looked like someone had lifted the entire room up, shaken it soundly, and set it back down.

"Girls? What did you do?" All the furniture was tipped over, including the bed. I had no doubt that given enough cause, that my flying hooligans could do this. But I couldn't fathom why they would.

"We no do." Leaf flew up to me with an earnest look. "We search."

Not sure how searching meant they didn't ransack the place.

Garbage flew up as well. "Was like when we came, but we find!" She grabbed a handful of hair and led me to the small closet. "Key!" She was scarily excited as she pointed to a hole in the floor.

I leaned forward and found it was a chest, which had a hole in it. The lid was up and in the darkness of the closet I hadn't noticed it at first. I patted the lid to make sure it was real, and it was. The hole in the bottom was a bit too odd to be normal, though. It looked like a tiny whirlpool. I started to lean forward to get a better look but was pulled back by a dozen pairs of tiny hands.

"Is no!"

"Sucking box."

I looked around the faeries. "Is the box the key?" I still wanted to look at it some more, but I had a feeling they would push me back if I tried.

"Is key. You no get yet." Garbage, Gracie Twinkleshine, and Leaf all flew back into the closet, then vanished into the chest.

"No!" I ran forward with the other faeries batting at me, but Garbage and the other two were gone.

Mathilda came running into the room. "What happened?" Then she looked around the room itself. "And what happened to the room?"

The vortex inside the chest had settled and now it looked like the inside of an empty chest. I was freaking out that the faeries were missing, but Crusty and the rest of the faeries seemed calm.

"Three of the faeries flew inside." I waved my hand as Mathilda arched an eyebrow. "There was a vortex, something blue and whirly inside that chest. Garbage kept saying it was the key, or the key was inside. They pushed me away from it, then they flew inside."

Mathilda looked at the chest again, then turned to the faeries. "Anyone know where your friends went?"

Crusty flew up closer. "Is key." She nodded solemnly and pointed toward the chest.

"Is the chest the key? Was the vortex the key? Did the key destroy this room?" I was glad that none of them seemed upset that their friends and the vortex had disappeared, but I was still concerned. The last vortex like that tossed Alric and me a thousand years back in time.

"No. Key coming." She smiled then and looked around the room. "We no do."

"If anything else happens, call me," Mathilda said. "I'm still trying to break Alric's spell on that fake wall of his. It is still connected to him and should have vanished when he passed out." She left the room.

I watched the chest for a few moments, but nothing happened. The faeries were puttering about so I called them over. "I know you didn't do it, but can you help me clean this up?" I still had no idea what caused it.

The faeries were already becoming bored, so they quickly agreed to help. Most things were fine, just tossed about. The small desk in the corner was shattered.

I went to that one as the faeries couldn't fix it. There were a few writing sticks and some paper, but not much else. I scooped up as many of the shattered pieces as best I could and had most of them in a neat pile when I saw the ball. Like a child's marble. At first, I thought it might be part of a necklace, but it wasn't connected to anything—just a soft, light blue orb. There was something about it that drew me closer. I reached for it almost against my will. The moment I tried to pick it up, it flung me across the room and into the closet.

Mathilda was there even faster this time. "Taryn! What happened?"

I used the edge of the chest to push myself up and got shoved back by three faeries flying through a new vortex also in the bottom of the chest. They were carrying something and yelling.

"Close chest!" That stood out from the rest of the gibberish, so I slammed the chest shut. It started rocking, so I sat on it.

My dagger glowed, sparked a bit, and then stopped. At the same time the chest stopped bucking.

"I think you might want to get up." Mathilda didn't have a sword, but she was armed with a stick I hadn't seen her with earlier.

I waited another moment, then jumped off the chest, out of the closet, and landed soundly on the bed. Good for me it was one of the first things we'd straightened.

Mathilda ran to the chest and slid her stick through the place where a lock would go. But there wasn't any more movement.

I turned to the faeries as they landed on the floor to gloat over whatever they'd come back with. "What did you get? And where did you go?"

"Key!" Five of them grabbed whatever they were cooing about and flew over to me. It was a heavy block of wood, about a foot long and carved into the crude shape of a dragon.

"Cute. Is this supposed to be me?"

"No. Is *key.* Now we have." Garbage had her why-are-you-so-stupid face on right now.

"Is it something I need to deal with right now?" It had been an extremely long day.

"No, is later." Crusty flew up and petted the wood. "Nice dragon."

I rubbed my forehead. "Mathilda? Do you have something I can drop this in for now?"

Mathilda snapped her fingers and a large traveling bag appeared. "This should work. I'd like to get a look at it as well, however, not here. There are some magic issues going on in this cottage, and none of them have Siabiane's signature."

"Okay so do we take this chest too?" I briefly filled her in on a chest being mentioned in a letter, but the cottage felt like it was listening, so I kept things vague.

"Yes." Garbage flew up and handed me one of her bags.

"The chest can go in one, but the key couldn't?"

"Yes." She motioned toward the chest.

I didn't know if removing the stick would be a good idea, but the bag managed to take in the stick as well.

Leaf flew up and tied a knot with the strings. "Is full. Keep safe."

I wasn't sure if she meant the bag, the chest, or both, but I didn't care at this point. I put the bag in my inner pocket.

"We can deal with these elsewhere." Mathilda rubbed her arms as she started out of the guest room. "I have Alric's spell down and sent Welsy and Delsy to go hire a carpenter. The door and wall need to be repaired without magic and quickly. I'd rather we waited outside, though." She glanced at the faeries still flying around the guest room.

"The stone!" I had almost left, but the faeries flying around the wreckage of the desk reminded me how I got into the closet in the first place. "I found something over here—it threw me across the room."

Mathilda came back and joined me in peering down at it. I didn't want to pick it up and it looked like she didn't either.

"What is it?"

"I was hoping you might know. This desk was the only thing destroyed and this was in the middle of the mess."

"I protect!" Crusty dove down before we could stop her and wrapped herself around the stone. She started bouncing around—rather, the stone she hung onto did—but she didn't let go.

"Let go!" I ran to catch her, but it and she were bouncing around too much. The rest of the faeries thought it was a game and flew behind us yelling and cheering.

Finally, after the third trip around the room, Crusty bounced close to Mathilda, who had a faery bag in her hand with the mouth open. "In here!"

Crusty and the stone bounced into the bag. Mathilda shut it for a few moments. When it started pulling near the mouth, she opened it, Crusty flew out, and the stone was left inside.

"Hello? We knocked, but no one heard us. We've come to replace a door and wall?" The gnome facing us looked more like he'd be more at home at the Shimmering Dewdrop. Three more stood behind him in the hall: two women and one round little man. All of them wide-eyed as they took in the still disorderly room and the shattered desk. It was a good thing they hadn't seen it before we picked things up.

Mathilda quickly slipped the bag inside her pocket and strode to them. "Yes, thank you for coming so quickly. My sister, Siabiane, had to go back to her country home unexpectedly and an experiment left her with a missing door and a missing wall."

I was going to add that it was actually two missing doors, but the gnomes were looking edgy enough already, and the interior door wasn't important.

The faeries tore out of the house without saying a word. Something grabbed their attention, but I'd have to find out later what it was.

The lead gnome nodded. "We noticed the front door. I can get two of my people on it immediately with the gear we have right now. Can I see the wall in question?"

Mathilda led them to the workroom. It was disturbing to see the wall almost completely gone. There'd been a lot of dust when it first collapsed, then Alric had the illusion spell on it.

The lead gnome marched over to the remains of the wall and started hemming and hawing as he looked at the massive hole from various angles.

"Impressive as to how it dropped like that while the structure around it is safe. We can do it in a week, for three silver, or a day for five gold."

I refrained from gasping at the gouging, but Mathilda didn't bat an eye. "Oh, we can pay the gold. Please do recall who you are doing the work for and be extremely conscientious. I don't believe we've met. I'm Mathilda." She extended her hand. There wasn't a threat indicated and she was even smiling, but the steel in her look made the gnome boss back down.

He shook her hand and then took a few steps back. "Nice to meet you. I'm Mclishian. I'm sure we can get it done by tomorrow morning for two gold, a deal for you and your sister." He smiled but he still looked wary.

"Quite generous of you. We will make sure to tell the palace of your assistance." She waved to Welsy and Delsy. "These two are my sister's stalwart companions. They will stay to make sure no one interferes with your work. A quick warning: when on guard, they don't sleep."

That was well played. The brownies were much shorter than the gnomes and wouldn't be a threat, beyond the fact she just told the gnomes they'd have awake watchers all night.

"Oh, and those faeries that flew out earlier might be coming by for checkups. They like to make sure things are being done right."

The gnome swallowed heavily. "Yes, yes, yes. Brownies and faeries. Odd combination, don't you think? Didn't think they got along. But we'd best get at it then." He waved to one of his people. "Go bring in the rest. We'll need everyone on duty for this one."

"Excellent. If you need us for any reason, send Welsy or Delsy." Mathilda tipped her head up and walked out like a fine lady. I did my best to follow.

Welsy and Delsy followed us out to the garden.

Mathilda turned to the brownies. "Thank you for bringing them. Mostly just make sure they keep working and that no one gets inside. If something goes wrong, find us at the healing house."

"We will watch."

"Everything."

Mathilda nodded and we left.

I looked around for my flock of faeries but wherever they'd gone they were out of sight now.

"Did you get everything you needed?" In all the excitement, I'd forgotten she was coming to get some items to help Padraig.

Mathilda patted her large bag. "I got what I could, everything but one ingredient. I had a feeling Siabiane wouldn't have warthin tongue. She probably does in her country house, but it's not a common spell element."

"You need a tongue?" I wasn't used to this kind of magic, but any body part was going to freak me out.

She laughed. "Oh no. It's an herb. One only found in the far north and a serious annoyance to retrieve. I know Lorcan will have some, as he does research on things that require it. But everything else, we have. The spell Padraig is under is related to both the trap they placed in him and how they managed to capture three such strong magic users." Her look went dark. "I will gladly rip apart whoever did this once we get them back. No one takes my little sister."

"I'll help you, if you don't mind." I never had a sister. Enough of my memories had come back that I knew I had been an only child. But I thought of my friends as family.

"That would be lovely."

We walked up to the palace and Mathilda glared at the knights.

Until one of them recognized her and smiled. "Mathilda! It has been far too long. Will you be staying in the palace or with Siabiane?"

Mathilda winced slightly but kept smiling. "Siabiane is having some work done on her place. I'll be staying at the healing house, working on some studies."

"Ah, I understand." The knight stood back to let us enter. "If you need anything, please ask."

"Thank you, dear boy." Mathilda swept past and we moved into the huge foyer. "Are they still looking?" She kept smiling and nodding as we worked our way through the palace entry.

I gave a quick glance to the front. "Nope, both back guarding the front door. Why? The one at least likes you."

"I know, and he is a sweet boy. But talks a lot. I'd rather people didn't know we were going into Lorcan's rooms. No one in the palace knows he's gone yet, and I'd like to keep any gossip about him or Siabiane down to a minimum. At least until we can wake up Padraig and find out what he knows. Then the royals really should be told." She grabbed my hand and darted down a side hallway, then two more before she came to a familiar stairwell.

I'd never approached it from this direction, but it was clearly the stairwell we normally used. We went up it quickly and stopped at the small landing with his door. Even though the hallway was empty, she still paused and looked around before tapping a few spots on the door. It popped open slightly and we went in.

Mathilda went right to the lab and I wandered in behind

her. So much had changed in a few hours. We weren't even sure what we were facing, and four of our magic users had been struck down in one way or another.

I followed her into the lab as she looked through various bottles. "Lorcan said they haven't been able to rebuild the shield because the magic of the elves had waned while in their enclave. You weren't inside, but have you noticed that?"

"No, not really." She paused in her searching. "I hadn't even thought about it, to be honest. But it does feel different than it used to. I wasn't here much after the shield dropped, so I assumed that was why. But there could be something to what you say, especially if Lorcan mentioned it. And no one investigated?"

I shrugged. "It sounded like they accepted it and adapted. Could that have anything to do with the attacks on the magic users here? I'm not from here, but something got my magic tied up. Then three powerful users get attacked, and even Alric, what he did shouldn't have drained him so badly." The more I thought about it, the more agitated I felt. The elves were losing magic and magic users.

"Do the king and queen know of this?"

"Not since we've been in town as far as I know. They certainly don't know about me or the others. I thought it was just something to us, especially with that visage of the Grimarian troll coming after me. But what if it also involves this city itself?"

Mathilda went pale. "You may be onto something. It would be like Nivinal to have left something, even when he was defeated during that battle that took down the shield."

"What do we do about it?"

"Right now, we get Padraig healed, then we get Lorcan and Siabiane back. I'm not sure why you were attacked unless someone truly does know what you are, but those three would have been the ones in the city most likely to notice a more subtle magic attack. We have to assume they were taken out for that reason." She looked through a few more bottles, then pulled out one in the far corner. "Finally." She grabbed some more bottles and a pair of scrolls. "Just in case." They all went into her bag and we quickly left. But not before she put a protection spell on all three doors from the inside. "Lorcan or I can get in, but I have no idea how long it will be before we can get him back. He has his own protections as well; I added an extra layer." She patted the final door as we left.

She took us a different route, and we ended up coming into the great room from the opposite side. I hoped I was never dropped in the middle of those halls and stairways. I'd never find my way out.

We made it back to the healing house with no further interruptions. The streetlights were coming on as we walked down the final block.

Ceithera was waiting for us as we got closer to the room. "Thank goodness you're back. I was about to find a way to knock Alric out. I swear he's gotten more stubborn as he's gotten older. And he was a difficult child."

Mathilda nodded. "I've only known him a short time, but I agree about stubbornness. Shall we see him first? I believe Taryn and I can help Padraig, but I don't want Alric fussing as we're working in the next room."

"I think after a good night's sleep, Alric should be fine," Ceithera said. "And it's good to know that Padraig will recover as well."

We all went into Alric's room. He was sitting up with pieces of paper all around him. Including three familiar pages. "I'm trying to translate this letter, which I'm beginning to think was part of the purpose." He sighed. "She knew that when we received it, I would be injured. A hundred years ago, she knew. Who does that? Why didn't more people listen to her?"

Mathilda looked over a page that was on the edge of

his bed. "She was also a bit mentally off and many of her predictions were dangerously wrong. But she meant well. After we get Padraig back, I can help figure it out. Well, tomorrow at any rate. I think a good night's rest for all of us will do wonders."

Alric perked up when she said Padraig. "You found a way to reverse what was done?"

"Yes." She folded her arms and glared. "And it will be done quite well without you, thank you very much."

"I could get the faeries again?" It was hard to keep a straight face when he pulled back in concern. Not to mention that I had no idea where they went.

"I'll stay for tonight. Are you two sleeping here?"

"Since Siabiane's place is out…?" I turned to Ceithera.

"Of course, you can even have the room you had two nights ago. Mathilda? It might be good to be near your patient."

"Agreed, and less likely I'd run into anyone I want to avoid here. The palace has far too many nosy people. We have knowledge they don't need yet."

I knew she was speaking on many levels and agreed that sorting things out first would be a wiser idea. Especially if dragging me forward was part of it.

"You sleep, we'll go work on your friend." Ceithera nodded and reduced the glows. "And put away all of your papers."

I went over and gave him a quick kiss, then we went to the next room.

The room was still soothing and peaceful, but the spell Mathilda had dropped over Padraig gave off an odd glow. "Is it supposed to look like that?" I hadn't noticed much of it when we left, but a greenish glow now covered him.

"No, it's not." Mathilda dropped her bag and went to his side. "Well, it is if it was attacked and its defenses came into play." She put her hands over the spell section. Then it dropped.

"Is that safe?" Ceithera was standing right next to her in case there was something she could do but she didn't look happy.

"It should be now. Whoever is at the other end couldn't bring him through to wherever they are, but they are really determined to use him against us. Not on my watch they don't." Mathilda grabbed her bag. "Can we pull up a table? And I'll need two glass bowls plus a large drinking vessel."

Ceithera went to go get the glassware while I pulled a small corner table next to Padraig's bed. He looked like he was sleeping at first, but then I saw his eyes. They were moving rapidly under his eye lids, and his jaw and hands were twitching. "Is there something to settle him down?"

Mathilda glanced over. "Right now, it might be good to leave him. I don't think they can come through again, but I didn't before either." She nodded toward his hands. "He's fighting back on another level and that is in our favor."

Ceithera came back with the bowls, large cup, and some utensils. "You didn't ask for them but thought they might help."

"Thank you, I'd not thought of them. Can you put a guard or two on the door from the outside? Warn them we will be spelling ourselves in here. They need to keep well-meaning people out and everything in here, in."

That was not comforting.

Ceithera didn't look happy, but she cared about her patients, Padraig, and the rest in this building. If something went wrong in here, she wouldn't want others to be in danger. She nodded and stepped out of the room.

Mathilda was halfway through her concoction when Ceithera came back. "We have guards, and they have orders to not back down unless I specifically say a set order of words. Or one of you do." She handed us each a slip of paper. "Don't say them until they are needed."

"Thank you, this is another layer against something going wrong." Mathilda dumped the final ingredients, the bottle she'd gotten in Lorcan's lab, into the first bowl and started mashing everything together. Then she poured half of the slimy looking mess in the smaller glass bowl. A few deep breaths and she cast a spell on the concoction. It flared purple, then lighter until the color was almost gone.

"Perfect. This is round one, and if things are going to go bad, this should be the stage where it happens. Since Taryn is currently magicless, I'd rather she give it to him to reduce interference. And if spells need to be thrown, it would be best if we were back here."

"I'm fine with that." I picked up the bowl, ignoring the fact that the liquids and herbs seemed to be moving, and waited while Mathilda told Ceithera what to be ready for. Ceithera might not be one for arcane relics and magics, but she was a strong healer and her magics were formidable.

Chapter Twenty Two

———•———

"Now, pour the contents of that bowl into the cup. Making him drink won't be easy, but I can make him sit up and function enough not to choke." As she spoke, vines that hadn't been there before pulled Padraig up and tied down his hands and legs.

I turned to her and lifted an eyebrow in question.

"You didn't think all of those vines on my cottage were for show, did you? Now go ahead."

I stepped forward and slowly poured some of the sludge into his mouth. He snarled but kept swallowing. Halfway through his eyes flung open, but they didn't look like him. He twisted, so I took a step back. I knew the amount we had was limited and didn't want him hitting the cup.

"Those eyes they aren't his…" I knew them. The Grimarian who'd been after me, or another of her kind was staring back at me from Padraig's face.

"Cover them!" Mathilda stayed back and so did Ceithera, but they both looked ready to fire spells.

I set down the cup and grabbed a pillowcase and wrapped it around his eyes. He still fought, but the vines held. I picked up the cup and poured some more in.

His fighting got worse and now he started yelling in between mouthfuls. It sounded so much like Padraig that I had to fight myself to ignore it and keep forcing the gloopy mess down his throat. He didn't spit it back at me, but he fought against the vines holding him.

Finally, I got it all down him. I was turning back to the others when Mathilda motioned at me and yelled. "Get down!"

I dropped to the floor as two spells flew over my head and crashed into Padraig. He'd gotten one hand free of the vines but collapsed when the spells hit him.

Ceithera sent a second spell at the walls around us as I got to my feet. "I'm securing this room. That was too close. Something is still trying to come through him."

Mathilda motioned me over to the table. "They are stronger than I thought, but I still have one more shot." She pulled out another vial, this one small and dark, and added it to the larger bowl. "I didn't want to use this, but right now we either get Padraig back or we lose him. I know he would choose death over being their puppet forever." Her face was serious as she lifted the larger bowl. "Be aware that it could kill him. It could blow up this room. It could save him. Three options and we won't know which until it happens."

I looked to Padraig; he was collapsed again, no movement at all that I could see. "You'll have to respell your vines and get him upright." I held my hands out to take the bowl from her.

"Are you certain? If something happens, it's not your fault. The foes we are facing are far stronger than I thought."

"Yes. I'd rather you were back here ready to defend us all. I agree, Padraig would want to die before his soul became a prisoner." She handed me the bowl. The new component made it darker and bubble a bit. But I walked back to him as the vines adjusted again.

His tossing had removed his eye cover, but I didn't think we had time to worry about it. His eyes flew open as I first poured the sludge in his mouth. Worse, this time it looked like him. His eyes were pleading at me—whether it was to stop or go on I wasn't sure. I finally focused my gaze on his mouth and kept pouring. The last of the sludge went in and an explosion of forced air came from him and shoved all of us to the far wall.

The room was filled with smoke, but somehow, I didn't think Padraig had exploded. I crawled forward—the air was better lower down—and rose onto my knees at his bed. He hadn't exploded. His eyes had rolled back, and he seemed to have no control of his body.

"He's trying to get out of the vines!" I didn't want to touch him but was on the edge of doing so if it looked like he was going to get free.

Mathilda crawled next to me, and a dark shape sitting near the door appeared to be Ceithera. It said a lot about her people that there was no yelling or pounding from outside, although they must have heard what happened.

"I think that might have been their final attempt." She smiled, then frowned. "Although if he is coming back to us, he is not going to thank me for the headache. That flis-han glove, the last thing I added, really does a number on the head. If the patient survives."

I felt silly, on my knees peering at Padraig, but the smoke was still lingering.

Finally, he groaned. "Where am I? Who are you? Why can't I move? Answer me."

Mathilda got closer and patted his arm. "You were attacked. We brought you back but Siabiane and Lorcan were taken. And you were a bit possessed."

"Mathilda? When did you come back to town? And why are you down so low? Taryn? What's this smoke? And why can't I move?" His first words had been rough and directed at his perceived attackers. His voice was softer once he saw us, but still not happy.

"In brief, you, Siabiane, and Lorcan were attacked at her cottage." She rose to look directly in his eyes. "We just saved you, and you are welcome."

Padraig smiled weakly. "Nice to know I was in good

hands. Are Siabiane and Lorcan recovering as well?"

"They were taken." Mathilda pushed him back into his pillows with a finger. "We will save them, but not until you have recovered. We believe our friends in the south have them." She clearly wasn't going to tell him that one of attackers had tried to use him to destroy us. Not yet anyway.

Padraig opened his mouth to argue and then shut it. "Hopefully with some rest more of what happened will come back to me."

Ceithera gave him a medicinal smelling drink and ushered us all out of the room.

I started across the foyer toward the stairs, then turned. "The faeries still haven't come back yet; will they be let in?"

Ceithera laughed. "I think they'd get in whether they were allowed to or not. Never fear, I will make certain they are watched for."

With a nod, I went to my room, got ready for bed, and was climbing in when a voice came from the darkened corner of the room.

"Taryn, we need to talk."

CHAPTER TWENTY THREE

—◆—

I WAS PROUD THAT I DIDN'T scream, but my bravado was reinforced by the sudden appearance of my sword. Which was good and bad, in that I hadn't thought of calling it. Which meant that it felt the situation was dire enough to pop in.

I automatically tried to call up the spell for a glow before I remembered my magic issue. I took a step back and tapped the pre-set glow near the door.

The corner was still alarmingly dark, but a faint light was emanating from it. A person-shaped light, but I couldn't see anything more than that. I held my sword steady. "Who are you?"

"A friend, you don't need to know more than that. Let's just say the enemies of my enemies are my friends. And you have made some interesting enemies. I can't help you all that much, not while you're up here. But if you do come to Colivith, I can help you and yours to get back what's mine." There was a soft laugh at their own joke. "I also know where your people have gone—your true people." The voice was not only cryptic, it fluctuated so I couldn't tell what gender the person was or even the species. "I have something to give you now but once I do, I'll be gone. This projecting takes a lot of power if one isn't willing to kill others to do it. I hope you and your friends are as smart as I need you to be."

The flash of light that followed was so bright that I not only had to shut my eyes, but I had to cover them with one hand. Even with that, I still saw spots when I finally opened my eyes.

Of course, my visitor was gone. Or so it seemed. The corner was still dark, so I walked forward, slowly swinging my sword a bit in case that person was there. And almost broke my neck tripping over something shin-high in the middle of the floor.

I was picking myself and my sword up from the floor when pounding rattled the door. Considering it sounded more like tiny beings flying into the door than someone larger knocking, I took the time to trigger another pre-set glow closer to the back corner to see what my visitor left.

A chest. Fairly large for doing the trick of sending it here when the person wasn't here, but another chest. *Damn it.* It was locked and I really wasn't up to dealing with it right now. I had a bad feeling that it was going to match whatever chest Nuthaina had talked about in her letter. Which meant even though she was off a bit timewise, she was still talking about future disasters and problems and not the ones we'd already faced. My sword vanished and I opened the door for the faeries.

Garbage led the band in a swarming circle around the room, then back to the chest and the corner my visitor had been in. "Where go?"

That was interesting; they knew someone had been here. Not terribly unusual as the faeries often sensed things others couldn't. But none of them seemed upset, so hopefully that was good. Or they were as confused as I was about the intentions of the visitor.

"Do you know what it was?"

"Not yet." Leaf flew up to my face.

"But you knew someone was here?"

The faeries collectively nodded.

"Was that person dangerous?" Maybe I could get something of use out of them. I shoved the fact that the person claimed to know where my people were into a dark corner of my mind. Getting my hopes up when dealing with someone who wouldn't even show who they were wasn't a great idea.

"Not yet." This time Leaf, Garbage, Crusty, and six others answered. Once they'd finished their laps of the room, they still looked more curious than upset. Well, everyone except Garbage. Annoyed was sort of her permanent state.

I took a deep breath. I was tired and needed to rest. "Are we in any danger right now? Is that chest going to explode? Or let in an army of deranged and possibly rabid squirrels?"

A few faeries laughed in the back but considering that some of them were landing on the chest and settling down, I figured we were safe.

"Is good. Now. Yet later might not be." Garbage tried out her wise sage look again, and I covered my mouth to not appear to be laughing at her.

"Then if no one is blowing up anything, I need some sleep." My sword stayed wherever it was it went when it vanished, so I grabbed the dagger and the sheath and put them next to my bed. "Hold up—don't tell me what you were doing for the last few hours, just tell me, is there any danger from it?"

"Not now." They all looked so happy, and at least they hadn't said "not yet," so I crawled into bed.

"Sleep where you want, but sleep. No roughhousing, understood?" There was a reason that at my house the faeries' little castle had been kept in the kitchen—the farthest room from my bedroom.

"We no sleeps. Things do." Garbage nodded to the group of faeries sitting on the chest. "They stay."

"What are you going to do?" I was too tired to care, but it might make me feel better later if I'd tried.

"Stuffs and things!" Crusty flew by sideways with a

twisting roll and crashed into two other faeries.

Garbage watched and shook her head. "Things. We do things. You stay. They watch." She pointed to the faeries now laying down on the chest.

I had a feeling by looking at them that they were going to beat me to sleep. "Stay out of trouble and please be quiet when you go through this healing house."

"We do!" Crusty had untangled herself from the two she crashed into and headed for the door. I tried to get out of bed to open it, but she sank through the door. With a wave, Garbage, Leaf, and the others with them also went through the door.

That had been a trick of theirs that seemed to come and go with annoying unpredictability. I turned to the faeries on the chest. "But why did you all knock if you can do that again?" Half of the faeries I was left with appeared to be paying attention.

"Is polite," Penqow, a black and white faery, said, then she belched and fell over asleep.

I turned off the glows and did the same, minus the belching.

———◆———

The next morning came far too soon, and being awoken by faeries who were obviously arguing, clearly trying to be quiet about it, and failing would not be my choice of how I woke up.

"Is too!"

"Is not!"

"Is!"

I rolled over and glared at the invaders having their face-off on the chest sitting in the middle of the room. There was enough light coming through to see them, which meant getting up now wasn't unexpected. I probably could have slept at least another hour or so, though. "What are you arguing about?"

Bad idea. All the faeries lifted off the chest and flew to me and my bed, all chattering at once.

"Stop. One of you, Garbage? Calmly tell me what happened."

I closed my eyes and fell back on my pillow, only to feel tiny feet stomping their way up my chest.

"You wake?"

I opened my eyes before she could do it. "Yes. Sometimes it helps me listen if I close my eyes. Tell me what happened and why you were arguing." I closed my eyes again.

"We go find others, bring here. They were away. Don't want to tell you message from bird lady."

That brought my eyes open. "You brought the faeries that had gone down with Qianru back here? And they don't want to tell me what?" I scattered a bunch of faeries as I sat up. There were more than before, but aside from a few I knew by name, mostly I couldn't tell who was new.

"Rosy Horsefly tells." Garbage turned and gave her one-eyed look to a pretty teal faery with striking purple wings who reluctantly stepped forward.

"We went with bird lady. She gives note but said no give yet." She started to reach into her pocket but stopped. Worry wasn't a common look for faeries, but her tiny brows were drawn tight.

"It's okay, sweetie. You can give me the note." There was no way to know if Qianru really wanted them to delay giving me the note, or they misunderstood. She'd sent away the faeries before she sent Grillion up north. And Grillion's note had caused a lot of trouble. "Actually, can you all wait? I'd like to get the others with us before we see it." And before I touched it. I was grateful for the dagger, especially since my magic was missing. But who knew what else she'd sent up here?

Rosy Horsefly smiled. "That good. Need others too." She shot a glance to Garbage that told me what at least part of the argument had been.

The faeries weren't moving off my bed, or me, so I shook my blankets. Tumbling and laughing as they flew into the air or fell to the floor, they might have been waiting for me to do that.

Once I'd showered and changed, I went downstairs. The door to Alric's sickroom was open but Padraig's was still closed.

Alric and Mathilda were in his room, chatting quietly when I got there.

"Perfect timing, we're going to go eat. Ceithera is setting up a place. Padraig is still asleep, and he should stay that way for now. He'll recover faster." Mathilda nodded to the faeries flying around me. "It looks like we have more?"

Alric was up and sitting in a chair and nodded as faeries swarmed him and patted him. "I'm fine, now. Thank you."

I laughed as the faeries kept landing on him. "Yes, some of them went back to Beccia and brought up the ones who had been with Qianru. I apparently have another note, but we all thought it best to read it when there were more people." I turned to Rosy. "Is this okay?"

"Is okay." She flew up to me, pulled out one of the faery bags, and handed me a folded note. Hers was in much better condition than Grillion's had been.

"Do we have anything to hold this with?" I had started to reach for it, but the same foreboding as before hit me. I kept my hand back.

"Is it okay if I take it?" Alric asked her.

Rosy frowned as she looked between us. "Is okay?" she asked me.

I didn't like the idea of Alric being letter-spelled any more than me, but maybe if the letter were aimed at me, it wouldn't react to him. "Yes."

Mathilda stepped closer and waved her hand over the letter as Rosy handed it to Alric. "I don't sense any triggering spells, but from what I saw of the last one it was old."

Alric took the letter and broke the seal. Everyone,

including all the faeries—even Crusty—
was watching as he unfolded the letter.

Alric scanned the letter. Well, the first page; it looked like there were a lot of pages which was far more typical Qianru than that single page she'd sent up with Grillion.

"She's first talking about the digs down in Notlianda and how amazing they are. She believes they might even have found evidence of the Ancients, although no one had previously believed they ever lived in the south." He and Mathilda looked over to me.

I shrugged. "As far as I recall we always lived up here. But I was young when everything went to hell, and I don't recall paying a lot of attention to history back then. Or those memories could be lost still."

Alric went back to the letter. "She's sending the faeries back to make sure you get this letter. There's nothing wrong that she can put a finger on, but there is something odd happening even further south than her location." He stopped talking but quickly went through the next two pages. "Most all of this is simply about her dig sites."

"Didn't you say she went south to find out what her people knew of the Dark? To rally against them?" Mathilda hadn't met Qianru, but she'd heard stories.

"Yes." Alric handed over the pages as he finished.

He was right; aside from a mention of some strange things in the kingdom further south of her, everything was digger talk. Then I noticed some odd spacing. I had been handing the finished pages to Mathilda. "Can I have the first one back please?"

She handed it back and I started swearing. "She's done a code in it. This line here?" I tapped the first page. "See how the spacing is odd on some words? It's a thief's code—she was fascinated with those." I started putting the pages out on the bed. It would take a while, but she had a message in here. "We need someone who knows this." Mathilda and I both looked to Alric, but he raised his hands.

"I might have done some thieving, but I wasn't involved with them like that. I can see the spacing you're talking about, but it doesn't mean anything to me." He put down the sheet he was looking at. "But we know someone who would."

"Grillion?"

"Yup. He bragged about growing up as a pickpocket and sneak-thief as a child in Kenithworth."

Mathilda read through the pages again. "Considering she went down there to find out about the Dark, and she sent all of her assigned faeries back up with a letter that really says nothing about anything, I'd say we need your friend. There has to be something to this."

"Rosy? How long ago were you sent back?" We knew it was before Grillion and crew, but it might have been anytime in the past five months.

"Is many sleeps." She tilted her head and flashed her hands open. Then again, again, and again. Then one open hand. "Got attacked, hide."

I was focusing on it having been a month and a half ago—give or take since I knew the faery concept of time wasn't a strong point. "Wait you were attacked?" None of the faeries seemed concerned, but usually they could avoid being seen if they wanted to. "Where? By who?"

Garbage scowled. "Squirrels. Always squirrels."

Rosy nodded. "Yes. Them. Outside of brownie town."

The faeries all nodded, but I was lost. "There's a town filled only with brownies?" That would be something to avoid.

"Is no, but many there. Ones captured from there," Garbage said.

"Hobbon? Hibben?" Siabiane had gotten the name out of them, but I really couldn't recall what it was called.

"Hobin?" Alric added.

"Yes! They send squirrels. Then bad flyers. Hide."

Bad flyers could mean anything, but I had a sick feeling in the pit of my stomach. The sceanra anam had been defeated by the chimeras in this very town. But not all were killed. They hadn't really been seen since then, so I was happy imagining them long gone and dead. "Do they look like this?" I took a paper and charcoal Alric had from yesterday and did a rough sketch, then held it up to the faeries gathered around Rosy.

"Bad flyers." Several of the faeries nodded. I turned the drawing toward Alric and Mathilda.

"We know where the sceanra anam went."

"Damn it. How and why did someone in a tiny fishing town have them and send them and squirrels after the faeries?"

"Are there any faeries in the south?" I was asking Mathilda, but Leaf flew up to me.

"Not now. All here."

"Not even the wilds?" Even though the numbers of faeries flocking around in overalls was growing, there had been far more who would appear from time to time who were still wild. They usually vanished into thin air, so it was hard to tell where they lived.

"No. Not go there." Leaf flew back to her friends, leaving Mathilda, Alric, and me all wondering what in the south could disturb faeries.

"But you were safe when I sent you there, right?" That was a horrifying thought.

Garbage flew up this time. "Is yes. We go, just not like much. But need to go."

We were back to where this adventure started with her convincing me that I needed to go south. Even though the faeries themselves didn't like it.

"We'll talk about that later." I turned to Mathilda as I folded up Qianru's note to give to Grillion. "How is Padraig? We could use his help with unraveling the issues here, as well as whatever Qianru is trying to warn us about."

"Which might have passed already," Alric said.

"Oh! That reminds me. I had a visitor last night. Couldn't see who they were—no, I don't think it was our Grimarian friend—but they left a chest in my room. Made a point of saying that it was a massive use of energy to send it to me, then vanished. They also said they knew where my people were." I added the last part softly. I might not want to believe it yet, but I knew the others should be aware.

"They know where your people are?" Mathilda watched me carefully.

"That's what they claimed. But I'm not really holding out hope."

Alric gave a small nod and changed the subject. "They left a chest? Maybe what Nuthaina was talking about?"

"I'd really hoped that she was talking about something in the past. Now we have Qianru being cryptic, Nuthaina being cryptic from beyond the grave, and some stranger leaving things in my room. While also being cryptic. I'm really tired of people not saying things outright."

"So, what was in the chest?" Mathilda asked.

I was glad they both let me drop the issue about my people for now. I wanted to find them, but I didn't want to get my hopes up at this point. "I have no idea. It was late, I was tired, and it has a lock." I folded my arms to stare them both down. I was as curious, or more so, than the average person—it came with being a digger. But I'd hit my limit by this point.

Mathilda patted my arm. "Let's go see how Padraig is, then go see about the chest."

I followed them out with the faeries fluttering around me. Apparently, we were boring now, as they started drifting toward the main door.

"We be back! Going to…check things!" She didn't even wait for a response before they flew out into the sunshine.

Ceithera was coming out of Padraig's room. "Good timing. He's awake, but still weak. He is insisting on seeing you all, though."

Mathilda stopped before she opened the door. "How does he seem?"

"Cranky, and he has the headache you predicted. However, he seems to be himself and is recovering quickly. I have to go check on some other patients, but if you need anything, please send someone to find me."

Alric and I let Mathilda go first. The room was a bit lighter than before but still darker than normal. Padraig sat up in bed. "Good of you to come visit."

Mathilda sat down next to him. "Do you recall anything new about the attack?"

Padraig sighed and shook his head. "The attack came with no warning. We were setting up in the workshop when we all started slowing down. Lorcan hid his faery bag; please tell me you found it?" At my nod he went on. "We couldn't move. No magic, nothing. Extremely tall and skinny dark shapes came through the wall, they grabbed the other two first. A third grabbed me but the wall seemed to be fluctuating. It felt like I was being torn in two."

That wasn't as helpful as we'd hoped. Although tall and skinny did exclude the Grimarian trolls, I still felt at least one of them was involved in this. We told him how we got him out thanks to the faeries.

"We have to find them." He started to rise out of the bed but fell back under Mathilda's glare.

"Taryn sent for me because you and Alric were injured— Ceithera and I spent a lot of magic trying to bring you back. You *will not* undo our work. We have something to look at in Taryn's room. Rest for now. We will get them back, never fear." She turned without waiting for his response and left the room.

I shrugged and followed. Alric nodded and followed me.

That Padraig didn't call us back spoke to how exhausted he was.

We went upstairs and I showed them the chest.

Alric walked around it a few times, tapping it in various spots. Mathilda folded her arms and glared at it. Finally, they both nodded.

"It's safe," Alric said. "Or as safe as we can hope for. Nuthaina gave a bit more description in her letter, and this does fit it better than the other chests we've found."

"We still haven't shown you the one we found in Siabiane's cottage, though." I looked closely. This one was heavier than that one and hopefully didn't have a vortex of any kind in it.

"We can look at that one later. From what you told me, it might be best to examine it far away from anything it could pull in," Alric said.

"Am I the only one certain that something is going to explode, jump out, or suck us in?" I was the closest but still hadn't moved too close.

"Neither of us sensed any magic triggers."

I shot Alric a glare—like that would stop something from trying to get us. I'd left my dagger up here, but I went and grabbed it now. Yup—it was starting to spark. "I have no idea what exactly this thing does, but I do know that so far the sparking hasn't been bad—not for us anyway. Wanna let us at the chest first?" I might not have the magic the two of them did, but I trusted this weird dagger.

Both nodded, so I approached the chest. The last one we'd come across, now hopefully still secure in the faery bag I still had stuffed in yesterday's clothes, had some nasty tricks to it. I almost wished for a faery or two to come back in case a vortex came out of this one too.

My dagger sent arcs forward, but it was almost like it was tasting the chest, checking it out, but not attacking it. Holding the dagger in my left hand, I flipped open the lid of the chest with my right.

And was faced with scrolls. A lot of scrolls. Covey would be in heaven, there were so many. And they were old. Some in elvish, which I couldn't read. A few even appeared to be completely in an old version of Ancient, which I found I could actually read a few words of. Most likely once my brain caught up, I could read those. I dropped down next to the chest, put down my dagger, and started leafing through to see if there was anything else—but it appeared to simply be filled with scrolls. I sat back on my butt.

"It's only scrolls. The person who showed up last night made it sound like it was a thing of massive importance and pointed out how much effort it took to get it here." While glad there hadn't been anything inside that tried to blow us up and drag us in, I was a bit disappointed. As a digger I'd always gone for artifacts over scrolls.

Both Alric and Mathilda moved forward as if the chest had been filed with gold.

Mathilda dropped down to the floor next to me. "Oh my. These are amazing."

"Look at their condition, they're astonishing. This is unheard of. Any idea where they came from?" Alric was holding each scroll like it was his first newborn.

"Look at these stamps, right in the corner of each." Mathilda held one up so I could see the tiny leaf and vine. "These had to have come from the library of Pernasi." She picked up another scroll and looked at it with tears in her eyes. "But that library vanished when half of Colivith was destroyed when Siabiane and I were children—long before we came to the north. How can this be?"

"I have no idea, but we need to protect this." Alric was still looking at the scrolls like he was envisioning his child taking its first steps. "We have to take it to Beccia."

That pronouncement made both Mathilda and me stare at him blankly.

"What?" I couldn't even get more than that out.

"I agree we need to keep these safe, but I was thinking the palace?" Mathilda had gone back to staring at the mountain of scrolls.

"I have a secret place in Beccia. No one knows about it,

and they can't get to it. It'll be safe there."

"Wait, what? Since when? You have a hiding spot in Beccia that you never told me about?" I was already feeling out of things since I'd barely heard of the long-lost library of Pernasi and these two were completely gobsmacked about it. But then to find out he had a secret place I didn't know about?

"Sorry, it was from before we met. Not too far from where Locksead and his gang had their hideout. It's a sunken elven ruin. But it's secure." He shook his head. "I can't get over these. My grandmother used to tell me stories of the library and some of the things it held."

Mathilda forced herself to look away from the scroll in her hand. "I still think the magic of our people and the strength of the palace could protect them better."

I sighed. "I don't like the idea of hiding things in ruins, but I think we have to consider how this enclave, and more importantly, the magic here, has been compromised. Your sister and Lorcan were grabbed right from her home. This place isn't safe."

"I guess you're right. And Alric has always been a rebel and in many ways so have I. It feels odd having such a find and keeping it secret."

I heard the catch in her voice and reached over to hug her. "We will get Siabiane back. Lorcan as well. I promise."

She smiled. "Thank you. Funny thing, she and I were limited to sendings for almost a thousand years when she was inside the shield and I stayed out. But I'd gotten used to her being around these last months."

"Have you tried a sending this time?" I had no idea on the distance limitations but people from the south kept being able to get up here.

Mathilda turned red. "I hadn't even thought of it. It always works better when we know where the other is, but our bond is close, so it's not as necessary. But since the people who took her are of an unknown magic level, this will have to be covert. I need to go into her mind."

"You can do that? Sort of like when I call to the faeries?" Or back when I could. I needed to ask the faeries about it. I realized that I wasn't sure if my problem had been because of the lack of magic or that they literally couldn't respond.

"Sort of. More two directional. If it works, I can talk to her and she should be able to respond. They can't see me, but I also can't see where she is." She walked to the far corner of the room and shut her eyes. A moment later she started to tumble over.

Alric caught her but she recovered almost immediately.

"I hit a wall. I think we have our guess confirmed that they took them to the far south." She rubbed her head. "Extremely far south, I'm thinking."

"We should find a place to put this until we're ready to leave." Alric was still staying close to Mathilda.

"I'd like to keep this chest in Lorcan's rooms. You both made good arguments not to leave it in the palace, but for now it is the safest place."

"Couldn't it go in a bag like the other one?" We were getting an extreme collection of items in faery bags, but they were handy.

"I'm not sure we should keep using them as much as we do," Mathilda said, as she and Alric went back to the chest and the scrolls. "I believe the items in them are safe, but not enough is known about those bags. These scrolls are priceless beyond measure, and I don't want to risk them. I would say when we move it to Lorcan's rooms, specifically in the lab, we glamour it but keep it out of the bags."

I waited a few minutes, but both were looking through the scrolls again. I might need to make sure Covey never saw these. "Okay. So, we move it now?"

Mathilda and Alric reluctantly placed the scrolls back. They both kept rearranging them until I finally came forward and started to shut the chest. "I think they are fine as they are. Do you want to lock it again? Just in case?" Just in case had become my mental motto during the search for the relics, one I'd gladly dumped for a week and now was having to pick back up again. It didn't make me happy.

Mathilda put another lock on, and Alric settled a glamour on the chest. It still looked the same to me. "I think I'm seeing through glamours again."

"No, I'm seeing the real chest as well." Mathilda turned to Alric. "You *have* been injured, you know. Maybe your magic is still recovering."

Alric gave a slight snarl and flung another spell.

"Nope. Still there," I answered and Mathilda confirmed it with a nod. Then she looked down at my dagger still on the floor next to the chest. He was slightly flickering green.

"Taryn? Can you take your dagger, sheath him, and step outside the room?"

When I did, Alric cast a spell again, and this time the chest changed into an old beaten sea chest with rusted bands.

"My dagger was stopping it?" I looked down, but the dagger wasn't even sparking right now. "Why and how…?"

Mathilda came out of my room with Alric and the chest behind her. "I have no idea, but I would say it has its own magical agenda."

It was still mid-morning, and most of the people passing by the healing house were heading toward the morning market down the road. I sighed. It would have been nice just to visit here, go to the market, and maybe have tea with Alric's grandmother.

"You might want to stay behind us. Let Alric go first, then me, then you." Mathilda looked down. "Your dagger was starting to spark as you got closer to the chest."

I dropped back. "I think it likes that chest. Maybe they're relatives."

The knights only gave a single look at the chest Alric

carried before stepping aside once he said it was for Lorcan. I had no idea how long we could keep the ruse up that Lorcan and Siabiane hadn't been kidnapped, but I agreed that the fewer people who knew the truth the better. At least until we knew what was happening.

Mathilda broke her spell on the door first, next Lorcan's protection spell was dropped, then she held the door open for Alric.

"Should we put it in the lab? Less noticeable if someone does get in."

Alric brought it into the lab and got it on the table. I stayed out of the way since I wasn't sure what my dagger would do as they set up more protections on the chest.

I was opening the front door to leave when I almost tripped over Welsy and Delsy. Judging by their raised hands, they'd been preparing to knock.

"We have important information."

They still had their name tags on, so bending down I could see Welsy was talking. "Please come in." I stepped back as they came forward.

"How did you find us?" Mathilda asked.

Delsy handed her a small bag, not faery bag sized, but more like a lunch bag. "We tracked. Siabiane gave us skills beyond other brownies. The gnomes are finished but found these items scattered in the back yard as they cleaned up. They were careful in their work and made sure to note they did not cause them to be in the yard."

Welsy nodded. "We believe it happened when you brought down the wall."

Mathilda emptied the bag on the table. Three faery bags, a wand, a ring, and two necklaces. "These belonged to Siabiane and Lorcan. That is his ring, her wand…but how?"

"The things could have been trapped in-between like Padraig was." Alric looked at the faery bags but didn't open them. "But did the people who grabbed them leave these or did Siabiane and Lorcan?"

Mathilda held the wand. "We know Lorcan hid one of his bags. I know Siabiane would have tried to leave behind anything she thought they could use, whoever they are. Her wand is old and precious, and she would have tried to protect it."

A soft noise behind us made us all turn to find Padraig coming in the secret entrance. He still looked pale, but he was up and walking. And looking pissed. "Lorcan would have guarded that ring unless he felt he couldn't protect it. I think Lorcan and Siabiane found a way to leave those behind when I was left behind." He shuddered. "The power of those who took us was terrifying."

"Does Ceithera know you're out?" I liked the healer, but I had a feeling she wouldn't be okay with almost dead patients out wandering about.

He smiled. "She came over with me to speak to Alric's grandmother." His smile dropped. "The king and queen are overdue for their return from the other enclaves, and Ceithera wanted to see if she knew anything."

"We should go talk to both. This isn't good news along with the other issues. And we need to tell Delphina about Lorcan and Siabiane." Mathilda scooped up the items the brownies had brought, put them back in the bag they came in, and put them in her huge cloth bag. "We'll have to sort these later and find out what's in the bags. But my good old trusty bag will keep them safe." She smiled and patted her bag. It looked like a normal bag used for going to market or about town, but knowing her it was far more than that.

Welsy and Delsy kept watching everyone as we headed for the door. "We go where?"

I started to say to guard Siabiane's house, but Mathilda had a thoughtful look. "Come with us for now. We'll have more tasks later."

They both grinned and followed us out.

Even though Alric and I had just been to his grandmother's quarters, I would have been hard pressed to find it again. Especially via the twisted route we were taking.

We finally got there and were greeted by a knight. There hadn't been one earlier, and I noticed that Alric's eyes narrowed when he saw him.

"Is something wrong with my grandmother?"

The knight shook his head. "Orders of the chancellor. He wants to make certain the higher-ranking officials are protected." He nodded to Mathilda. "We were notified that your sister and Lorcan went to her house in the country. Please pass along our offer of protection."

Mathilda smiled as if that was the truth. "I shall, but they are likely to be there for a bit." She patted his arm and knocked sharply on the door. "Thank you, though."

Padraig had stayed back but now stepped forward. "Is there anything we should be concerned about?" Both he and Alric were technically knights, but they were also nobles.

"No, sir. Just being cautious." The knight resumed staring ahead as the door opened and Alric's grandmother motioned for us to come in.

"What is that about?" Alric asked as we came into the room. "Knights? At doors?"

"Yes, not a good morning, although I am glad to see you all. Ceithera has been informing me about Siabiane and Lorcan. We gave them that story of where Siabiane and Lorcan had gone to keep them from searching for them." She looked down as Welsy and Delsy came in. "Hello, Siabiane told me of you two. I am glad to meet you."

"We are here to help. And are glad to meet you as well."

Once we were all seated, Mathilda turned to Delphina. "What have you heard from the king and queen? It's not like them to be late."

"No, it's not. I've heard little, which is also disturbing. Especially with attacks against some of our most powerful magic users."

"Who rules if the king and queen are absent?" I didn't think I was going to like the answer; Nivinal had been highly ranked. Maybe he wasn't the only one leading a duplicitous life.

"Lorcan would be first, followed by the chancellor, then myself. Siabiane is a powerful advisor and could step in if she felt she needed to, but her official position in the hierarchy is more fluid."

"And the chancellor is the one who ordered the knights?" I didn't need to say what I was thinking; from the looks on their faces I wasn't alone.

"But Lord Sealia has been part of this enclave since before the Breaking. He's a good man." Delphina looked around but there was doubt even in her eyes.

"Maybe he's not him?" From the looks around me, I wasn't the only one thinking that.

Alric shrugged. "It could be, or it could be that the magic issue is unrelated to anything else. Lorcan and Siabiane could have been kidnapped because of their connection to someone or something else." He looked to me.

"I think we need to get Taryn and Alric out of here," Padraig said. "Mathilda and I as well. Either it is all connected, in which case more attacks will be coming, or they are after Taryn."

"And more attacks would be coming." I sighed and sat back in my chair.

Alric looked around and nodded. "We were planning on leaving soon anyway. I hadn't figured on Padraig joining us, but it might be good to make it harder for them to find him. The four of us can leave soon."

"Six," Welsy said, as he and Delsy stepped forward.

"We go with you." Delsy nodded.

I'd sort of thought they'd want to stay and protect Siabiane's cottage, but then I realized, constructs or not, they loved Siabiane and knew we were going after her one way or another.

Delphina smiled. "Okay, six of you. But in case it is some-one connected to the enclave, we should have a plan." Her gaze seemed to linger on Alric and me, which sadly wasn't shocking. "I believe Ceithera and I saw you all heading off to join Siabiane and Lorcan at her country cottage. And since getting there if she hasn't invited you is extremely difficult, it should give some breathing room if someone is following you."

Everyone got to their feet and Delphina came and gave me a hug. "Thank you for saving my grandson, again." Then she hugged Alric, whispered a few things, and we all headed for the door.

Mathilda turned to Alric and me. "I can mask our exit at least until we are out aways. Then we'll—"

Delphina cut her off. "Don't tell us where you'll be. You *will be* at Siabiane's cottage."

We left quietly and Padraig led us down a few side hall-ways to get to Lorcan's rooms.

I wanted to ask questions, but it felt like silence was the wisest choice right now. I waited until we got into Lor-can's rooms.

"I'll need to call the faeries, or should I wait until we're out of town?" I still wasn't certain if my ability to call them was related to my magic or not.

"Probably a good idea to wait until we're on the road." Padraig glanced around as he and Mathilda pilfered what they felt they might need from Lorcan's books and supplies. "I think we've taken anything I can see us needing—or that Lorcan wouldn't want someone else getting."

Mathilda sighed as she looked around the room. "I would love to go to Siabiane's country cottage and pick up things there as well, particularly if we are going to bat-tle. But we don't have the time, and even for me, getting there without her guidance would be difficult." She went to the front door.

I opened my mouth to ask about this battle, then shut it

silently. I'd found over the past two years that fights don't always involve giant masses of armies.

CHAPTER TWENTY FOUR

———•———

ALRIC PICKED UP THE CHEST again, still under its glamour. I walked ahead with Mathilda, followed by Padraig, then Alric with Welsy and Delsy running the back guard. My dagger played nice and wasn't going green or reaching out to anything, so we wanted to keep it that way.

We quickly loaded up our things from the healing house and Padraig ran to his house for his own supplies. We were waiting for his return when two healers approached.

"Ceithera said you were going on a long journey and would need provisions. We hope this is enough." They set down two large baskets.

Mathilda smiled. "Thank you, this should be fine. Do thank her for us as well. I'm afraid we must be off before she'll be back."

"I have the cart ready and everything," Padraig said, as he came up behind us and smiled to the healers.

They both bowed and then left. His smile dropped immediately. "Mathilda, could you check the things they gave us? I'm sure they're fine, but I found evidence that someone broke into my house. Nothing important was taken, but we need to be careful."

Mathilda looked around, then said a few words as she leaned over the baskets. She stood upright. "They appear clear. Shall we?"

We each picked up something—packs, baskets, and chest

were all moved out the front door. The cart, as Padraig called it, was a full carriage. There were two horses pulling it and the three we'd come in on were tied behind it.

"I figured we might as well be comfortable on our trip. And this has a deflect spell already built in. Won't last long, but it will get us out of here."

Welsy and Delsy darted about securing our things faster than any of us could have. The chest stayed in the passenger section of the carriage.

We were all onboard, with Alric and Welsy in the front, when I heard horses riding up. I looked out the window to see Flarinen and four other knights blocking our path.

"The chancellor inquired if you would like an escort to wherever you're going?" From the bored arrogance in his voice, he wasn't up to anything bad—but the chancellor obviously wanted to know where we were going.

"Thank you, but no. We're going to Siabiane's country cottage and you know how difficult getting there can be for someone not invited."

I could only see the side of Flarinen's face, but the wince was still visible.

"Yes, my brother and I are in her employ and we must get there in haste," Welsy said.

Delsy leaned out of the window. "Is there a problem, Sir Knight? Our mistress does need us."

Flarinen looked at the brownies, then to us, then shrugged. "No problem, I will inform the chancellor that you are fine." Without another word he turned his horse around and led his knights away.

Alric waited a moment and then got the horses moving. We would be cutting through the city in case anyone saw through the deflect spell. It was a subtle one, but even I could feel it. Interesting, since that meant I hadn't completely reverted back into my magic-sink status. I'd take whatever good news I could get.

I waited until we were mostly through the city. "Should

I call for the faeries now, or still wait?"

"I would do it now," Alric said from the driver's seat. "It may take a while to reach them, and I'd like to get the Chawsia path open quickly. The paths draw a lot of magic and as soon as we've cleared the city, I want to be off."

That explained why no one was worried about going far out of our way. They were planning on using the magic path Alric and I utilized coming in. Considering how that ended up, I wasn't sure about it. Yet, we needed to get to Beccia and the longer we were on open roads, the easier someone could find us.

I closed my eyes and tried calling for the faeries. After a few minutes of silence, I was about to see if Mathilda could reach them. We needed to get on the road, but I wasn't leaving without the faeries.

A bunch of welcome thumps on the top of the carriage, along with squealing laughter, made me realize they'd found us. And that calling them was probably not related to my magic status.

A group of them started swinging into the open windows to join us, but clearly more were riding on top. I was sure Alric loved that.

Garbage, Leaf, and Crusty flew in and landed in between Mathilda and me. "Is good go. Bad place." Garbage didn't seem upset.

"The enclave was the bad place?"

"Is yes, all magic tingly." Leaf held up her hands and wiggled her tiny fingers.

I looked to Mathilda. I wasn't sure if I were up to playing let's-catch-the-disaster with the faeries.

"Girls? Is it something we can stop?"

"No, need leave—save others." Garbage looked like that answered everything.

Padraig pulled out a handful of sugar, which succeeded in bringing the rest of the faeries into the carriage. "Settle down." He covered his hand before they could get it. "Now, slowly, one of you say what's wrong with the enclave and how our leaving will save them."

The faeries all stared at each other and started muttering in faery. It appeared they were trying to sort out their answer.

Crusty was finally pushed forward. "This. Problem here." She pointed to me, then lower to my sheath with the dagger. "Is not bad. But peoples want. Hurt others. Already hurt others." She scowled and narrowed her eyes.

"Wait, are my friends in danger?" I didn't want anything to happen to the elves, but neither did I want anything to happen to my friends in Beccia.

"No? Yes? Not sure?" Crusty shrugged but the faeries behind her applauded, and even Garbage looked proud.

"So? Are we going with the plan?" Alric had missed Crusty's less than helpful presentation.

Mathilda watched the faeries for a moment. "Yes. Our Grimarian friend triggered something when she tried to attack Taryn and when she suppressed her magic. We should protect the dagger as it is an item of interest by those who would hurt us. Also, Beccia is safe for now, but that might change soon."

All the faeries ran to her and hugged her, then ran over to Padraig for their sugar.

As I watched them and Mathilda. I had no idea how she got all of that from what Crusty said. "How? I don't understand."

She reached over and patted my hand. "You will. Keep in mind I've been around them for longer than you have."

The faeries quickly went to sit along the benches, the floor, or anywhere they could, and settled in with their sugar.

Delsy watched them carefully. "Siabiane told us of the faeries, but until yours came to town, we'd never seen them. They are…most interesting."

I looked around at them. "That's one way to put it."

The carriage picked up speed. "Hang on, there's someone following us through the woods," Alric yelled back to us.

I knew we weren't on the secret path yet because Mathilda or Padraig would have had to do it. Alric had done one too recently. Which meant it was probably someone from the enclave. I was closest to the small window between us and the driver, so I slid it open to talk without yelling. "Couldn't they be on the road on their own?" I was as paranoid as the next gal, but maybe this time it wasn't something to worry about.

"They aren't on the road and are trying to stay hidden— there are at least two and they aren't doing a great job." Alric kept his voice low but got the horses moving faster.

Unless they were in dense brush or close trees, a horse with a single rider would always move faster than a carriage. That wouldn't stop Alric from trying, however.

Padraig slid over to the window and pulled back the curtain. He started swearing. "They are now in a section of thinner forest coverage. Those look like knights. They're even wearing some armor. Not all of it, but I see chest pieces. Idiots." He took out a small crossbow from the folds of his clothing. I'd never seen it before.

"You're going to shoot them?" I know he just called them idiots, but that seemed a bit extreme.

"I'm going to be ready. They may not actually be knights, or they could be. Either way I think stopping and confronting them is better than trying to run." Padraig kept watching them.

Alric didn't say anything, but did slow the horses a bit. I was watching out the window along with Alric, and the two horsemen rode toward us.

"How are we handling this? Whoever they are they had to have come from the enclave." Alric slowed the horses down further.

"We stop and see what they want." Mathilda hadn't been

looking out the window, but a frown was growing on her face. "There is something strange about them."

"Everyone, make sure you're armed." Alric pulled up the horses to a stop and yelled into the woods. "Hello, can we help you with anything? There's room enough on the road for all of us." He pitched his voice to carry, but it had just enough of a twang that it didn't sound like him.

I wondered if he missed pretending to be other people all the time.

Our horses, including the three behind the carriage, were nickering softly, but that was about the only sound I heard.

"Hello there! In the woods. We do see you."

I thought about pulling out my dagger but focused on my sword instead. It took it a few moments, but eventually it appeared. It was far more impressive than my dagger, but a bit awkward in the confines of the carriage.

The faeries had still been rolling about in a sugar crash, but most perked up when my sword appeared.

"Is fight!" Garbage yelled, as she pulled out her war stick and led her flight of faeries out the window before I could say anything.

"Damn it, should I call them back?" Of course, they were all flying into the wrong side of the forest at the moment.

"Don't know that you could." Mathilda shook her head. "I think we need to deal with whoever our friends are." She pushed open the carriage door and stepped out. Padraig was right behind her and I followed.

Alric stayed in his seat but had his sword out. Padraig's appeared a moment later. Delsy started to come out of the carriage but Mathilda shook her head and waved him back. She nodded to Welsy to stay put as well.

"I believe my driver asked you a question?" Mathilda hadn't glamoured that I saw, but she was standing taller and had a haughty stance as she faced the woods.

The shadowy shapes came forward and even though only two had been visible before as they moved it was clear there were six.

They weren't knights, at least not elven ones. Only two wore armor on their chests and they didn't appear to be fitted properly. More like they'd picked it off others.

"We won't hurt you, we only want your money and jewelry." The one closest drew out a large crossbow, then he tumbled over as a smaller bolt hit him in the throat.

Padraig reloaded his small crossbow and raised it again. "I don't think so. Now get back on your horses, and ride far away."

"You're still outnumbered."

"No not!" The faeries flew over the carriage in a swarm.

I was watching the faces of the bandits and none of them looked surprised. Not a good sign. Common bandits wouldn't have been expecting a bunch of faeries. People looking for us would. I started to say something when one long arm pinned my own and another covered my mouth. My sword vanished with horrific timing and I stomped on the attacker's foot. Luckily for me, while he had boots, they weren't metal. I also bit his hand. He still didn't let go but by then more attackers on foot moved in and my friends were fighting.

Mathilda put a shield of protection over the carriage and stepped forward with her stick and started bashing heads. Alric had dropped down from the driver's bench and was fighting two of them.

The faeries started swarming, then saw me as my attacker lifted me off my feet, flung me over his shoulder, and started running. I kicked and hit him a few more times, but he still didn't let go. The faeries were right behind us when he turned around halfway and flung a packet at them. I couldn't see them well but yelled as they all crashed to the ground. His hand was back pinning my legs to his chest. My other friends all looked up but none of them could get free of their opponents.

My arms were flung over his back, but a jab in my hip

reminded me of my dagger. This guy was determined to keep running so I worked on getting the dagger out.

The yelling from my friends had faded by the time I felt the handle of the dagger in my hand. My plan had been to stab him somewhere vital in the back, but I was bouncing too much. Not to mention my dagger had other plans. I was holding it, trying to time at least a decent strike, when the dagger started its nice green sparking. I'd only seen it respond to non-living things, so I wasn't sure what to expect. It crackled a bit, then green sparks shot out all over my attacker.

He screamed and threw me off him as he frantically fought the green sparks. I couldn't figure out what they were going after—then I saw it. They were going after anything metal in his clothes and on the armor he wore. And from the yelling, they hurt like hell.

Once he'd dumped me, he started backing away, thinking the sparks would stop. They didn't, but they did make him keep running.

I slowly got to my feet; that had been a hard fall. I looked down at the dagger. "Thanks, little guy. I will think up a name for you, soon." He wasn't sparking anymore so I put him back in his sheath and gingerly jogged back to where I could still hear fighting. My sword came back, scaring the crap out of me, but it would be good to have if there was still swordplay.

I ran into the faeries first. They were awake now but staggering about and none of them were flying. I tried to pick them up, but they kept falling out of my hand and I was still holding a sword. I nudged and pushed them toward a boulder. "Stay here until you can all fly. I'll be back for you." A few nodded but all of them were still disorientated. At least the boulder should keep them from being stepped on.

I continued running and got to the carriage just in time to see the last attacker get punched in the gut, then smacked in the head by Mathilda's stick. "I want one alive."

Padraig nodded and grabbed the unconscious attacker.

"Where's Alric?"

They both turned. "He went to get you once we'd gotten these ones under control," Padraig said. "You didn't see him?"

"No and I was yelling the entire way." There was no way I could have missed him. I started to turn back, then remembered the faeries. "Can I borrow Welsy and Delsy?"

Padraig was tying up the one Mathilda had knocked out, and Mathilda nodded as she went around making sure the others were dead.

Welsy and Delsy came to me, and the three of us ran back to the faeries. A few were walking normally and one or two gave small flying leaps. One was Crusty. "Delsy, stay here and help the faeries. If Alric comes back this way, stop him." I grabbed Crusty and two others who looked close to flight and set them on my shoulder. "Hang on, girls. Welsy, you're with me. Can you track Alric?" Non-construct brownies could be excellent trackers when they put their minds to it. I hoped that Siabiane gave her constructs similar abilities.

Welsy nodded, then tilted his head and started running. It was in the same general direction my attacker had been dragging me but veering toward a pile of rocks. I finally saw Alric. He looked unconscious and was being carried by a huge troll, one I knew I hadn't seen in the original group. Another person, semi-transparent, was waiting near the largest part of the pile of boulders and was creating a vortex.

There was no way I could get there in time, and the faeries I had weren't flying well, nor would they be a match for that thing. So, I took my dagger and threw it.

The semi-transparent being held up a hand and the dagger flew back at me. Stabbing me in the hand wasn't something either of us expected to happen. I screamed and a bolt of green fire ran through me and out from my other hand into the rocks, shattering the transparent image, the vortex, and obliterating most of the rocks. The troll dropped Alric and ran away into the forest.

I dropped to my knees in pain and shock as the dagger pulled its way out of my hand, the wound closing itself up as it went. Good thing too. There was a lot more of my blood on the ground than I liked to see. It still hurt like mad, but not gushing was good. I put the dagger back in its sheath and ran to Alric.

He had a darkening bruise on his forehead but was slowly coming around. Crusty and the other two faeries dropped to him and started patting his face.

"It's okay, girls. I think he's waking up."

His eyes fluttered open, and then immediately shut again.

Crusty stomped up his face and sat on his cheek. "Is there?"

"Too close. Way too close." Alric's words were low but I could hear him.

"Yes, Crusty, he's there. Maybe all of you should back off a bit." The three all flew up. That was good. "Are you okay?" I helped him up.

"Yes, but it's getting disturbing how many times you've been saving me as of late." He rubbed the back of his neck. "That damn troll came out of nowhere and bashed me as I was running after you. Are you all right?"

"I hurt my hand, but I can explain later. Let's go pick up the rest of the faeries and get back to the others." I'd thought since they could fly, Crusty and the other two might take off, but they remained nearby. Welsy also stayed close and was watching the woods as we started back.

"Do you sense something?" Alric asked Welsy, but the same could have been asked of the faeries. All of them were extremely watchful. Uncommon for Crusty.

"Bad things." Crusty flew closer to us.

"There is something in the air." Welsy was a little less

cryptic than Crusty but not much.

Nothing happened on the way back to the rest of the faeries. Delsy was chastising one as we walked up. "They tried to leave. I explained they needed to stay here. I don't believe they are fully recovered."

I kept from laughing at his face. He looked like an annoyed mother with misbehaving children. "Thank you, Delsy, they can be a bit difficult." I turned to Welsy and Crusty. Do you still feel whatever was wrong?" Alric and both brownies started picking up the grounded faeries. About half were flying now, but even Garbage landed on my shoulder instead of flying.

"Is no. Back there." Crusty landed on my head and patted my hair. "We go that way." A tug on my hair told me I was supposed to go back to the carriage.

"Do you sense anything? Magically?" I asked Alric, as he finished getting the faeries onboard.

He sighed. "No, but my head is pretty scrambled. That troll really got me, and I don't know how we didn't see him before. They aren't known for being quiet." We started back toward the carriage. Everyone was quiet, even the faeries, but I know I didn't hear anything.

Padraig and Mathilda had moved the bodies away and had their captive tied up to a tree. He was still out, but his chest was moving so he was still alive.

"What happened to you?" Padraig walked up to Alric and looked at his face. "Did you run into a rock?"

The faeries who had been riding Alric's shoulders fluttered to the ground and ran into the carriage along with all but Garbage, Leaf, and Crusty.

"A troll ran into me. Full speed for both of us and I didn't hold up well." He looked to their prisoner. "We'll fill you both in later; did you get anything from him yet?"

He'd been unconscious when I left, and he was again. But Mathilda nodded. "More than he would have liked. That too, should wait until we're not here. I will kill in defense, but not in cold blood."

Padraig shook his head. "I won't either. And he won't recall much of what happened. But we should leave soon. I'd like to get to Siabiane's cottage before dark."

Either they believed their prisoner was awake but faking it, or they too sensed something or someone else out here in the woods.

Crusty was still on my head and Garbage and Leaf fluttered in front of me. "No good. Need hide."

"We're working on that, ladies." I paused. "Is it okay if we get back on the road?" The faeries had their own way of seeing the world, but sometimes they saw things we couldn't. They were acting extremely odd, even for them.

Crusty flew off my head and the three held a brief but animated conversation. Finally, they broke up.

"Go. Now." Crusty flew up and started pulling my hair. The other two didn't go for hair but they were trying to push the others into the carriage.

"Maybe we should get moving quickly? Ow!" Crusty pulled harder, as apparently, I wasn't moving fast enough. I climbed into the carriage and was joined by the others except for Alric and Delsy, who took the driver's bench.

I wasn't sure if it was the faeries or something else, but a skin-crawling feeling hit me, and the dagger started glowing in his sheath. I'd sent back my sword when we grabbed the faeries, but it popped back now across my lap.

Alric clicked to the horses and they quickly started running. We'd only traveled for a few minutes when he opened the secret path, and a large pressure wave caught the back of the carriage.

CHAPTER TWENTY FIVE

THE CARRIAGE ROCKED BUT DIDN'T slow down. "Hold on!" Alric yelled, as we veered to the side. As far as I knew these paths just had one direction once they were created, so I looked out to see where we had veered.

Not a good idea. The tunnel around the path was swirling like crazy, and more tunnels kept shooting off it. Before I could stop them, a group of faeries flew out the window and up to Alric where they started yelling directions of some sort. He raced down another tunnel and they settled down. But none of them came back into the carriage. After a few minutes, the tunnel settled down to what it had looked like on the way up here—minus the black spot.

Alric slowed to a more reasonable pace, and I swore the horses tied to the back of the carriage nickered in gratitude.

"Anyone want to tell me what happened?" It hadn't gone unnoticed that during our wild ride Padraig's sword appeared, and both he and Mathilda seemed to be preparing spells. My sword vanished when Alric slowed down.

Padraig had leaned over to the window on the other side and was watching the slowly swirling tunnel. "There was someone else out there, or at least nearby. Someone threw a spell as we entered the vortex; it could have killed us by collapsing the tunnel around us."

"Who captured Alric?" Mathilda had released the spell

she'd been holding and was shaking out her shoulders.

I quickly explained how I'd found him and that the thug who had grabbed me had been prepared for the faeries. The more I spoke, the darker their faces grew.

"Maybe the enclave really wasn't under attack—it could be trying to get you and Alric." Mathilda watched the faeries who'd stayed in the carriage sit and chatter among themselves. "I wish I knew what they'd thrown on them. It's not easy to disable a faery."

Welsy picked up the two faeries closest to him. "Do you have a piece of fabric?"

Mathilda looked around and found a bit of fabric from the inside of her bag. "Will this work?"

Welsy nodded and thoroughly shook both faeries over the fabric. A light blue dust drifted down. He then did the same with two more. The faeries didn't mind and must have thought it was some sort of game as they lined up in pairs.

Mathilda held up her hand after the third pair. "Thank you. I believe I have enough to determine what it is. Although, given what you told me, and the color of this dust, I can make a guess." She said a soft spell over the fabric, and it sealed in on itself, securing the light blue dust. "This is varlick powder, taken from the bark of trees native to the islands below the southern continent. Someone mixed it with a natural sedative. Enough could knock out a person or ground some faeries." She looked up. "Someone was expecting the faeries and had done a lot of research."

"But why take Alric and me? And if we were the targets all along, why did they grab Siabiane, Lorcan, and Padraig?"

"Because, aside from Mathilda who hadn't been involved until you sent for her, we were the ones most able to protect you. They took away your power to defend yourself first, then tried to take us out."

"That's why the troll grabbed Alric? But they already had me at that point." This wasn't making sense, and if they were going to keep picking off my friends, I was going to find a way to stop them. "Unless that's why they're doing it." I was answering my own unspoken question, but both heard me.

"Unless that's why they're doing what?" Mathilda had that kindly, are-you-going-crazy look in her eyes as she leaned forward.

"Sorry, talking to myself. My response in my head was that I'd go wherever they were taking my friends, or Alric. We're back to them picking off everyone I know if I don't go down there." I flung myself back into the seat. "They could have picked up the faeries as well once they'd taken you all out."

"That does seem to be what's going on, but why?" Mathilda shook her head. "I don't think that many people know what you really are."

Padraig moved the chest closer. "I think when we get to Beccia and someplace reasonably safe, we need to look over those scrolls you spoke of. I wouldn't trust whoever sent them, but the enemy-of-my-enemy-is-my-friend can have validity. Someone might really want to stop whoever is doing this for their own gain."

"We're closing in on Beccia," Alric called back to us. "When the tunnel stops, we'll still be about an hour out. I don't want to get too close."

"In case whoever threw that spell is right behind us, I assume?" I was already tired of being chased.

"Most likely. There wasn't a strong magic user in the lot we fought, but like the troll who grabbed Alric, I think we can be sure not everyone showed themselves." Mathilda folded her faery dust cloth up, put it into her bag, and moved some things around inside it. "When we're wher-ever we're going, I think we should look at the other chest and the key the faeries gave you."

I'd forgotten about both. I still wasn't sure how a chunk of wood could be called a key, but I was certain it made sense to the faeries. "Oh, and that odd ball from Siabiane's guest room, the one Crusty was bouncing around on." Forgot about that too, until she brought up the other two.

She frowned. "Depending upon how secure the place we are in is. That had an awful lot of force for something so small. I couldn't tell what it was or what was causing it to do what it did. We'll need to be careful with it."

The tunnel ended and I found myself looking at the outskirts of the Beccian ruins. No diggers would be out this far, and the road was rarely used. The faeries all flew out the window, and I heard a few grunts from Alric as the ones riding on him took off as well.

"We must be close enough for them." I watched them vanish into the forest. It already seemed like it had been far more than a few days since we left.

The ride back was peaceful, but I was surprised when Alric led us up to my house. I had no idea where his hidden spot was, but I doubted my place was secret. He got down from the driver's seat and started untying the horses from the back.

"Your hidey-hole is at Taryn's house?" Padraig said it before I did, but I assumed we were all thinking the same thing.

"No, but this carriage is noticeable enough, I don't need the added strain of hiding the extra horses."

I heard the gronking first, then Bunky, Irving and the entire pack of faeries, including the ones who had been with us, came swooping down the street from the general direction of the Shimmering Dewdrop. Followed by Covey, Grillion, and Harlan.

"Okay, none of that is going to be subtle." I was glad to see my friends, but we needed to get that chest and the other weird assortment of things we'd collected to somewhere safe. I would say Alric made a mistake coming here first, but with the constructs and the faeries leading the way they all would have found us regardless.

Bunky swooped down to try to head bump Alric and it was a near miss.

"Good of you to come back." Covey jogged up ahead of the others and greeted Padraig and Mathilda. "And you're friends with brownies now?" She took a step back upon seeing Welsy and Delsy.

"It's okay, they're friends. Like Irving and Bunky. They're Siabiane's friends." I felt too exposed to talk about things out here. Maybe hanging around Alric so much was making me as paranoid as him. Not that he was necessarily wrong.

Covey nodded as she caught the construct reference. "Nice to meet you then, Welsy and Delsy." She'd peered at their name tags. "Siabiane isn't coming down too?"

Padraig stepped up. "No, she and Lorcan went to her place in the country. But we'd like to drop this carriage off before we get into things. We're leaving the extra horses here."

Then Harlan and Grillion caught up to us. Harlan never ran unless someone was trying to kill him, and Grillion seemed to be of the same mentality. I quickly introduced Grillion and the brownies. The feeling of being watched was growing. Padraig and Mathilda brought out everything that had been in the carriage—except the chest.

"I'll go return this, then come back here. We can catch up at Taryn's place." Alric swung back into the driver's seat but didn't say anything when Welsy and Delsy joined him.

"I could go with you?" Grillion stepped up. "Lots of exciting bar fights to talk about."

Alric waved him off. "Get settled in here. It'll just take a bit." He got the horses moving.

Everyone turned to me, even the faeries. "Okay, then. Why don't we all go in and make ourselves comfortable." Grillion didn't appear worried, so I hoped the house looked okay. I would have rather chatted at the pub, but this would be more secure from prying ears and eyes. The faeries and constructs buzzed through the house and then back out.

"Back later," Garbage said as they flew off.

I shook my head and went inside. The house looked better than when I left.

"I did some tidying while you were away, cleaned up the sofa, and restocked your food." Grillion stood back proudly as we entered, as if it were his home.

"Could I bother you for some tea?" Mathilda had her innocent old woman appearance on, and Grillion practically tripped over himself getting to the kitchen.

"Tea for all! Never can have too much tea. And cookies, I picked up some of those as well." If anyone had ever thought he was some sort of master criminal, that was gone now. He was almost giddy at serving tea and cookies.

All of us sat and I lifted an eyebrow in Mathilda's direction. She leaned in close. "I might have overdone the charm a bit. Do we think he's trustworthy? Or should I slip him a little something stronger?"

I watched Grillion buzzing around my kitchen with mixed feelings. I wasn't up to entertaining, and although the wound had closed, my hand still hurt. Still, it was a bit odd to see someone else in my kitchen. I didn't know him well enough to know what he could be trusted with. Aside from my house, that was.

Covey sat next to me on the sofa. "He's been fine while you were gone. Helpful and not too much of a problem. Those fights he was talking about weren't even out of the normal, nor was he involved."

Padraig also kept his voice low and faced both Harlan and Covey. "Would you trust him with any of the relics?"

Covey and Harlan both pulled back with varying looks of panic. "They're back?"

"No, but there are things like them. And it's appearing like that's the level of trouble we're in." I was watching Grillion and he was about to leave the kitchen.

They glanced at each other and then shook their heads. "We don't know him well enough," Harlan said.

"Never fear, I won't hurt him." Mathilda sat back as the tea and cookies were served.

"You didn't bring Hass back I see. The elves kept him, didn't they?" He nodded as he sipped his tea.

This we could talk about. I gave him an abbreviated story of what happened and ended up with the vanishing of Fealk, the troll, Hass, and the death of Domniall's changeling.

Grillion's eyes were about the size of his saucer and his mouth dropped open. "So that thing…wasn't a necromancer at all, but a changeling? And it killed itself?" He set down his tea. "I don't know which is worse." He picked his tea back up and downed it quickly.

Harlan and Covey sat in silence, but from the way they both kept glancing at Grillion, I knew a big part of it was wondering what they should say in front of him.

"You know? I'm glad you're back. Yes, indeed. But I think I need to go lie down for a bit. Too much excitement for one day, you see." Grillion started listing to one side.

Padraig grabbed Grillion's teacup before it slid out of his hand, and Harlan pulled him to his feet.

"You do look uncommonly tired, my friend. Maybe a short rest." With a shrug to us, Harlan walked the almost staggering Grillion down the hall. He came back a few moments later. "Never let me do anything that makes you mad, Mathilda. He was asleep the moment I dropped him in the bed." He started to pick up his tea, then froze. "It wasn't something in the tea, was it?"

Mathilda laughed and took a sip of her own tea. "No, it was a suggestion spell only. But I do love tea."

We quickly filled Harlan and Covey in on what had happened in the past few days. Harlan's eyes were round, but Covey looked annoyed.

"I told you not to go on adventures without me. So,

what happens now?" Her arms were folded a little too tightly for my comfort. She did that when she didn't want to strangle someone by accident.

I hadn't mentioned the chest Alric was hopefully now hiding in whatever secret hidey-hole he had. I wished I'd gone with him to see where the place was, but it might have made it harder to keep Grillion from wanting to go.

"Now we make plans," Mathilda said. "Something is going on to the south, the far south. I believe some of us will need to go down there to get Lorcan and my sister back." She looked to me. "And some need to stay here, like Taryn."

It was a good thing I'd sat down my teacup as I leapt to my feet. "I am the one who can't stay here. Didn't we just discuss this in the carriage?"

The door opened and Alric came in with a sack. "I only overheard the last part, and I agree with Mathilda. I secured the carriage and the chest, don't worry. But I did go through a few of the scrolls and brought back the ones that seem to be related. It's hard to tell since reading them fully will take a while. I don't think we can let Taryn go down south." He went to the dining table and took the scrolls carefully out of his sack. "I left Welsy and Delsy guarding the rest."

"What are those?" Covey looked at all of us. "And what chest?" Her nose was practically twitching as she stalked toward the table. Alric wisely stood back.

"I thought it best to tell them about those, and it, when you got back. I didn't know you were bringing some out." Mathilda also went to the table, but less aggressively than Covey.

I quickly summarized the chest but stayed out of everyone's way. Padraig had been told about the scrolls and their mysterious arrival, but he hadn't seen any of them. Covey and Harlan were in danger of damaging them by drooling.

"These are from the library of Pernasi? And someone

simply appeared and gave them to you?" Covey didn't look toward me as she spoke; she just kept looking at the scrolls.

"Yes. Maybe it's more common in the south, but an apparition appeared and gave me the chest with those scrolls in it. As for what they are? I'm taking Mathilda's word for it." Even when I was still actively digging, I preferred tangible finds of a civilization over scrolls.

"These are amazing, and I can't even read them." Covey reverently held one up to Padraig. "Can you read them?"

"Probably. It might take us a while, but Mathilda, Alric, and I should be able to get through some. But it's mostly an old form of elvish."

"What I want to know is why everyone thinks these indicate that I should stay here, while you all go south to save Siabiane and Lorcan." I really couldn't believe that I was arguing to go running into danger. But the image of Alric being carried to that vortex was terrifying.

Both Alric and Mathilda started to answer at once, but he gestured for her to go first.

"Thank you. I have a feeling that they are taking only those people around you. Note that your closest friends remained unharmed because you were not here. If we are not with you, then we cannot be used as leverage to get you to come south."

"Except that I would be imagining all of you being taken while you're gone and most likely follow on my own." I held up my hand. "And, they could be targeting people they have seen me around—with or without me being around them." It made more sense in my head, but we had little to go on.

"They want your blood." Alric's voice was low and he held a small scroll. "I couldn't help myself and as I was picking which ones to bring back, I skimmed a few. Most are such an archaic version of elvish that I couldn't really read them, at least not quickly. But this one I could." He handed the scroll to Padraig and Mathilda, while Covey peeked around them. "Not all of your people stayed in the north. Long before the incident happened, there were Ancients living in the south. Then the evil mages moved in from whatever hell they came from. It was an alliance of hilstrike mages, necromancers, and more. According to this, dragon's blood can give unimaginable powers to the right magic users."

I sat back down and looked at all of them. "But that's a myth, right?"

"Your people were not in our lands when Siabiane and I were growing up, not even as a myth." Mathilda shook her head. "The magic users referred to in this scroll were known to us, however. They were called the Jerinthati. There are massive dead holes in the land, worse than the most lifeless deserts, which are said to be their final battle areas. They destroyed themselves thousands of years ago—possibly after killing or at least chasing away your people."

"I'd say someone is bringing back the old ways." Padraig finished reading the scroll and stepped back to let Covey in closer to the rest of them on the table.

I had no idea what to say. Nothing. "How do we stop them?"

Harlan came back with me and dropped down on the sofa next to me. "We protect you. You don't go down there, you let the others stop them."

The sincerity in his face was brutal. He wasn't a fighter by any means, but he meant each word. I started crying as I looked at my friends—my family. "I can't let them destroy you to get to me. There has to be another way."

Loud laughter filled the little tunnel the faeries used when my door was shut. Not the most appropriate given the situation but it did make me smile.

Harlan wiped my tears away as the faeries flew in.

"We here!"

"Need in."

They flew around the door handle until Harlan went

and opened the door. Bunky and Irving flew in with a huge basket of food. And Amara was right behind them.

"I thought you might need some food and if the tension coming from this house is any indication, none of you were planning on leaving to get it." She held up her hands. "No, my goddess powers are not back, so no one die any time soon. But there are enough magics still in me to sense when things are wrong." She peered up at all of us, then settled on me. "This one is the worst. Taryn, what's wrong?"

Again, the full summary, this time with no hesitation. Amara had brought Alric back from the dead, she could be told anything.

I wasn't sure what I'd been expecting, but pure anger was not it. I swore I saw her face turn dark.

"Hilstrikes? Grimarians? Necromancers? In the south? Any evil plant worship in those scrolls? My people weren't the type of goddesses to stay in one area. It was my sisters and I who finally put an end to the Jerinthati uprising over five thousand years ago."

"Could you do it again? Even without your goddess standing?" There might have been a bit too much hope in my voice.

"Sadly, no. Even if I were still a goddess, I couldn't do it alone. It took all of us to stop them last time." She looked to the scrolls but didn't pick them up. "Those might help you. I will say one thing: the beings we stopped long ago were so powerful it was felt in every land. Even without all my powers, I would have felt it if they had somehow returned. No matter how far away they were."

"That doesn't mean someone isn't trying to resume what they started. Were the Dark involved?" Mathilda asked.

"The Dark were not around when this happened, the elves were still young. However, they could be working with whoever is behind this now. Obviously, Foxy will have to go with you."

I did a double take. "What now? Wouldn't it be better if you went?" I adored Foxy, and he was great to have in a non-magical fight. But up until a few years ago, he rarely left the pub, let alone Beccia. Not to mention traveling to an entirely different continent.

"I can't. I was able to move about at great distances from my tree because I was a goddess. However, now I am only slightly more magical than a normal dryad. My days of going far outside of Beccia are over." She didn't seem that sad, and I wondered if the pain of being the last of your kind negated the helpfulness of being a goddess.

"That explains you staying here, but why do you think Foxy needs to go?" Alric pulled himself away from the scroll he was trying to read. No one was able to read them quickly, but all three elves were slowly getting through them.

"He and I have had a long talk. I wasn't sure what was coming, but I've felt off for the past few days. My tree felt it too. Then when you got closer, I sensed another major shift. This information has settled things in my mind. I can't explain it, beyond that he needs to be there."

"A prophecy?" We'd had what we thought were a few prophecies pop up while looking for the relics—none of them were accurate. Well, maybe the faeries ones had been but since they really weren't good at explaining, we'd never know for sure.

"Sort of?" She shrugged. "I can't really explain. But trust me, you know I would never send him away, certainly not to face what might be down there, without a powerful reason. This is a major world change. Like when you sent your people away and changed the syclarions." She nodded to me and then looked around. "It's not all doom and gloom. I will be able to communicate with Foxy and one other. Taryn would be the best, if she will accept it."

I looked at the others, but they were as confused as I was. Or at least projecting that. "They were trying to keep me here. What do I have to accept?"

Amara gave a sad smile. "A simple mark, a tattoo of a sort. Foxy has his on his calf, but I can put it on your arm if that would be easier. It is part of my remaining magic and will allow me to communicate with you from any distance through the power of my tree. I can't go there, but my memories of that place and those people are strong. I can help guide."

"It would be helpful, right? Because I *am* going." I glared at the others, softening it a bit when my gaze hit Alric.

Amara tilted her head. "Of course, you must go. You are possibly the only one who can stop what they are trying to bring back."

Alric stepped closer. "They want her blood to increase their magic. It's in this scroll."

"And were you planning on letting them have her?" She looked around. "Any of you? I know Foxy wouldn't."

"That isn't always enough," Mathilda said. "We need more protection, and I don't know that we have time if what you sensed is true—and I think we can believe it is."

"You have some already—those scrolls. Have other items come into your possession in mysterious ways? Prophecies always find a way to get things to people, even if the person doing it has no idea. I've never liked that part about them." Amara rubbed her eyes. "I know I sound like an avenging goddess and in my heart, I still am. But I know this is something that has to be done."

"You're saying Taryn has to go, and Foxy. Anyone else?" Harlan had been watching everything closely, but I noticed he was standing back from the scrolls.

"I really can't see that. And whoever goes has to be aware that they may not come back." She'd started crying but smiled. "Trust me on this, even Foxy might not return, and telling him about this almost killed me. But it has to be done. I fear far more than the fate of your missing friends hangs in the balance."

"Harlan shouldn't go." I was off to the side but also a bit behind him. I saw his shoulders drop at my words. He'd never been a fighter and honestly, I was surprised he survived the adventures he had joined us on. But he was also an extremely proud and stubborn cat. "We need someone to stay here, to help Amara." I was scrambling; honestly, even de-goddessed I had a feeling Amara could hold her own—not to mention Dogmaela and the rest of the pub staff.

"I suppose Orenda would be most put out if I left. She still hasn't come home and there is something going on with the elves. I might be needed to help." Harlan nodded as if he was thinking about it, but I saw relief in his eyes.

Covey clapped him on the shoulder. "Thank you for staying here. We need to know Beccia is safe."

I knew their relationship had changed, but that touched me. Covey knew he wasn't a fighter and was trying to make him feel better about not going.

"It's settled then. Will you be taking all the faeries? The constructs?" The relief on his face was clear, but he was still going to do what he could to help.

I looked to where the faeries were digging through their playhouse. "It has to be up to them. Up to all of you. Each being decides whether they stay or go. Constructs included." We'd have to speak to Welsy and Delsy; they needed the chance to help bring back Siabiane.

Crusty flew over to me, even though I swore she'd been with her friends in the dollhouse. "Is you. Follow you." She pushed one tiny finger into my chest, then looked around as if she lost something. "Where key?"

Mathilda went to her bag and pulled out the piece of wood with the dragon carving and handed it to me. Not subtle if they were after dragon blood.

Amara immediately came to my side as I held it up. "Oh, this is magnificent." Her eyes were almost glowing bright green as she looked up. "Can I touch it?"

I handed it to her. I knew she got excited about living trees, but didn't know she'd react to an obviously long dead one.

She ran her hand over it with the same reverence that a banker handled money. "Do you know what this is? Where did you find it?"

Several details got dropped during the initial run-through of our story, so I caught her and the others up on the key.

"You found this in a room? Just a room? No one gave it to you?" She seemed to be studying each tiny section. The thing was only about a foot long, but at the rate she was going it would take her an hour or so to look it over.

"Well, there was a chest in the closet of Siabiane's spare bedroom. But I don't think it had been there the night before. Three of the faeries went into the chest, which seems to have a vortex in it, and when they came out, they had this."

Crusty flew to Amara and sat on the wooden piece. "Is good. Need key. He help." She patted the wood. She also called my dagger he, so that wasn't too unusual.

Amara smiled. "I believe he will. It is good to see you again, old friend."

I looked to the others in case they were seeing something I missed. Crusty talking to a block of wood wasn't shocking, but Amara doing so—more importantly, now tilting her head toward it as if it was speaking back—was.

"It is okay, I am not crazy. Part of what drove my sisters and me to go fight five thousand years ago was what the Jerinthati were doing to the sentient trees. This was once a tree named Oak-far-from-river. A massive tree who could have covered all of Beccia." Her face fell. "We didn't get there in time to save him. After the battle some of the remaining pieces were carved and given their own spirit names. I don't know what he is a key for. He doesn't either, but he is good to have on this trip."

I really wasn't sure what a semi-sentient piece of wood

that probably couldn't talk to any of us was going to do, but it couldn't hurt to bring it along. Probably. My new mantra was that anything could hurt you if it tried hard enough.

"Do you have the chest with the vortex?" Alric hadn't been with us when we found it. I was surprised he held off asking about it for this long.

Mathilda nodded and pulled out her faery bags. "There do seem to be a lot of bags, aren't there? Some are Lorcan's that he managed to leave when he and my sister were taken." They carefully moved some of the scrolls over, and she started taking things out of the collection of faery bags.

A pile of books came out of one, and Covey not so subtly drifted over to try to look at them, then a familiar chest came out of the second. I reached for the next bag, but it felt like it was moving. "Is this what I think it is?" I held it carefully. The twitching was subtle but there. Nothing should be twitching in one of these bags. I had no idea what to call an insane, odd, glowing, and destructive ball but I didn't think we wanted to take it out.

Mathilda nodded. "I think that needs to stay inside its bag. Unless you know of some glowing ball that destroys rooms and is part of anything important?" She turned to Amara.

Crusty ran across the table and jumped up to my hand and the bag. "Is mine!"

I pulled my hand back and closed it tightly over the bag. "It is not. It was bouncing all over with you on it."

"Sounds like Crusty," Harlan said.

Amara watched as Crusty tried to get to the bag in my hand. "I have to say that I don't know of anything like that, but I wouldn't get rid of it. It might have come to you for a reason. Or it could be something that bounced through that chest vortex."

Padraig and Alric stood near the chest. "So, can we open it?"

I found they were both looking at me. "Sure? I mean does anyone have a reason that we shouldn't? Aside from the fact I saw a swirling vortex in there before?"

"I say let's see what we have." Covey had moved closer as well.

"Okay, but no one flies into it this time." The grunted mutters I heard behind me pointed out that the rest of the faeries were out of their playhouse, and that they'd planned on diving into the chest as soon as it was opened.

Padraig looked over to them. "I'll make sure they don't go in."

Even Crusty sighed in defeat at that, but since she was still far too close to the table and the chest, I grabbed her, after handing off the weird bouncing ball faery bag to Mathilda. I could hold Crusty in one hand but wanted a second one free in case anyone else got bright ideas.

Alric opened the chest slowly and Padraig stood nearby in case something came out. Or tried to suck Alric in.

"Nope, there's nothing in it." He leaned forward and tapped the sides. The rest of us peered in as well. A nice empty chest.

"There was a vortex—honestly. Three of the faeries even flew into it." I stepped back as Crusty started to squirm.

"Is gone?" She kicked at the right spot and my hand flung open. She flew to the chest and was followed by the rest of the faeries—even the ones that had stayed here during the earlier trip and not seen that chest before.

"There's nothing here." Padraig still had his hands on the top of the chest to slam shut if needed, but let the faeries see for themselves.

Garbage flew into the chest, made a few laps, and then flew up and into my face. "You lost! Where go?"

"Girls, I can promise you I had nothing to do with the vortex being lost. Whoever set it up probably closed it." I glanced over to Padraig for confirmation. I had no idea how vortexes worked, and I wasn't sure it was something

I needed to know.

Padraig nodded. "Vortexes can be tricky; this one might have had a short timer set on it. I'm more concerned about who put it there and why. I don't recall anything odd about the guest room when we got there, but Siabiane led us straight to the workroom."

"Good point." Alric picked up the chest and tapped around the outside. "It seems like a normal chest."

Crusty had drifted away from the others and before any of us could stop her, she grabbed the bouncing faery bag from Mathilda and threw it into the chest. The faeries all cleared out as it was coming in, so Padraig slammed shut the lid on it.

"And why did you do that?" The thumping inside the chest pointed out that either the ball had gotten far more active inside the bag, or she'd untied the bag as she threw it.

"Needed go back—make the pretty booms again."

Oh no, back to boom.

"Do you mean the vortex? That weird ball is somehow related to the vortex?"

"Boom make ball. Ball make boom." Garbage linked her fingers together.

"Ideas?" I looked around but everyone was watching the chest.

"Might as well find out what it did." Covey put her hand on the lid and Padraig didn't stop her. He did have a spell ready in his hand. So did Alric and Mathilda. Harlan and Amara looked curious, and I'm sure my face held an expression of fear.

At first it seemed like the chest was the same. Then two balls bounced out of it and a weird glowing light was reflected up.

"And down it goes." Covey shut the lid while the rest of us dodged the light yellow-green glowing balls.

Except Amara. She yelled some strange words and held

out one hand palm up. The two balls bounced a few more times, trailed by squealing faeries, then landed in her hand. They were still moving a bit, but only slightly.

"There was only one before." I glared at Crusty, but she was too busy looking at the balls and grinning.

Amara patted both. "Oh, more friends, long lost and well met." She looked up at us. "I think I know what your key might be related to. These are tree spirits, extremely old tree spirits, which are somehow getting through to us from that vortex. Can I see the key?"

I handed it over. The little balls rolled a bit as she took it, then both bounced toward the wood and vanished. The edges of the key glowed a bit.

"Does anyone know what happened?" Covey asked.

"Someone is sending you help." Amara smiled and handed me the wooden box. "I recommend that Taryn keep this with her."

"Can I keep it in a faery bag? It's not that big but if we're traveling light, it might be an issue. But why me? And are more balls going to come out of that chest?"

"She's the Ceisiwr, isn't she?" Mathilda looked ready to hug me. "Oh, I do wish Siabiane were here. Lorcan too. They would be fascinated to know the ancient myth is coming alive. Not sure it said the seeker would be a dragon, though."

"The Ceisiwr?" I had no idea what she was talking about but judging by the facial expressions of my friends—they did. Or most. Harlan looked as confused as I felt.

"You really think she is the one? Dragon aside, she does fit some of the criteria." Covey was nodding and appeared to be studying everything about me.

"The one, what? Can someone please fill me in? Is this an elf thing?"

"The Ceisiwr, or the finder or seeker. An avenging spirit said to come and right the wrongs of the world." Amara was starting to glow with excitement.

Alric looked dubious. "It's not an elven thing, although we've passed the tales along. It's older. I think from before even your people. But it's a myth."

Mathilda wagged a finger at him. "You of all people should know myths sometimes become reality. If the stories are true, they are the people who created the *tir cudd*—the hidden pockets. Like where we found the diamond sphinx. They are said to be the founders of this world, or at least this half of it. The *tir cudd* existed long before you created your staff of relics, yet somehow that pocket of magic called a piece of your staff, the diamond sphinx, to it after you'd vanished."

"Doesn't an avenging spirit need to be, well, a spirit? As in dead? Pretty sure I'm still alive." I went and sat on the sofa. They were making things more complicated rather than less.

"You don't have to be dead, although that is usually the case with spirits." Padraig was starting to get into it now. "Technically, when you flung yourself forward in time, were you alive?"

"I have no idea." Up until a few weeks ago, I hadn't even known what I had done or who I really was. I certainly didn't remember the trip to this time.

Alric secured the vortex chest with a lock and came over to the sofa. "Siabiane believed whoever is blocking Taryn's magic had used the power of time, adding in the thousands of years that she came forward. Would that make a difference?"

Amara was watching me carefully. "It could. How did Siabiane stop the drain? I would think the purpose of the spell would have been to remove all of her magic. But I can still feel it there and your description of the power you shot into the visage, and the rock sounds like your magic got a jump start from the dagger."

I rubbed my palm. It still had a phantom ache. "A painful one. So, my magic really isn't gone for good?" That was something hopeful at least.

Mathilda responded to my question. "I don't think so. I wish I knew what my sister did to stop the drain, though."

I reached inside my shirt and held up the amulet she'd made. "She gave Alric and me these—or rather we made them per her instructions. I couldn't be near Alric before she gave it to me."

Mathilda and Padraig both leaned forward to look at the pendant, then Alric held up his as well.

"Yes, among other things, these would cut off the time portion of the spell being used against you. That might do it. I think everyone who goes on this jaunt, needs to have one of these amulets. Even your sleeping friend back there." Mathilda pointed down the hall toward the guest room and then started fussing in her bag.

"But Siabiane said these were to block magical possession—the fact it enabled me to be near people who had trained me, like Alric, had been a bonus." Or so I thought. The quick grin Mathilda flashed before she went back to looking in her bag told me Siabiane might have put more things in these amulets beyond what she told me.

"Can I touch the amulet?" Amara was suddenly next to me. I'd left it on the outside of my shirt but nodded.

She gently held the amulet and then turned it over slowly. "She did a good job. I knew I liked Siabiane. There are layers of protection on here, ones that go beyond when she told you." She spun to Alric. "May I?" She motioned to his amulet.

"Sure." He leaned forward a bit as she took both amulets in her hands.

"Very well created by our sneaky Siabiane. Others won't sense them at all, nor how powerful they are." Her smile turned into a confused scowl. "But you said they were trying to take Alric through a vortex set upon a rock?" She released both amulets.

"Yes, he was unconscious but the thing carrying him

was running toward a visage standing against a boulder. Too faint to see, but it might have been a Grimarian." I shrugged. It happened too fast. "I didn't have time to stop them, I was too far away. So, I threw the dagger."

"And the visage threw it back."

"Yes." That was another issue I needed to have explained. There were way too many of these visage things who were able to move objects on our side.

Amara shook her head. "They couldn't have dragged him through. This amulet would have blocked them from taking Alric through a solid object. That is a standard way to pull someone through a vortex and what it sounds like happened to Siabiane and Lorcan. But it couldn't have happened to Alric in that manner—not against a rock."

"These amulets stop them from dragging us through a vortex?"

"No. Just a vortex based on a solid object on this side. They can be built in the air or water, but both are much more difficult. This won't block against those, the casting of them is too complicated."

"Then what were they doing with him?"

Padraig shook his head and frowned. "It wasn't him, it was you. They were testing what you can still do. I'd say that dagger flew back exactly where they intended it to."

"They sacrificed their own people just to see what I could do? I'm pretty sure the troll holding Alric died when I sent that bolt. He ran off but was in bad shape. And if it's possible to damage someone in a visage form, the one casting the spell was fried."

"These people don't think like us," Padraig said. "They wanted to know if you had your magic. If you had been completely drained, nothing would have happened when the dagger hit you. Besides pain, obviously. That dagger is focusing your remaining magic somehow. I'd bet on it."

Mathilda turned to me. "I hadn't thought of that. But no one really knows how Robukian pieces work. Might I look at it?"

I felt reluctant to hand over the dagger but did so.

The faeries had scattered about the room once the chest had been shut, but now they flocked around Mathilda. Garbage, Leaf, and Crusty flew closest to her.

"Is friend." Crusty smiled to everyone as if she had been the one who brought him to us.

Mathilda, Padraig, Alric, and Amara all clustered around the dagger.

I was still on the sofa and Covey and Harlan came to sit with me.

"You really didn't have to go to this extreme if you wanted another adventure, you know." Covey shook her head but couldn't stop grinning. "The seeker? The Ceisiwr? That's deep even for my studies and is usually part of the myths and fables curriculum."

"I do wish I could go." Harlan held up his paw before we could speak. "No, I agree someone should stay here. But to see the lands of the far south, if that is where you end up. Think of the relics down there." He leaned forward. "If you can find something small, maybe from the early period, that would be lovely." His grin told me he was only half joking.

"Somehow I think we'll be busy trying to get our missing people back and stopping whatever this group of misfit magic users is up to. And finding a way to get my magic back." I patted his arm. "But if we can, I will bring back something." I knew he was saying it to distract me from what we were doing and what they were implying I specifically needed to be doing. I also knew he wouldn't object to a trinket.

Grillion stumbled out of the hall, looking like he'd been woken out of a dead sleep. His straw-colored hair was stuck up at odd angles. "Why is there a swirling lady in my room?"

CHAPTER TWENTY SIX

H E RUBBED HIS FACE BUT didn't appear any more awake. "Kinda looks familiar."

Padraig and Alric were closest to the hall and ran past him. Grillion kept stumbling forward and fell face first into the sofa. The rest of us went down the hall.

"Another visage. Seriously, how much power do they have that they can burn it like this?" Alric was at the door to the guest room but kept it mostly closed.

"Another vortex?"

He and Padraig pushed open the door completely. "No."

I peeked around him and found myself looking at a watery Qianru. The visage was so distorted that Grillion in his groggy state couldn't recognize her.

She was still blurry and the way she kept squinting told me we were fuzzy to her as well. "This is costing a lot of magic, I'll be brief. Under no circumstances are you to cross into the southern continent. Not at all."

I waited for the reason. "Why? There are some serious things going on."

"And some deadly things down here. I'm not sure what you've done up there, but there are a lot of rumors. And the Angari are coming out of the hidden past because of you."

I was about to ask who that was when Mathilda and Amara both gasped. "We know, will explain later. How does she know?" Mathilda spoke first, but Amara nodded.

I was getting tired of people going back and forth on where I needed to go. "How do you know? How are you doing this? Why can't I come down there?"

"I have friends who are doing the magic to open this and they can't hold it. We are part of a resistance. The Angari are growing. They will destroy you." There were more words in between those, but she faded out as she spoke. She vanished, and then came back. "Guard the chest! I'll try again when he's stronger." And she was gone again.

"What and who are the Angari? And which chest? If we count the one from the Dark, hidden in one of Lorcan's bags, we have three."

"I'd forgotten about that one." Padraig slowly walked to where Qianru's image had been. "What made you think of that?" He kept slowly walking through the area. I couldn't see anything, but maybe there was magical residue.

"It's the only one she would have known about. Unless she's able to spy up here in secret, the other two wouldn't be known to her. Are the Angari part of the Dark?"

"No," Mathilda answered. "The Dark might have become part of the Angari, but even if there was only one left, no Angari would join a group unless they were the leader. However, they could have gathered Dark, Grimarians, hilstrikes, and many more if there was still one alive."

"Aren't they, like Ceisiwr, a myth?" Covey hadn't come into the room but was staying right outside the door.

"Like the Ceisiwr, they are a myth with a basis in reality. Think of them as sort of where all the bad came in the world." Mathilda started back to the front room.

"Let me guess, they are also on the southern continent."

"In the far south, or at least that's where they originated." Alric left Padraig to his searches in the guest room. "But they were myths. I know, myths can be based on truth, but why would some cabal of evil from thousands of years ago come forward now? If they were real, they were destroyed long ago. How are they coming back?"

"I have no idea." Mathilda stopped and watched Grillion sleep. "Nor am I sure what he can be told."

"Maybe someone wants everyone to think they're back? They were destroyed long before I was even born. My people may or may not have come from the southern continent, but we'd been up here a long time before I started flinging them about. But what if this is a ploy by the remnants of the Dark?"

"I think you may be partially correct. The Angari were a subset of the larger group, the Jerinthati, whom my sisters and I destroyed five thousand years ago. And I do mean, destroyed." Amara drummed her fingers on her arms. "I wonder what I'm missing. As for why now, you might not have felt it, but when you reclaimed your power during that last battle, an echo went across the world. All that power that had been missing for so long. It made a big echo in the deep places."

Mathilda, Padraig, and Alric all looked at her.

"I didn't feel anything." Mathilda responded but the other two looked like they agreed with her.

"You don't have the connections to the earth that I do. That I did. When the realization of who she was and the memories came back, there was a vibration through the land." Amara gave me a small smile. "That's honestly what pulled me close enough to you to save Alric."

"I did feel something, but there was a lot going on at the time. I caused them to come back? These Angari?" I dropped down on the small section of sofa not being taken over by Grillion.

"No. Not you specifically. And they would have existed already; nothing could have brought them back otherwise. The power from you caused them to focus on you." Mathilda looked around. "And they think you are a dangerous sort. You do have power, even with your magic blocked as it is, but not what they think."

From where she leaned against the wall, Covey nodded. "So, we go south, without Taryn, get Siabiane and Lorcan back, then come home, and avoid triggering another twenty-five-hundred-year magic build-up in Taryn. Sounds like a plan."

I was about to point out a few dozen issues with her plan when something pounded on my door. "Doesn't anyone just knock?"

Covey got to the door before I could, only to find two annoyed and disheveled brownies. "They have attacked!" Welsy and Delsy ran in both looking ready to start cutting people off at the knees.

Alric ran forward. "Who? What's happened to the chest?"

"You were wise to be concerned, and the spell bubble you put over it still holds, but there is an attack on the room." Welsy waved a tiny sword about. It was covered in what looked like green blood.

Everyone started for the door, including the faeries, Bunky, and Irving.

"Wait, someone has to stay here. We still have things they might want." I looked back at Grillion, who was still drooling on my sofa.

"I can stay." Amara stood firm in the middle of my living room. Harlan nodded as well.

"Just in case this is a ruse, I will lend support on this end and guard the house. Go find out what has happened."

The faeries were flying around in the street as if they had no idea where we were going. Alric took the lead with Welsy and Delsy sprinting alongside. Their legs might be short, but they could keep up a good pace.

We ran along the road for only a short while, then Alric darted down a side path that led around the ruins. He'd said his spot was in the older ruins, where no one went, and he wasn't kidding about them being remote. I was ready to fall over by the time he stopped and held up his hand.

I didn't see anything but massive Gapen trees.

He waited until all of us were together, then stepped sideways around a massive tree and vanished. The brownies were almost on his heels and I was right behind. At first, I thought maybe Alric had been snatched when I didn't see him or the brownies. Then I saw the odd line past the closest tree. It was an illusion spell, but even without that this place was extremely well hidden. Just beyond the spell was a broken staircase that went below ground.

Glows bobbed along the way, but I was only halfway down when an explosion rocked the staircase and the area beyond it.

Alric swore and as I got to the ground floor, I saw him fighting with what could only be a Grimarian troll. Far uglier than it had been as a visage, and even worse than Zirtha. "Is it drooling?" No answer, but it looked to me like it was.

The others fanned out around me. Not that a Grimarian in person wasn't a danger, but there was only one. And we had the faeries. I looked around. "Where are the faeries?" They'd dropped behind us on the way here, but I hadn't noticed them or Bunky and Irving taking off.

"They were behind us. Then they started yelling about sweets and took off. Bunky and Irving followed." Covey was flexing and unflexing her clawed hands; waiting for the right moment to jump into the fight was my guess.

Damn it. Someone probably drew them away. Someone who knew how Zirtha died. Not good. But all of us against one? Still in our favor. I hoped.

The ground started cracking behind the Grimarian as we advanced on the fight. Alric was flinging spells more than sword fighting, but his sword was ready. His magic was keeping the Grimarian back, but she got a few strikes in.

Dark and wispy arms reached up through the floor, followed by the thin dark shapes I'd seen in Siabiane's guest room. But then the shapes changed into creepy-looking short, skeletal beings. These looked far too real. They weren't really skeletons, but gaunt enough to just be a missed meal away from being that.

"Stand back!" Alric yelled, as the creatures ran forward. Then they all zigged and ran up the stairs.

"What were those, and why did they take off?" I had my sword out.

The Grimarian clucked and shook her head. "And yet you are the threat we've heard of?" She was facing me but spun on Alric and hit him with enough magic to make him stagger back a few feet.

"I have to go after those things." Padraig was torn between helping Alric and the flight of monsters that ran out.

"Go, all of you. I can handle her." Alric recovered and responded with his own spells.

Padraig and Covey ran out. Welsy and Delsy paused and then followed. I had no magic and if even Alric couldn't get close enough for sword work my odds were not good. I put my hand on the dagger, but there was no spark. I had a bad feeling that if I threw it this time, I wasn't getting it back.

"Hold her as long as you can." I ran up after the others but stopped when I got a few feet from the entrance. Someone or something had pulled away the faeries. Again. I wasn't so much afraid of them being hurt, but they could have been trapped in that tree for a long time before we found them when they had been pulled away before.

I took out the dagger. There was a light crackling of green around it now. Clearly, it didn't like that damn Grimarian any more than the rest of us. I held it in my hands, hoping whatever magic it contained could help. Then I thought hard about the faeries. I put everything I could think of into the thoughts. Begging, pleading, wishing for them to come back to me.

"You called us?"

My eyes popped open to see Queen Mungoosey flying in front of me. The only cat faery I'd ever seen, she looked exactly like a four-inch gray cat with wings and a scarily smart expression. She didn't look angry, but her tail was twitching slightly. She had a few hundred faeries with her, but none of mine.

"There's a Grimarian down there. Somehow, they've drawn away Garbage Blossom and the others. We can't stop her."

Queen Mungoosey's tail poofed out completely and the lashing became stronger. "A Grimarian? Here? Against the treaty?" She waved one paw. "To war!"

The wild faeries steamed down the stairwell. The queen nodded. "Thank you again for this prey. This is twice they have sent one north against the treaty. We will deal with this." She gave a curt nod and flew after her faeries.

I had no idea what treaty she spoke of, but apparently a lot of folks weren't supposed to be this far north. I kept both my sword and dagger out as I ran down the stairs.

This Grimarian was apparently made of sterner stuff than Zirtha. The faeries were attacking but only a few were getting strikes in and many were on the ground. Stunned, and moving slowly, but not dead.

"She's got up a new shield of some kind," Alric yelled as he made another move toward her. He was staying on one side and the faeries were on the other, but the Grimarian was still holding her own.

My dagger was crackling away now. Little arcs of green lit the area. "Should I throw you?" I wasn't really expecting an answer, but I felt one anyway. Nope. "Charge her?" Really hoped for a no on this one, but it was shaking with the power of yes.

Crap. The Grimarian was holding her own, but had completely discounted me. She must have been the one who stole my magic and figured it was too tight in here for me to change into dragon form.

She wasn't counting on a violent dagger who didn't seem to like her.

The faeries swooped in as Alric made a lunge and cast a spell. I ran forward in between both with my sword high and my sparking green dagger low. I wasn't sure who was more surprised when I found myself plowing through her magic shield and right into the Grimarian, knocking us both over with my dagger going right into her. The crackling increased and soon was coming out of her mouth and fingertips. The faeries pulled back and I thought Alric did as well, but I couldn't lose focus to look around. This thing had to die.

Unfortunately, pulling away as she started splitting into shards of green probably would have been a good idea.

CHAPTER TWENTY SEVEN

———⋅———

S HE EXPLODED, SENDING ME, ALRIC, and a few faeries across the room. Along with an unfortunate amount of Grimarian goo.

Queen Mungoosey had managed to avoid the slime and was helping the downed faeries to their feet. The ones around me yelled and shook their war sticks. Which resulted in more slime being flung about.

"Eeewww!" I shook my hands, but the goo was all over me. I'd need a few weeks of baths to get rid of this. Luckily, the interior of a Grimarian wasn't red and bloody but green. But still, I knew what was on me.

Alric helped me to my feet. He too was slimier than he started, but I think I got the majority of it.

The faeries around us thought it was hysterical but then went to help their queen with the ones who had fallen.

Queen Mungoosey flew to me. "They will be okay, but I have worries for the ones who are missing. I'll send some out to look for them." She tilted her head. "There is a battle in your town, but we cannot help with that. I will find your faery friends." The snarl on her face told me she'd also take care of whoever had them. I'd like to know why it was okay to fight the Grimarian but not whatever those other things were, but now wasn't the time.

I thanked her and the faeries, then Alric and I ran up the stairs. After he checked the battered spell bubble he had placed on the chest.

"What did you do?" Alric led us back to town.

"It was him, the dagger. He really didn't like her." I mentally sent a thank you to the still nameless dagger.

Alric looked back briefly with a raised eyebrow and shook his head. Then he kept running.

I knew he wasn't running as fast as he could because I was keeping up, but still he was moving fast enough to dry the goo.

Beccia looked calm at first, then I heard the yelling. "What were those things that ran out?" They may have started looking like the wispy creatures both me and Padraig had seen, but they didn't end up that way. Maybe the tall, thin, and smoky look was a visage for them. Neither look was comforting.

"I have no idea. They aren't rakasas, and those are the only monsters I know that come from underground. They almost look like…no." Alric slowed down as we closed in on the noisiest part. I still couldn't see the fighting, but something was obviously happening as we neared the main street.

"No what?"

"They almost looked like small dwollers. Dwollers started as small underground scavengers. They evolved to the things we know and hate today a few thousand years ago. If those things were dwollers, they are some sort of primitive throwback."

We'd gotten close enough to the Shimmering Dewdrop to be overheard. "Aye, that's what Padraig said when he took off after them." Foxy was standing with Lehua, both armed with large pikes, in front of the pub. There were dozens of faces peering out of the windows. "Dogmaela is guarding the back. He told us to get as many people inside as possible and guard them. Then he and Covey ran that way. As did those wee brownies." He didn't look happy about that, but clearly wasn't going to argue if we were now aligning with brownies.

"Have you seen the girls? Or Bunky and Irving?" Most likely if the faeries had been drawn off, Bunky and Irving had followed them.

"Nay. Are you sure you don't want me to join?" He looked hopeful, but I had to think if Padraig set him to guard, there was a reason.

"Stay here. If you do see the faeries, send them our way." I flashed him a smile as Alric started moving again. I had no idea where exactly the ruckus was coming from, but elven ears were better than mine.

He led us down a side alley and up a few smaller streets.

I started to realize where we were headed. "Seriously? They're on the Hill? What for?" The Hill was the area where the rich and infamous had their mansions. They were the true rulers of Beccia. I'd only been up there a few times and the place almost bothered me as much as some of the worst neighborhoods.

"No idea why, but that's where the fighting is happening." He slowed down at the corner of a house and waited until I caught up. Then both of us peered around the corner.

We were still on the lower part of the Hill, and the houses here were big but not massive. But there was a wide-open area that lead to the massive ones and that seemed to be under attack.

The people who lived up on the Hill all had mini standing armies—okay, armies of usually fifteen or twenty guards. Men and women whom the rich kept on staff in case the riffraff became aggressive. Right now, it wasn't the riffraff they had to worry about.

The odd creatures, throwback dwollers, whatever they were, were charging into the open area. I would have estimated a dozen or so had run past us when we were in Alric's hidden room, but there were three to four times that many now. They weren't trying to fight the guards, just get around them. Since the guards were paid good money from what I heard to not let that happen—bloodshed was ensuing.

I saw Padraig and Covey in the middle of the fight at the same time Alric must have. He grabbed my hand and ran around and through the dwollers. Since we weren't getting in their way, they mostly ignored us. I did glance at one who was chewing on a guard. The guard was winning, it looked like, as he was stabbing the creature—but that didn't slow the dwoller down.

"They don't look bright." The main experience I'd had with a dwoller had been the crime lord, Cirocco. Scary smart. Until someone cut off his head. These weren't focusing on anything except their goal up the hill.

"They aren't," Padraig yelled, as we got to him and Covey. "But their numbers keep increasing. No idea where they are coming from."

Covey was grabbing them as they ran by, snapping them in half, and throwing them back behind her. A bit gruesome, but I appeared to be more upset about it than the surviving dwollers.

"What are they after?" There were more coming from somewhere down the road. They could win by sheer numbers as they were wearing the guards down.

Alric shook his head as he looked up the hill. "It could be anything up there, but I've no idea why. They don't look like they want riches and gold."

I looked around. A few got past the guards and were curving up the hill toward a large white and gold house. "They are going for Qianru's house!" I had no idea what she'd left behind when she left Beccia all those months ago, but there was something those mini dwollers wanted. Or more likely, something that Grimarian troll and whoever she'd been working with wanted.

I took off toward her house, with Alric, Padraig, and Covey around me. I hadn't seen Welsy and Delsy in the fight, but they broke free from wherever they were and joined in.

Five of the dwollers had cleared the twenty-foot-high wall around Qianru's home and three more were trying to. Covey sped past us all and took care of the three on the wall.

It took spells from both Alric and Padraig to break the gate in the wall. We ran in to see the dwollers shattering Qianru's front door and running inside.

The place was far emptier than it had been when I'd been inside long ago, but there were still relics and art strewn about. Obviously, they were the lower-end pieces that Qianru didn't feel were worth hauling around with her. Considering I saw more than one piece that would make a serious collector cry, I added that to my list of things I needed to talk to her about. Whenever I finally saw her again.

The dwollers headed straight for one of the back rooms. Either they knew exactly where they were going, or they had a sense for what they were looking for. Considering how simple they were, I was betting on the latter.

"I'll stay here and stop any more from getting in." Covey's grin said she was having way too much fun fighting the dwollers. Welsy and Delsy grinned and stayed with her.

The three of us continued down to what was probably Qianru's bedroom. The bed was larger than my entire living room. She'd left bedding on it, as if she were just popping out for a bit, but it looked older and probably was something she didn't want.

The dwollers were diving into the bed. Literally. Their hands had claws, and they were tearing through the stuffing. I started to run forward, but Alric held me back.

"Let's see what they are after." Padraig was a foot or two closer to them but stayed put.

I heard fighting out front, but no yelling. Part of what was disturbing about these dwollers was their silence. Finally, the ones inside the bed came out. At first, I thought they were each holding a body part but then realized they were parts of a statue. One that was missing at least two pieces from what I could tell.

They ran toward us and the door. Alric sliced one in half, but the piece it had went flying up and another grabbed it. I tackled one but it decided to fight back this time and swung at me, breaking free as I scrambled out of reach.

Padraig threw a spell at the door to stop them, but they went right through.

"Covey! Stop them!" I scrambled to my feet and we all ran out. I had no idea what those pieces were, but Alric and Padraig looked extremely upset, so I was guessing they knew.

Covey and the brownies were still fighting more dwollers coming in the door. Clearly, they'd overrun the guards at the bottom as there were too many for Covey and the brownies to keep up with. And the dwollers were fighting back more. Covey had marks on her arms and a slash on her face.

That didn't slow down the dwollers we were following much. They turned, tore through the front room, and crashed out the window. Qianru was not going to be happy.

Padraig and Alric leapt through and I followed a bit behind. The dwollers with the pieces tore out into the open space, then vanished into a small swirling circle on the side of a neighbor's wall. The ones fighting Covey and the brownies did the same. Then the swirling vortex closed with enough force to knock us all off our feet. Not all the dwollers had gotten inside before it shut and dwoller parts went flying.

Seriously. I was going to need two months of baths.

CHAPTER TWENTY EIGHT

ALRIC HELPED ME TO MY feet. Neither of us looked good at this point. "Are you okay?"

I tried brushing myself off. "I'm not hurt, but not really okay. People have to stop exploding around us."

Covey and the brownies joined us. "What was that? And what were they carrying?"

"That was a vortex. Even with our Grimarian friend gone, there was someone back where they came from keeping their end open. It was probably tied to those dwollers," Alric said.

"As for what they had? Three of the six pieces of the seeker's chest. A religious artifact destroyed five thousand years ago by a group of tree goddesses." Padraig dusted himself off.

"Oh. That's not good. But it looked like body parts?" I wasn't excited about stone body parts either.

"It is in the shape of a prisoner, bound for all eternity in a kneeling position. It is a chest, or so the tales say, but it is gruesome. I'm sure Amara can tell us more about it."

We started walking away from the house when Padraig turned and cast a spell. Even though I'd seen the damage happen with my own eyes, it wasn't visible now. "I can't set a true guard spell on it. The ones Qianru had are still partially functioning. But this should keep curious people out."

We were mostly silent going down the hill. "Why would Qianru have those pieces in her bed, and why would she have left them behind?" That seemed unlike her.

"Something we'll have to ask once we catch up with her." Alric shook his head. "I think we have to consider that she might not be on our side after all."

I wanted to argue but realized there was too much I didn't know about her. And there were layers of evil. Some people might think they were on the right side but were helping the wrong one.

I watched for the faeries or Bunky and Irving the entire way back to my house but didn't see them. Padraig had detoured over to the pub to tell Foxy things were clear but rejoined us right before we got home.

"Halt!" Grillion jumped out of my neighbor's bushes with a pot on his head and his sword wavering. "Oh, sorry. Things were a bit tense there." He stepped back, and then yelled over his shoulder. "It's okay, it's them!" Then he looked at us, particularly Alric and me. "What is on you?" His nose wrinkled. I couldn't smell anything, but I took his word for it.

"Good to see you came through intact. If a bit fragrant," Mathilda said from where she and Amara stood right inside the doorway.

"I know this is your house, Taryn, but you two look and smell awful. Maybe we could get some water on you first?" Grillion asked.

I shrugged. I wanted to get home, but I also wasn't happy with goo all over me and certainly wouldn't want it in my house. "Sure?" I'd agreed when Mathilda pulled in what felt like an entire pond and dumped it on us. Grillion was too close so he got a nice drenching as well.

Amara grinned, raised her arms, and a lovely fresh-smelling wind dried us off. "Some of my magic still remains."

We were heading inside when I heard Bunky and Irving gronking. They were flying low to the ground and seemed to be having trouble. We met them in the street and Irving crashed in my arms and Bunky in Alric's.

"What's wrong?" Constructs could be destroyed but they were extremely tough.

Irving opened his mouth. A pile of faeries was in there.

"Are they…?" I couldn't even say it.

Bunky also seemed to have some, but managed to get some words out to Alric which he translated for us.

"He says they are only unconscious." He looked around. "We probably want to get inside."

My neighbors were pretty good about ignoring things, but even they were starting to come out.

We all went inside my house. Harlan had stayed back toward the kitchen and was waiting with a large stick. "Just in case they got through everyone else." He quickly moved everything off the dining room table.

Alric and I put Bunky and Irving on the table. They both did some odd convulsions and two piles of knocked-out faeries appeared.

"What's wrong with them?" Crusty was on the top of the pile closest to me. She looked like she was sleeping.

Mathilda came up and looked at Crusty's wing, then rubbed her fingers. "A lot of it has rubbed off, but yes, they used varlick powder. Again. We can assume it's the same group, although it's mixed stronger. That Grimarian has a favorite weapon against faeries."

"Can you reverse it?" The last time they hadn't been out this long.

"Yes, but this is a bit different. I think they all need baths as well."

Grillion ran to the kitchen and started filling up pots and bowls with water. I had been about to suggest dumping them all in my bathtub, but this way worked. And we could keep an eye on them without a handful of people in my bathroom.

We got them all in the various pots and bowls and slowly

they started waking up. I went and closed the door to the faery tunnel. "Someone knows too much about them. Yes, that Grimarian is dead, but those dwollers got away."

We all sat around the table and filled the others in. Amara almost choked about what we found in Qianru's house—or rather what the dwollers found.

"That can't be right; those pieces vanished when my sisters died. We disassembled that chest when we freed the south."

"Did the pieces vanish or were they destroyed earlier?" Padraig put a comforting hand on Amara's shoulder, but she jumped when he first touched her.

"Both, sort of. We destroyed its power by making sure the pieces could never go back together. Then we tied the pieces to ourselves, making sure they would vanish as we eventually died." She looked around earnestly. "There was nothing more we could do. But my sisters are gone—there should only be my piece left."

The faeries took that moment to all wake up, fly out of the water, yelling and jabbering, and tear off for the door. I was so glad I'd shut their passageway.

"You let out!" Garbage was furious but not at us. "Bads! Lots of bads!"

"We know, sweetie. It looks like you and your friends got taken out of the fight. Queen Mungoosey came to help us take care of a Grimarian, and we mostly handled the dwollers."

"No fights?" Crusty was the last to wake up and hadn't flown over to the others. "Wants fights. This not good."

"No fighting now, but there will be. And it will be deadly." Amara had turned her fear at the returning chest pieces into focusing on the faeries. "I can't go where this needs to happen. But can I make you all my helpers?"

I wasn't sure what she was doing, but the faeries all flocked around her. "Do!" They started chanting.

"I need you all to put a hand on me." She looked up.

"Can't hurt for the rest of you as well, but the faeries are more in touch with nature so it will be stronger for them."

We all looked at each other and then touched Amara. I felt a brief shock go through me and an image hit. The chest as it had been. A focus of vile magic. Then it exploded.

Amara was chanting something and then she stopped.

"What was that?"

"It was a link to the parts of the chest that Qianru had. I will have an extremely serious talk with her as to where she got them. But right now, they to be brought back here to be dealt with."

The tingle from Amara's image was still with me. "I think that might have done something else." I held out the hand I had touched her with and focused on magically creating a glow. At first, I didn't think it would work, then a small and rather faded glow appeared. It wasn't giving off much light, but it didn't vanish either.

"How is this happening? Do you have your magic back?" Covey was watching the glow like it was going to grow a few limbs.

"I don't know. Something about what Amara did helped, but I think it was the death of that Grimarian." I gently lifted the glow up and it hung in the air.

"Then there are others working with her as we suspected. They are doing bound spells so the death of one won't end them, but it did weaken the spell's hold on your magic." Padraig watched my glow, but he wasn't smiling.

"But that means I can get my magic back if we destroy enough of them?" I wasn't violent; I'd rather have settled down and grown old with Alric. The world didn't seem to want that to happen. So, I was going to have to make it happen.

"Possibly. I've felt your magic the entire time, and I do think it's working through your dagger friend," Mathilda said. "The bulk of it still is."

Alric came closer to me. "I still would rather that you

stayed here."

I leaned into him. "I know. But we know I can't. I need to help get Lorcan and Siabiane back. I know there is something in my blood that they want, but my blood might help me find my people. If there's a chance…" I looked into his eyes.

He sighed and rubbed my arms. "I know." More might have been said or done, but we both remembered there were a lot of our friends standing around us.

Amara smiled. "I am going to go see how my love is holding up. I will have him here first thing in the morning, ready to leave. You can't afford to wait."

I wanted to ask her how she knew, but it wasn't that hard to guess.

The others left as well. Harlan and Covey went to their homes. Amara offered Mathilda and Padraig guest rooms and the brownies went with them. Which left Alric, me, and Grillion. Plus, some still annoyed faeries and a pair of exhausted constructs.

Grillion went out to the pub, but I managed to convince the faeries to stay in. I will admit having used a fair amount of chocolate that Harlan had left with me.

"This might be the last night we are alone for a while." Alric kissed me once the last faery had collapsed into a chocolate stupor.

"You are a wise elf." I kissed him back and we stumbled back to my bedroom.

———◆———

The next morning, I heard the ruckus before I opened my eyes. Alric wasn't in the bed with me, but his side was still warm.

The noises out front didn't sound like mayhem or murder, so I took time to shower and find fresh clothes before I went out there.

There were debates about what to take down and what

to leave. Eventually Amara convinced Covey and Mathilda that the bulk of the scrolls would be safe with her.

After a half hour, during which Harlan had come to play negotiator, decisions were made. The risk, of course, was that we might need a lot of things. But bringing them with us meant we were risking the people in the south getting ahold of them.

After an hour, everyone was packed, Amara and Harlan had a cart of mystical items to be stored, and I had a nice new tattoo on my upper arm. A green vine that didn't hurt at all when she put it on.

Amara smiled at the delicate green lines. "This will help me see what you see when you wish it. And communicate with you." Her smile dropped. "I will warn you, if there are any of the Jerinthati still down there, they will know this mark."

"Let them. Maybe they'll think twice about taking me on."

We all got our packs and supplies on the horses, said our goodbyes to those staying behind, including Welsy and Delsy, who were going to stay at the pub, then headed south.

The trip to the docks and the ship that would make the crossing was about a week, and if all went well would give us time to all be completely bored. I liked the idea of boredom right now.

Eight days after leaving Beccia, setting up camp had become a routine that we all knew by heart. Most of us remained lost in our own thoughts as we traveled, and even Grillion seemed to be pondering things. I wasn't happy about going on a long trip, but I wanted my friends back. And if there was even the slightest chance that the mystery person in Colivith, who dumped all those scrolls on us, knew when or where my people were, I had to take it.

If we could get on board the ship, we should be fine. Just one more day.

The attack hit us fast and hard ten minutes later.

Masked fighters focused on Padraig, Alric, and Foxy first, until Mathilda and Covey jumped into the fray. Grillion fought but he wasn't a great swordsman, and he didn't have magic, so he mostly stayed toward the edge of the fighting.

The faeries flew up in one giant wave around Mathilda and all crashed to the ground a moment later.

"They have that dust!" Mathilda yelled and bashed an attacker in the head. She stepped away from the fighting and was chanting something. One by one the faeries slowly flew up. They were flashing colors, which meant they were holding their breath. That explained the time Mathilda spent doing experiments. That dust must need to get inside of them to work.

Flashing various colors, the faeries fought to get close to any of the attackers.

"And they have a magic dampener," Alric yelled as two of them jumped him.

The attackers ignored me, I assumed because I was at the far end of the camp and had about twenty feet of solid rock behind me. But ignoring me was a bad move on their part. My sword appeared as soon as the yelling started, and I was scared enough to use it. I ran toward the fighting. I wouldn't have thought fear would be a good motivator for good swordsmanship—in fact, pretty sure I'd been told to stay calm.

At first, I thought they were common thieves; after all we were in a desolate part of the land—attacking strangers was probably status quo. Then the one facing me swung his sword high, and I saw the damn tattoo on his wrist.

"It's the Dark!" The one I was fighting had a cloth band over his ears and was wearing mud or makeup to disguise his features, but I was sure he was an elf. The rest of them as well. Could be their non-elven minions, but they were fighting too well.

I dodged from the one I was fighting and pulled out my dagger. He was glowing like a lightning storm. I held him high as I fought my opponent. The dagger crackled and sent static charges into the man I was facing. I still wasn't sure how I felt about my magic funneling through a dagger, but if I were blocked from my magic directly, at least I could still use it through the dagger. And the magic dampener didn't appear to have any effect on the dagger—most likely the spell didn't recognize what the dagger was doing.

My opponent swung high, trying to avoid the green strikes, but they went into him anyway. While the bolts hit him, I ran him through with my sword.

I pulled free as he tumbled to the ground. Three more opponents were coming my way right as a vortex opened in the air at the far end of the camp where five of the fighters were attacking Alric. He was one of the best swordsmen I knew but it was five against one. And the pile of bodies around them pointed out that Alric had won most of his fights. One opponent gave him a sharp rap to the head, and he dropped. His sword vanished as he fell.

"Alric!" I yelled, but I was too far away, and my friends were all fighting for their lives. Even the faeries were being held back. And there was no way I could throw my dagger this time. There were too many friends between me and the swirling vortex. The people attacking us had managed to separate him away from all of us.

Fury hit me as I watched them dragging him toward the vortex. The change hit me, and I crossed the camp in two strides as I changed. I grabbed one of the men holding Alric and flung him into the air, not caring where he landed, only that he wasn't in my way. A second one screamed in pain as I ripped her from the entrance to the vortex and threw her behind me. Two got through the vortex with Alric, and it slammed shut on the last one. I stomped what was left of him into the ground in my anger and fear.

The rest of the attackers ran, but whether it was from me, or they'd gotten what they came for I wasn't sure. I saw the magic dampener hovering a bit below my eye line and smacked it with my tail. Mathilda and Padraig sent spells after the fleeing attackers. Covey ran them down. The faeries and the constructs were right behind her.

I transformed and crumbled to the ground. I was still too angry for tears, but they were there anyway.

Grillion ran to me, along with Foxy.

"They got him?" Grillion patted me on the shoulder but didn't seem frightened. Considering he had never seen me change before, a part of my mind was impressed.

"Yes. I couldn't…why take him? Damn it, if they want me, why take him?"

Padraig and Mathilda came back into the clearing. They were both bruised and looked angry enough to start ripping heads off anything in their way. "Because of what you just did," Padraig said as he wiped off his sword. "It was hard for a twenty-five-hundred-year-old syclarion to fight you and she still lost. They know they can't get enough forces here to take you down. At least not without killing you."

Mathilda leaned heavily on her stick. She wasn't bleeding that I could see, but she still could have been hurt. "I'd say he's right; they want you intact and alive. And they are going to make you come to them."

I looked around as Covey, the faeries, and Bunky and Irving came back. "Then I have to go alone. We killed the Grimarian, but they will keep picking my friends off, endangering everyone I love until I turn myself over. I can't be responsible for this." Yup. Still angry but I felt hot tears flowing down my face. "I need to go alone. I can't risk more of you."

Foxy came up and hugged me. Like lifting me in the air and I couldn't breathe, hugged me. He was murmuring something and patting my hair. I freed a hand to try to push him away.

He sat me on my feet, but he was crying almost as much as I was. "We can't let you go alone, at least I can't. Amara sent me to help protect you and get the others back and I aim to do that. And she fears what is growing in the south. We need to stop it."

I opened my mouth to argue, but the solid look on his face said I might as well argue with the rock behind him.

"I can't speak for the others, but we knew the risks. They tried to take me, did take two dear friends, and now the one I think of as a brother. I *will* get them back." Padraig had that regal and stubborn as hell look. The blood seeping through his shirt from his wounds just made him more dangerous. The one you couldn't argue with.

Covey started laughing. She'd changed into a controlled berserker during the fight and was only now returning to normal. Her lip lifted in a snarl. "There is no way in any hell or heaven that I'm letting you go without me." She flicked her talons one more time before they returned to fingers.

Mathilda and all the flyers nodded their agreement. Right now, Garbage and her faeries were going around making sure all the enemy fighters were dead. If they hadn't been dead already, they were after the faeries stabbed them repeatedly with their war sticks.

"We get back." Satisfied all were dead, she flew up to me.

"Protect." Leaf was right behind her.

"Tree!" That was Crusty's comment, but she shouted it in the direction of my inner pocket where the key was. I hoped it was a key that could help us.

"Was anything else taken?" Most everything we were carrying with us was in the tiny bags, which meant that whatever bags Alric had on him were gone now.

"Nothing that I can find." Grillion looked overwhelmed and had stayed silent during everyone else's declarations of loyalty.

I put my hand on his shoulder. "You don't have to stay with us. No one would blame you at all, and if you go back to Beccia, I'm sure Harlan would welcome the help." He wasn't a magic user or a serious swordsman, and this was a dangerous trip even for those who could fight.

"True. But I don't like being used, nor attacked." He took a deep breath, then nodded. "Alric and I were thieves, but he never cheated me and often saved my ass. It's time I try to return the favor."

Without even much debate, we repacked the camp and took off again. I was tired, but I couldn't sleep where Alric had been taken. Padraig packed up Alric's things first and stored them with his own. He also tied Alric's horse behind his. I couldn't say much but I gave him a hug. Being around Alric's possessions without him here would be far too hard.

We rode for another two hours before exhaustion eventually took its toll on all of us. Well, most of us.

"We go!" Garbage and her faeries wanted to keep going.

"Honey, we're too tired. We can't keep going." The terror of Alric being taken had kept me going initially, but even that could only last for so long.

"We protect."

"And we'll help."

I almost jumped a foot in the air at the voice behind me. Welsy and Delsy, who were supposedly staying in Beccia, stood in the bushes.

"We are sorry we couldn't catch up before the attack, but we are here now."

Mathilda came over. "Aren't you supposed to be staying to help guard the scrolls?"

"We were but Harlan said elves were there now and they could guard." Welsy turned to me. "Amara had a dream three nights ago; you were being attacked. She wanted to send us."

I looked over to the others. "Sending them back wouldn't really change anything. And right now, we could all use some sleep. If they can stand guard?"

Everyone nodded.

"I'm not tired. I can stay up a bit with them. We can talk of Amara." Foxy grinned and made a fire.

I didn't think I could sleep, but exhaustion smacked me, and I was out.

The next morning was quiet as everyone was lost in their thoughts. I was finishing packing when I heard what sounded like a small dog. I looked around but the others were talking. I turned back to my things and this time I heard a cat and a dog.

"Garbage?" The dog was confusing, but I knew who dealt with cats.

"Is yes?" Garbage flew up behind me.

"Why am I hearing a cat…and a dog?" Who sounded like they were playing somewhere. In the middle of a forest.

"Is okay, ours." She waved toward a teal and purple faery riding a cat coming out of the bushes. "Rosy Horsefly and Rainbow cat." Then a puppy also being ridden by a faery, this one was fuchsia and yellow. "That Gracie Twinkleshine and war puppy, Candy." She flew closer and dropped her voice. "But no eat him."

"Why and how are they here? And a puppy?" I was waiting for a pack of cats to come out of the trees, but there didn't seem to be any more.

"Puppy because Gracie sneeze on cats. They here for war."

"Two?" I wasn't going to complain. But traveling with a cat and dog might make things tricky.

"Rest here too!" Leaf flew up and waved a green and brown bag at me. The two faeries got off their steeds, Leaf flew down and the cat and puppy vanished into the bag.

I just looked at them for a few moments. "They're okay in there?" This was a new trick and a new bag.

"Yes! How else we get them where go?" Garbage looked at me like I had taken too many hits to the head. Again.

I started to say something, then shrugged. "You're certain they are all okay in there?"

"Yes!" All the faeries joined in on that pronouncement.

I finished packing and we were on our way. I'd warn the others about our cat and dog collection when we were on the ship.

We got to the docks by mid-morning of the next day. The travel papers we had taken from Hass and Fealk had been magicked by both Padraig and Mathilda to include our entire group. And they would let us take the horses.

Of course, the passage hadn't been fully paid far and the cost was exorbitant—the captain knew we were in a rush. Padraig and Mathilda eventually bargained him down to something we could pay, and we all boarded the ship.

The trip would only be a few days; this was a channel passage not an ocean voyage. We had the largest room, but it was still extremely small. We moved our things in as the ship left the dock. I waited until we'd been moving for a bit and then went up on the deck.

The flock of faeries and Bunky and Irving flew out ahead of the ship. The captain seemed a bit uptight about them, but for what we were paying for passage they could sit on his head if they wanted. Besides, his issue had mostly been with them *on* his boat and right now they weren't touching it.

I looked out over the water. While I knew logically that there was land ahead of us somewhere, and it wasn't nearly as large as the ocean, this wasn't going to be a great passage for me. Water was still not my friend and probably never would be.

"We'll get Alric back, I promise." Padraig had come up

beside me so quietly I hadn't known he was there.

"We have to. Or they will find out what real dragon's blood can do."

The End

DEAR READER,

Thank you for joining me on another adventure with Taryn, the faeries, and the gang. As always, I appreciate you for coming along on the newest escapade. The next book in the series will be out fall of 2021, if not before.

If you want to keep up on the further adventures of Taryn, Alric, and the faeries, make sure to visit my website and sign up for my mailing list. *http://marieandreas.com/index.html*

If you enjoyed this book, please spread the word! Positive reviews on are like emotional gold to any writer. And mean more than you know.

Thank you again—and keep reading!

About the Author

Marie is a multi award winning fantasy and science fiction author with a serious reading addiction. If she wasn't writing about all the people in her head, she'd be lurking about coffee shops annoying total strangers with her stories. So really, writing is a way of saving the masses. She lives in Southern California and is owned by two very faery-minded cats.

When not saving the masses from coffee shop shenanigans, Marie likes to visit the UK and keeps hoping someone will give her a nice summer home in the Forest of Dean.